More . . .

THE AWAKENING (Book II):

"An intriguing portrait of vampiric society, reminiscent of Anne Rice and Laurell K. Hamilton."

—*Library Journal*

"L. A. Banks has taken her Huntress series to another level; the action, adventure, and romance have readers tingling with anticipation. I am not normally into science fiction or the vampire genre, but I find myself addicted to this series. The characters are strong and compelling, and following them throughout this series is a thrill. I highly recommend this book to others."

—Book-remarks.com

"With *The Awakening*, Banks solidifies her intriguing, dark series as a project worth watching."

—*Booklist*

"Again, Banks brilliantly combines spirituality, vampires, and demons (and hip-hop music) into a fast-paced tale that is sure to leave fans of her first novel, *Minion*, panting for more but nothing seems quite as hot as the steamy, often tense relationship between Damali and Carlos . . . a new-comer to the vampire genre . . . [Banks] lends a fresh and contemporary voice."

—*Columbus Dispatch*

MINION (Book I):

"Banks's mastery of character creation shines through in the strong-willed Damali . . . a sure-fire hit . . . pretty dramatic fiction."

—Philadelphia Daily News

"[Minion] literally rocks the reader into the action-packed underworld power struggle between vampire rivals with a little demon juice thrown in. Nothing less than the future state of the universe lies in the balance . . . it furthermore blasts open the door of the vampire huntress theme to future African American writers . . . [a] groundbreaking concept . . . Minion is the first appetizer setting up the next course. As in any delectable meal, it is the savory morsels of each bite that count. So fasten your seatbelt and enjoy a ride littered with holy water, vamp ooze and a layered web of political intrigue ingeniously woven from the mind of Banks. Cutting-edge wit and plenty of urban heat flies from the pages of this quick read."

—Philadelphia Sunday Sun

"Minion is arguably superior to the Buffy franchise . . . while Banks relies on an established vampire-slayer mythos for part of her story, she is also wildly creative and invents a totally new and refreshing milieu. Its social hierarchy and politics are fascinating, and the author's reinterpretation of the seven levels of hell is brilliant. Another inspired detail is her explanation for how some otherwise 'normal' humans end up as cannibalistic serial killers. Minion is an entirely delicious read, leaving the reader licking one's lips and wanting more, cursing the cliffhanger ending. Luckily, this book is the beginning of the Vampire Huntress series, so there's more to look forward to."

—Fangoria

ST. MARTIN'S PAPERBACKS TITLES BY
L. A. BANKS

Minion
The Awakening
The Hunted
The Forbidden

THE ℬITTEN

A VAMPIRE
HUNTRESS
LEGEND

L. A. BANKS

St. Martin's Paperbacks

THE BITTEN

Library of Congress Catalog Card Number: 2004051163

ISBN: 0-312-99509-1
EAN: 9780312-99509-6

Printed in the United States of America

St. Martin's Griffin trade paperback edition / February 2005
St. Martin's Paperbacks edition / January 2006

St. Martin's Paperbacks are published by St. Martin's Press, 175 Fifth Avenue, New York, NY 10010.

10 9 8 7 6 5 4 3 2

DEDICATION AND
SPECIAL ACKNOWLEDGMENTS

I would like to dedicate this and all my work to the Creator, Who teaches us to look upon trials and tribulations not as the sum total of punishment, but as the fire that hones to allow growth and subsequent rebirth. It is not about punishment, but about love, peace, learning, abundance, and grace. The light provides good things, always. So if it ain't good, needless to say, let's not blame the Creator. Knowing that there is redemption, and more to this life than meets the naked human eye, is a matter of faith in the promise that we are all God's children. To that end, bring positive energy into your consciousness and may it also provide you with comfort, abundance, inspiration, and renewed purpose.

We dwell in the midst of infinite abundance; all else is illusion. The Creator provides for all our needs, and wants us to live in radiant health, with positive purpose and the blessings of enriched, fruitful relationships, uplifted spirits, and plentiful resources. That is the Divine plan. That is the Divine promise. Believe it.

Loving acknowledgment goes to: Manie Barron, always; Monique Patterson, forever; Amanda Maxwell; Harriett Seltzer; Monica Peters; Liza, my sister; Althea, who sees the divine; Hilary Beard, my soul sister; Joanne White, Bill Harvey, and Dr. Xu, for your depth of knowledge and understanding; Derrick, Jermaine, Dame, Virg, and the squad of RBG, for your music; Michael Storrings, for his fabulous designs; Eric Battle, Vince Natale, and Chris Bonelli, for your art; Tony Nottingham and Charles Holmes—thanks for getting my paper straight, brothers! To my husband, children, and my spiritual crew of friends, extended family, sister/brother authors, and guides . . . my village, my compound, and the very foundation of my soul—thank you!

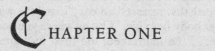

CHAPTER ONE

The lair in St. Lucia

"TELL ME your darkest fantasy," she murmured against his ear, gently pulling the lobe between her teeth.

Carlos smiled with his eyes still closed, too exhausted to do much else. Damali sounded so wickedly sexy, but why did women always go there—dredging for answers to questions that they really didn't want to hear, especially while in bed? "I don't have any, except being with you."

"Tell me," she pleaded low and throaty, her tone so seductive that he'd swear she was all vamp.

No. He was not going to go there, no matter what. He was not going to stare into those big brown eyes of hers and become hypnotized by them. Dark fantasies . . . She had no idea what went through a master's mind. Despite himself, his smile broadened. The things he'd seen . . . *sheeit*. Had she any idea of the lifetimes of vampire knowledge he'd acquired from Kemet through Rome and beyond, just by being offered a council seat? And Rome . . . damn . . . no way.

He stroked her still-damp back, his fingers reveling in the tingling sensation her tattoo created as he touched the base of his spine, hoping she'd let his love be enough to satisfy her.

"You're my fantasy," he finally said to appease her when she became morbidly silent. But he'd also meant what he'd said, albeit skillfully avoiding the question she'd really asked. "You're this dead man's dream come true, baby."

Her response was a chuckle, followed by an expulsion of hot breath that caressed his ear. "Liar," she whispered, as she slid her body onto his. "I know where you want to go."

"D . . ." he murmured, too tired to argue with her, and much too compromised by her warmth to avoid being stirred by her butter softness. "C'mon, girl . . . stop playing."

His hand continued to stroke her back, finding the deep curve in it that gave rise to her firm, tight bottom. He allowed his fingers to leisurely play at the slit that separated both halves of it, enjoying the moistness that he knew he'd created there. Her immediate sigh made him shudder and seek her mouth to kiss her gently, half hoping to shut her up, half hoping to derail his own darkening thoughts. Without resistance, she deepened their kiss, rewarding his senses with a hint of mango, the merest trace of red wine, and her own sweetness fused with his salty aftermath as his tongue searched the soft interiors.

Damn, this woman was fine . . . five feet seven inches' worth of buff curves packaged in flawless bronze skin, a lush mouth, brunette locks that kissed her shoulders, and a shea-oil scent that was slowly driving him crazy. It always did. He breathed in the fragrances held by her still-damp scalp: vanilla, coconut oils; and then there was also the scent of heavy, pungent sex hanging in the air.

"You always smell *so* good," he murmured, kissing the edge of her jaw. He could still taste her on his mouth when he licked his lips. "Hmmm . . ." Sticky, sweet-salty, female. The way she breathed against his neck, and her head found the crook of his shoulder, she fit so perfectly, like a handmade blanket on him. Even exhausted, her slick wetness made him want to move just to maintain their friction, their pulse. Merely thinking about it made him hard again.

"I know you have to eat," she said in a husky tone against the sensitive part of his throat, her tongue trailing up his jugular vein, causing him to tighten his hold on her.

"Yeah, I do . . . in a few," he admitted quietly, now too distracted to go out hunting.

The way she tilted her hips forward—ever so slightly, a tease, an offering, just a contraction of the muscles beneath her bronze skin—fought with the hunger and was winning. They'd been at it all night, and he glimpsed the moonlight that washed over her through the deck opening. Silver blue hues shimmered on her smooth ass, and he touched the light with his fingers a millimeter above her skin. She shivered at the almost-touch. That was always her most powerful weapon; her reaction to whatever he was doing to her just blew him away. One more round and he'd have to go before dawn trapped and starved him.

"What's *your* darkest fantasy?" he said smiling, turning the question on her, and not caring that a little fang was beginning to show with his smile. He passed his tongue over his incisors, willing patience as he played the game that she seemed to be enjoying.

Damali brought her head up to stare into his eyes with a mischievous smirk. "My darkest fantasy is fulfilling yours."

He laughed low and deep and slow. "Yeah?" He raised an eyebrow in a challenge. "But I don't have any really dark fantasies . . . this is all I need."

"Liar," she said again, chuckling from within her throat and planting a wet kiss on his Adam's apple in a way that made him swallow hard. "I bet I know what it is, even if you won't tell me."

She was rocking against him harder now, although she hadn't allowed him entry. Faint sounds from the slick rub of wet skin against skin added to his agony. She had his full attention, his awareness of her engaged. The teasing sensation accompanied with her well-placed nips along his chest made him suck in a hard breath between his teeth.

"This is working just fine," he murmured, tracing her sides and finding both of her breasts to gently cradle.

"But there's always more," she whispered, lowering her mouth to roughly suckle one of his nipples.

"Curiosity killed the cat," he told her, arching, trying to penetrate her without success.

"But satisfaction brought her back." She lifted her head and stared at him hard, her smile strained with anticipation, intensity boring into him from her expression of unmasked desire.

For a moment, neither of them spoke. The exchange was telepathic, electric, and he found her neck, kissed it hard, then her shoulder, licking a path down her collarbone. When she moaned, he almost lost it and bit her.

"Tell me what you want," he murmured hot against her breast, before pulling a taut nipple between his lips.

Her inhale was a deep hiss, a sound that traveled through his body, igniting his want for her that never seemed to disappear. Whatever she asked for, he'd give her one last time before dawn. Didn't she already know, *por ella seria capaz de cualquier cosa?* Yeah, he would do anything for her. "Tell me," he whispered, "and it's done."

"I've already told you," she said in a rasp, moving to allow him to slip inside her, then contracting around him before withdrawing.

"C'mon, baby," he said, feeling his voice tighten with the contraction. "Right now, I'm—"

"Getting too hot to think about it?" She laughed and mounted him with a hard lunge that forced a groan up from deep inside him.

"Yeah . . . something like that." His lids closed on their own volition, his eyes rolling toward the back of his skull—the sensation was so gloriously sudden.

"Then don't think about it," she whispered, moving away, but then coming back with quick jerky circles before plunging down again.

"Oh shit, woman . . ."

"I know, baby," she murmured, her motions becoming more driven, but then backing away so that only the tip of him was within her drenched, slick valley. "But let me see if I've guessed it right. What would a master vampire's deepest fantasy be? A possible throne-level council member, at that?"

"You have no idea . . . what you're doing to me." That was the pure truth. A scent that had been locked in the deep registers of his mind filtered into his awareness, gradually at first, until it was all-consuming. Every inhale now was riddled with the maddening aphrodisiac that he'd sworn he'd forget—had to—but it moved his body, banished a portion of his control. Master or not, Neteru was entering his system and slaying him. If she kept this up, he'd slip and take her to the vanishing point with him for sure.

Her hard shudder and the rhythmic squeeze of her inner thighs against his hips was practically his undoing. But it was also her boldness when she threw her head back and breathed out, "I know *exactly* what I'm doing to you."

He wasn't prepared to argue with her, not now. Didn't she know that that was one of the things he loved best about being with her—she was his match, a pure equal, and had had this effect on him before he'd ever been turned? But there were still some places he wasn't prepared to go with her. Not if he wanted to ever retrieve his soul.

But she was messing with his mind, talking all low and sexy, husky and deep, down the side of his throat, and into his ear, saying crazy things like, "C'mon, baby, tell me what you *really* want . . . I'll give it to you," knocking at the guarded black box of his senses, prying him open for a total mind lock while making him want to cum so badly his balls ached. He could feel every cell in his body poised, readied, a burn of pure energy threatening to split them, beginning to deconstruct him down to hot vapor, and her along with him.

Her skin was covered with a light sheen of perspiration, and she slid against him like water flowing over rocks, liquid fire motion, hips undulating in a slow, rolling current, with eddies that spontaneously spun, lurched, took him in to the hilt, then washed him ashore, leaving cold air to knife at the hot surface that had been ejected from her body. His tightening grip would each time be enough to summon his return to her warm, wet center, only to be cast ashore by her fickle tide again and again, until he flipped her on her back and was done playing.

"Enough." There was no nonsense in his tone. He was beyond games as he stared into her eyes; saw a glow of red reflected back from her dark brown irises, knowing it came from his. Her scent bathed him, made him shut his eyes tight as he breathed in deeply and entered her hard. *"That's* what I want."

His fingers tangled in her velvet-spun locks, and her arches finally met him in a rhythm they both knew by heart—no stopping, no more teasing, just hard down, uninterrupted returns until he felt his gums give way to the incisors he could no longer hold in check, no more than he could hold back the inevitable convulsion of pleasure that was about to rip through his groin.

Nuzzling his throat, her fingers wound through his hair, and he was surprised by the force of her pull, that her fingers had made a fist at the nape of his neck, and that one of her palms slid against his jaw to push his head back, her breath on his throat in the way he'd always imagined. Trembling with need, the sensation was so damned good . . . if only . . . she could . . . just once . . . *Oh, baby* . . .

Then she suddenly shifted her weight, her legs a vise, and rolled on top of him. Her strength came from nowhere. It happened so quickly. A sharp strike as fast as a cobra's tore at his throat, making him shut his eyes harder, his gasp fused with a groan that transformed into a wail, and the pull that siphoned his throat sent the convulsion of ecstasy throughout his system, emptied his scrotum until his body dry heaved, made his lashes flutter from the rapid seizure, where every pull from her lips erupted hot seed from him into her, sheets gathered in knots within his fists before his hand again sought her skin, shards of color ricocheted behind his lids while he cradled her in his arms, stuttering, *"Don't stop . . . take it all."*

His body went hot, then cold, minutes of unrelenting pleasure—her hold indomitable, a physical lock of sheer will, as she moved her hips in a lazy rhythm, ignoring his attempt to rush her with deep thrusts and staccato jerks, his voice foreign to him as it reverberated off the walls of the lair, echoed back, and taunted him . . . a master vampire, done for the first time, by what could only be a female vamp. *A master female.* One conjured from his darkest fantasy, riding him with more than skill, precise slow torture that he couldn't stop, even if he'd wanted to.

Winded, siphoned, turned out, he could barely open his eyes—but he had to. Which one of them had taken Damali's place, stolen her form? Damn, his territory had some shit with it, but never in his wildest dreams would he have imagined it to be like this. If Damali ever found out . . . And how did this female get in here? Where was D?

She smiled, looking down at him, and wiped her mouth with the back of her hand.

"Who made you, baby?" Dazed, that was all he could ask.

"You did," she said, chuckling low, and pressing an index finger over one of his streaming bite wounds to help seal it before stemming the flow with a soft kiss. Then she slowly licked her finger and smiled before sealing the other so he wouldn't entirely bleed out.

"Seriously . . . look. I've got a lady, and—"

"You're damned straight you do, brother." She cocked her head to the side, giving him a curious glance. "You should have told me that's what you really wanted. It was good, though, wasn't it? The first time's always the best."

There was no denying that fact. Carlos blinked twice, staring. "Damali?" Two inches of fang glistened crimson in the moonlight within her lovely mouth, and a thin red line of blood had dribbled down her chin between her breasts. He resisted the urge to sit up and lick the dark trail to her stained lips.

"Who else?" She shook her head, sat back with him still in her, and folded her arms over her chest. "Oh, so you had some other Jane on your mind while I was working?"

"No . . . Oh . . . shit . . ."

He grabbed her by her hips, and extricated himself from her to stand, stumbling a bit, but he needed motion—fatigue and the siphon notwithstanding. He had to break the physical contact with her. The pleasure wave of aftershocks were impairing his judgment, and if he bit her in this condition, he'd flat-line her for sure. Even standing away from her, he could still feel her hot seal. "No, no, no, no, no—this *cannot* be happening."

"That's not what you said a minute ago, baby. Last I heard you were hollering, 'Don't stop,' and some *por favor* mess before you went over the edge. Men." She laughed and flopped back on the bed, lazy and sated, twirling one of her locks around a finger, then closed her eyes. "Damn, that was awesome. We should get you something to feed on, soon, though. I'm two quarts to the good, myself."

He could feel panic bubbling within him, and he had never been the kind of man to outright freak about anything. But this, of all the things he'd seen and been through so far, was scaring the hell out of him.

"No!" he said fast, walking in a circle, then going from the deck back to the side of the bed, gesturing with his hands in a naked frenzy. "Something went wrong. I have to get you back to the guardians—to Marlene, your mom . . . baby, you're turning—"

"Turned," she sighed with a smile, "and I love it. Relax. What's done is done."

"You're supposed to be immune to my bites! What the fuck? *No.* I'm not having my woman go out like that—oh shit, baby—"

"You're panicking because you need to eat." She ran her finger down the side of her throat, summoning him with a lopsided grin. "You didn't finish . . . or did you want to save it for when we wake up?"

He shook his head no, and backed away from the glorious temptation.

Damali yawned and nodded toward the opened deck doors. "Suit yourself, but it's late, it's almost dawn, and it's time to go to bed, honey. Just—"

"Oh, my God, D—"

When she hissed and held both sides of her head and glared at him, he could feel hot tears begin to form in his eyes. He could call on the Almighty, but the Neteru couldn't? What the hell had he done?

She was sitting up now, seeming thoroughly annoyed. When she stood to fetch her white silk nightgown, she almost glided; her stride was so smooth, supernatural. Horrified, he watched her sashay out to the deck and turn her face up toward the moon, as though to bay at it.

"I'm going to get us something before the sun fries us both," she muttered, and then was gone.

It took him a moment to process what he'd just witnessed. The edge of his lair was built into a cliff with no passable roads leading to it. But she'd walked down the stairs to the mountainside and was nowhere to be found in the dense, tropical foliage. However, he was painfully aware that the sounds of the night had gone still. *She'd turned.* Even the creatures knew it.

Instantly, he sheathed himself with a pair of pants and his boots. Near dawn, his woman newly turned, and he was running around two quarts low on blood.

Carlos rounded the deck, stood out on the cliffs, and willed Damali's return. If he'd made her, then she had to come when he called . . . Then again, she still had a lot of Neteru running through her, not to mention general-purpose stubbornness that not even the underworld could probably sway. But what had gone wrong? Marlene had told them both that Damali was immune. All Neterus were supposed to be able to take a bite and survive it, unturned. He'd held off until she'd crossed over to full huntress . . . and when did she die? In his arms?

Memories bound him as he thought back on night after night of sweet indulgence with her, no will as her barrier, no prayers to protect her from him; he was welcomed, wanted, considered a Dark Guardian, but approved by the team, nonetheless . . . and deep down, she'd found his Achilles' heel, the one thing that he knew he could never have with her. A true vampiric bite, in the throes, at the moment of truth—something he had not allowed any female vamp in his territory to do to him, *yet* . . . Something that, until now, Damali would never be able to do . . . or so he thought. Guilt stabbed at him. If he'd done this to her, God help him.

Yet, at the same time, what she'd done to him had been so powerful, totally unforgettable. So where did that leave them? Between another rock and a damned hard place. One taste of *that* was *not* going to be enough. That was raw truth. Lying to himself about it wasn't a viable option. He had to take her home, before she came to him like this again.

He had to get Marlene to give her something to turn her back, if there was such a potion or spell—which meant confessing how and when he'd seen her first crest of fangs. Yeah, right . . . explain to this girl's mother-seer that he'd been hard-rocking her Neteru's world every night for almost a month, siphoning a pint from her until one night she had bitten *him*? Marlene was gonna have a cow and Shabazz would rightfully mount a posse of Damali's big brothers with stakes in their hands. He couldn't blame them.

But they were the least of his worries. Father Patrick and the Covenant would go nuts and the Vampire Council . . . there were no words. He was supposed to be protecting their vessel until her next cycle, a ruse to buy him, Damali, and her crew some time. *This was not supposed to happen.*

But he could have sworn that he felt her ripening right underneath him. The scent of her was undeniable, and the sweet essence of her still lingered in the back of his throat. If her body changed while they were together—it was over. She would be his, pregnant, and there'd be no going back. Yet, how was that even possible, especially if she were already turned? It was like her system was going haywire . . . Marlene had to fix this, because he sure as hell couldn't, had no frame of reference, nor a big black book of ancient text for answers. This was definitely some new whack shit. Still, the worst part of it was, his woman could be among the undead—the one person on the planet that he never *ever* wanted to see that way.

Marlene *had* to bring her back.

CHAPTER TWO

YONNIE STOOD on the roof of Club Vengeance and breathed in the night air. For he'd gambled right, had chosen to ally with Carlos Rivera, and had been handsomely rewarded. He'd been given management of the club with nearly free rein. Rivera was cool like that, it seemed.

A blue haze filtered across the moon and he smiled. It was in the air, a surge of power that all vampires had to acknowledge. The blood in the territories had more adrenaline kick to it, the kills were more satisfying . . . existence was good. To be a third-level vamp and take a club from a second-level just by strategically aligning with the right man, was unprecedented. All of a sudden he cocked his head to the side, briefly shut his eyes, and felt the powerful surge of sex in the air. Damn! Even the sex in the territory was sweeter under Rivera's rule. He just wished he knew who the vamp female was that Rivera had just turned. It was a fresh turn. Her vibe set his teeth on edge. But she felt stronger than a second . . .

"Damn, sis," Yonnie muttered as he strolled to the edge of the roof and peered down at the small specks of humanity beneath him.

"Enough to give a brother wood." All he could do was

shake his head as he wondered what it would be like to become a second-gen vampire, or even a master.

Yonnie chuckled to himself. Maybe if Carlos remained in a particularly generous mood he might share his new lair kitten. Yonnie quickly banished the thought. Not a strong female like that—she was destined for a throat mate-marking, for sure. No sense in a man getting his heart ripped out by the boss over wishful thinking. But to be able to transform into pure vapor and fuse with the blue haze of the moon . . . To be able to attract all the females that the master had no further use for, have them trembling for one vein hit. Yonnie shook his head as he balanced on the drain gutter, tempting his good fate. Rivera had been cool enough to give him Club Vengeance and let him run the other clubs in the network; pushing his luck farther to ask for more would not be wise.

He turned his head and looked at the metal door leading to the club. He could sense the approach of a guard. He smiled. That was odd. As a third-level, he had some precognitive skills, but he had never been able to sense another third-gen like this.

"Yo, man, what's up?" Yonnie said, thoroughly amused by his new strength.

"We just got back from Philly," the guard said, shaking his head and raking his fingers through his ragged Afro.

Yonnie allowed his gaze to roam over the thickly built vamp. His boy's army fatigue vest was in shreds, his jeans were dusty, his Timberlands were crusted with mud and old blood. None of which was a good sign. Old human blood, yes. Black blood from the empire, no. Stack's normally deep brown color was dull, which meant he'd been in battle and hadn't stopped to refuel. Stack had been in a hurry. What had gone down in Philly? His euphoria quickly faded. If Rivera came back and found out that he and his boys couldn't hold it down . . . He didn't want to think about it.

"What the fuck happened, Stack?" Yonnie said, walking up to his friend. He smoothed the front of his electric-blue suede jacket and hitched up his black leather pants. "Man, we just got this promotion. You know the boss's rep," Yonnie warned, speaking low and firm. "You fuck this up and there's no tellin'—"

Stack stepped away from Yonnie. "It ain't like that. You shoulda been there. We was checkin' on the Philly clubs, like you said. We was up in North Philly—where they have all them damned row houses stuck together so you can run a whole block roof to roof, if you get in trouble. But you have to be careful, because the humans got storefront churches in them houses, so some of the roofs are hot, and—"

"Aw'ight, aw'ight, I get the picture. So, you was up in the badlands. The humans got outposts, so who hit us?"

Stack stared at Yonnie for a moment and then looked away. "Humans."

"What?" Yonnie was incredulous. "The Guardian team is in LA, man. How you gonna tell me that—"

"No, man," Stack said, grabbing Yonnie by both arms. "Can't you feel it in the air? We were in one of our clubs, everything was going smooth, the girls were dancing the poles. We were about to do a little dinner theater—chick about fifteen or sixteen. You know, blood sacrifice for the crowds, when the fucking door blew in and these big, burly, black motherfuckers came in and lit the joint up. Rowdy black giants, and shit, are what they call themselves."

Yonnie opened his mouth and closed it. Stack dropped his arms and walked away.

"Lost three of our boys. They have one about the size of Damali's big man, Mike. And a smaller version of Shabazz. Like ten or eleven of 'em, and they roll fast, combat-style, then be gone. We got our asses kicked, man. They drew us to the rooftops. We thought we could escape, but that's their backyard. Lost one of our boys on a disguised roof—was hallowed ground and he torched on impact. Then that big Hannibal-looking guy threw a hammer at our other boy, and the way it hit him, it dazed him, and he fell wrong off the roof—two of them got him on the ground before he could get up. Third one got wrapped up in motorcycle chains— pure silver dipped in holy water—strangled to death. We was out."

"You sure they were human?"

"Man, they bled red blood, okay?"

Stack let his breath out hard and leaned against the metal door and shut his eyes.

For a moment, Yonnie didn't move. He became so still that he didn't even breathe, sensing the atmosphere.

"You feel like you're getting stronger?" Yonnie whispered to his friend.

"That's the crazy thing about it," Stack said quietly, peering around nervously. "We felt strong as shit going in. Every one of us was on top of our game. We were drinking toasts to you for getting us aligned with Rivera, and they were saying that even back in the day under the old regime, we'd never had the blood flowing like this. At one point tonight, it was like the females were *all* in heat. You could feel it in the air."

"Yeah, I know, man," Yonnie muttered as he began to pace. "That's what's so freaky about humans taking you out like that."

Both vampires looked at each other for a long time but said nothing.

"If we're getting stronger, it has to be because he's getting stronger." It was more a question than a statement.

"Then, it makes sense," Stack said, but his voice seemed unsure. "If our side just kicked up a notch, then the light maybe kicked up a notch?"

"That has to be it." Yonnie continued to walk back and forth, running his palm over his jaw. "See, you guys probably ran into a regulation Guardian team—there's like a hundred forty-four thousand of them bastards in hidden cells scattered throughout the globe. So, what happened in Philly was good. We'll explain to Rivera that you tracked down a splinter Guardian unit in his territory. Cool?"

"Right. Makes sense. We tell him that we were holding down his club, and we drew fire. Then, we can ask him if he wants us to take a small army back there to deal with the Philadelphia problem."

Yonnie was walking in circles now, perspiration making

his black silk shirt cling to his body. "Yeah, man. That could work."

Stack wheezed as he pushed himself away from the metal door.

"You need to eat," Yonnie said with concern. He slung his arm over Stack's broad shoulders.

"Let it go, man," Yonnie told him. We've gotta take this shit like men. We'll feed, get laid, and be merry since tonight might be our last night once Rivera blows in here."

Berkfield walked the perimeter of his suburban home one last time before he set his top-of-the-line security system. His wife thought his job was making him paranoid; it was better that she and his teenage son and daughter believed that. They didn't need to know that his floodlights were special UV halogens, nor did they need to know that the lawn and garden sprinkler systems contained holy water.

If his family knew he believed in monsters, they'd have him committed. Then what would happen to them? Who would take the special precautions that had become a neurotic routine?

He scanned the short hedges and peered into his neighbor's yard. All seemed well. It was still light out, nearly dusk, and people were about, messing with yard equipment, calling children in for dinner, and washing their SUVs and minivans after work.

Maybe he was crazy, but he'd witnessed his partner's shot mysteriously turn on him when he'd tried to shoot a guy with fangs. Carlos Rivera had dropped a gold mine of info on the local drug lords in his lap. Then Rivera had disappeared and he'd come up empty on all his searching into Rivera's territories. There was something very serious going on . . . Then again, maybe he was just crazy.

Berkfield's shoulders sagged resignation as he slowly walked toward the garage.

A bee sting on his calf made him wince. He hated yard work and he hated bugs. He grunted with exertion as he leaned on the workbench to pick up the garage-door opener that had fallen—and froze when he saw a shiny pair of military-issue black shoes on the other side of his minivan. Then everything went dark.

Groggy, Berkfield woke with a start, his gaze darting around. He was in a van. A gaunt, older, Caucasian male with dark sunglasses and a shock of unruly white hair leaned in close and shined a penlight in his eyes, causing him to squint.

"You'll be a little disoriented for a moment," the man with the light said, "but it will wear off. Our apologies for the way we had to collect you."

"Who are you?" he said, his voice tense and angry. "What do you want? Where's my family?" He let his mouth snap shut. What if his captors didn't know that he had a beautiful wife, daughter, and son? Damn it! Whatever they'd given him had made him sloppy.

"That's why we have taken you," the strange man said.

Berkfield studied his abductor intently. He had a wild rush of silver hair all over his head, piercing gray eyes, and a seeking expression. He looked like someone's professor. His accent was foreign, but hard to place. His demeanor was calm, almost too calm.

"What do you want?" Berkfield noted the four heavily armed men on either side of the professor.

"We're trying to protect you," the man said.

"Protect me?" Berkfield's eyes narrowed. "What branch of government are you from?"

The man offered a patient smile. "What's about to happen is an international issue. Not just an American issue. But you, my friend, are at risk."

Berkfield ran his sweaty palm over his bald scalp. His objective was singular—get home to ensure that these nuts hadn't harmed his family. "I'm just a cop on a local force— not worth much to anybody," he hedged.

The man's face became stern and the polite smile vanished from his face. "Let's stop playing games, Detective

Berkfield—or is it Captain now? You are lucky to have so narrowly escaped death at the hands of your partner. And even more lucky to be placed under the protective seal of the master vampire in this territory, Carlos Rivera."

Stunned, Berkfield leaned forward. "You've seen him? What do you know?" His voice escalated. Someone else, somebody in authority, knew there was such a thing as vampires! Berkfield grabbed his captor's arms. The henchmen bristled, but the man before him remained calm. He nodded reassuringly.

Gently extricating himself from Berkfield's hold, the man sat back and removed his sunglasses. "They are the most fascinating creatures we have yet to study," he said. "They have abilities that we could never fathom. Until we found out about your situation, we thought that they didn't have anything resembling a conscience—that their capacity to discern emotions, like empathy, was impossible. But they can, which means there may be hope."

Total confusion kept Berkfield riveted, but there were so many questions that he needed to ask that he couldn't contain himself.

"You actually *know* there are such things as vampires? You guys *study* them? You've *seen* the vampires? You know about Carlos? When did he become one? How? We'd just seen him taking a stroll by day, then, bam, just like that, he's a creature of the night— And the girl. Is she one? *I'm* not bitten, am I? You guys work for the feds, black ops? CIA? You said my family is at risk. Why? Some-fucking-body talk to me!"

"Take a deep breath, Mr. Berkfield," the man ordered. "Yes, to all of the above, except we don't work for the feds. Every government has been searching for its next weapon of mass destruction. They've each set up very small, well-funded, independent science teams to research these areas. But a few years ago, several of us broke away from our countries and banded together under an international umbrella. Once the governments saw that they'd lose their top scientists and that their threats had minimal effect on men who'd lived their entire lives on a quest of knowledge, they begrudgingly funded our group. Currently, we're made up of all the global superpowers. Recently we began to follow up on some old German research."

The man's eyes contained pain, and his voice became weary. "Our directive, when attached to our respective countries, was simple. Find a way to harness the paranormal, if it existed, and give it to the highest bidder within our respective military units. Phase one was to determine if there was such a thing as a paranormal plane. We succeeded with those tests. But as we gained further insights, it became apparent that the dark energy was limitless and stratified—almost like finding out there's an entire universe within a universe . . . space exploration is *nothing* compared to what we've uncovered. Yet, it's all linked; the esoteric sciences are just as real as hard quantum physics."

He gazed at Berkfield, his beady, gray eyes shining. "We also found out that there was another side—a side we hadn't considered. If there's a Hell, there's a Heaven," he whispered. "You cannot even begin to quantify the energy of that realm. Since we couldn't capture it, they wanted us to abandon that as a potential source for weaponry and to focus on dark matter. That's when the group fractured . . . Several good scientists died or, better stated, were murdered or driven mad. Those of us who survived now pretend to go along with the demands of our governments."

Berkfield sat very still. "So, you guys are like a hostage ghostbusters team?" he said as he continued to look for a possible escape route.

The man sighed. "Don't be foolish. We found hard evidence behind every myth and legend. We've catalogued demon fila, Detective Berkfield. The ancient high priests, warlocks, witches, generals, you name it, called on deities to assist them in wartimes. The new era of so-called reason has made us forget their power."

"So, you plan to do what with me and my family?"

Raking his fingers through his hair, the man looked Berkfield in the eye. "Listen carefully. We don't have much time.

There are two sides of this organization—those insane enough to believe that they can open up the gates of Hell and contain what comes out of it, so that they can proceed with imperialistic desires to rule humanity. And those of us who, after having studied the phenomena, have enough respect for it to leave it alone. We know that chaos will ensue. Therefore, the group is philosophically at odds with itself and threatening to implode. That means that valuable and dangerous research will spill out into the various nations that support this work, and as we all know, anything is for sale on the black market. Do you follow?"

Berkfield nodded, but he still didn't understand his role. This whole story was too bizarre to wrap his mind around.

"You, my friend, are currently under the protective seal of the master vampire who controls this region; therefore, right now, you're in full favor. The dark side essentially has a no-hit policy on you, and the Light apparently has you covered, as well. However, the way the power shifts seem to work within the vampire world are very much like old feudal law—they wipe out anything once associated with the outgoing incumbent. Understood?"

Terror halted Berkfield's breath for a moment. He touched his throat and then his fingers slid down to the small gold cross that he never took off. "But I'm a believer," he rasped. "How could I be marked by the dark side?"

The scientist calmly reached beneath his olive green flack-jacket and pulled a long chain from beneath it, bearing a sterling silver Star of David. "I'm a believer, too. The mark isn't physically on your body. It's in your aura. That's what we measure—energy fields, if you will. Our equipment cannot pick up much more than that. All we can ascertain is that a very strong energy from the nether realms has been gathering in the region, and it has been sending out sensor tentacles in your direction. Time is nigh, my friend. We're not exactly sure what this means, but it cannot be good."

"My wife, my kids—how do I get this fucking seal off me? I didn't ask for it, I don't even understand it!"

"That's why we want you to make a decision—quickly—to come work for us. Maybe, just maybe, you hold the key to bringing both sides to a standstill, a stalemate. You were deemed a good man by both sides. You could be the key to creating world peace. We must have an opportunity to study you, understand the conditions that led up to—"

"No! I don't know! This is all so crazy!" Berkfield put his head in his hands. "I want my old life back, my kids and wife safe. I want to read the damned paper, drink beer, and worry about gas prices. I do not want to be a guinea pig, nor do I want my family traumatized."

"Then you should have never become a crime fighter, never should have made that bargain in that alley, never should have started researching otherworldly phenomena and come up on our radar. I am a man of logic. I'm a scientist with thirty years of hard research under my belt and degrees that would . . ." The man stopped, swallowed hard, his voice gravelly with emotion. He spread his hands before Berkfield, imploring him to understand.

"I'm no cop. I'm no weapons designer. I opened a gate in a lab and found Hell," he said in a barely audible tone. "I thought I was losing my mind, and I cried out to God to save me, and another door opened and bright light bearing a blade shut the gate. We all saw it—and all of those colleagues joined us that day." The man's gaze slid away and he held the hair at his temples in clenched fists as he stared at the locked back door. "Some said it was a group hallucination. We told our superiors and they gave us an unlimited budget. That's when I knew we were in trouble." His voice dipped to a scratchy murmur. "They don't open the financial floodgates unless they know you're close. We're so close, and so are they."

"I thought I was the only one . . ." Berkfield said, dazed.

"So did we," the professor said sadly. "Then we began religious research, started looking at texts we had never considered in our scientific quest." He glanced up at Berkfield. "Ever wonder why you were spared that night in the alley where your partner double-crossed you and pulled a gun on you? Ever wonder what higher purpose you are to serve?"

The two men stared at each other, only the faint sounds of traffic droning on in the background.

"But my family—"

"Will be relocated and re-identified, just like ours had to be."

"But we can't just leave our home—"

"You make your informants do it all the time. Think of it as a witness protection program for scientists, and like I said, we're well funded."

"I can't make a decision like this without talking to my wife and my kids, and—"

"All you have to tell them is that one of the drug lords you've put away is out now and looking for payback. They know what you do, so that's not too far-fetched."

Berkfield sat back. "Why me? What special skill do I bring to the table?"

His abductor leaned forward and touched his clasped hands. "You're sane, you're not on the take, you've been spared because you're a good man, and you can call this master vampire to you. We need to speak to him. Plus, you know the inside of the American legal system like the back of your hand, and you have connections. And we may need sanctuary."

"But why now?" Berkfield asked, not convinced that this was his problem or that he needed to get swept up into the madness of trying to solve it. Truthfully, it was enough that he'd learned that vampires and demons were real. He didn't need to know more, or want to know more—except how to keep them away from him and his family.

"We've forecast a problem that is about to blow up on American soil. The dark-side energy levels are off the meters. We have a small sample of its atmosphere contained, and it's expanding exponentially within the vacuum containers in the lab. More current is being drawn into it, and its density is increasing. Disturbance locations in the U.S., where we know there are dark energy fields, are almost, for lack of a better explanation, harvesting power."

The van came to a sudden stop. Berkfield and the scientist's gaze locked.

"You have twenty-four hours to make your decision. Push nine-one-one on your garage-door opener between now and then, and we'll come collect you. They won't expect the code to be imbedded there. Ignore our offer, and you're on your own."

A henchman motioned for Berkfield to open the door. "You're home. You never saw us. We do not exist."

CHAPTER THREE

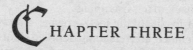

CARLOS STOOD outside the compound door, his arm draped over Damali's shoulder, willing his breathing to normalize. He wasn't sure if it was his proximity to her, or the fact that he had to explain some real bad news to her people.

Regardless, he hated going into her compound, which looked like a maximum-security prison. The concrete walls, iron-sealed windows, floodlights, and lack of trees until you hit the property border a mile away, gave him the feeling that he was walking into the federal pen. Maybe he was. He just hoped that he'd get out alive this time.

Besides, this whole situation was bullshit. He'd had to splatter the front of his Beverly Hills lair with a courier's guts, all because Damali was trailing ripe Neteru scent and the dumb bastard had reached for her. Damn straight he had to rip out the brother's heart, but he also had to clean up the mess before any neighbors noticed and wondered why there was black blood dripping down the white marble columns and the huge oak-paneled door, and why the stained-glass windows were streaked with innards.

Carlos let his breath out hard in disgust. He loved this woman dearly, but she always created drama! Council was right. It was time to get some guards at his doors, some security measures in place. He had descended and couldn't roll solo anymore. If he were in his right mind, he'd just make Damali his queen and battle the expected consequences. He glanced at her. No. He wasn't in his right mind to give her back to the Guardians.

When Carlos heard the locks engage, a thousand ways to begin the dreaded conversation tumbled through his brain. There was no easy way to say any of it. Worst part was, he had no idea how Damali would react when she found out he was taking her there for good—not just until he came back up from Hell.

"Que pasa?" Rider shouted, pounding Carlos's fist with a wide smile as they entered the outer safety chamber.

"Everything is everything," Carlos said, returning the pound, but keeping a watchful eye on the team's sharpshooter as they all moved deeper into the interior hallway. He immediately scanned the tall, muscular white guy with dirty-blond spike hair, and returned his smile—once he was sure that Rider wasn't packing. Even if the guy was in his forties, Rider was an all-pro vamp assassin.

"Hey y'all!" Damali hollered. "Can a person come home and get some love?"

"You know that ain't no problem from me, D," Jose said, embracing her quickly, then stepping back.

"We got nothing but love for you, li'l sis," Rider said laughing. "C'mon in . . . er, uh, him, too?"

"Yes," Damali said, slapping Rider on the back. "If he wasn't cool, why'd y'all leave me with him for a month?"

"Point taken," Rider said, stepping aside. "You're in."

Carlos moved forward with Damali next to him. The young bucks were no problem. Jose looked like his younger brother and had a soft heart, would hesitate if something ridiculous jumped off. However, he paused when he saw the quick flash of resentment on Jose's face. Something primitive and possessive rose in him and he fought it back down. Had to be Damali's Neteru still working his system. Jose wasn't a contender. He was family. He shook off the sensation. Kid was just probably still spooked.

His gaze scanned the others, sensing for signs of resistance. Dan was a nervous, wiry blond with no real combat under his belt. But J.L. had some Jet Li moves on him . . . Carlos gave the Asian kid a nod, then issued his most disarming smile to the others.

"Long time no see, *hombre,*" Jose finally said, laughing tensely, using his head to motion for them to enter beyond the first isolation chamber.

Good. The noses, Rider and Jose, were out front, and hadn't picked up anything unusual. Everybody had on T-shirts, jeans, sweats, no place to conceal a weapon, or get to one quickly. Big Mike, their audio sensor, had lowered his shoulder cannon and was all smiles. However, he wasn't sure he liked having a huge, six foot eight, two-hundred-and-seventy-five-pound, old school linebacker walking behind him. Big Mike was usually cool, but even Carlos knew to always keep an eye on the team's giant.

He also noticed that the tactical sensors were hanging back. Shabazz, Dan, and J.L. just nodded, and Marlene had her arms folded over her chest. Not good, especially the positions of the two older ones, Shabazz and Marlene. However, if J.L. was out front, then maybe he'd temporarily abandoned the monitors before he could pick up two cold bodies incoming.

But Carlos wisely noted that Shabazz was strapped—openly had a Glock on his hip and one in a shoulder holster, sending a quiet message to be cool, no doubt. Carlos scanned the streetwise Guardian from the 'hood. Instinctively he knew the old dude could feel trouble. It was as though Shabazz's shoulder-length locks telegraphed the vibrational changes, almost like a current, and Marlene was a freakin' seer. She had on a long, flowing, African-print robe—a great place to hide anything with a silver tip. The two of them together, late forties, early fifties, would surely be able to tell that something wasn't right with their girl. He just wanted the chance to explain.

"Oh, so now I'm like chopped liver," Damali said, laughing when no one else immediately moved forward to greet her, then she embraced her team members one by one. "Dag, you all act like I'm a stranger."

Carlos hung back in the entryway, watching as the tactical Guardians bristled slightly from her hug.

"Thought you weren't coming home, you were gone so long, kiddo," Marlene said with a sly smile, but her eyes were carefully scanning Damali the whole time. "Doesn't leave much time for us to get ready to do the Australian gig and all that goes with it."

"Yeah . . . well . . . what can I say?" Damali replied, her smile widening as she glanced at Carlos. "Let's go inside and catch up. Y'all got anything good in here to eat?"

Carlos didn't say a word as he monitored the uneasy glances that passed between the Guardians. But they followed her down the long cement corridor to the back of the facility; half of the team in front of him, the other half behind him, making him feel boxed in and claustrophobic. As they walked, he glanced up at the holy-water sprinkler system, hoping that there'd be no accidental discharge. He shook his head. No, it wouldn't be an accident at all.

Damali headed straight for the kitchen, and he was glad she hadn't gone straight for the weapons room. If he had to make a hasty exit, at least there weren't UV lights in there that could fry him—only harmless fluorescents. But the fact that she wouldn't give off a reflection in any of the stainless-steel appliance surfaces was going to be hard to explain.

"So, how were the islands?" Rider asked cheerfully, taking a backward seat in one of the wooden kitchen chairs.

"Beautiful . . ." Damali crooned in a distracted tone as she hunted for what the compound cupboards didn't have. "The water there is the prettiest blue, even if I did only see it at night."

Dead silence surrounded them.

Carlos glanced at the large picnic-style butcher-block oak table. Wood. Matching wood chairs. If the big brother got hyped, there were eight chairs that could easily be broken down to make fast stakes. Shit.

Big Mike leaned on the door frame, catching something unspoken in Shabazz's rigid carriage. Marlene hung back, and leaned against the sink, watching Damali begin to root inside the fridge. Jose, Dan, and J.L. took their time finding seats at the table, their glances nervously darting from Carlos to Damali and back to the team. J.L. fidgeted with a set of sharp knives that protruded from a wooden carving-set holder. Jose's eyes were practically welded to Damali, following her every move around the room. Dan's line of vision darted between Jose's and J.L.'s, then kept monitoring Marlene's unreadable expression.

Carlos found the closest spot by a window and vent near the far end of the oak cabinets, then leaned against them. Even the thick bulletproof windows were sealed by steel grates. Yellow designer mini blinds were ludicrous; it was still a prison.

"You only saw the islands at night?" Marlene asked coolly.

This could get ugly. Carlos studied the group's reaction and hoped Damali had enough sense not to just blurt out the truth.

"Well," Damali said, not paying Marlene's tone the attention it deserved, "we mostly stayed in during the day and slept."

"She did the day thing by herself for a while, but something happened down in St. Lucia," Carlos said quietly. "We need some advice, Mar."

All eyes were on Carlos as Damali slammed the refrigerator door and put one hand on her hip. He held up his palm, and begged her with his eyes not to start.

"While you're here, D, I order you to not harm anyone in this compound, or any other human. I don't care how hungry you get—that's nonnegotiable. Got it? Call me if it gets bad."

"Who are you *ordering*? Have you lost your mind? And why would you try to out me like that in front of my people? Damn, Carlos. Very uncool."

"Oh, shit," Rider muttered, standing slowly and backing away from the table.

Rider's slow withdrawal made the other younger Guardians near him stand and ease back. Only Jose stood his ground. Marlene covered her heart with her hand and remained frozen, centered between Damali and Carlos. Her gaze immediately went toward the stainless-steel stove, then tore back to Damali, and back to where there was no image of Damali to be found. Marlene's eyes then narrowed on Carlos.

Big Mike moved from his leaning position on the door frame with slow caution. Shabazz fingered the holstered weapon at his hip. Jose casually retrieved a crossbow from beneath the kitchen table and held it at his side.

"Talk to me," Shabazz said in a quiet voice. "Fast."

"It wasn't supposed to go down like this," Carlos said in a near whisper, shaking his head.

"Like what, brother? What did you do to li'l sis, man? Speak now, or forever hold your peace." Big Mike had raised the shoulder cannon again, positioning it in Carlos's direction.

Shabazz drew like lightning, the Glock muzzle pointed at the center of Carlos's forehead.

"Put it down, Mike," Marlene ordered. "You wanna hit a gas line and blow up the whole frigging kitchen? Stand down for a second, 'Bazz. Please, gentlemen."

"Something went wrong," Carlos said in a slow, controlled voice, "and I think she's turning."

Carlos had less than a second to duck before Shabazz and Rider emptied half a clip each into the kitchen wall behind him. He was immediately forced to fake right to avoid the crossbow stake released by Jose, who was reloading. Before J.L. could reach for the stashed lights, Carlos sent them crashing to the ground.

"Yo!" Carlos yelled, avoiding the onslaught in the close confines while trying not to hurt anybody. "Chill, I'm on your side, remember!"

"Fuck you!" Shabazz shouted. "Kill this mother dead, *now!*"

Carlos had taken a crouching position on the ceiling. He could smell the compound being flooded by the holy-water sprinkler systems; the heat of UV lights trapping him from a hallway exit was leaving him limited options; he might have to take a body to get out of there. "It didn't go down like you think and I thought you all said she couldn't turn after twenty-one! Why would I bring her back, if I'd meant to turn her? Think about it!"

"She isn't supposed to turn after twenty-one!" Marlene shrieked. "What type of dark energy did you hit her with? I'll climb up there on the ceiling and stake your ass myself for this!"

"Naw, Mar," Mike said, aiming the shoulder cannon in Carlos's direction. "I got him."

Immediately Carlos vaporized and reappeared on top of the gas range. "If you hit me here, we all go up, Mike. We need to talk."

"This is waaaay out of hand, people." Damali shook her head and suddenly laughed. "Carlos is tripping about nothing worth getting all hype about. You all are bugging." She walked away and flopped down in a kitchen chair, leaned her head back, and blew out a long breath of annoyance. "This shit don't make no sense."

The members of the Guardian team cast nervous glances in each other's direction, their gazes settling on Marlene. Carlos glimpsed the bullet-ridden kitchen wall, destroyed cabinets, and shards of glass and dishes. Damali was right, this didn't make any kinda sense—but he could understand it.

"Stand down," Marlene finally said, breaking the standoff and breathing hard. "If we kill him, we won't know what we're up against or how she . . ." Marlene's voice trailed off. "I can't even say it." Her eyes narrowed on Carlos as her tone became lethal. "What did you do to her?"

"Yeah!" Shabazz yelled. "Talk to us, man."

"Fuck talking," Jose said, tears standing in his eyes. "Kill this bastard, finish it, right here, right now!"

"Hold up," Rider said, and pulled his gun barrel back,

pointing it to the ceiling away from Carlos. "The only thing that is making sense is that he brought her here."

Mike nodded with Dan and Marlene.

"Speak," Shabazz ordered, his jaw pulsing with rage.

"She bit me," Carlos said, his voice low, shame almost burning the words from his mouth.

For a moment, no one spoke. Jose looked away and folded his arms over his chest. Finally, Rider was the first to break the silence with a full, tension-relieving belly laugh.

"Damn, man, is that all? You almost got yourself smoked in here because we thought she'd *really* turned." Rider glanced around and watched his teammates begin to slowly relax. "Oh, God help us all. Young bucks. Well . . ."

But Rider's voice trailed off as Damali brought both hands to the sides of her head and winced.

"Yeah," Carlos said with more authority in his tone. "Like I said. She bit me. Dropped two inches of fang in my jugular and came away with a coupla quarts. You feeling me?" He glanced at each member of the team, vindicated yet sad that their semi-amused expressions had gone ashen.

"You weren't complaining when—"

"D, that's *our* business. I ain't going there, not here in front of everyone," Carlos warned. "I just want to ask Marlene why. How could something like this happen?" Even the now-drawn weapons couldn't keep him from materializing in the middle of the kitchen floor and pacing. However, he kept his motions slow and steady as he stopped in front of Marlene, his eyes searching her wise ones for answers. "Mar, you gotta believe me. I didn't mean for this to happen to her."

"Y'all young bloods never do," Marlene said flatly, swallowing hard and fighting back tears. "Everybody drop your weapons. Shit. This is a family crisis. I'll rip his fucking heart out myself with my bare hands if he fangs-up in my presence. Right now we need answers."

Nobody moved as Marlene brushed past them and left the room. The fact that *Marlene* had cursed, *like that,* and had pushed a master vampire out of her way without a trace of fear was not lost on a soul in the room, especially not Carlos.

"I knew she would take it hard . . . but . . ." Damali said in a far-off tone, her eyes following the path Marlene had taken. "But shit happens."

"You okay, D?" Jose said, his voice strident with worry. He went to her side and placed a hand on her shoulder. She touched it and nodded yes, but Jose never drew away from her.

"Look, man, I'm sorry," Carlos muttered, trying to offer Shabazz a truce, even if an allegiance was impossible. But his glance kept traveling back to where Jose stood—way too close to his woman.

"Save it, motherfucker. If Marlene can come up with a cure, then I might forgive you. If not, I will smoke you, if it's the last thing I do."

The expression on Shabazz's face went beyond rage. His gaze was straight ahead, looking past Carlos down the hall in the direction Marlene had gone, totally stoic. Carlos simply nodded. He knew that place where Shabazz was, well past rage and so totally done that there were no words. He'd lived there most of his human existence.

"Once a dealer, always a dealer, right, Rivera? Damn, man, I expected better from you. D is like your family, but you got her all turned out with that 'first hit's on me' vampire bullshit." Big Mike sucked his teeth. "I might *never* forgive your trifling ass."

Carlos nodded and studied the terra-cotta tile floor. He could dig it. What was there to say? They would never understand.

It felt like it took twenty years for Marlene to come back into the room, and if looks could have killed, they'd all be goners, especially him. She shot each one of them the most lethal glare he'd ever seen, then slammed a huge black leather-bound book in the center of the kitchen table.

"The *Temt Tchaas* has *nothing* in here to deal with a situation like this!" Marlene rubbed her palms over her face. "Does Father Patrick know about this yet? Does he?"

"No," Carlos muttered. "I'm going to tell him later tonight."

Damali hung her head. "Ouch. I forgot about the priests."

"Well you two need to take it from the top and explain *exactly* what happened—so maybe, just maybe, I can jook-up some sort of antidote . . . I just don't know. How far gone is she?"

The fifty-million-dollar question, and he didn't have an answer. "I don't know," Carlos said honestly, tension winding its way down his spinal column. Suddenly he looked at Jose hard. "If you know like I know, you need to back up off her, man." The two men's eyes locked in a silent standoff, until finally Jose left Damali's side.

"Oh, that's just *beautiful*," Rider said, slapping his forehead. "The man lays down a turn bite, and as a master, doesn't even know when—"

"That's the point!" Carlos shouted. "I never did! I mean, I never meant to turn her; there was no will behind the action. No intent, man, for real."

"So, you all just talk about me like I'm not here, why don't you?" Damali was on her feet.

"Okay, okay, okay," Marlene said quickly. "Everybody take a deep breath. Let's summon calm so we can get some answers. If I have to conjure, then I need a brainstorm, and information, and plenty of prayers." She cast a hard glare at Damali. "And, yes, you will have to suffer through each one of those prayers, sister. Have a seat. It might be a long night."

Quiet filled the kitchen as Marlene took a deep breath, closed her eyes, then let it out slowly to center herself. She said nothing for what seemed like a long time, and then finally opened her eyes, her gaze going right for Carlos.

"Talk to me," Marlene said in a quiet voice. There was no judgment in her tone this time, just a weariness that he could appreciate. "How many times have you bitten her?"

The question caused him to glance at Damali, who shrugged and looked down at the floor. Total humiliation stripped him in front of her team. He should know things like this—but they just didn't understand what being with her was like. "I don't know," he finally admitted. "A lot."

"Jesus H. Christ!" Rider said, disgusted, kicking over a kitchen chair and walking to stand by Shabazz.

When Damali covered her head with her hands and gasped, everyone merely stared.

"It's like that," Carlos said, going to Damali, his palm stroking her soft locks as he stooped beside her. "I don't know why I can take it . . . hear the sacred names . . . but, now, she can't. It's fucking me up. I'm the one who's been banished by the Light. Mar, you've gotta make her better. My baby can't go out like this."

He wasn't sure whether it was the simple truth that seemed to galvanize the team, the fact that he didn't care that they saw just how worried he was for her, or if it was the fact that they were finally understanding just how serious this was. But the tension in the room eased, weapons got lowered in earnest, and a few younger Guardians moved toward the huge oak table to sit down again.

"I'm gonna do what I can, Carlos," Marlene said, a promise held in her voice. "She's our baby, too, and we know how you feel."

"Mar, honest to goodness," Carlos said, his tone fervent while double-checking himself not to say any words that would hurt Damali. "At first, things were cool. Just like you said. If things got . . . intense, and I bit her, it was all good. I had enough discipline not to flat-line her." His gaze swept the group, hoping for understanding, while feeling so stupid for even being in such a predicament. A council-level master, no less. This was beyond embarrassing.

When Rider rolled his eyes, Carlos pressed on, ignoring him. "I knew to siphon less than a pint. I wasn't trying to kill her."

Carlos could feel the tension in the kitchen gathering like a slow storm, but knew an explosive reaction was soon coming. He could hear the energy whining like a turbine. As the thought formed, Jose blew.

"Are you out of your fucking mind? There was no reason to bite her, man! I'll fucking kill you!" Jose spun toward the older armed Guardians at the door for a second and quickly raised his crossbow, holding Carlos in his sight. "'Bazz, let me put this bastard down once and for all!" He held out his hand toward Damali to come to his side of the room, but she just looked at him.

Only when Shabazz didn't move did Carlos stand and stalk away from Damali's side, far away from the group. From his peripheral vision, he saw Rider touch the young Guardian's arm, and saw how Jose angrily jerked away from his older, wiser comrade, following but not liking the silent message to stand down. He'd misjudged; the young bucks were a problem. A hair-trigger variable. He should have known better. The young ones weren't as effective, but were always shaky, nervous, and too stupid to know they'd die trying. However, if the old boys were holding steady, then he had a chance to explain. But he kept his primary line of vision directly on Marlene—the only reasonable one among them.

"Most of the time, she'd hang out on the beach, dozing during the day, or doing whatever, while I slept. Then at night, we'd go out on the town, chill, listen to some music, check out a festival, get her something to eat, go back to the lair. Everything was peace," Carlos finally said in a controlled tone.

Jose's eyes glittered raw fury, just like Shabazz and Big Mike's did, but . . .

"Just groovy," Rider muttered, with a scowl. "Okay. So, since everything was copacetic, when did you notice girlfriend had fangs and couldn't do a day at the beach even with sunblock?"

"Last night," Carlos said under his breath. "Everything changed last night."

"Why?" Shabazz asked, his tone so tightly controlled that it made Damali look up.

"I'm not exactly sure," Carlos admitted, glancing at the same spot on the floor Damali had focused on. Marlene's appraisal was also too intense to continue direct eye contact with her at the moment.

"All right," Marlene said, her voice like a schoolteacher dispensing facts. "For twenty-eight days and nights, everything was fine. I take it you bit her multiple times every one of those nights—no need to answer. Fact one." Her gaze went to Damali. "And, during said time, there was no fight, no resistance, correct?"

Damali glanced out the kitchen window. "No."

Jose walked so far away from the group that he was nearly beyond the kitchen entry. Carlos glanced at him, expecting to see worry, but the glare Jose gave him was almost a direct challenge. He could feel himself begin to bulk, but willed away the sensation. The young blood was definitely working his nerves.

"Herein lies the beginning of our problem," Marlene said on a long sigh. Disgusted, she put the reading glasses that dangled from a silver-beaded cord about her neck on the bridge of her nose, and opened the *Temt Tchaas* hard in the middle of the table. "This is partly my fault."

"How's that?" Shabazz holstered his gun, folded his arms, and stared at Marlene, unconvinced.

"The Neteru physiology is designed to create vampire antibodies under battle conditions. When fully amped, in a bloodlust, in the heat of battle with adrenaline pumping, everything in her whole system works as a unit to seal the wound, kill the attacking virus. But with a serious endorphin rush happening with every bite . . . no anger, no fear, total open trust and willingly offering her throat . . ."

"No," Shabazz said, his words seething past his lips. "They would have had a seduction provision in there, knowing that a Neteru could get within intimate proximity to a master vamp while on the hunt and possibly get hypnotized, whatever. It's not your fault; that much I do know." He glared at Carlos. "The bastard wanted her like this all along—you and I both know that, Mar. Subconscious intent was there from the door."

"Shit." Carlos just closed his eyes. "I should have seen this coming."

"Poor choice of words, dude. We're still armed."

He refused to dignify Rider's comment, but it was a direct blow to his ego. The way the muscle in Jose's jaw pulsed grated him. Carlos turned away toward the sink, now unable to look at any of them.

"Then, you mix in the normal fluctuations that happen to a normal female's body chemistry on a monthly basis," Marlene added, her voice pained as she spoke, "and we have a recipe for disaster. A variable. You're the only one she would have allowed to be with her like this, and there's nothing in the *Temt Tchaas* about a Neteru falling head over heals for a master vampire—ever. This wasn't a vamp seduction or treachery that would have had resistance still lingering in her subconscious; she wanted to be with you, that's the issue. There was no resistance to fire her system up to fight the turn."

Damali stood and went to Carlos's side. "It wasn't his fault, y'all. It wasn't anybody's fault. I didn't know; he didn't know; you guys didn't know."

Her voice had become so tender that he almost reached for her.

"There was nothing to resist," she said, still defending him. "He was supposed to be a Guardian, and he is a good man. Carlos didn't *want* to turn me . . . it just sorta happened."

He had to get away from Damali's sweet words, so he concentrated instead on Marlene's eyes, the pain and anger he saw there. He had to stay focused, so the group's mother-seer could save Damali. He just wished that he hadn't blocked the older woman's second sight from entering his lairs. Maybe she could have prevented this.

"We're not here to cast blame, honey." Marlene's voice was gentle. "But we have to find a solution, or by the end of the night . . ."

"The hunger is gonna hit her," Carlos said, giving his back to the group again.

When Damali touched his shoulder, he turned slowly and lifted her chin with one finger. "Baby . . . I'm so sorry.

They're gonna have to lock you up, and seal you in a room without sunlight until—"

"Oh, hell no!" Damali snatched away from him, and started for the door, but stopped as Big Mike, Shabazz, and Rider blocked her exit.

"I might be the only one who can feed you, until Marlene figures out a way. Call me, if it gets real bad, and I promise, I'll come to you. From my veins is the only way, at the moment." Carlos looked at her team. "And you all are gonna have to be cool and let me in so she can feed. If she gets out I don't want her hunting alone—she might take a body. That can't happen. Or another male might approach her and feed her. That *definitely* can't happen."

"No, it can't," Marlene said, ignoring Damali's stricken expression.

"But there's one other problem," Carlos muttered.

"What the hell else could be worse than this?" Jose walked into the kitchen again to stand by Shabazz, Rider, and Big Mike.

"I think she's ripening early," Carlos said in a distant tone, his gaze going toward the window. "So you've gotta find a cure fast, because I won't be able to come in here and just feed her. Understand?"

"You have *got* to be bullshitting me." Rider let his back slam against the wall and he closed his eyes.

"Wish I were, man." Carlos went to Damali and touched her hair. "That's when the shit got really out of hand . . . last night. One hit of her fragrance, and I was near gone. If she hadn't siphoned me first, I would have flat-lined her. You have no idea how close it came to that."

Shabazz had taken two paces in Carlos's direction, but Big Mike grabbed the back of his shirt.

What could he say? It was the cold-blooded truth. Carlos spoke slowly; he needed them to understand. "A mind lock went down, she took a walk on the dark side with me. She bit me, took two quarts, and the virus is all through her . . . not just from my bites, but now from a total blood exchange—a double plunge. She woke up hungry, and watched me drop an international courier to feed her without batting an eyelash."

Fuck it. This wasn't the time for shame or games. Carlos looked at the group hard. "You remember what our international messengers look like, don't you?"

"Huge mothers," Big Mike replied, nodding. "She made you take one of those, then, forewarned is forearmed."

Both men nodded.

"But she didn't die," Marlene said in an urgent rush. "That may be our only hope."

"You sure she didn't?" Jose asked, his voice cracking from his obviously dry throat. "I mean, I'm not trying to be negative, or anything . . . but how do we know?" His eyes darted between Damali and Carlos, then back toward Marlene.

"Jose's got a point," Dan chimed in. "No offense."

"No offense taken. Definitely a valid point." Carlos could almost feel Marlene's gasp pass through his skeleton. "We shouldn't take anything for granted. There were periods when I wasn't conscious."

"C'mon, man," J.L. protested. "Wouldn't you know if she died on your watch, even if it happened during your daytime sleep?"

A slight smile tugged at Carlos's mouth. "That's not necessarily when I was out." They just didn't understand.

"Je—"

"Don't say it, Rider," Marlene warned, holding up her hand. "If she died in your arms, and came back . . . say within minutes . . . oh, I don't know."

"I will kill you," Jose said slowly, moving forward in preparation for a foolhardy lunge, but was stopped by Shabazz's arm.

"Gives a whole new meaning to petite mort," Rider chided, shaking his head.

"How about a grand mal seizure," Damali whispered, sidling up to Carlos. "Let's get out of here, baby. We told them enough . . . and I'm hungry. I can tell you're starved, too."

Again the room went stone-cold still.

"No," Carlos said firmly. "Baby, listen. I've gotta go to Hell, handle a few things—"

"Do you *hear* yourselves!" Rider was walking in a circle, arms outstretched. "Where's my fucking clip?"

"Got one you can borrow," Shabazz said, tossing Rider the spare ammo clip from his shoulder gear, and pulling Sleeping Beauty from his hip again.

Jose eyed the crossbow that Rider had discreetly taken from his side, noting that it was too far away for a quick grab. Opting for the available, he unsheathed a bowie knife, stripping it from Rider's belt. In a lightning move, J.L. had snatched the largest knife from the carving set, and had tossed Dan one that was only a bit smaller.

"I take it this has hallowed-earth-packed rhinos locked and loaded?" Rider asked Shabazz with a sneer in Carlos's direction.

"You know me, brother," Shabazz said in a tight voice.

"Would you people relax?" Damali said, thoroughly annoyed. "We're just going out and will be back in a few."

"No, D. They're right. That's how this all got started in the first place. Me and you were gonna go and just *talk* at Father Pat's . . . and it got crazy. Then, you were gonna take the shortcut home from Brazil, and wound up staying waaay too long in my Rio lair. Then, St. Lucia was supposed to be a one-night pit stop, but lasted longer. So, I'm out. Remember what I said—no humans, ever."

"Oh, so you're just gonna leave—just like that?" Both hands were on Damali's shapely hips, and the outrage that glittered in her eyes was like a magnet.

Carlos paused, then shook off the temptation. "I have to." He had to get away from her before he changed his mind.

"Yeah, he does," Marlene agreed, telling Carlos with one look that it was time to go. "He's getting stronger, though . . . each time we see him—I don't know if that's bad or good."

"Bad sign," Rider said fast. "We were real happy to have you on our side down in Hell, and in the Amazon, but turning our li'l sister was not a part of the dealio."

"You got that right," Jose said, his voice low and dangerous.

"Mar," Carlos warned, ignoring the other guardians. "She was made by a master with council-level lineage. Hear me? From all indications she rolls like a female master, not a second-generation."

"Marlene, what's he talking about?" Jose stood back to allow Carlos an opening to pass.

"All I'm hearing is the part about council-level lineage," Shabazz said slowly.

"Council-levels make masters. Masters make seconds. If he was the one who made her, he just made a topside female master, people. When Nuit bought it, then Damali dusted Vlak, Carlos must have descended—that's the power shift. Brother just moved a level up in the vamp food chain." Marlene shut her eyes. "Oh, Lord . . ."

Damali weaved and held her temples. "Mar, please . . . gimme a break!"

"Yeah, Mar. Dead on." Carlos looked at the team and lowered his gaze. "It went down something like that. Open territory. I was next in line. Mar, see if the book says something about a councilman's bite. I'm way more than a master these days, sis."

"Oh, and you couldn't have dropped that little bit of info on us before we let you take her to your lair in Rio! Are you nuts?" Rider was holding his gun so tightly that it shook.

"Get real," Carlos said. "I'm a damned vampire, not a saint."

"As far as us watching her, what does this mean?" Jose asked, his eyes searching Marlene's face.

Carlos brushed past the Guardians at the door, who gave him wide berth, then stopped in the hallway and turned to look at them all hard. But for a split second his concentration fractured. Something strong and distant was calling him. It was a garbled, muffled, indecipherable call that had become muted within the prayer-guarded walls of the compound. He had to get out of there. *Now.* He could feel it, knew he had to address the 9-1-1 pulse within his territory.

Shaking the distraction, Carlos glimpsed at Jose, knowing that Guardian would be the weak link in the chain. If Damali needed to feed, Jose was dinner. "What I'm telling you all is, her mind lock is beyond the strength you can imagine—I almost couldn't fight it."

"No, you couldn't, could you?" Damali casually leaned against the refrigerator and smiled. "But you are not leaving me here, with them."

Carlos ignored her, and kept talking to the group. "The master vamp powers of seduction are deep, trust me. But don't make me have to come in here and take a body for her—it's in my nature, what can I say? Don't ever forget she's my woman." Although his statement was issued to the entire group, and his eyes scanned each member of it, his gaze lingered longest on Jose.

"Shit . . ." Rider walked away deeper into the kitchen to get out of Carlos's possible swing range when Marlene bristled.

"No male in this joint is immune," Carlos muttered, still holding Jose's line of vision. "She will do *anything* to get out of here, and she went into the turn with Neteru strength . . . whatever she got from me, I don't know."

"You know what I got from you," Damali murmured, the barest hint of fang glistening in the fluorescent kitchen light.

Carlos swallowed hard, but motioned with his head toward her. "I want you all to see this, so we're all clear before I leave. It's in your best interests not to have any illusions."

He walked back into the kitchen, stood before Damali, embraced her, and exposed his jugular to her. Her body fit against him, slid against all the right places so smoothly that he fought not to groan—respect for the family. Her hunger was palpable, just like her desire to be alone with him. She raised herself on her toes, pressing her abdomen against his, belly-to-belly, nearly climbing up him to reach just the right spot. *C'mon, baby, get it over with, before I drag you out of here.* He could feel his lids go to half mast as he struggled to keep his own incisors from lowering. Her family would be traumatized enough, they didn't need to also witness him feeding from her. But she was mentally coaxing him into a double-plunge. "Uh-uh, not in front of family," he murmured. They had no idea what resisting this urge was like.

"Right. What was I thinking?" she whispered, and then nuzzled his throat. "Later."

"Just do it," he said tensely, then shut his eyes, blocking out the stricken expressions of her family.

When the strike came he closed his lids tighter and mentally blocked out the gasp that rattled the group. He'd vowed to never do this in public, but this was necessary, and it took everything within him to break from Damali's hold without biting her in return. Girlfriend was all pro, had pulled blood from his veins with the intensity of a master, sending pleasure throughout his system to block the pain, a smooth siphon that made sweat form on his brow and caused an involuntary shudder throughout his body. It felt like an eternity as he waited for her to lift her head. He opened his eyes, only to be met by hers and a sexy smile. Her tongue ran over her crimson bottom lip, leaving it moist.

"Want some?"

He ignored the generous invitation. This was not the time or place. Winded from her feed before he'd hunted and fed, he kissed her hard and staggered away from her, fighting the urge to take her to his lair to finish what she had started. He dabbed the corner of his mouth with the back of his fist, his mouth practically watering. Humiliation made his face burn, but he looked at her team, nonetheless. "Now, do you see what I'm talking about?"

Quiet tears streamed down Marlene's face. Dan turned and vomited on the kitchen floor. Rider and J.L. were taking in slow sips of air. Jose's face crumbled and he turned toward the wall. Shabazz and Big Mike stood motionless, their eyes moist, their glares unmoving.

"Fix this shit, Marlene," Shabazz finally grumbled. "Tonight. I don't want to ever see this bastard in our compound again."

"She'll be all right for the next twenty-four hours," Carlos said without emotion. He understood. It was horrifying. And there was no one to blame but him.

His fingers traced Damali's cheek as he watched her begin to normalize—but her family would never be the same. "I'll be back," he told Damali, "and Marlene is going to make this all right. Stay in, and don't fight them when they try to help you—promise me?"

She nodded and pressed her fingers to his throat wound, then licked them. That was Big Mike's last straw. When the big brother broke down and cried openly without shame, Carlos was out. He couldn't watch pain like this. They were family.

The ground was pulsing. Clouds of bats filled the night sky, screeching his name. Council had sent out an all-points bulletin for him. He could tell by the look on Father Pat's face that Marlene had already filled in the Covenant. News traveled fast, especially bad news. They all stood on the cabin steps, not speaking, but he knew a new round of prayers now barred him entry to what had been his safe house. Father Lopez, the youngest of the priests, looked away as silent tears slid down his brown cheeks. The Moor, Asula, was practically gray. Monk Lin turned away and swallowed hard.

"But I love her," was all Carlos could say. "No matter what."

"I know," Father Pat said quietly, his tone gentle. "But now we have a situation. It's greater than you can imagine, and the timing . . ."

"Do whatever you can to get her straight."

The old priest nodded. "We'll do whatever we can. We'll take a blood supply to her. In two days, you won't be able to."

"Thank you." That was all there was left to say before Carlos turned toward the night wind and was gone.

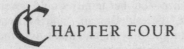HAPTER FOUR

·❈·

CARLOS'S GAZE narrowed on the dark blue horizon as he opened his arms, feeling the wind gather about him. Going down to Hell alone was not an issue at this point. One more night of freedom—for what? He was so worried about what might happen within the compound that he just willed himself to council chambers without waiting for the formal VIP escort that was on its way.

As the earth split at his feet, emitting a black cloud that swirled around him, pulling him down, he could sense slippery things reach out for him, then think better of it. Even the demons knew he was not to be messed with right now.

As soon as he landed in the black-stalactite-studded outer council chamber corridors, the messenger bats screeched their confusion, gossiping wildly, stirring their putrid ammonia-ridden stench. Several hooded domestic couriers stepped out of the sulfur fumes, and materialized from behind slick stalagmites, their eyes glowing red.

Two scythes dropped before him, blocking his approach, and the bolder of the two messengers that stopped him hissed its concern.

"Master Rivera, it is customary to be escorted to chambers by VIP escort at your level when the chairman has summoned you. We believe your furlough expires tomorrow night. Then and only then does your full installation as a councilman occur."

The tunnel went silent, all entities waiting for the proper response. From the corner of his eye Carlos could see the narrow path that led to the molten sea of Perpetual Agony that surrounded the main chamber. For a moment, the sight of the howling, begging, lost vampire souls within it gave him pause. Their relentless shrieks always made the hair stand up on his arms, but that would be the last thing he'd have to worry about if the chairman decided he didn't like what he had to say.

"I didn't send for a courier, because the international one I summoned broke protocol and reached for my package." Carlos gave the smaller, domestic couriers a threatening smile. "I had to . . . fire him. The chairman needs to know about things like that. Besides, I'm responding to a nine-one-one."

At once the corridor erupted with screeches and squeals of delight—juicy gossip always fed the blind. The messengers raised their scythes, and hissed their approval, signaling that Carlos could pass.

"How did you kill him?" a voice echoed behind Carlos.

"Tore his arm off when he reached for my package, then ripped his heart out."

A chorus of delighted squeals cheered Carlos as he walked away.

He crossed the bubbling pit on a six-inch band of earth and once at the massive, black marble double doors, Carlos steadied himself before reaching for the golden, fanged door knockers and submitted to the required serpent strike on his hand that would identify his black blood for entry.

The doors slowly opened, and he was once again standing before the ancient power center. His footsteps echoed on the black marble floor veined with blood. Carlos held his head up, his jaw set hard, his eye contact with the chairman never wavering as he approached the pentagram-shaped council table. Dense smoke from the iron wall torches plumed in a spiral upward, joining with the ever-present black transport tornado that circled high above in the ceiling's arch.

Everything seemed to be in order, calm. He nodded at the chairman, who returned the gesture, lacing his long, clawed fingers together under his chin. Carlos then acknowledged the two remaining council members, detecting a level of nervousness.

"Mr. Chairman," Carlos said in his most confident voice. "Gentlemen. It is good to be back at this table."

The chairman stood and issued a sly smile with a raised eyebrow, and put his hands behind his back. He took his time rounding the table, his long onyx-colored robe making a soft swishing sound as he neared Carlos. The blue blood within his veins moved slowly under his paper-thin gray skin. And although that was a good sign that the chairman's mood was calm, even the cloud of transporter bats high above in the arched ceiling fell eerily silent.

"How were the islands?" the chairman asked, his tone cooing, almost amused.

"Fine, sir, but that's not why I'm here, right? You sent a high-priority message for me to . . ." Carlos's statement died as he watched the chairman continue to move toward him.

The chairman circled him slowly and Carlos knew better than to move. His body temperature dropped to a nervous twenty-eight degrees when the chairman came close enough to rip his heart out.

"You had one more night before your furlough expired." The chairman put a hooked claw to his lips and made a little tsking sound. The other senior members shook their heads, then began filling their golden goblets with blood that oozed from the table's pointed edges.

"Mr. Chairman, we've got major problems topside," Carlos said firmly, his chin still held high, his gaze level with the chairman's.

"I *know* we have major problems topside!" the chairman shouted, fangs suddenly eight inches and growing longer by the second as he grabbed Carlos by the throat. "We got a visit from the seventh level last night. They sent harpies to inform us that the Neteru might have turned. Speak to me, *now!*"

The force of the chairman's grasp was crushing his Adam's apple, but Carlos managed to croak out, "She's not turning. She's in flux."

The chairman dropped him and began to pace. "Explain," he said in Dananu.

Thinking fast, Carlos threaded every truth he knew with the best lies. The fact that the senior council member had asked the question in the old language was not good, but it also meant that he was unnerved by the level-seven inquiry, and that was potentially advantageous.

"As you gentlemen know, I have been protecting this package since the day I was turned." Carlos took his time. This had to be an airtight game. "After the incident in Brazil, where we lost Counselor Vlak, and with Nuit's seat also open, our council was suddenly and extremely vulnerable. We need five points of the pentagram territories inhabited by a throne-level master to keep the power flow at peak levels."

"Dispense with the history," the chairman snapped, his patience gone. "Explain the flux."

"You gave me a month to work on her, to keep her confused, in an open state. I marked her, and even her family had its guard down after my team's performance in Brazil."

Carlos glanced at the still-seated councilmen, who nodded their approval, and he could feel his body temperature begin to normalize as the chairman moved away from him to take a seat at the table. But their icy glares said they were waiting for more answers.

"The repeated bites I delivered were not enough to turn her, just influence her. I know that she cannot be allowed to die, or be compromised."

He waited until the old chairman nodded.

"But I still had the tracer of ripening were-demon on me from . . . let's say . . . a brief indiscretion I had while tracking the Neteru."

Again, he waited, and when the old men around the table smiled, he began to relax. "Bottom line is, the scent caused an international courier to get confused, try to rush the Neteru, and he nicked her," Carlos said, puffing up to seem indignant. "To keep her family placated, I took her home so they can perform whatever rituals are necessary to flush her system of the bite overdose—the courier's is now added to mine. Her womb has to remain inviolate."

"That fool!" the chairman exclaimed, aghast. "If you had not exterminated him, surely I would have."

The chairman's statement was met with a round of murmurs from the others at the table.

"My point exactly," Carlos replied with confidence. "I had to smoke him right in front of her. But it worked to our advantage."

"The Guardians will be able to rectify this?" The chairman's eyes searched Carlos's.

"That's why I took her to her compound before responding to your urgent page. Nothing short of a serious emergency would have made me do something like that, Mr. Chairman."

It was a standoff. He could feel the chairman trying to break through his mental barriers. All he could hope was that the Covenant had not rescinded the prayers they'd had around him that created a Vampire Council blind spot.

Finally, the chairman sat back and closed his eyes. "Our apologies," he said in a soothing tone. "You do appear sufficiently alarmed by the incident. We are all under duress."

Carlos nodded and let his breath out slowly. "Thank you."

"The timing of this situation is very delicate." The chairman was on his feet again, slowly pacing behind the table.

"Don't worry, I've got this under control," Carlos said, holding up his hand, hoping to arrest the old man's agitation. "It was perfect."

All eyes were trained on Carlos as a lopsided smile tugged at his mouth. "I saved her, yet again, from danger when I dropped the courier. I brought her to her people and asked them to pray away the turn, to find an antidote. I, a vampire, asked *them* to pray."

The chairman stood so still that Carlos wasn't sure if the old man was even breathing. "Brilliant," the senior vampire whispered. "What then?"

"She argued with them, because, of course, they were angry at me for putting her in harm's way . . . but she went against her entire team and even the Covenant . . . *for me*. We have fully co-opted the Neteru, gentlemen." Carlos allowed the silent awe to sweep through the three elder vampires.

Triumphant, Carlos lifted his chin higher as fanged smiles slowly opened on the faces around the table. The chairman threw back his head and laughed.

"Rivera, each time you come to council chambers, you delight me. And, your plan, now, young man?"

This was it: the bargaining hour. Time to call in more resources, and to buy him and Damali more time.

"I still want her people protected until the very end so she doesn't get nervous and think I've started picking them off one by one. I've invested a lot to keep her on my side."

"Done," the chairman murmured, rubbing his long, pointed chin with satisfaction.

"I can't travel down here by courier for a while, even though I know the two empty seats creates a power drain, but it'd only be temporary. I can come down for serious business, meetings on significant topside matters, but I shouldn't risk going back and forth unescorted on a regular basis. I need to stay topside to keep the vessel out of harm's way. None of us knows how many scattered rebel forces from the civil war still remain at large."

All the bald heads around the table nodded their consent.

"These are indeed unstable times, Rivera. You have been our best insurance, thus far."

"But my lairs are wide open. I haven't had time to set up lieutenants I can trust. So, I'll need some Hell-dogs to watch my back while I handle my territory realignments."

"There are four other masters topside, Mr. Chairman," one of the other councilmen said with concern. "Each continent has one. Nuit's old territory was ceded to Carlos, and it is vast with breechable borders. Surely we can authorize some safeguards for our esteemed Councilman Rivera?"

The chairman nodded. "Absolutely. While he is in-lair, his perimeters must be held. But, as you travel you'll need bodyguards, of some sort."

"I'll work it out. I can make some bodyguards; that's not my primary concern. I just want to be sure that I don't get smoked in my sleep."

"These are dangerous times to be at our level, Carlos," the chairman said carefully. "Fallon Nuit's coup attempt has given the other masters ideas . . . and none of them is pleased with our choice to promote you before them. Envy is such a powerful emotion."

Carlos watched the elderly vampire's eyes, slowly becoming aware that while the Neteru situation was a problem, something much worse was brewing. When the chairman glanced at the other seated council members before proceeding, he was sure of it.

"Sir," Carlos asked with total deference in his tone, "if there's something compromising our position, I need to know."

The old vampire closed his eyes, let out a long, weary breath and laced his gnarled fingers together. "Your territory had a key hidden within it, as all the territories do. The gray zone of choice is where the catalysts of the Armageddon lie."

Cool beads of sweat crept between Carlos's shoulder blades until they united into a silent trickle down his spine. "You said, 'had' . . ."

"Damned scientists," the chairman muttered so quietly that no one at the table breathed for a moment. "Their ignorance . . . lack of knowledge and understanding."

Carlos and the others watched the chairman battle repressed rage, a slight tremor running through him as he stood and swept past the table to stop before the torture wall. He opened his fingers wide, stretching them until the ancient skin seemed like it would rip. They all watched as each digit soon glowed with an eerie red heat, and when he was satisfied that enough energy had collected within his now blue-white palm, he pointed to the wall, scorching it with laser-like flames as he drew the diagram for them.

"There is a key for the Seven Seals as specified within the sixth chapter of Revelations—contained within the book we never mention. Someone from the sixth realm—a master vampire—has stolen the key that will unlock the sixth seal."

Carlos was leaning forward so far in his throne that he almost fell to the floor. *The key to the sixth seal had been stolen?*

"When opened, the sixth seal turns the sun to ash, making it black like sackcloth . . . perpetual night." The chairman paused as murmurs swept the chamber. "The moon will turn to blood. Heaven will roll away as though a scroll taken up." His hard gaze stabbed into every set of pupils that remained riveted to his. "The opener of the seal would be powerful enough to mark his territory with the sacred number of our empire. He would not need a daywalker bloodline, as night would be eternal! The sun would be forever banished. Heaven would have rolled away, giving rise to earthquakes and landmass realignments—our territories would be in chaos . . . and this victor would rule under a blood moon, rendering this council obsolete as a ruling body!"

All Carlos heard was the part about not needing a Neteru to make daywalkers. That meant Damali was instantly at risk. The only thing that had ever kept them from trying to kill her was the possible use of her womb. If that option vanished, her protection would disappear. Carlos was on his feet.

"But if this was already prophesized in Revelations, it was only a matter of time—"

"Our time!" the chairman shouted, pointing a bony finger toward Carlos to correct him. "Our Dark Lord has always been in pursuit of these hidden keys and seals. He, and he alone, would have handed them over to the most deserving realms, and our level-six council would have been the epitome of his empire. The daywalkers were our insurance. No one knows the true hour of the Armageddon, and for centuries we have all been in wait."

Weary resignation entered Carlos's body, just as it seemed to have slowed the chairman's complaint.

"Sir, you said it happened in my territory. North America, I take it?"

"Yes," the chairman hissed, as he slowly made his way back to his throne. "Your borders were weak, there were many insurgents—but that would not have been enough to find the keys." His lethal gaze swept the table. "*Scientists*. Bloody, foolish scientists have been conducting experiments to find and monitor our energy fields. They have created disturbances, opened portals, and demagnetized some force fields that once hid the seals and keys from us. They were doing advanced weapons research in the U.S., experimenting with electromagnetic fields, and that's how one of our topside masters came to know that the most critical of the keys was hidden in North America." He released a pained chuckle. "They wanted the ultimate weapon, and they have indeed created it."

"If a master vampire has his hands on the key, then we'll just have to jack him and get it back—basic," Carlos said, making a tent with his hands. "Assassinate the sonofabitch."

The chairman smiled. "While we all like how you think, Mr. Rivera, the critical element is we don't know which master has it." He glimpsed the other more senior councilmen. "You see, Carlos, that is why we summoned you. When the Neteru began to turn, and this all occurred in your territory, we had to invite you down here for an appraisal. Our initial assumption had to be governed by logic versus loyalty. If your bite turned her, and the threat of this council, as well as the loss of the opportunity to start a daywalker empire, was not enough to make you garner restraint . . . then we could only assume . . ."

"I understand, sir." Although Carlos was offended, he could appreciate the precaution and simply nodded.

"We now believe that she turned because of the power shift," one of the councilmen at the far end of the table admitted. "A Neteru, post-twenty-one years of age, should never turn. Not like that. Not within the same night. This happened when the breach occurred. When one of the Keys of Light fell into the hands of the Dark Realms, some of her immunity was possibly compromised."

Carlos concurred with a nod. "If you don't know who took it, please tell me you do know where it was taken from. North America is a lot of ground to cover on a treasure hunt."

"A church in Boston," the chairman said, wiping his brow. "Seems energy fluctuations reduced the barrier to evil around the key holder and exposed it, and he had a weakness . . . shall we call it a proclivity for little boys. The master who came to him trailed illusion and transformed into an irresistible youth, sources tell us, and was thus able to sweet-talk the cleric into fetching the key in order to make an impression."

The chairman let his breath out in disgust. "Everybody has a weakness, every power structure has an Achilles' heel— ironically, theirs has now become ours." He chuckled sadly and closed his eyes, the strain clear in his fatigued expression. "Almost karmic, wouldn't you agree?" When Carlos didn't reply to the rhetorical question, the chairman calmly returned to his seat. "Our only chance is the fact that they've never kept the keys with the seals. Each seal, we can only determine via logic, is most likely kept far away from each key. The quest then is to secure either the key or the seal to have bargaining power with the master who is attempting the coup."

"Or we can eliminate the bastard from the game before he can play it." Carlos stared at the chairman hard and could feel the electric agreement of the others course through him as they hissed their approval.

The chairman smiled.

Carlos stood and began to pace. "All right. What does the key look like?" His nerves were drawn so taut that he had to put his hands behind his back as he paced.

"It's blood," the chairman whispered. "It's the blood of the Lamb. It's the Key of Life. When the blood is spilled upon the seal, it opens. The priest showed the master vampire a holy vial, which was then stolen."

Carlos stopped walking. *The blood of Christ?* Carlos

chose his next words carefully. "The Light is going to send a *serious* militia for it. You know that, right?" He hesitated. "I can't imagine that they'd just sit back and—"

"Even their normal Guardian teams are gaining strength, becoming more aggressive. You are correct, Mr. Rivera. This has already begun to create repercussions that we are monitoring to develop a damage-control strategy against."

"Even if the priest left hallowed ground, the master wouldn't be able to hold onto the vial. If this blood really came from—"

"Yes," the chairman said quickly, again cutting Carlos off. "A human helper had to do the master's bidding, but the key can be contained within a living body. We must find the human that has been given the blood, and that human must be slain on the seal as a perfect sacrifice at the appointed hour. If we do not find this human before the other master uncovers the location of the sixth seal, existence as we know it is over."

"If I off the master vamp who did the heist, and bring you the key—"

"The Neteru is yours, fangs and all. We would have no more use for her and she would be less problematic as your vampire bride, Carlos, than as a huntress."

Carlos returned to his throne very slowly. The threat was implicit. *Bring us the seal or we kill Damali.* It was so obvious, yet so subtle, a knowing so clear that the chairman didn't even have to say it. The old vampire understood by now that Damali was worth more to his existence than even infinite power. The realization that the chairman recognized that deeply held secret left Carlos feeling naked. They could trust him to bring them the seal and not use it himself—it made too much sense.

He sat with great effort and in deep contemplation. What would he tell Damali? Every fiber within him knew that she'd never allow such a trade; her life for the sixth biblical seal. She'd fight to the death to protect it, even with fangs. That was her nature, just like to negotiate to the bone to save her was his. Another variable had arisen, but it was one he might not be able to live with.

"You seem hesitant," the chairman said, threading new tension throughout the chamber.

Carlos shook his head. "No. I'm trying to figure out who could have crossed my borders and when. It probably went down when I was in Brazil or in the Caribbean. The northern borders would have been wide open for a month." Renewed rage and frustration lowered his incisors as he raked his fingers through his hair. Damn!

The chairman sat back in his throne, appearing relaxed.

"Perhaps as the newest council member, I may call a topside meeting. The others, after all, are a level of power lesser than me, right? That is my prerogative." Carlos watched the chairman for a reaction.

"Do not take these old masters lightly, Carlos," the chairman warned. "They are shrewd and deadly. We cannot afford another power drain to the table. Do not act on an ill-conceived plan developed in haste and frustration."

"I know better than to go in blind-swinging because I'm pissed about a border breech." Carlos tried to temper the indignant tone that was making his statement too brittle. Mellowing slightly to show respect, he took a deep breath before continuing. "I just need a little time to work some things out, but duly noted. If they've lasted this long topside, against all the Neterus they've historically encountered, I have respect for what they can do." Carlos leaned forward and filled his goblet without looking at it, his gaze holding the throne-seated vampires' steely glares. "But they also need to respect this council."

The chairman smiled. "We had not made your descent full public knowledge while you were away . . . for your safety, and for that of the Neteru's, since she was your traveling companion. Perhaps we should?"

"Rub some salt in the wound and see who bristles the most," Carlos said, taking a casual sip from his goblet. "That ought to bring out the claws, and I can pick them off one by one."

"You are talking about wiping out four masters?" The councilman seated closest to Carlos stood and ran his palm over his bald scalp.

"If I have to." Carlos didn't blink as he stared at the group. "You can make more, we all can make more, if it comes to that. But what we cannot allow is for this council to be overturned. I just need to work out a plan to get them all together under the same roof. We have to be sure of where any allegiances may lie—more than one of them could be in on it."

The chairman's smile broadened. "It will represent a temporary and significant power drain, but well worth the topside purge under the circumstances. Very wise. Once the seal is opened under our control, the power drain will be inconsequential. Yes, and I have every confidence you will develop a suitable plan," the chairman said, raising a goblet to Carlos. "Come, sit, drink, and let us enjoy the evening. A couple of dogs are available to aid in your security—they're more loyal than men."

With a casual wave of his hand, the chairman dispatched a ceiling transport bat, and Carlos waited for his resources, trying to stay cool. A loud commotion beyond the council walls made everyone train their attention toward the sound. Bats screeched in terror, and incessant growls and barks careened through the cavernous space. The front doors blew open, and four super-strength international couriers paired off to hold the two beasts they held by chains.

Carlos noted how the couriers' bulging arms strained, and massive chests within their hooded messenger robes expanded and contracted under the exertion. Red eyes glowed in the faceless dark hollows of their hoods, flickering out and occasionally disappearing as they tried to control pit bulls from level seven.

Just as before, when he'd asked for assistance in Brazil, he'd been given beasts, each with six yellow glowing eyes that ringed the circumference of their huge skulls, standing three feet high at the shoulder, their muscular black chests rippling as they scrabbled against the slippery marble floor to get to Carlos. Their jaws were so packed with fangs that they couldn't fully close their mouths, and foamed, slick saliva dripped from them, leaving acid burns in the floor. They flapped their leathery wings, half flying, as they pulled the couriers along the floor, slashing at them with their spaded, double-blade tails.

The chairman turned to him and chuckled.

"You approve?" he asked. "The last time you declined my offer to adopt Brutus and Bath Sheba. Just look at them . . . they're beautiful."

Carlos wasn't sure how to respond. "This time I accept," he finally said with a nod of gratitude. "They are truly magnificent creatures." There was only awe in his tone. He'd never seen anything like them.

"Don't worry, turn them loose on your lair grounds, and we're fairly confident that you will have no intruders—day or night."

"Just let them go?" Carlos asked, very unsure.

"Pop the chains," the chairman said with a wicked grin. "Let them get to know their new master."

Before Carlos could object, the dogs had broken from their hold and were making a snarling hurdle toward him. He could feel the chairman silently communicate to stay seated—show fear, and they will not obey, might even attack. Every instinct within him was poised to bulk and do battle.

When the beasts got to the table, they slowed, sniffing each seated entity, passing them by until they spotted Carlos, then they sat back on their haunches, threw their heads back, and howled.

"Give them your fist so they can get the scent of your territory, and transmit who is considered off limits," the chairman said calmly.

Too on guard to speak, Carlos slowly extended his fist to the snarling beasts, projecting images and scents of Damali, her Guardians, the Covenant, his family—even that crazy cop, Berkfield. Immediately one of the dogs opened its jaws, and clamped down on his fist, drawing in his arm all the way up to his elbow—but never bore down. He could feel acid bubbling on his skin, but then the creature whimpered, and licked the ooze off, wagged its savage tail, nuzzled his leg, and dropped to Carlos's feet.

A trickle of sweat rolled down his temple. Had he been less than he was, he would have shit his pants. The second creature loped up to him, wings still flapping, muscles twisting and knotting in its back as it approached. It sniffed the creature that was lying on the floor, then went to Carlos, flicked a long, green forked tongue at him, and licked the sweat from Carlos's cheek, before flopping down with a satisfied grunt.

"Marvelous, aren't they?"

"Un-fucking-believable," Carlos murmured, still shaken. And he'd thought Nuit's panther had been something.

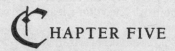 CHAPTER FIVE

"FOLKS, WE have us a real situation," Marlene said, but too calmly for the occasion as she sat down at the kitchen table.

"You ain't said a mumblin' word, Mar," Big Mike uttered on a long, tired breath. "You think the bedroom locks will hold?"

"I hope so," Marlene said, letting her head drop into her hands. "I'm just glad that she willingly went in there after she'd fed. I'm not worried about tonight—it's *tomorrow night* that concerns me."

"Yeah, but if the reinforced equipment that me and Jose installed fails," J.L. said slowly, "then what?"

"I honestly don't know," Marlene whispered.

"You don't think she'd bite anybody in here, do you, Mar? I mean . . ."

Marlene looked up at Jose, and cast a worried glance around the team. "You heard the man, and saw the transformation with your own eyes. Plus, we don't even know if Carlos's orders will hold up. This wasn't a normal vamp turn. We don't know to what degree she's beholden to follow his instructions. And if she fluxes hard, coming out of this vampiric state with her body chemistry all whacked out only to go into a full ripening—she's not the only one we have to worry about."

"He's coming back for her," Jose said in a quiet voice.

All eyes were on him as he hung his head. "I don't know why, but me and Carlos have a connection. I can feel where he's coming from . . . I wouldn't leave my woman, either, under the circumstances."

No one spoke for a moment as their thoughts went to the lost Dee Dee.

"Yeah, but Carlos saved a lot of lives, folks. That counts for something."

Marlene sighed as she studied the newest Guardian. "We like him a lot, too, Dan. But we have to also remember what he is."

Dan nodded. "But, Mar, check it out. Remember the old priest said that there had to be faith, hope, and love?"

"If she goes into a turn," Jose said, "I'll stay with her . . . I've got the faith, hope, and love for D. I'm not afraid of her."

"That was before dude did our little sister, man. Get a grip. Rivera is all vamp, so is Damali at the moment. No heroics, Jose." Rider crossed his arms over his chest and looked at Jose hard. "Don't be the weak link in this chain, brother. That gets us all fucked up."

"The faith, hope, and love thing was supposed to be between li'l sis and Rivera to keep the bite from going down like it did," Big Mike told Jose gently. "Ain't no percentage in you putting yourself, or anybody in this compound, in harm's way by letting her out till we get her straight."

"I hear you, Big Mike," Dan said calmly. "But aren't we all out on a crazy limb as Guardians, anyway, with nothing to go on but a whole lotta faith, nothing but hope, and love for each other?"

Big Mike nodded and let his breath out hard. The group studied Dan while he spoke, his words of inspiration holding them all for ransom.

"Well," Dan pressed on, "she loved him, too. Still does. Maybe that's enough to keep her bound to her promise?"

"Kinda ironic, though, don't you think?" Rider said, his gaze going toward the sealed compound windows.

"How so?" Marlene gave him her full attention.

"She helps Rivera fight his worst enemy, Nuit, who was also her worst enemy. In exchange, her accidental brand saves Rivera's life. Then, he helps her fight the biggest battle of her life over in Brazil, an external force, only to wind up fighting the biggest internal battle she's ever had to deal with. Namely, turning into the same thing she's been fighting, while also trying to stay away from him, which is the other pull she's been fighting ever since she was a kid—just like he's been fighting going to her all these years. It's like one big circle of madness between them."

Rider raked his fingers through his hair. "I'm just a nose, not a tactical sensor, but the electricity was in the air. He wanted her throat *real* bad, but had respect. I'll give him that. I don't think he meant to turn her—or why else would he have brought her home?"

"Rider, sometimes you can be deep." Marlene smiled at him and covered his hand with her own.

"I try," he said sheepishly.

"You just gave me a wild thought, though." She sat back and then leaned forward on the table, making a tent with her hands. "The planets forecast it, but like all things, we can never truly know what they portend until the action starts."

When everyone looked at her, Marlene tilted her head and shut her eyes. "Mars came the closest it's been to the earth in sixty thousand years this past August. And all these cosmic events seem to happen around our girl's birthday and close to home." She paused, looked at the group, and let her words settle in before continuing. "Mars is the planet of war, and we've seen new and awful wars erupt everywhere on this planet during this transit. Just like before, I thought that only had to do with what we were up against in the Amazon."

"Meaning what, baby?" Shabazz asked quietly.

"I know he's a sore subject, but back in Brazil, Kamal told us that Damali was fighting *herself,* the other half of who she was. That's an *internal* battle—close to home for her, for us . . . for Carlos." She sighed hard and shook her head. "When we get spiritual messages, there are always layers of meaning in them."

"True dat," Shabazz muttered. "Brotherman was right on all counts, 'cause she's definitely fighting herself, and a pull to the male energy that's the opposite of what she is—was."

"Right," Marlene said, her gaze searching each face in the room. "If this Neteru, sent to our charge, is fighting the biggest spiritual battle of her life during this rare war transit—something very different than fighting an external demon . . . while her soul mate, her almost-lost Guardian, Carlos, is also doing the same, fighting what lies within . . . then this thing that they're fighting might be the beginning of the real McCoy of biblical proportions. Maybe the universe is spiritually imploding, concentrating everything inward, instead of outward—just like they are . . . needing to purge internally to bring forth the Light. We have to get to their core before it draws everything down into it."

"The real McCoy?" Big Mike rubbed his palm over his bald scalp, dispersing the beads of nervous sweat in the process.

"The Armageddon," Shabazz said flatly. "Parent against child, husband against wife, internal battles of the most insidious kind. Seas offering up their fishes—an internal purge. Plagues sweeping the land—an internal purge. Even the church is purging itself of terrible secrets and deviant acts. Everything is getting turned out from within—vomited up, so the hidden truths can be known. Ruthless government schemes are being outed. Environmental disasters . . . earthquakes, tornadoes, floods—nature's internal purge . . . and the whole world at war. Think about it—everything is purging internally . . . countries are fighting internal civil wars; families are fighting horrific domestic battles—internal. Major corporations are purging their ranks, finding thieves—internally. The big red planet just came its closest ever to us; Rivera is trying his best to pull away from the dark, while Damali is pulling away from the light, roles are reversing, the signs are everywhere. Implosion, contractions, even time feels like it's speeding up for something big."

"Well, shit," Rider said fast, standing. "Without getting all philosophical, Shabazz, the bottom line is simple: we can't let him bite her again, especially if she's ripening. If she's in some kinda funky mid-turn or Neteru system fluctuation, we'll have to help her purge it, before it goes too far. And we also can't be too hasty to do him, because he might be the tipping weight toward our side, just like he saved our asses twice. Dan is right about remembering that. But if the two of them get together before they make the wise choice—"

"That could be the beginning of the daywalker empire that the Vampire Council was planning to shift the balance once and for all, regardless of Fallon Nuit. *That's* what we have to purge—from within our own ranks as Guardians." Shabazz closed his eyes.

Jose found a stool in the far corner of the weapons room and sat on it slowly, just staring at the floor.

"Dude, talk to me," Rider said, his voice brittle from worry. "I thought we'd squashed that issue for the time being, after we beat Nuit? Then we just went through this same mess in Brazil, with a near-daylight hijack by the were-demons trying to form an alliance with the vamps. C'mon, y'all, gimme a break."

"Were it that simple," Shabazz said quietly. "We all thought it was done for a while, too. But if it's back again, that makes the third time, a trinity."

Growing more agitated as Shabazz's words sank in, Rider opened his arms, leaning forward, ignoring the ringing telephone. "That's why we got the millennium job?"

Shabazz and Marlene simply nodded.

When the ringing stopped abruptly and then suddenly began again, Marlene stared at the phone. "Pick it up. It's Father Pat."

Damali walked the floor in her room like a junkie, perspiration beading up and running down the center of her back. The soft yellows and greens and cream hues of her bedroom swirled and taunted her, echoing the fact that she was indeed trapped within them.

If this was anything like what Carlos had had to endure in

the safe house, all she could do was weep for him like she wanted to weep for herself now. *She'd turned.* Had actually become a vampire. Had tasted blood. Her hands began to tremble just thinking of that sweet nectar.

How in the hell could something so bizarre happen from loving a good man? And yet the mere thought was laughable. She truly believed a master vampire was good—her, a Neteru. But Carlos wasn't just some master vamp. He was her man, a good man. She sat on the edge of her bed for a moment, trying to still her pulse. It was beating an erratic thud in her ears till they rang. Her clothes clung to her, matted to her body from the hunger sweats. The need to hunt, to be free, almost made her cry out. The need for him, insatiable.

If he would just come to her, and break her free of this prison, get her away from the people she loved before she did something she'd never be able to live with, or die with, whatever her fate at this point. Prayers gave her a headache, but she tried anyway. It was hard to breathe. The air in the room was stifling, but as she looked at the clock, fear coursed through her. Near dawn. She immediately knew that she couldn't breathe because the damnable light was taking up precious oxygen, burning it away, like it might now torch her flesh.

Damali pulled herself into a tight ball on the bed, and closed her eyes. She was supposed to be the Neteru, the one to battle demons and vampires and ugly things of the night. A single tear rolled down the bridge of her nose and plopped on her lemon-yellow duvet. They'd even taken Madame Isis from her, along with every other weapon she'd owned. She'd failed. She wasn't worthy to have the blade of the huntress. She couldn't be trusted—couldn't even trust herself. Now, she was just a common creature of the night.

He sat in the dark in his Beverly Hills lair, sated from the newly refreshed blood tanks, but nothing close to fulfilled. The hunger was gone, but the ache in his soul would never be healed. *She'd turned.* His precious baby had turned, and from his bite. There was no one else to blame but himself.

No matter what else was going on, no matter what supernatural forces had been tampered with, Damali wouldn't have turned if she hadn't been bitten.

If he found the key or the seal, he had to turn it over to the council. There would be no acceptable excuse this time if he didn't satisfy their demand. There was no back-door option, no game he could run. Even the Covenant and the Guardians had shunned him and rightfully so. He just hoped that if she'd died, it was with a prayer in her heart—the only thing that had halfway saved him. If her soul got lost in the realms, he'd turn over every stone and root out every snake until he found hers.

But if she'd died the way he was pretty sure she might have, a salvation prayer was probably the last thing on her mind. Bitter, perverse, cosmic injustice . . . she'd told him to pray on his dying breath, and he had. She knew to call for help and to seek redemption at the final moment. But when she'd slipped to the other side, she was probably calling his name with her last breath—the last entity that could save her. Too fucked up a situation.

He winced and closed his eyes in the darkness, then shifted his body to lie down. Suddenly the hidden, all-black marble subbasement beneath the Beverly Hills mansion felt like a cell. No amount of fine accoutrements, top-of-the-line electronic gadgets, solid gold fixtures, or expensive plush furnishings could make it be anything but what it was. This was no different than the monk's barren quarters—it was empty existence. At least there, he had someone he trusted to talk to. But now sprawled out in the center of a custom-made king-sized bed, the black satin sheets made him feel like he was drowning in a dark sea.

Damali's frustrated mental call to him was so piteous that even by day, rest would be impossible. He knew the suffering well, had lived it. Answering her by thought would only make her initial hours into the turn worse. He remembered riding it out in the safe house, like teetering on the edge of an orgasm for days . . . weeks . . . months, unable to hurl himself over the edge. Oblivion was always beyond reach.

No peace, just unrelenting pent-up desire that broke your ass down for just one more time and stole your pride. You'd do anything or anyone just to get out and into the night . . . and into your lover's arms. It was a physical want so intense that there was only one answer for it—and without the bite, there was no way to quench it alone. Yeah, he remembered all too well.

Then a hunger came that literally ate your insides out. That he'd visited this horror upon her was beyond forgiveness . . . and that she couldn't even pray for assistance was thoroughly messed up. Her options were worse than his had ever been. At least he'd been a criminal, knew it, and there was a bounty on the recovery of his soul. Who came to look for willingly turned Neterus, he wondered? The answer was basic: he would.

If Marlene couldn't come up with a quick cure, Damali was a sitting duck in the Guardian compound. Her seven teammates, along with the Covenant brethren, would surely plant Damali's own Isis in her chest to save her soul—just like he'd been forced to plant a stake in Alejandro's to save his brother's.

Even if he got her out of there, once the Vampire Council found out that she had fully turned and could no longer produce a daywalker line, if he didn't deliver the seal or the key, they'd hunt her down—just to punish him. Whether the sick old bastards harvested her lost soul and tortured it in order to slowly rip his heart out, or passed her around to every topside male while he was held prisoner and unable to help her—either situation was unthinkable. And, despite knowing that, he wouldn't have it in him to dust her. Besides, without his protection, if there was a chance that she was still fertile, and ripening, her compound would be the epicenter of a major vampire invasion by every topside male on the planet now that borders were shaky, chaos was in full effect, and everyone was vying for world dominance. But if he got to her, he'd also start her worst nightmare . . . making her the mother of something unspeakable. Then, again, did any of that matter? If he didn't find the seal, it was all over anyway.

Carlos willed the tears in his eyes to dry. He was supposed to be her protector, from the very beginning, and had fucked this whole thing up big time. Her life was ruined, all because he couldn't keep his hands off of her. That was pathetic. No sense of control, no discipline when it came to her.

By rights, Damali should have been out there hunting down the bastard who stole the sacred key. That was her job as a Neteru. But because they'd both been off the job, and his love bites had turned into more than they'd both bargained for, he'd put his baby in a position where the clerical forces might have to smoke her. Now he understood everything Father Pat had been trying to tell him. They should have left him to die in the desert.

He sat up as her calls intensified and leaned his head against one of the cool black marble bedposts. He could feel the ache on the entire surface of her skin, even past the near sunlight, even past Marlene's new ring of prayers. If she would only just take in a slow breath through her mouth and let it out through her nose to summon control. She had to regulate her breathing, slow her heart rate. The more she fought it, got hyped, the more her heart raced, the hotter the burn . . . A master burn was no joke, but he couldn't afford to reach out to her in a mind lock to explain all that. Whenever they connected telepathically it was too volatile. But not watching her struggle was impossible. Just seeing her so aroused was messing him up. It was lowering his defenses, turning him on, jacking up his control, and when she cupped her breasts he tried to pull out of the vision.

He could already taste the salt of her tears in his mouth, smell every bead of sweat that had exited her pores as her dampened body tossed on her sheets. And she was *so* wet, and so ready . . . his hands began to tremble, he needed to touch her so badly.

The moment he'd fully entered the turn, the full impact of what it meant to be a vampire became an unforgettable, defining moment that dragged every vice, secretly harbored desire, and lust to the surface, along with the insatiable need to feed. The vibration within Damali rippled through him like an electric current, bonding them regardless of the barriers. He now understood, even if it was for a moment—she was *his* turn, and would home to *him*, also sadly understanding the rush that turning a human produced in his kind. What had he done?

Carlos pulled in a steady breath, willing his pulse to slow to a near halt. He had to. Going into her mind now to talk her down was definitely impossible. She was too strong, wasn't a second-level, nor a mere human. That would have been easy. But this was master to council, and there was nothing in his line's knowledge base to deal with that. There had never been, to his knowledge, a topside female master to connect with a male of the species at council level. Thus, two senior levels had never been forced to separate like this—ever. Who would be a worthy enough adversary to make them do such a thing, if one had been made? And if Damali seized upon his mind and locked it, come nightfall, he'd be over there taking a bullet. He was nearly ready to chance the sun, as it was. Not to mention, that was the last thing she needed. This was best. If they locked, he told himself firmly, he'd telepathically siphon her for sure. Her system couldn't take another nick. But when her palm slid down her stomach, he shivered.

For a long while he just sat there with his head leaned against the marble post, a thousand thoughts feeding his despair, her insistent but confused calls making him want to jump out of his skin. *Oh, baby . . . just stop struggling with this thing. No, I can't come to you. It's almost daybreak.*

Seconds elongated to minutes. Whatever Neteru was still left within her sliced through the approaching dawn and held him hostage. "Damali, cut it out . . ." Carlos murmured, as her thoughts gripped his in a mental vise, nearly strangling him with desire.

She'd broadcasted her intense call on an open channel that static-charged the air around him. He tried his best to put a privacy seal around it—all they needed was for council or the remaining topside masters to hear her . . . and Marlene and Father Pat!

Carlos locked in on the register of her voice and put a black box around it, but even holding it at mental length from him was nearly impossible. The transmission was so hot, coming to him as though broadband video images, he could only hope that the fact that she was still the Neteru would mute some of it to anyone but him. Then her complete thoughts broke through the compound barrier, adding the element of touch to the sound of her voice. The Guardians had left a hole in their seal!

Carlos groaned. "No, no, *no*—how could y'all forget to mentally block her, too?" They had sealed in her physical presence, not her telepathy . . . had sealed out both of his methods of coming to her, but had left the door wide open for her to mentally escape! He had told them, *shown them,* that she was as much a vampire as he was, in this fluctuation state. But they were still treating her like a human, only physically barring the windows and doors! That would never be enough to contain her.

The moment he felt her hands slide down his chest, he opened his eyes, trying to break the mental connection. There was no way this could end well, and she had no concept of the torture she was about to trap them within if she started something that couldn't be finished. "Stop," he said in a forceful whisper. "I'm not playing, D. I can't bite you to take you over the edge."

In his mind he saw her tremble, then felt a hot rake score his shoulder and collarbone as her cheek grazed his skin hard and her lush mouth pulled the lobe of his ear between her lips. "For real . . . stop," he murmured, his voice catching in his throat as his eyes slowly closed. The nip at the vein in his wrist did it, and when her tongue trailed up his forearm to the inside of his elbow, completing the sensual sweep with her deep, wet kiss at that sensitive pulse point, his shudder connected to the contraction she'd sent through his groin. He soon felt himself sliding down the marble post to lie on his back, his chin tipped toward the ceiling as her suckles intensified. "I mean it, baby. Stop."

Oh . . . no . . . she was rewiring him, placing a physical

mark . . . just like a master, doing to him what he'd done to her. Everywhere she kissed up his forearm he'd felt down the length of his shaft. His hand balled into a fist as she nursed and licked the skin inside the bend of his arm, and against his will, he felt his hips begin to move to her rhythm, the agony concentrating as though she had the head of him in her mouth. He was connecting with air, nothingness, yet needing to be inside her. He could mentally see her pelvis working against the tangled knot of sheets on her bed, could feel the tension in her building and demanding an answer. But there was no way to reach her. A groan traveled through him . . . she had no idea what she was doing to him.

Suddenly her slick, scorching heat sheathed him and the sensation was totally unexpected. Intense pleasure made him cry out and hold himself. The pressure that lodged in his shaft throbbed so badly tears came to his eyes. Pain collided with fleeting gratification, making him sweat. Her voice escalated an octave, driving him to the brink of his sanity.

Knowing that the rough sensation his palm offered compared to her was futile, only made matters worse, but didn't stop his frenzied strokes that now matched her movements. Why did she start what couldn't be finished? His touch soon became her wetness, and then evaporated to once again only be his dry palm. The barrier was maddening. He dropped his hand away, hoping that might ease the torture. But the instant vacancy of warmth, the lack of sensation, was so visceral that it almost made him sit up. He covered the central ache like a wound, applied pressure to staunch the throb, and just held it, trying to will away the pulse that was wed to her insistent thrusts.

Trapped without an option, he was breathing through his mouth, hyperventilating like her with ragged inhales and exhales, and he gripped the mattress, his nails ripping through satin sheets and ticking, exposing stuffing as he arched hard. He needed her skin against his, instant friction to meet the burn. He needed her in his arms beneath him. Every pulse point he owned was lit on fire for her.

Sweat soaked him as his stomach, his thighs, his buttocks, and back muscles clenched and released to the pace she set. "Baby, stop . . . please," he said out loud in a pained rush through his fangs. When she arched again the back of his head dug into the pillows. But as long as she moved, he couldn't stop lifting his hips for her, couldn't stop the hard stroke of his hand that again felt just like her, couldn't catch his breath, much less form the words to break the connection that would haunt them both for hours.

Nearly sobbing with frustration, his mouth hungered for her kiss so much that he dropped his plundered defenses. Immediately he felt her mouth upon his, consuming it with a phantom kiss, her tongue dancing with his, planting the burn within his groin there, too, making him moan from deep within his chest. The side of his throat was on fire, needing her instant strike as much as he needed release. Her softness covered him, and he ran his hand over her round, tight behind, touching the air above him, feeling her as though she were there.

"Don't do this," he begged, edging toward the point of no return. Each of her hard nips along his chest and his shoulders and the side of his jaw were layering sensations inside his thighs, mirroring the unfulfilled pleasure that was now oozing from his shaft. "You don't understand."

A soft kiss grazed his temple, trailed down the bridge of his nose, but then became aggressive again as it captured his mouth and pulled a groan up from his gut. The way her lips hovered just a fraction of an inch above the aching skin at his jugular stripped his breath, turning the pace of his exhales into shallow pants. Then she mastered him with a long, rough lick up his jugular, the heat of it searing his oversensitive skin's surface, making him arch hard as though a high-volt electric current had hit him. That's when he lost it, couldn't think about the state of her turning or the consequences.

"Deliver the bite!" His eyes were practically crossing beneath his lids. If she was strong enough to open-channel seduce him at dawn, maybe . . . "Baby, *please*—do it now!" He could feel her struggling with the knowledge, trying to learn master technique on the fly, needing to respond to his request as much as he also wanted that, but her fangs hadn't lowered . . . a psychic siphon took practice.

She stared into his eyes, the look in them pained and confused as she edged toward a climax that faded. *We were so close,* she murmured. *Why—*

"That's what I've been trying to tell you . . ." His voice was a harsh whisper. The connection was so strong that each sensation that eluded her also summarily vanished within him, leaving them both precariously hovering on the precipice. And from a deep reservoir of knowing he understood all too well that the fact that she still had Neteru flowing through her was blocking the full knowledge transfer from his line. Everything in her makeup was designed to fight a turn. "Baby, without the final bite, there is no end to this. You can go all the way up to the door, but won't be able to open it. Now stop. All right?"

Part of him took very small comfort in the fact that her system was purging on its own. However, right now, it was a serious impediment. But it was better this way. Less complicated. He tried to steady his breathing and resolve himself to the inevitable—a very long and sleepless day within his lair.

She just stared at him for a moment. *I've never felt like this in my life* . . . She closed her eyes and threw her head back and began moving against him again. Her fluid thrusts quaked him, and every tremble that contracted her body around his made him gasp. *We have to finish this,* she murmured, her tone urgent just like her movements had become. *I can't take it.*

If she couldn't do it, he had to. She had to go beyond level-one thought, actually had to manifest the nick and draw blood. Had to transform matter into energy at the speed of light. He'd show her how, maybe could talk her through it? Oh, *man,* he had to . . . if the prayer barrier wasn't blocking him, he'd take her to V-point on the spot. But that was crazy; he knew he shouldn't teach her something like that . . . her team would be at risk . . . she might hurt a

Guardian or worse. But she felt so good, was crooning in his ear, was promising him in fits and starts that she'd only siphon him. *Just do it.*

It was an offer he couldn't refuse, not now. He focused on her throat, could feel her pulse thudding in his ears. No problem, he'd release them both from this torture. Just a nick, not a full siphon. Just one more time. His incisors lowered another lethal inch, but the barrier wouldn't allow his penetration. Damn!

"Focus, baby," he pleaded. She had to do this. "Sync up with my pulse. Ride it hard and drop fang, then open the vein."

He could barely get the words out and was literally shaking with anticipation as he mentally braced himself, watched her draw a deep breath, then stare at his throat, and come in against it hard. Just as suddenly, he felt the bite. It was a human one that sent ripples of pleasure through him, but it wasn't enough to take either of them to oblivion. She hadn't gathered enough atomic velocity in the thought when she delivered the strike. She had to break the skin. He could feel her frustration wash through him as her head dropped back, no hint of fangs in her mouth.

The near miss made him inhale and exhale hard; he'd show her how this was done. Neither of them would last more than twelve hours messed up like this.

Reflex made him roll over onto his stomach to gather her beneath him for leverage, but the compound barriers made her vanish as his intent to bite her became laser. All he had in his arms were black satin sheets. He brought them to his face in defeat and felt her shudder the moment her near-orgasm dissolved with her moan. Her tears ate away at him, making him need her even more as only the echo of her frustrated sobs remained.

He knew exactly how she felt; he needed to cum so badly he was ready to cry himself. Pure agony became one with panic as he flopped over onto his back again, hoping she was still focused enough to broadcast. *Damali, come back . . .*

The thought was almost a prayer that shot from his brain in the tone of a command. Damn, why did she start this mess? "It's all right, *mi tormenta,* stay with me," he said gently, but deeply conflicted, and wondered why he was submitting to such agony.

She covered him immediately and he nearly wept it felt so good. If she hadn't been able to come back, he would have lost his mind. The unrelenting tension was giving him a headache. A hard bite against his femoral artery almost convulsed him and made tears fall in earnest this time. "Don't do it." If she went down on him he'd open the lair for sure. Cancel that. He couldn't take it without knowing there'd be an end in sight.

Hot moisture slid from beneath his lids and ran down the sides of his face, meeting the sweat that was coursing down his temples. When he felt her kiss the tears away from his lashes, another futile reflex made him attempt to knock her chin back with his jaw to find her throat, and he again held his length within a firm grasp. Every place that he'd ever bitten her glowed red, became an infrared beacon bearing his mark, but he couldn't get near a single pulse point. A blue-white layer of dangerous heat covered her skin and barred his incisors entry. An agonized groan swept through him as her tongue found his navel. She was trying to make him break through a barrier that simply couldn't be crossed. It wasn't about not wanting to, some things just couldn't be done.

"I can't!" he finally yelled, his voice echoing through the lair. "You have to come to me!"

I don't know how to . . . Every time I get close—

"Then stop," he said as his voice faltered. "Just go to sleep."

I can't.

They both knew what she'd said was the truth. As her torture wore on, he began counting the hours till sunset with his eyes tightly shut. Just one more time. *Anything,* for just one more time . . . Her voice carried his name like a blade against his senses. Each time she said it, his name got lower in octave until it filled her abdomen, the register of it was so low and sensual it had gone beyond a croon to a desperate whisper. He could feel it vibrate inside her like a depth charge, then his name broke up into two low timbre syllables as she shuddered, *Car-los*.

She had to stop, but if she did he'd risk sunlight. He was mentally stuttering her name in three-part harmony, *Da-mal-i* . . . Then she seized upon the thought, mounted him, bore down on him, arched in a hard snap that made him call her out loud by name. Her response was instantaneous; she sent the message to him as a challenge, using his own past words to tease him—*That's what I was waiting to hear, baby.*

"*Un mordisco! Por favor* . . . Damali, *ahora*. Baby, it's almost *entumecido*." He was nearly weeping for release as she moaned in his ear and stopped moving against him, holding his hips down firmly. What was she doing to him? A sly smile crossed her kiss-punished mouth.

She let go of his hips as he thrashed against her hold. She allowed the sensation of being inside her to ebb as she pulled back and made him slip from her warmth. *Stop struggling with this,* she murmured in a tone so seductive that it made him pump wildly against the air.

"I can't," he admitted in an urgent rush. "Finish this now!"

I thought you wanted me to stop and go to sleep?

All he could do was surrender. "No, don't," he said between his teeth. "You win."

You left me—

"It won't ever happen again."

Promise?

He nodded and shut his eyes tighter. "I promise I'll get you out tonight—as soon as it gets dark . . . baby . . . just . . . try one more time."

You pissed me off, and really hurt my feelings. I don't know that I should . . . maybe I'll just go to sleep, like you said to.

"No. Please don't do that," he said quickly. He could hear her thoughts but could no longer feel her touch. "I swear, girl, I'm sorry." She was making him beg, and that didn't make any sense. She had his dignity in shreds and fury was only stoking the burn. He tried to summon some control, throttle his impulses, tried to regulate his breathing, to ignore her, but then she pulled him into her mouth. "Please don't stop," he whispered, trembling as she left him again and became nothing but air.

If you promise not to leave me, I won't leave you . . .

There were no words. He was beyond speech and in no position to negotiate as he leaned his head to the side, exposing his jugular with hope, begging her not to break the touch transmission. *Just try,* his mind demanded . . . *for both of us.*

A hot breath scored his throat. Behind his tightly shut lids he could see her throw her head back. A gorgeous pair of fangs lowered, parting her lips, making him shudder and forcefully lift his hips trying to enter her. The sight of her incisors glistening within her darkened bedroom sent a shiver through him that locked each vertebra in his spine together disc by disc. Hope lit a fuse that might detonate with salvation. Their eyes met for a second. She coated him like hot butter and he winced at the long-awaited sensation. One strangled word escaped from his mouth when she sheathed him: *"Please."* Then a razor strike opened his jugular lengthwise, threatening to bleed him out, not two neat puncture wounds like he'd anticipated. It was thoroughly primal, so erotic what she'd done that he thought he'd go blind. *"Oh, baby!"*

He came so hard, so fast that it felt like his testicles were being sucked up into his abdomen with every spasmodic convulsion. Each contraction of hers fused with his, her guttural moan working its way into the open vein like a pleasure stab as she climaxed. His wail got trapped in his chest for a moment on a sharp gasp, then broke free in jerky, stuttering increments. Thick emulsion ran over his fist, ejecting from his body in molten waves to the same rhythm of her throat siphon. When she threw back her head again just to breathe, he futilely tried to bring her back. "Don't stop, *not now.*"

Her gasping murmur was passionate, yet logical. *I'll flat-line you—*

"Then do it!"

Immediately, she returned to his neck and pulled hard. Beneath his lids he saw flashes of light that married the pleasure, setting off another wave of ecstasy so profound that his body went into a cold sweat. She was bleeding him out to the bone—like a pro. Oh, shit, it felt so good . . . Blood was running down the sides of her mouth, dribbling down her chin, she couldn't take it all in fast enough. He was going into pleasure shock, shivers hitting him in tidal waves till he nearly blacked out, but she kept him from probable extinction by finally covering the open wound with her hand to seal it.

Get a bottle from the kitchen. Now, she said quickly. *You won't make it through the day.*

He didn't argue, just weakly materialized private label from in-lair stock and popped the cork with his thumb. He was still trembling as he leaned over the side of the bed and turned the black bottle up to his mouth. He sighed hard after downing half of the magnum, and then wiped his seed-covered hand on the sheets.

"Damn . . ." he murmured, flopping back against the mattress. Her first night as a turned vampire and she'd done him like that? Had worked a mind lock so hard she'd made him see stars? Then the way she'd opened him up—lengthwise—and passionately marked him like he'd never even dreamed was possible? He shuddered as just the mere thought made him feel it all over again in quick phantom pangs.

"Baby, listen," he said through harsh, intermittent breaths. "We've gotta stop, it's almost full daylight . . . we both have to regenerate—I mean, I have to, and you've gotta purge. Please. I can't take another round like this last one." That was no lie. He needed her to be physically with him, if she was going to take him there with a lateral nick. The delivery was so awesome it could have passed for a battle bite. His fingers went to the side of his throat and he shivered at what she'd done.

A gentle kiss swept his mouth, and he could feel her pull

back and release her hold on him. He almost dropped the bottle he was clutching on the floor. Relief, fatigue, bone-deep satisfaction claimed him, as did renewed worry. He was so spent that he couldn't even lift his head. How was he going to keep his hands off her now? "Good night, baby," he whispered, too tired to say much else. Her soft reply stabbed at him and made him renew his promise. "I love you, too. I'll be there tonight." He nodded. "Yeah." This dangerous situation had gone too far.

As soon as it got dark, he knew he had to go to her, and he also knew that if they didn't get the seal or the key, he'd have to smoke her, then stake himself . . . just to be sure the council wouldn't torture her. Ironic—that's just how her parents had died.

The options narrowed down to the basics: break her out, bring her to the lair so she could feed from the tanks, love her hard to stop the burn, and then find the key. The big question was, where? The other major question was, would he risk alerting Father Pat or Damali's squad? If the humans freaked and jumped the gun with a sloppy plan, then all their asses would be in a sling.

He needed more time to think. But time had never been a luxury he'd owned.

HAPTER SIX

BERKFIELD STOOD in the archway that separated his kitchen and dining room. He watched his wife move between the sink and the dishwasher, the counter television blaring a sitcom. He glanced up toward the ceiling, willing away sudden tears. The sound of heavy metal was coming from his son's room. Robert would go deaf by twenty, he mused, then sadness chased away the thought.

Before the scientist had briefly detained him, he knew for sure that his children would outlive him, no matter what statistics proved. He was a cop; he knew he might die young. His family was supposed to be inviolate. This was a perversion of the way things were meant to be. He closed his eyes to fight back the tears and listened for his daughter's voice, already knowing that Kristin was on the telephone with one of her girl friends. It pained him to think of the trauma he was about to visit upon them all.

His attention returned to his wife. She looked so pretty in her wrinkled khaki capri pants, her pink T-shirt, and little white sneakers. Marjorie was a pretty woman, still, at forty-two. Sure they'd had their ups and downs, but he still loved her smile, the way her eyes crinkled at the corners when she smiled . . . her form was rounder, softer these days, but it was also comforting and matched his own.

As she continued to bend and pivot and rinse dinner dishes, he found himself drawn to her. He watched the setting sun glisten in her short blond hair, and then reached out to cup her cheek.

She stopped, holding a dripping dish midair. "What's wrong, honey?"

He shook his head. "Nothing. I love you."

She set the dish down carefully, her eyes searching his face. "No one died at work, did they? Your new partner . . ."

He shook his head no and tucked a wisp of hair behind her ear. "No. Everything and everyone at work is fine. I just wanted to tell you how much I appreciate you . . . how much I love you." He smiled. "Why don't you make me and the kids help you out more?"

Marjorie chuckled, and began working on clearing out the sink beside him. "Because it's easier not to fight with you guys and just get it done myself." She kissed his cheek. "Some battles you learn, over the years, are not worth the energy." She offered him a sly pout. "So, either you're angling for a second Wednesday night this week, or you just bought some more electronic gizmos that this house doesn't need. Which is it?"

He cast his gaze out past the breakfast nook to the sliding glass doors. How did a man protect his family from the night?

"I didn't buy any more stuff, and I'm getting used to rations," he said, trying to tease her.

"Oh, ho, ho . . . Very funny, Mr. Berkfield. You might have to get used to sleeping on the sofa, if you don't watch it."

Her laughter and the twinkle in her eyes made him know what he had to do. It broke his heart to steal her joy, but he wanted them all to survive. Even if this scientist had been wrong and was just a nutcase, it was better that his family not be around until he figured it out. Yet, the fact that the scientist had seen the same things he'd seen made him slow to judge the man as a lunatic. Deciding to err on the side of caution, Berkfield took his time to explain.

"Marj," he said quietly, in a tone that stilled her mirth, "I need you and the kids to tell people that you're going to visit your sister in Iowa for a while. There's this priest I met, uh . . . a Father Patrick that I need you to stay with for a bit." He waited until his wife nervously nodded. "Remember after what happened in the alley, I told you he came to me while I was looking for that guy, Rivera? If something happens to me, you and the kids will be safe with him. Do you understand?"

He caught the glass that was in her hand before it fell to the floor.

"There are some men I put away, years ago . . . I want you and the kids to lay low until it gets sorted out. I don't want you to go with anybody except the priest. I don't even want any of the guys at the office to know where you are, in case there's another bad apple in the department."

He watched tears fill her pretty blue-green eyes; he almost couldn't breathe as she wrapped one arm around her waist and covered her mouth. He stared at her glistening tears, loving how one eye seemed blue and one seemed green. It was as though he needed to recall every facet of her in great detail and brand the memory of it into his mind.

"I knew this would happen one day," she whispered. "You've put so many criminals away . . ."

She touched his cheek and he drew her into an embrace, burying his face against her neck.

"The children . . ." Her voice faltered and he hugged her tighter.

"Only trust that priest. *Only him*," he said, firmly holding her back from him to look into her eyes. There was no way in the world he would entrust the lives of his family to some unknown group of mad scientists that had abducted him and threatened him in his own driveway.

"When my old partner went bad, Father Pat came to me and told me a lot of things were happening around Carlos Rivera that I didn't understand. But he's a man of the cloth, and he said if Rivera's word ever got shaky or if he was compromised, to come to him immediately for safe harbor. He's linked to the Vatican, and they have resources that can keep you safe and comfortable until this all blows over."

"You're going with us, right? You aren't staying here!"

He cradled his wife in his arms and kissed the crown of her head. "No, honey. I have to bring closure to this thing, and I want you and the kids safe until this is finished. I'll be all right. Just go with the priest, tonight. Call a few girl-friends and spread the word that you're visiting relatives, and then make the call. I'll joke around with the guys about hanging out for beers while you and the kids are in Iowa. I want everyone to think everything is fine, got it?"

"But you don't trust anyone in the department? No one?" Her eyes scanned his face as tears streaked her ashen cheeks.

Berkfield kissed his cross, then kissed her lips fast. "No. Your mouth to God's ear, you are going to visit your sister tonight, with the kids. Make the calls, get the bags from the garage that I always told you to keep ready, and drive. You get in the car and dial the priest's number—memorize it when I give it to you. Okay?"

Marjorie only nodded, obviously too traumatized to speak. Her stricken expression cut into his conscience. What if this was all pure insanity? He'd made his wife memorize safe-house numbers, keep clothes in a garage to escape at a moment's notice as though they were fugitives. He'd run drills with his children to keep them readied . . . all the while telling them that mobsters were the culprit, that his job had hazards that could spill over to them . . . but he'd never imagined the danger would be vampires.

He'd vowed to give the Guardians the early part of the evening to purge Damali, but Carlos knew it would be impossible to make it through the entire night without going to her. Still, there were security issues that he had to address, if he was going to keep her safe. That reality held him steady, honed his focus to razor clarity. It was about finding the motherfucker that had breeched his borders and had put his woman at risk.

When the earth opened and the swirling blackness died down, Carlos stood on the front grounds of his Beverly Hills lair, huge chains wrapped around both fists, a beast at either side of him, straining to break free of their leads.

"Chill," he said firmly, his head tilting. He heard it, too. Damali's bloodcurdling screams slammed into his brain. Not a good sign. The sound agitated the hounds, but it drove a spike through his skull. The Guardians were not confining his baby; they were torturing the living shit out of her! The only relief was that they hadn't dusted her.

Carlos closed his eyes. He had to give them time to work on her. He had to ignore her call. She had to ride it out to become human again. Only his council-level status gave him the wherewithal to resist her cries, but even that power was questionable. He let his breath out slowly and wound the chains in his fist tighter. It was about caring for her enough to let her live the way she was intended.

He forced the dogs to heel, giving them a hard tug by their chains, and began walking the perimeter of his grounds with them so they'd know the borders that they were confined within. "Not the postman, not the cops, not a kid chasing a ball—only I feed you," he muttered as he walked the monsters, noting how they snarled, sniffed, and occasionally looked at him confused when Damali's voice pierced their senses. "I know," he said, dropping the chains and stroking their ugly heads to calm them. "It's fucking me up, too. Stay!"

The more aggressive of the two animals growled low in his throat and walked in a circle, going from the edge of the land back to Carlos, but then settled down. He had to feed these creatures—go find a miscellaneous vamp or local demon so the animals could get a topside feed on, even though they'd fed well on the way up.

It had sent a serious message within all the lower levels he'd passed, and the news was out, couriers were on notice. Every region was now aware that a council master was going topside and was taking no prisoners, if crossed. Courier ranks stood aghast as he donated a few of them to the cause of proving his point. Even the were-realms were giving him wide berth. The little stop down there garnered respect with Hell-dogs at his heels. And every region knew that council masters didn't do topside, unless there was a serious mission at hand.

But the other issue was he had to do something, anything, to get the sound of Damali's cries out of his mind. As her voice escalated, he gave his dogs a hard glare. "Conceal. Stay. Guard." He watched them sulk away, dematerializing as they took winged flight and bent the top branches of a mature oak tree as their lookout post. Only their glowing eyes told him where they were.

Blood Music made the most sense as a primary feeding ground, to his way of thinking—it had been the epicenter of Nuit's territory. The hounds would get the scent from Nuit's tracer in the meat, and any old dons left, rebels, or human operatives marked from that region, would be blocked from ambushing him. So, he went there.

"Good evening," Carlos said with a calm smile as he materialized in the plush outer lobby of Blood's sixty-sixth-floor penthouse. He remembered being brought here when first turned . . . ironic how life . . . and death could be. At the bottom one minute, at the top the next, but wasn't the promise that in the last days, the first should be last and the last should be first?

He studied the sumptuous leather seating, dark marble along the walls, and the huge reception desk of the same materials, bearing the Blood Music insignia crest and logo— that would have to go. So would a few of the tired human artists on the label. But all things in good time. Too hasty a move would further alert the four topside masters, and unfortunately, Nuit's music empire was still producing plenty of negative results for the vamp nation. It was already tense in the empire, given that a councilman had not elected to stay seated on a subterranean throne.

As he moved toward the front desk, the pale, willowy

vamp receptionist at the front desk blanched and held her breath for a moment before responding.

"Master Rivera, uh, oh, a . . . good evening. We didn't know you were coming or when you'd want your new offices readied." She jumped up from her desk, and hit the console. "We'll have that immediately rectified, sir. How can I make you comfortable in the—"

"I want a board meeting of all my vice presidents, now, in the war room." He smiled at her more broadly and gave her a wink. "You can chill. Only top brass changes in a hostile takeover."

"Got a bad feeling, man," Stack said, peering around the new additions to Club Vengeance.

Yonnie only nodded and continued to sip his drink. Downing it quickly, he ordered another round for himself and his partner. "Two Chivas, double color. Top shelf," he told the bartender without glancing up, waiting as the bartender mixed liquor and blood. He knew Rivera was close. The hair on his neck was crackling with electricity. Every curly strand of his Afro felt like it was on fire.

Accepting his drink, he suddenly stood as he watched Stack nearly topple his short rocks glass when he knocked back the shot and set the drink down hard. "It's time."

Stack was slow to get up and follow him. Yonnie brushed past the eager females that greeted them as they cut a swath through the frenetic club crowd. Almost as quickly as their popularity had been ignited, he could feel it wane as he wound his way up the spiral staircase and crossed the first floor on his way to Carlos's old office. The females in the club had their line of vision trained on the boss's VIP booth. Furious energy radiated from it nearly twenty-five yards away.

"Whatchu gonna tell him, man?" Stack whispered.

"The truth, and beg for mercy," Yonnie said, no quiver in his tone, his gaze straight ahead, his pace steady as they walked. "If we bullshit him that's a sure death."

Heads turned slowly as they passed. All eyes were trained upon the two young lieutenants walking toward the booth. The music seemed to get quieter as they approached. The entire club froze, then gasps rippled through the room as two Hell-dogs appeared and snarled to stop Yonnie and Stack's approach.

"Gentlemen," Carlos said, materializing out of a beam of blue club light. "I like what you've done with the establishment." He stroked the heads of his beasts and snapped his fingers twice, commanding the dogs to sit, and then extended his crest ring for Yonnie and Stack to kiss.

"We added a new subterranean level," Stack said quickly, bowing and stepping back from Carlos after appropriately acknowledging his rank. "While you were gone, we converted the basement level for VIPs so the club can stay open twenty-four hours without a light intrusion. It's fully stocked with top-shelf and the territory's best females."

Carlos nodded and smoothed the front of his black Armani suit, his gaze sweeping the club floor. His line of vision settled on Yonnie, who looked him square in the eyes. He liked that. A man with courage. A man of few words, wise enough to hold his counsel until he was asked to speak. Carlos smiled. The collective tension in the establishment abated. The music resumed.

"Walk with me, Yonnie. Let's have a conversation."

Yonnie nodded and neared Carlos.

Appearing relieved, Stack stepped away from his partner's side, his eyes holding an expression of pity. Carlos watched Yonnie stiffen from the corner of his eye.

"Feed the dogs," Carlos ordered as they left Stack. "They require a hundred and eighty pounds of meat. Take it from the old inventory in the freezer. I want that bullshit out of my club, understood? Only top-shelf from Nuit's old holding in here, but no new bodies." He glanced at the dogs, angry that he didn't consider feeding them the leftovers from Blood Music. Carlos resumed walking with Yonnie a few paces behind him.

They climbed the stairs to Carlos's old office, and for a

bit, nostalgia settled into Carlos's bones. He approached two bulked security vamps who parted for them to pass. The good old days, when he was alive and this club had been the crown jewel of his human empire. So much had changed in such a short time, and he'd learned just how relative time was.

Carlos took in his environment, walking around the spacious room, remembering, and fingering objects on his old mahogany desk. The room now seemed so small, so plain, compared to what he'd experienced since then.

"Sit," he bade Yonnie, as he found his old high-back leather chair and sat in it. He was amazed at how ordinary it felt in comparison to his council throne.

But Yonnie didn't sit. He stood before the wide desk, his eyes glittering with both fear and respect as he stared at Carlos.

"Sir, we have a problem."

Carlos laced his fingers together and made a tent. "I know."

"Philadelphia was a disaster."

A slight smile tugged at Carlos's mouth as he stared at the young vampire. Yonnie couldn't have been more than eighteen years old when he turned. He wasn't concerned about Philadelphia. But he was aware of the strong Guardian nest that had been uncovered there. Perverse amusement filled him. He now understood the chairman's reactions to his visits to council chambers. So he waited, gathering the patience to watch how Yonnie would function when there was bad news to deliver to the boss.

"We got blindsided there," Yonnie said, his expression stoic, but the beads of perspiration forming on his brow gave away his calm exterior. "We'll go back and address it, will root out all Guardian teams in your territories. Our resources had been strained—"

Carlos held up his hand. "Let the Guardian teams, wherever you find them, be."

Yonnie blinked twice. "Sir?"

"Strategy," Carlos said, his gaze assessing every inch of the young vampire. "When their side gets that strong, it's because our side has kicked up a notch. If Guardian teams are flooding my zones, then it stands to reason that the light has picked up on more than me in the area." Carlos's smile disappeared as Yonnie's body swayed. "This is why I asked you to have a seat."

Yonnie nodded and sat slowly, his attention riveted to Carlos. "You were breached by another master?"

"Appears so," Carlos murmured, renewed fury making his incisors lower a half inch.

"We'll take him," Yonnie said quickly. He stood again and began pacing, his agitation creating a crackle of electricity throughout the room.

"Your men couldn't take a well-fortified Guardian team," Carlos said in a blasé tone. "You're third-gens, and that's my fault."

Yonnie stopped pacing and horror filled his eyes.

Carlos shook his head and stood. "I should've had seconds in there watching my back." He began walking in a wide circle around Yonnie. As he watched pure terror reflect back at him from the vampire's young face, an old wound opened inside him. Alejandro should have been here. Julio should have been here. Miguel should have been here, just like all the others should have. "All my family is gone . . . all my old *hombres,* at a time when I need them most." Carlos chuckled, and a sad, hollow sound echoed throughout the room. "Fate is a curious thing. I didn't think I'd survive this long without them."

He stopped and stood before Yonnie. He reached out and placed a hand on Yonnie's shoulder. He wasn't surprised when Yonnie closed his eyes, resigned to his fate.

"How old are you, man?" Carlos asked, his voice low and gentle. It hurt him that Yonnie was trembling.

"I was turned at eighteen."

"Open your eyes. Talk to me. How long ago were you turned?"

Seeming surprised, Yonnie opened his eyes. A silent understanding connected them. They both knew that Carlos could have dredged him for the information, but hadn't invaded his mind.

"Respect," Carlos murmured. "Some things, between men, are just not done." He dropped his hold on Yonnie's shoulder and appraised his light almond complexion, wiry light brown Afro, and hazel eyes. "You've got a Southern accent," Carlos said, leaving Yonnie and walking to the far side of the room toward the bar. He studied his old crystal decanter, which was now filled with blood, and poured a half goblet, offering one to Yonnie. "You ever miss your living family?" Carlos asked, extending the tumbler.

Yonnie accepted the glass and took a shaky sip, his eyes never leaving Carlos's. "They're all dead by now," he admitted quietly. "I was made just before Nuit overthrew my master. A lot has changed in the world since then."

Intrigued, Carlos stared at Yonnie, as the vampire polished off his drink and set the glass down carefully on the edge of Carlos's desk.

"That was in the plantation days," Yonnie said slowly. "You cannot imagine what those days were like."

Carlos nodded. That was the stark truth, if ever he'd heard it. He didn't know much about this kid, but he did know an honest man when he saw one. But the irony of it all was not lost on him. In human terms, Yonnie was most likely two hundred years his senior, but in vampire terms, because he was a third-gen, he was a junior ranking officer now in his camp. Twisted.

"I gotchure back, man," Yonnie said in a quiet voice. His eyes searched Carlos's as he spoke. "I got into this by accident . . . it was more like a dupe. Had heard your turn went down like that, too. All of us from the old generation were rooting for you in that drag race, brother. We wanted to see one of our own, somebody who'd been played get the upper hand. So, when you came out holdin' aces, it was one of the proudest moments in my vamp life—and that's no bullshit. Go 'head, scan me, test me, but I mean what I'm saying, no matter how this night ends."

Emotion filled Carlos, but he kept that locked within him. He could appreciate where Yonnie was coming from, and didn't need a mental probe to test for authenticity.

Without fear, Yonnie stepped closer to him. His gaze locked with Carlos's, and Carlos could feel the invitation to peer into his mind. He nodded his acceptance of the offer and allowed his hand to again rest on Yonnie's shoulder. Horrible images filled his inner vision. A pretty, ebony-skinned young slave woman raped and brutalized by barbaric overseers. An almond-colored baby born and snatched from her arms, while she was forced to work. A child abused and beaten when it cried for its mother. A tender caress in the dead of night to soothe a frightened little boy . . . who became a man who ran into the woods one night to find a way to save his momma from her misery.

Tears streamed down Yonnie's face. Carlos closed his eyes.

"They told me that this old woman knew a man with power . . ."

Carlos stepped away from Yonnie and nodded, not sure that his dead heart could withstand the story he knew too well. "And he promised you power like you'd never imagine."

Yonnie simply nodded, then drew a ragged breath. "I wanted to get them back for what they'd done to us. I wanted to give all my boys the chance to live forever and to be strong. Two of them had tried to run and go north, but Alabama was a long way from the Mason-Dixon. They dragged them back, strung them up, and burned them alive for us all to see. That night I stole away and got made."

"And it wasn't what you thought it would be," Carlos said flatly. "It never is."

Yonnie wiped his face and nodded. "No, brother. It's not."

"Stack's been with you since then?"

"Yeah," Yonnie replied, drained. "All my boys were made by me. That's the tragedy." He quickly looked up, becoming tense. All vampires knew it was forbidden to speak ill of the eternal dark life, and he'd admitted his displeasure to a councilman.

"It's cool, man," Carlos said with a wave of his hand. He

sat on the edge of his desk, emotionally spent. "This shit is not what it's cracked up to be, even at my level."

Again, a silent understanding bound them as they stared at each other.

"But it is what it is," Carlos finally said. "We are where we are, and what we are. So, the only option is to make the best of it."

Yonnie nodded and found his empty chair and slumped in it. "After two hundred years, man, there are some nights when it all seems like it was yesterday. Then, there are some nights when it seems like it will never end." He laughed sadly. "And it won't."

Carlos rubbed his jaw, hearing everything Yonnie had said. He was only a year old in his vampire life, and already it had been too long. He could only imagine the boredom and pure agony of hundreds of years of existence . . . and the master vampires who were very old had that reality as their Achilles' heel.

"You know," Carlos said, his voice a low murmur, "as a councilman, there are some wrongs I can right."

Yonnie stared at him, new tension ebbing back into his body.

"I need men I can depend on, men who died with honorable intent."

Yonnie had stopped breathing. Carlos stood.

"My borders are shaky; another master has come into my territory and poached it." Carlos walked to stand before Yonnie and motioned for him to stand. "If you don't know anything else about me, you know I ain't having that."

"No. I didn't expect you would."

"I have certain rules about how I handle my business." Carlos stared at Yonnie hard. "No women and children. No elderly. No innocents. It's a long story, but it has to do with how I was made and who's still under my mark. It has everything to do with how they half ate my brother when they turned him."

Yonnie nodded. "Nuit's bite was nasty, man. We all hid from him. You ain't got no problem from us. Where we came from, none of us has the stomach for babies and old folks . . . hate seeing sisters diced up and left on the morgue slabs. What humans have done is worse than what we've ever imagined."

"That's why I want the dead meat out of my freezers. That's why I don't want any more floor shows with underage chicks. I want all my establishments run on the up and up, like we're going legit—so the humans don't swarm us. Top-shelf is siphoned from willing human donors only, already compromised motherfuckers who have lost their souls while still alive—and there's enough of them walking the planet to fill vats."

"Got it. We stay off radar until the heat dies down."

"Correct."

Carlos extended his hand to Yonnie. And when he accepted it, Carlos pulled him in close. He studied the junior vampire's jugular and waited until Yonnie threw his head back in submission. "You ready for a demotion to second-level, man . . . with the power to deliver this to your boys?"

Tears of admiration filled Yonnie's eyes as he choked out the word, "Yes."

"Make 'em all seconds with you," Carlos whispered as his fangs lowered to a deadly eight inches. "Do it tonight. After that, your bites will make thirds, and unless I sanction the turn, you make none without my permission."

He could feel Yonnie trembling as he held him in a steel embrace. Yonnie swallowed hard, on the verge of weeping as a current passed through them. "I'd always wished . . . but never dared dream."

"I know," Carlos crooned. "With this bite I give you the flight pattern to my lairs—guard them well. Watch my back. Protect my woman. Protect her family. Honor my strategy. Never question my judgment. Bring me information about which master has been in my yard."

"Done," Yonnie murmured.

The strike was so swift that Yonnie's knees buckled. The shock of energy transfer coursed through the room, toppling chairs, shattering glass, and eliciting a garbled groan of pleasure from the junior vampire. Years of Yonnie's torment entered Carlos and fused with his own, making Carlos's hands tremble as he siphoned away the pain and wrapped it in a pleasure bond. Prisms of dancing lights formed beneath Carlos's lids as he made his first lieutenant.

Winded, he dropped Yonnie to a chair and staggered away from him, torn. Part of him knew that the power transfer was a necessary evil to shore up his territory, but another side of him was deeply troubled. The pleasure that came from such power was nearly maddening. Now that he'd learned what it was like, he wondered if he'd ever be able to give up this new, dark life.

He brought the back of his hand to his mouth and dabbed away the black blood. He stared at Yonnie, who was prone, breathing heavily, eyes closed, as though he'd just been with a lover. The image disturbed Carlos and he crossed the room for much-needed space.

Without turning around he knew the vampire was slowly opening his eyes, which now glowed red. He watched Yonnie stretch out his arms and stare at the blue-black electric current running down them. Instantly, Yonnie stood and walked around in a circle, becoming giddy, almost as though he were high.

"I descended," Yonnie said, laughing. "Oh, shit, you made me, man! I'm your first lieutenant—*Carlos Rivera's* first lieutenant!"

Carlos poured a drink and downed it, his tone even, his nerves shattered. "Yeah, man. Congratulations. Go celebrate."

CHAPTER SEVEN

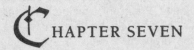

FINALLY MARLENE opened the bedroom door with Shabazz, Big Mike, and Rider leveling weapons in Damali's direction. It hurt her soul to see her team's expressions, each member meeting her at the front door armed, and prepared to fire. J.L.'s hand hovered over the hallway holy-water emergency levers. Tears were standing in Jose's eyes and he couldn't even hold up his crossbow against her. But it was that look in everyone's eyes that cut more than any weapon ever could.

"Let's do this in the weapons room," she said softly.

Father Patrick nodded, and unsheathed Madame Isis. Her team allowed her to pass slowly, each person watching everyone's backs.

The walk down that hallway felt like the longest road she'd ever taken. When she entered the room, the teams filed in behind her, everyone standing far enough away and taking strategic battle positions.

Damali's gaze settled on Marlene first. She was the only one unarmed, and the two women exchanged a silent understanding. They both knew that the teams had been trying to bring her out through a gentler method to no avail. Now, the options were severe.

"After Raven . . ." Marlene said quietly. "I can't put down another daughter."

"I know," Damali said, holding her head up high. "Father Pat and Imam Asula have to be the ones. Marlene . . . Mom . . . just know that I love you, 'kay?"

Rider's shotgun was tilted up, even though his finger was on the trigger. His face appeared so worn and his eyes were so red that she could barely look at him. She saw Big Mike waver, too, his shoulder cannon position was not dead aim like it should have been, but would only slow her down enough just to wound her. Shabazz held the line, but his gun shook as he aimed it at her, his eyes containing so much pain that the tears that glittered in them seemed like crystals. Dan, Jose, and J.L. had crossbows, but their aims were off, too. Only the Covenant held their weapons at full military readiness. That was to be expected. Family could never easily put down their own.

She smiled sadly at them. "I love you, too," she whispered. "I am so sorry, big brothers. God only knows how much."

"What did you say?" Shabazz whispered, lowering his Glock, and stepping out of the battle stance.

"I said," Damali repeated, "that I am so sorry. I never meant for this to happen."

They all continued to stare at each other.

"She said the name of the Almighty," Father Lopez whispered. He closed his eyes and made the sign of the cross over his chest, lowering his battle-ax.

"At a time like this," Damali said, confused, looking at each person in the room, "don't you think that makes sense?" Then eerie awareness entered her. She'd turned, had been in some sort of horrible flux, where she was banished from even the name of the Most High. The nightmarish reality brought hot tears to her eyes. She'd been stripped of her mission. She was no longer the Neteru. She wasn't even sure if she was still human.

When no one spoke, she opened her arms as hysteria began to claim her. "Kill me now, but say a prayer over me— let family do it, not the dark side!"

They were shaking their heads, tears standing in their

eyes. Their mute response tore at her, and her voice escalated as hot tears coursed down her face. "I messed up! Not
him. I baited Carlos into the bite. But I am not a creature of
the undead! I refuse to feed off the living and suck the
lifeblood from living things. I want to at least die with honor.
That deserves a prayer on the way out, doesn't it?"

"You thinking what I'm thinking, Mar?" Shabazz said,
ignoring Damali's impassioned outburst.

"I'm praying what you're thinking, baby," Marlene said
in a quiet rush.

"We might still have a chance," Father Patrick said carefully. "Three eves have not passed. The Neteru is strong.
And given that the Vatican told us that the holy key is missing, as I said when I arrived and Damali was still confined,
the warrior angels may be battling to preserve her for the intended mission." Father Patrick looked at Damali hard.
"Child, we need you on our side, but must also do what we
must do . . . if that isn't possible."

For a moment, Damali couldn't answer. She covered her
face with her hands and breathed into them slowly. Hope and
a host of other emotions had closed her throat, and new tears
stung her eyes as a sliver of a chance hung in the balance
there in the weapons room. But she sucked up the sob that
tried to force its way out, swallowed it away, and stood firm.
"Make me whole again. Human," she whispered. "Whatever
the mission, I'll always fight for the Light."

Uneasy smiles began to slowly dawn on the faces before
her. All except on Marlene's. When Jose totally abandoned
his weapon and moved to go to Damali, the older woman
placed her hand firmly on his shoulder and stopped him.

"He got to you telepathically through my strongest prayer
line, and a cleric team's prayers with an entire monastery
backing that up. Nothing should have been able to get in or
out of here from the dark side."

Monk Lin bowed in Marlene's direction, lowering his
samurai sword. "We set the perimeter prayer to let no evil
enter this compound, and to let no weapon formed against
us or her prosper. We asked that only good things come to

her, and that no force that would harm her be allowed to breech this house. We said to keep Damali safe; we called her by name. But we never said not to allow *Carlos Rivera* to gain entry. Dear Marlene, could that have been the cosmic loophole?"

"He was able to connect with her," Dan said slowly, "because he didn't mean her any harm."

Pure shame burned Damali's cheeks as she dropped her hands away from her face and wrapped her arms around her. "I baited him into that, too," she said quietly. "He *didn't* mean me any harm. Never did. When the man said there was no intent to turn me, that was the truth."

"I don't *believe* that that motherfucker might still be on our side," Shabazz said, wiping his face with his free hand, and walking away shaking his head in amazement.

"I told you to have faith," Father Lopez said, as he hung his head back and let out a hard breath of relief.

"Yo, she's standing before us, not trying to run or attack, talking about dying with honor, just like a Neteru," Jose said fast. "It's gotta be cool."

Asula wisely held up his hand, stopping the group from moving toward her. "Rivera said that Damali had been turned by a council-level vamp, making her extremely treacherous. Be advised, this night is not over yet. We need to perform some tests."

Damali nodded. "The man speaks the truth. I don't know how much of this is still in my system, or if I'll have some sort of lapse."

"I don't care, D," Jose said quietly, his gaze holding hers. "I got your back."

Father Patrick let out his breath slowly and motioned for Damali to stand by the cleared-off table, using the Isis blade to direct her. "I hope that we have not lost either of you. We have not removed our prayers and hope for his redemption, but we have barred him entry to the safe house until we know for sure which side he's chosen. The hour is short. He cannot enter this compound until we have certain assurances that you are yourself. My hope is that somehow this new experience and knowledge of the dark side will aid us in reclaiming what has been stolen from our holiest orders."

Nervous glances ricocheted around the team, but Father Patrick shook his head. "Until we know how your condition will evolve, you are not privy to Guardian information." He watched shoulders slump around the group, but drew a shaky breath as Damali thrust her chin up and nodded her understanding.

"Marlene will set up a named barrier to keep him out," the elder cleric said in a weary voice. "Then, we are going to recite the Twenty-third Psalm in unison while I walk around you, making a holy-water ring. Father Lopez will be swinging frankincense and then will read the communion prayer and offer you the sacrament. If your system can bear it, you will then be anointed with blessed oil at your forehead, your temples, your throat, over your heart, inside your wrists, and at the bottoms of your feet."

Asula nodded. "Then, a blood pack will be set before you, along with human sustenance. If you cannot consume real food, then all may be lost . . . and you know what we'll have to do."

"Each member of the team is going to read a scripture from each of the twelve holy books, from the twelve scattered tribes and twelve major religions, and you will be touched by the symbols of those faiths and if your skin doesn't burn, we will use the lights," Monk Lin said. "You will have to pass through the UV lights."

"Before the lights, though, I'll prepare you a white bath, filled with garlic cloves and myrrh, and holy water," Marlene said, her expression so tormented that it forced Damali to look away.

"It will be painful," Father Patrick warned. "Any residue of vampire abomination within your system will be purged. But the choice is yours. If you cannot submit to the tests, and even if you do, but do not pass any of the tests, we will have to end this quickly so your soul can rest in peace. You know the code of the Neteru, and of the Covenant."

"For the good of all mankind, the Light is my only path,

and only the light that casts no shadows. Death with honor before dark disgrace," Damali murmured, her gaze holding Father Patrick's until he nodded and looked away.

Damali fully understood. The choice was simple—she wanted to live and to give Carlos a fighting chance to reclaim his soul. She owed him that much. "Bring it."

Berkfield stood in his darkened garage, clutching the door opener and staring down the driveway behind the disappearing taillights of his family's minivan. He knew he had to punch in the number on the keypad soon, to call the scientist who had changed his life. He had to know, had to bring closure to this whole mystery that had haunted him since that fateful night in the alley when Carlos Rivera made him know there was a whole other universe out there that he didn't understand. But where was this man, this enigma that had shattered his neat world?

"Heard you were looking for me," a deep voice said from behind. Berkfield pulled his revolver and spun to meet the sound. "Your mental calls have been drilling a hole in my brain for a long time now, *hombre*."

Berkfield watched in horror as Carlos Rivera stepped out of the shadows. Sweat made his grip on his gun unsteady, and he reinforced his hold.

"Put it down," Carlos ordered. "You and I both know that's useless against my kind."

"What do you want? Where did you come from?" Berkfield asked nervously, stepping back without lowering the weapon.

"I came from Hell," Carlos said in a bored voice. "But I also came to call in a marker."

"Stay back!" Berkfield shouted as Carlos casually walked forward. "I have hallowed-earth-packed bullets, holy water, a blessed crucifix, and—"

"Good," Carlos said in a weary tone. "I'm also glad you sent the wife and kids to Father Patrick. Wise move." He smiled. "Don't look so shocked. I always know where everyone under my protection goes."

The fact that Carlos knew where his family was headed made Berkfield bold. "I will blow you away if you come near my family. We clear?"

Carlos nodded. "I want them safe, too. So you can dispense with the drama. I wouldn't have gone through all the trouble to put all of you under my protective seal if I wanted you dead. Use your brain. *Think.*"

Berkfield lowered his weapon. Carlos mentioned a protective seal, the same thing the scientist had said. "I need some answers."

Carlos nodded. "We both do." He walked over to the workbench and leaned against it, folding his arms. "You're a good man, Berkfield. That's why I'm here."

Berkfield just stared at Carlos for a moment. "I've been losing my mind, seeing crazy things, thinking . . ."

"You haven't lost your mind," Carlos said in a quiet voice. "But the whole thing is insane."

"I want this seal off of me! Whatever this shit is you did—some black magic bullshit, I don't know, but I—"

"In these unstable times, you do not want my mark off of you," Carlos said very slowly. "I gave you all the drug dealers, kingpins, led you to drug busts that would have taken years, and—"

"But I did not agree to sell my soul for it, and didn't agree to a deal with the Devil."

"Correct," Carlos said, beginning to lose patience. "Which is the only reason you're still standing here."

Silence had created a stalemate, and after a moment, Carlos let out his breath hard, pushing away from the workbench.

"Listen, Berkfield. I gave you a lot of information when you needed it, now I need some help."

When Berkfield didn't respond, Carlos pressed on. "Something very valuable was stolen from my territory by a human, but if it falls into the wrong hands, it could be disastrous. My empire is very—"

"Empire?" Berkfield said, cutting him off. Then he chuckled and rubbed his moist palm over his balding scalp. "I've lost my damned mind. I'm worried about vampires and werewolves and madness, and you're still just a drug lord." He shook his head and put the safety on his weapon.

Carlos studied the man before him. Time was of the essence and Damali's purging process was shattering his nerves. To make Berkfield understand, he went for shock value.

"Let me explain this to you slowly and carefully, and I'm going to stand here and not make a sudden move toward you so that your dumb ass doesn't have a heart attack," Carlos said in a smooth tone. He allowed his fangs to lower inch by inch as his body mass doubled, annoyance flickering his pupils gold and red. "I am of the highest level of my kind. There's an entire empire of us out there. But you got lucky. I've marked you. Not for food, not for bait, not to be a human slave, but have given you a protection voucher." Sending a dark current toward Berkfield, he slammed the garage door closed behind them and sealed the barrel of his gun.

He could feel Berkfield's heart beating erratically, a scream lodging in the man's throat. His blood pressure was spiking, his jaw had gone slack, and his bladder was about to empty. Carlos waved his hand to assist the human. "Chill, man," Carlos said as calmly as he could while normalizing. "I'm not here to hurt you—never will. All right?"

Berkfield clutched his chest and staggered toward the wall to slump against it. "What do you want?"

"Information," Carlos said coolly.

"About what?"

Carlos considered where to begin and sighed. "I didn't start off like this, *hombre*. I got jacked in the woods where you found my shit. I had the same reaction you're having now. Thought I'd have a fucking heart attack. But, bottom line is, I am what I am. Only good thing about it is that I can serve a little justice from this side, now. So, in that regard, we're *compadres*."

Berkfield's hand went to his cross and he fingered it nervously as he spoke. "You've been helping me all along? From behind the scenes? But you're dead?"

"Fucked up, ain't it?" Carlos shook his head.

"And Damali Richards . . ."

"She's all red-blooded human, but, yeah, she's my woman." Carlos smiled. "So, I can't be that bad."

"My family—"

"Is in the safest place on the planet," Carlos said, all amusement gone from his tone once again. "With the clerics on hallowed ground. Your gut hunch was right about sending them there."

"You said you needed information," Berkfield rasped, his voice cracking.

"Yeah. Seems some scientists have been dicking around with Mother Nature, magnetic fields—the kinda shit that keeps my universe somewhat separated from yours. They're doing experiments, trying to find the ultimate weapon, and may have opened up Pandora's box." Carlos began pacing. "Some places I can't go. Only a human can get inside to do the detective work, which is your specialty." He looked at Berkfield hard. "So this is where you come in. One of the master vampires, guys with power almost as serious as mine, may have come stateside and hijacked a key to one of the biblical seals. If he's able to open that seal, then everything you learned in Catholic school will go down. All Hell will literally break loose, *hombre*. You feel me?"

"I don't understand. What can I do? I'm just a—"

"You're just a man with knowledge beyond the average man. You've got skills for finding shit, and I need you on the case to bring me that key before some crazy shit jumps off."

Berkfield shook his head. "You think I'm a fool? If I did know where this so-called biblical key was, why would I give it to you? A demon? I did learn something about—"

"You will give it to me because your alternatives are very limited. The master who stole it isn't going to stand in your garage, have a nice chat, and negotiate with you." Carlos sent a searing strip of flame across the garage to make his point. "He will rip your fucking human heart out. He will turn your wife and children into the undead. He will do things to you that will make you know that Hell exists. So, my goal is to try to spare you that experience." Carlos took in a deep breath to steady himself and put out the flames. "Because you are under my seal, I know your every move. A scientist came to you, let's start there. What do scientists want with it?"

Confusion riddled Berkfield as he tried to process all that he'd witnessed and been told. "I was in the garage, had just come in, and they doped me up, I went out, and when I woke up I was in a military van."

Carlos began pacing. "Humans. All right."

"But the guy was trying to help me," Berkfield said fast. "He also told me about a faction of scientists who disagreed with this madness. They said everything you just said, and gave me a number to punch into the door opener. They said they would send a squad to put my wife and kids in hiding. But he also said that I was in some sort of danger, something about my aura and your mark, a buncha stuff I still don't understand."

"Yeah," Carlos said. "Neither do I and I don't like it." Carlos studied Berkfield and rubbed his jaw. "It was a smart move to get your family under Father Pat's wing, but the thing that troubles me is, why would they come to you?"

Both men stared at each other.

"If I'm supposed to find this key for you, man, you oughta know it is sacred blood."

"I know. Humans extracted it from the Shroud of Turin; it was dried in powder form and always kept on hallowed ground. There was a problem with the guy watching it this century. The situation went down in Boston."

Berkfield staggered over to the workbench where Carlos had been and leaned against it. "Well . . . Thanks, man, for the heads-up . . . and for watching my back, for taking care of my family. I owe you."

"We're even, if you bring me info that can help me find the key." Carlos spit on the ground and looked up. "You call me if you get yourself in a predicament. My advice is that you follow your family and stay with Father Pat's crew. If you can make some inquiries using your cop resources by day, get a bead on those scientists and where they hang. The master working with them can be traced, if he's marked a human helper."

"But I don't understand how you'd be working with and helping clerics."

"Long story. Like they say, politics and business make for strange bedfellows. Just like you and me ain't exactly a matched pair, but wound up on the same side."

Carlos began walking away into the shadows, Damali's torturous screams making it difficult for him to think.

"Hey!" Berkfield yelled. "Two questions. How am I supposed to find out who has this blood key now, and how in the hell do I call you?"

Carlos didn't turn around as he dematerialized into wind. "Work with the cool scientist and learn as much as you can about the black ops boys who are building weapons. And, as for calling me, I'll pick you up on the bat channel," he said, laughing. "If your ass gets in a sling and you start screaming, I'll hear you."

It felt like they were peeling her skin from her bones as they dunked her in the putrid white bath. Garlic fumes singed the insides of her nostrils, and the second round of holy water in the tub ate at the first- and second-degree burns on her entire surface. Vomiting and screaming, and twisting against the torture, she could feel her gums rip as Big Mike and Shabazz forced her head back from their arms.

"What the hell is happening?" Rider grunted over her screams, struggling with one of Damali's slippery legs.

"She's rejecting the cure," Father Patrick said, dangling a long crucifix over the water, while Marlene pushed Damali's torso under it and poured more bath water over her face and head.

Damali arched and wailed in pain.

"But she made it through the other tests," Jose said, clutching his weapon, on guard at the door. "The sight of the blood nauseated her, and she took the fruit and kept it down!"

"The baptismal ritual is the more arduous test, and will either shock her system back . . . or . . ." Father Patrick's words trailed off as another wave of screeches and curses came from Damali's twisted mouth.

Monk Lin, Imam Asula, and Father Lopez keep a trinity of loud chants going over the commotion, while Dan assisted J.L. in monitoring possible incoming from Carlos.

"Dude must really be gone," Dan muttered. "Big Mike's ears are bleeding. If he doesn't come for her through this . . ."

J.L. shook his head. "Marlene's new prayer line with the Covenant is blocking him. But look alive, stay alive, young brother, and man your post."

On the third dunk, Damali could feel her skin bubble up and begin to peel away, dissolving into the acidic bath. Totally submerged, she went into a convulsion, and the water went red around her until she could no longer see the faces beyond the surface.

"Jesus, Lord," Marlene croaked. "I can feel her skin coming off in my hands, Father! Drive the Isis in her heart, man! This is no way to kill her!"

"Stay steady, Mar," Shabazz ordered. "Let the man work. She's not struggling in our hold. Bring her up slow."

A collective gasp passed through the Guardian team as they brought Damali's limp form up from beneath the water's edge. Her once beautiful bronze skin was festered and split; huge boils and blisters covered it. Where she'd been touched by religious symbols, the blacked images were branded.

"Mike, take her out and put her on her bed in the center of the garlic ring," Marlene whispered.

Big Mike dabbed the corners of his eyes on his wet T-shirt with a shrug, and followed Marlene's command. Marlene stooped beneath Damali's form as Big Mike stood with care, checking the Sankofa tattoo.

"It's burned off," Marlene said, tears dropping off her nose as her voice broke.

"Put her down slow, Mike," Shabazz said, while he, Rider, and Jose flanked him with weapons.

"We did the best we could," Father Patrick murmured. "Bring the lights, J.L."

"No, guys. Enough," Rider said, choked. "Enough."

"But, we can't give up on her," Jose said, panicked, "We have to keep trying!"

"Bring the lights, J.L.," Marlene repeated in a far-off tone. "If that doesn't work, then *I'll* plant the Isis in my baby girl."

Carlos watched with disinterest as the two hounds snapped at each other, snarling over the two limp vamp bodies at his feet. Yonnie had routed out two territory sniffers and delivered them, just as Carlos had requested. But they held no information; therefore, they were as useless as dog food.

One creature had one leg of a body, the other had an arm, and they were ripping it apart, pulling in opposite directions, each trying to get more than their fair share of the gruesome remains.

Suddenly he looked down at his arms and saw how the skin went raw, then immediately healed. He closed his eyes and took in a deep breath as the slurping, cracking sound of the dogs eating became a faraway echo in his mind. The foul stench of garlic and incense attacked the back of his throat, and Carlos hawked and spit. The dogs stopped feeding for a moment, monitoring the new scent and growled, dragging the carcasses away from the offending smell. Carlos couldn't hear Damali screaming anymore.

His line-knowledge was enough to tell him what they'd done to her. But he'd gambled that they'd never go that far. This was the old way, followed up with a medieval, Vatican-style cleansing. All he could do was send healing thoughts to her and hope. If he'd known they were going to go the Full Monte and not just dust her quick . . . or even just accept her back with a few modern tests . . . But, then, hindsight was always twenty-twenty.

The pain was so intense that she slipped in and out of consciousness, feeling hot, then cold, now warm again. A bright-

ness just beyond her lids made her try to cover her eyes to
block it at first, but then the warm sensation against the back
of her hand made her reach for it. An eerie peace covered her,
and she felt like she was floating away. She reached harder
toward the source of comfort, anything to stop the pain.

She tasted tears and could feel them slide from beneath
her shut lids, down the sides of her face. Light, blessed light,
her mind seized upon it, remembering, holding the image
of the light in the long tunnel . . . yearning for it, seeing
bright forms in it that she couldn't quite make out—but that
she knew meant her no harm—were calling to her, beckoning, reaching for her to touch her hands and pull her . . .
then she saw a pair of deep-set, concerned eyes, and a
strong hand extended toward her. She grasped it, heaved,
and sucked in a shuddering breath, then opened her eyes to
Shabazz.

"Come back to us, baby," Shabazz whispered. "Please,
darlin', just come back."

The images around her were blurry. The point of the Isis
blade was centered over her chest, held by an old man in a
blue robe. The glint of silver made her squint.

"Wait, Father Pat," Marlene said loudly. "Look at her
skin! The wounds are healing."

The blue image moved away with the silver. Faces slowly
came into focus. The burns on her body began to abate, and
a shiver ran through her, then became a sudden seizure. A
white blanket immediately covered her, and through her eyelids she could almost see shadows of Marlene's frantic motions passing over her.

"She's going into shock," Marlene yelled. "Bring her
out, turn off the lights. Circle of three! Healing touch. Bring
her out!"

He sat on the front balcony railing of the mansion for a
long time, his head back, his eyes closed, his thoughts cen-
tralized . . . stroking her hair with his mind, his fingers gently caressing every blistered, scarred surface on her
battered body. His will for her to live transferring through

the night air; his hope an airborne message, her torture—his torture.

"I would give my life . . . let the pain come to me," he whispered to the nothingness. "Bring her out," he murmured. "Just bring her out." They were supposed to be professionals at this; he'd trusted them, and had banked on their knowledge. But something was going very wrong.

Patience began sliding down a very slippery slope within his mind. Damali was still screaming. This was her trial, and she had to ride it out—take it like a woman, that had been her choice. But they were botching the job, and she had no concept of what level of torture a bite purge could inflict. Panic had been his enemy, now it was his best friend. They were botching the fucking job . . . *hell* no. Amateurs!

His hand reached toward her, flesh of his flesh, bone of his bone, love of his life, spirit inside his spirit. Angry, thunderous storm clouds split the blackening sky and gathered above his head as his thoughts concentrated. Every power that he'd come into, every lifetime that had been held within the dark throne, ran down his arm, burned his fingertips black as the energy exited his body, lit the night, and resounded with a sonic boom.

A shock wave rocked the compound. All lights went out and not even the generators booted up.

"Heads up, people," Shabazz said fast. "The brother obviously ain't having this shit."

"Stay with her," Marlene said, as Damali convulsed and stopped breathing. "Keep the circle unbroken around her."

"Are you people fucking *nuts*?" a voice said, ricocheting off the walls in a low, even baritone. "You should have brought her out slower!"

On the last part of his statement, the back bedroom wall blew out as Carlos's form materialized. Mike leveled, aimed, and fired his cannon, discharging a hallowed-earth grenade that knocked his shoulder back.

The team watched as the shell spiraled, slowed, and stopped, hovering inches from the target. Jose stepped forward, but hesitated, weapon drawn.

"Do not make me take a body up in this joint," Carlos warned. "I didn't come here for that. I came for my woman."

As other weapons discharged, he stepped aside and let the cannon shell whiz by him to explode in a dirt hill beyond the ridge—sending every bullet behind it like heat-seeking missiles with a wave of his hand.

"I told you I was not in the frame of mind!" Carlos snarled between his teeth and walked calmly toward the bed.

Ignoring the stricken faces around him, Carlos stooped and picked Damali's limp form up in his arms, the white blanket billowing in the wind.

"You do not think we're just going to stand here and let you walk out of here with our baby girl," Shabazz said, catching the Isis from Father Patrick's toss.

Jose was holding his empty gun with two hands. "Word. You ain't taking D nowhere, man!"

Rider was on his flank, crossbow raised. "Not."

Carlos reached out his hand, breaking Shabazz's hold on the Isis, drawing it toward him. The sword spiraled and lodged into a cinder block behind Carlos. "I'll bring her back when she's better," he said, retracting his fangs.

He turned and stepped over the wall line with Damali in his arms. He grabbed her sword from the wall, resealed the compound, rebooted the lights, and was gone.

When he landed on the mansion porch, his Hell-dogs immediately lunged at him. He drove the Isis blade into the dirt, slowing their now-stalking advance. The garlic and incense and prayers Damali trailed had obviously confused their senses, bristled the hair on their backs, and formed acid foam at their jaws.

"No!" he ordered, making them completely stop, sniff around confused, and retch up half digested body parts.

"Not this scent, either," he said, his voice dropping to a threatening low that cowed their aggression. *"Never.*

"Stay. Guard. Watch," he said, turning his back on them and taking Damali into the house.

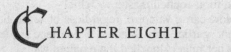

CHAPTER EIGHT

NUMB, BERKFIELD punched the code into the garage-door opener that he'd been given by the scientist. He waited as the door slowly opened and stood, transfixed, in the same spot where he'd been when Carlos disappeared. Every belief he'd once held had been shattered. In a place beyond fear, he stood watching the horizon—traumatized.

He didn't move as a black van without windows pulled into his driveway. He just stared at it. But when six burly guys climbed out of it bearing a strange crest on their black fatigues, the hair stood up on his arms.

"Where's the old guy with the white hair?"

Berkfield began to back up as he spoke. The scream that was bubbling within his chest never reached his throat as two icy hands held the sides of his head from behind. He couldn't speak, couldn't move. Paralysis swept through his body.

"Dr. Zeitloff was a problem," a strangely accented voice murmured close to his ear. "He's dead. Your protector is battling a Guardian team and coping with domestic problems with his wife. And you, my friend, are soon going to become my living key."

"Did you see that shit?" Rider said quietly, sitting down slowly on the edge of the bed.

"He walked through every prayer line we'd laid down," Father Patrick whispered, looking at the team members.

"He more like blew through them," Shabazz muttered. "Even for a council master . . . shit."

"How can a vampire, regardless of level, be immune to prayers, garlic, holy water . . ." Marlene's question trailed off as her fingers touched the repaired wall.

"He's hybridizing," Father Patrick said, running his fingers through his shock of white hair. "She's in him, as much as he's in her," the elder cleric said in a far-off tone. "They've soul-joined . . . that's why he could speak the name of the Almighty, break the new line—but he didn't attack."

"What have we got here, Father?" Big Mike asked as he lowered his weapon. "He's still all vamp and if the traditional methods don't work . . ."

For a moment no one spoke as the impact of what they were now facing settled into their awareness.

"We need the team of seven around the table so I can try to locate them." Marlene looked at Father Patrick. "Then you and I can link thoughts, and the three remaining members of the Covenant can find the lair."

"Yeah, Mar, but that ritual needs a twelve-man team." Shabazz looked at the clerics. "Carlos had always been your fifth man over with the Covenant, a dark Guardian—but a Guardian nonetheless. It's a risk that his energy might get pulled into the mix."

"We don't have a choice," Marlene said quietly, despair making her voice barely audible.

"We just saw how strong he's gotten, Marlene," Rider said, taking sides with Shabazz, and glancing around the team for agreement. "We can search for her by day. Forget the mind lock to her. If she's still alive, Carlos is all inside her head."

"I'll take the weight," Jose said fast. "I'll go in with Marlene, if you all won't." His intense gaze swept the team. "She went to Hell for me to break Dee Dee's bond, that's the least I can do."

Father Patrick nodded. "Marlene's right. Time is of the

essence, and the risk is of no consequence." He gave Jose a nod of respect. "We'll still have to do a daylight recovery . . . but we need not waste another moment in divining her location tonight. They'll be on the move from this point forward as a mated vampire pair."

Every place her skin touched his, sizzled. Carlos pulled in a deep breath and covered Damali's mouth and nose with his lips, and pushed the breath of life into her lungs.

When she didn't respond, he willed himself not to panic. He dropped to his knees on the foyer floor, laying her flat, as he massaged her heart, continued to breathe for her, with her, into her, spitting out the nasty taste of whatever they'd made her swallow in the process, until he was left with no option but to pound on her chest.

Her body convulsed, shivered, and her eyes opened, glassy and dead. The sight of it nearly stole his breath, and he scooped her up, taking the stairs two at a time, too rattled to even dematerialize. Dashing down the hall, he willed on the shower, thrust her into the cold spray and began gently washing the horrible oils and residues off her pretty brown skin.

Fury roiled within him. They should have brought her out of the turn slowly. But not this—a total flat-line.

"C'mon, baby. Come back to me. Fight it. I'll take the pain—don't run from it!"

He lathered her hair and skin and hands, gradually warming the water by will, hoping that would help her to slowly come around, stepping into the shower with her to keep her lifeless body pressed to his, sending her his life force, breathing into her, cleaning her, begging her with his mind to come back.

A sob of total defeat claimed him as he rocked her and just held her head against his shoulder, petting her drenched locks, finally abandoning his attempts to revive her.

How many lifetimes would he have to live through to purge this pain? "Oh, God . . . I'm so sorry . . . for everything," he whispered, his head back, eyes closed against the splash of the spray in his face. "Don't do this. Don't take her away from me like this."

The water beating against the tiles droned out his quiet sobs. He stood there, just rocking her, nuzzling her cold body, trying to build enough acceptance to will his legs to move her out of the shower. There was no way to make this right, no game to play, no option to explore. There was only one ultimate power that held sway now. He believed now. The dark side didn't have nothin' on this.

Carlos drew a ragged breath and let it out slowly. He'd take her back home so they could give her a proper burial on hallowed ground . . . Then he'd take the Isis, allow them to plant it hard in the center of his chest—with honor. That was the only way to go out. His baby was right. Always had been.

A sudden gasp passed through her body, into his chest, and into his splayed palms upon her back. It forced him to jerk his head down, to roughly take her jaw into his hand. He shook her hard, grabbed the hair at her skull when a flicker of life stirred within her. He frantically tilted her head, and covered her mouth again, forcing another breath into her, then slapped her face hard.

She opened her eyes, stunned, disoriented, weakened, her irises glittering gold, then normalizing to deep brown. He breathed into her again, until she gasped on her own, and began coughing and sputtering, while she clung to him. As he held her head hard against his shoulder, he felt her jaw fill, and instinctively knew that she needed to feed.

He tilted her head back, lifting her mouth to his throat. At first, her strike was weak, clumsy, but he held her to him, letting her renew herself, siphon slowly. Then the siphon changed, becoming more aggressive as she filled herself, fought to live, battled to survive at any cost.

He staggered against the tiles as she began to bleed him out, but he held her close, letting her take what she needed. Even if she flat-lined him, it was all right, just as long as she survived.

When she finally lifted her head, he was semiconscious. Her beautiful mouth was dripping red water, the shower washing the blood away. Her skin was no longer cool and pallid, but flushed and warm. All he could do was reach out and trace her jaw with trembling fingers and brush the stray locks away from her face. She nuzzled the inside of his hand and brought her mouth to his to exchange a kiss, which he returned so tenderly that she deepened it immediately.

Relief buckled his knees as his arms enfolded her tightly and they fell against the tile wall. His fingers wound through her hair, caressed her back, pulled her so hard against him that he was afraid he might hurt her. He kissed her face, her neck, her shoulders, her throat. Then he hugged and rocked her. A dead man's prayers had been answered.

Through her shudder he felt it, but hesitated to act on it. She'd seen this before—this had happened in the compound . . . the shower. Yeah, he remembered her premonition, too.

She looked at him, their minds locking with the shared gaze. She nodded and smiled. The offending scent now washed away, the raw essence of Neteru ran all through him. He shook his head no. He didn't want to tempt fate.

"The purge shocked your system," he said, panicked, trying to extract himself from her embrace. "You've ripened early." He closed his eyes, tilted his head, drew in a deep breath and shuddered. Then he spoke to her through suddenly lowered incisors. "I've gotta get you home."

"They'll torture me again," she said quietly, standing an inch away from him, water cascading down her naked form, her eyes glittering. "You were the one who understood . . . brought me back."

"But I'm the one thing right now that might kill you," he said, her fragrance destroying his resolve. But neither of them moved. He couldn't even look at her. Not standing there naked, dripping, with a plea for sanctuary in her eyes, a half inch of fang showing and Neteru scenting the air.

She reached out and cupped his cheek with her hand. He turned into it and pressed a deep kiss in the center of her palm.

"You are the *only* one who accepts all of me—the good and the bad, the strong and the weak. You'd take me with a halo or with fangs," she said quietly, smiling sadly and moving in closer to him. "To be with you doesn't require that I play some role, or be something special, and when I fall, you don't even care about that. You were that way with me before and after your turn . . . strength of character, Carlos—you've got it. So, if fate has it that I die with you, isn't that an honorable way to go out?"

Her words were shredding him, and he tried to remember that he was indeed talking to a female master, as her gaze held his defiantly. Life was ironic, death was even more perverse, because here he was backing away from a gorgeous, naked, wet, ripe, seductive vampire.

"Damali, I actually *prayed* that you'd get a second chance to live," he said, pushing a stray lock over her shoulder. "In this condition, you could conceive, and we wouldn't know whether what you were carrying was good or something . . ."

She pressed her index finger to his lips to stop his awkward tumble of words. "Nobody knows what will come out of this next generation. Life is a gamble, just like death is a gamble. The way I see it, we've got a fifty-fifty shot."

Water beat on the tiles, just like her words beat on his conscience, both standing so still neither was breathing. Then she made the fatal mistake of moving a millimeter closer, her breasts brushing his chest when she lifted herself on tiptoes to take his mouth.

Prayer was forgotten, his conscience was banished. Her hair filled his hands, and his mouth captured hers. The steam carried her scent. As his reason melted, so did his clothes. The hard rake of her nails down his back dragged his hands the length of hers. There was one single objective: enter this woman, or lose his mind.

Her short pants were now the pace of his pulse. Her back hit the wall, knocking the wind from her lungs. He caught the hard exhale in his throat and thrust his tongue into her mouth.

Tearing his lips from hers, his jaw collided with her cheek, forcing her head to the side so his incisors could drag a hot trail from the edge of her shoulder to find the sweet spot midpoint on her neck. She held his shoulders tight, pulling him against her as though trying to fuse with his skin. His hands flattened at the small of her back, then moved over her supple behind, lifting her off her feet.

Writhing under his hold, her eyes shut tight, anticipation in every breath, waiting for the double entry. A swift strike came with the deep thrust, her voice rising with the steam, creating so feral a sensation that she let go of his shoulders and flattened both palms on the tiles.

From some remote place of awareness, he knew he had to pull out of the siphon. Her body was going limp; the punishment too intense. Yet need created by the scent of ripe Neteru was beyond even council-level control. He should have fed, first . . . but how in the hell . . . when she shuddered like she did, her moan deep and guttural, her legs now clamped around his waist, and every returned thrust sending intense pleasure through his groin.

He could feel his incisors about to sever the vein, hit muscle, cartilage, and penetrate her esophagus. A long, hard shiver sent shock waves down his spine as he tore his head back, kissed the wound to close it, and rested his forehead against the tiles, sucking in air.

"Don't stop," she whispered hard against his ear, still moving under him, cradling his head, running her fingers through his hair.

"I have to feed," he said, breaths staccato, words running together. "I'll kill you."

"You can't, not this way now that I'm already turned . . ."

"Not permanently."

Her head was tilted back, her neck arched, breathing irregular through her mouth. The words, the timbre of the plea, the invitation, were a double-edged blade—slicing reason, while snapping it back into focus, if only for a moment. He pulled out hard, causing her gasp to stab him. She turned away and pressed her cheek against the cold tiles.

"You're right, you're right . . . okay," she said between her teeth after a moment.

But the sight of how the water played over her shoulder

blades, the definition of her spine flexing drew his fingers to each vertebra, lingering to kiss them with his touch, making him take one step back to admire the form of her wet ass.

His hands slid over the high, glistening cheeks with the water, and he entered her, hard from the rear.

He cried out as her stomach hit the wall. He slid his hand between the tiles and her wondrously smooth belly, pulling her into him, against him, to keep her from being slammed into the wall. Using an outstretched arm with his elbow locked to brace the impact, shelter her skull, his breaths became a chant. He needed to feed.

With his head thrown back, his eyes shut tight, he tried to reason with her, slow his motions, his pulse, the inevitable. "Downstairs in the lair, on tap," he said between pants. "But you have to stop moving."

"I can't." Her voice broke, and she reached back, holding his hips, refusing to allow him to break the seal of their bodies. "Not yet."

"It's now or never," he told her honestly, gathering her in his arms, his hands sliding up her slick torso to mold her breasts. "Let me feed, so we can both live to do this again tomorrow night."

Grudgingly, she moved, disengaging their bodies and allowing him to turn her, shuddering when the connection was lost. He embraced her and nuzzled her hair. With a thought, they were downstairs, dripping water on the black marble kitchen floor.

She backed up to the sink, baiting him with her eyes. "Turn on the tap," she ordered. Her voice was low, and husky. Lethal.

He nodded and it ran blood.

Without his looking at the cabinets, they slammed open—and a crystal goblet materialized in his hand. She inched over and let him fill it, watching him with burning intensity as he downed two glassfuls quickly.

"Can I taste?" She smiled, her fangs glistening in the darkness, her eyes flickering gold.

"It's got a kick to it . . . not like feeding from me, or the packs."

She nodded, her hot body sliding beneath him. She dipped her finger in his glass, put it in her mouth, and closed her eyes, pulling her finger out slow and wet. "Yeah . . . it does."

He let her take the glass. She took a deep swig, dropped the glass, and let it shatter. With feline agility, she pushed herself up on the counter and leaned back and her eyes said it all—no mind lock necessary.

More stable now, he took his time, his lips finding her eyelids, the bridge of her nose, but denying her ready mouth his kiss. It was about finesse. A sad knowing overcame him as he honored her body—she was too far gone, the purge hadn't worked, and she'd turned. Instinctively he knew that while female vampires could not reproduce the scent of ripe Neteru, a master could reproduce any illusion that he had intimate knowledge of. In this case, he'd made a female master with Neteru DNA. He wanted to weep.

"I'm so sorry, baby," he whispered, swallowing away his tears.

"If I had to be bitten and turned," she whispered, stroking his hair, "I'm glad you were the one who did it."

Carlos nuzzled her neck. He'd never forgive himself, but vowed to spend eternity making it up to her.

Breath warm and coating teased her throat, a nip, a flicker of tongue, making her squirm in frustration as she waited for his bite and entry. Deep, long kisses sucked her collarbone. A gentle caress lifted her breasts, causing a shiver. Gooseflesh from anticipation made her arch to make contact with his mouth, the tips hardened, ready, but ignored, then suddenly captured. The sensation almost blinding, then gone.

Moistened thumbs traced a lazy circle around edges of her nipples in a burning tease. A light kiss on her breastbone made her belly quiver. A long, sweeping lick down her abdomen—impossible to hold her head up and watch. A tongue circling her navel, then penetrating it, causing a slow moan . . . a series of advancing kisses, nips, that forced her to lift her head with hope . . . then he looked up at her and smiled.

Her thighs opened wider on their own accord. But the place that she most needed to feel him, he ignored. The tender insides of her thighs were on fire. Every swipe of his tongue, every deep French kiss against them, made her lift her hips and contract, not knowing when the kiss there would come.

When his hands slid down her sides and over her thighs, water came to her eyes, blurring her vision. His caress was so lazy, almost hypnotic, were it not for the white-hot burn it created.

"You always smell *so* damned good," he murmured into the soft down as he kissed it.

His words vibrated against the tender place, sending a hard contraction up the core of her. Her face felt hot, and she licked the tiny beads of sweat that had formed just above her lip. But when he separated her with his tongue an electric current straightened her spine.

The slow suckle of the oversensitive bud that he'd found made her hips move to the pulse of his tongue. And as his mouth explored the tender folds around it, she arched to try to return him to where he'd just been. But he wasn't having it. He'd found a deeper region, and he circled it before plundering it, her cries nearly shattering glass.

His mouth wandered, leaving her aching, another site abandoned, his fingers adding delicious, torturous penetration, but a poor substitute. He chuckled, reading her mind, knowing, finding the place she needed him to kiss most, and he allowed his tongue to salsa it until she grabbed his hair with both hands.

Hovering on the edge of certain madness, she could not understand her body. It wouldn't yield, wouldn't obey her and just plunge over the edge of the near orgasm. Instead, it teetered, going close, then stepping back, ignoring her will. Her moan became a whimper, then a plea of despair.

"I know," he murmured against her thigh, hot and thick. "*Now* do you understand?"

Her voice caught in her throat. She nodded with her eyes closed, but knew he was watching her face, triumphant.

His kisses trailed up her middle, his hands leaving a burn as they stroked her. "I was right there, just like that . . . on the brink *for months*."

She wanted him so badly, she nearly wept when he covered her. She struggled beneath his hold, trying to offer him entry, but he just lay refusing to come in.

"For us," he murmured into her hair, winding it through his fingers, "release is impossible without the bite." If she'd turned, he had to teach her. She was his woman, his wife, and had to know all there was to thrive in his dark world that had become hers.

He was in full control, and she knew it. She could feel his fangs tease her skin, his hips lowering slowly, calmly.

"Please . . ." Her hands scrabbled at his shoulder blades, but he shook his head no and chuckled low in his throat.

"Uh-uh. Not yet." She had to learn patience, how to seduce prey, how to co-opt would-be aggressors. She had to learn how to function within the sixth realm.

Only a millimeter in, he withdrew from the bite, as he entered her agonizingly slow, kissing the nick at her neck. Then he kissed her hard, pulled back to look into her eyes. She ran her tongue over her fangs and she tried to catch her breath. He smiled and closed his eyes.

"Yeah, baby, now you're ready."

She felt herself falling, his arms tight around her as her back met red satin sheets. Crimson rose petals stuck to her legs, the aroma making her heady, his touch now bold and firm. His eyes flickered in the dancing torchlight as he looked down at her. She could feel perspiration dampen his back, and she arched into him, hoping he would take her quickly.

The strike was so sudden, so hard, it made colors dance behind her lids. Her body convulsed as he penetrated her once again. He was in so deep that she could taste her own blood in her mouth. He'd found that elusive spot and stroked it over and over again. She dug her nails into the smooth, hard globes of his ass.

Every muscle in his back worked in harmony with her breath-chants, his thighs pushing them up the bed, dangerously near a marble post. He reached out, not breaking stride, and slid them away from it.

She sobbed his name in refrain and he pulled out of the bite, threw his head back, tears streaming down his face. *Now she understood.*

Offering her his throat, even while he continued to lunge against her, she knew what he needed. His anticipation of her bite made his breaths become ragged. The moment her mouth neared his neck, she could feel him begin to shudder. She leaned up and licked the sensitive surface of his neck and he moaned. The sound of his voice convulsed her womb. They struck at the same moment. Blinding pleasure almost made it impossible to siphon. Every convulsion that ripped through him entered her, recycling itself back to him with her heat contained within it.

She could barely breathe and had to pull up. Her heart felt like a tight fist was crushing it—the waves of ecstasy were so intense. But his tortured plea not to stop now brought her mouth to his throat again.

A prolonged wail traveled up his torso, entered her veins through his bite, made him seek air, refuge from the sensory overload. Carlos's fingers raked the sheets, shredding them in the wake, while she tightened her legs and arms around him and tried to hold on.

Carlos dropped his head to her shoulder, his face burning, hair soaked, breathing erratic. All she could do was pet away the shudders until his body stopped jerking.

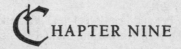

CHAPTER NINE

THE GLARE of harsh hospital lamps made him squint as he came to. Berkfield immediately tried to sit up, but realized instantly that his hands and feet were strapped to a cold metal table. He tried to cry out, but his vocal cords were frozen. White-masked men in green surgeon's gowns peered down at him.

"Is the key ready?" an eerily distant, accented voice asked.

One of the masked men around the table nodded and held up a huge needle containing a silvery red fluid. Terror seized Berkfield as he stared at the epidural-sized syringe. He shook his head no, wildly resisting in vain. That only produced strange, out-of-body laughter from an unknown source within the sterile lab.

"Inject him," the voice said. "Then bring him to my chambers for the ritual."

Seated comfortably in the rec room around the poker table, seven guardians sat in a circle, hands joined, eyes closed. Four members of the Covenant stood watch, each positioned in the four earth directions, north, south, east, and west. The men at the Guardians' backs kept vigil to prevent evil from attacking from all directions, murmuring prayers in different languages. Marlene's mouth moved, her silent meditation calling down the Light to watch over them, requesting discernment to open their eyes, to sharpen their gifts, and to locate their baby girl.

"I can't see her and I can't feel her," Marlene said quietly, her voice tight with frustration, "and I've been trying for nearly an hour."

Beads of sweat dotted her brow, and she dabbed at the offending moisture with the back of her forearm, not breaking the human circle.

"They're obviously blinding both the seers in the group to their whereabouts," Father Patrick said. "But they can't block all of us."

Marlene nodded. "We'll have to track them through a back door. If one of the other members at the table can pick up a sensitivity, then we might have a chance. One of us will eventually feel their vibrations, or hear them, perhaps pick up a scent."

"Up to now, Marlene, you've been trying to get an immediate sightline on them. Let's see if we can redirect that energy to the olfactory sensors, or the tacticals. Maybe Mike can hear something that will clue us in?"

"It's worth a shot, Mar," Rider said. "If Jose and I can pick up some kinda tracer, then Father Pat's crew can trail it. We'll talk them through on walkie-talkie while keeping the circle connection going."

"All right, people," Marlene said on a weary sigh. "Let's clear our thoughts, stretch our minds. We know she mentioned a lair in Beverly Hills, so envision the environment, the surroundings, the streets, feel the trees, and see the colors, close your eyes, open up your minds, hear the traffic, smell the freshly cut lawns, let your gifts guide you and send those impressions to each other, then to me."

Only the sound of deep, steady inhales could be heard. Air-conditioner compressors around the compound hummed in the distance. A wall clock ticked ever so slightly. Water from a faucet in the next room dripped.

Then Jose breathed in deeply and tilted his head at the same moment Father Lopez did.

"Talk to us, Jose," Marlene said, her voice low, melodic, calm. "Impression . . . scent?"

Jose took a deeper breath and squeezed Rider's hand harder. "Smells so good," he murmured.

"Rider," Marlene said, keeping the group steady, "you picking up?"

"No, Mar. The young buck got this one. I'm not picking up anything."

When Jose shuddered, everyone opened their eyes and stared at him.

"Stay focused everybody, keep hands joined, stay relaxed. Jose, where are you?"

A palpable tension could be felt in the room. The squat white candle in the center of the ring of hands sputtered and flickered as an energy charged the atmosphere around it.

"I don't know, but *shit*."

"Are you hurt?" Marlene asked quickly, but her voice was still low and controlled.

"No," Jose murmured.

"Are you by yourself?"

He shook his head no. His breathing deepened as his T-shirt became damp from sweat.

"The scent, is it vampire?"

"No," Jose said on a heavy exhale. "Female, straight up."

"Mar," Rider said. "He found Damali. Think he's got a lock with our girl."

"Yeah, bro," Jose said, slowly. "Roses . . . blood . . . *oh, baby*."

Marlene stiffened. "Roses . . . are they outside?"

"No," Jose whispered. "Red everywhere . . ."

"He's picking up tactical senses, which is beyond his gift range. Mar, pull him out."

"No, Shabazz," she said through clenched teeth. "He saw a *color*, which means that he's got a visual, something we haven't been able to get."

Shabazz eased back in his chair, casting a concerned glance around the team. Father Lopez stepped forward, bringing the other three Covenant members to the table with him, walking almost in lockstep with them so they wouldn't lose their protective directional position. Father Lopez laid his hand on Jose's shoulder.

"I'll connect with him directly, stay with his spirit to guide him and to be a second source of strength." Father Lopez looked away shyly. "I feel things . . . and no offense, but I picked it up before Shabazz and J.L. did. I guess I'm a tactical sensor, too."

"Good," Rider said, nodding. "We almost lost our brother once before to some freak accident and I don't want to go there again."

"No lie," Big Mike said.

Once Father Lopez was squarely at Jose's back, Marlene began her inquiry again, pushing harder for answers.

"Red," she told Jose, "concentrate on red. Is it blood?"

"No, soft . . ." he said and sighed. "Satin and roses."

"Why am I not surprised?" Rider asked, blowing his breath out hard.

"Rider, please," Marlene warned. "Jose, baby, open your mind's eye wider. Let Father Lopez's energy help you. Work with it."

"It's all in the air . . . Neteru," Jose said, taking in a deep breath and shuddering. "Her skin is like butter . . . and her throat." He licked his lips, and squeezed his shut eyes tighter.

The group went still.

"Where?" Marlene's voice was strained. Her gaze bore into Jose as sweat coursed down the sides of his face.

Father Patrick put his hand on Marlene's shoulders. "Steady, Mar. You'll lose the connection if you panic."

"In the mansion—"

All of a sudden Father Lopez dropped his hands from Jose's shoulders and backed away from the group, hugging his arms about himself. "I cannot do it," he said, shaking his head. "No."

"What did you feel, or see?" Father Patrick asked.

"It wasn't what I saw," Father Lopez said quietly. "It was what I *felt*." He staggered over to the wall, and leaned against it. The front of his black robe had a darkening stain that spread down his leg.

The team watched horrified as blood splattered the top of his shoe and oozed out onto the floor.

"It's his femoral artery! Break circle! Now!" Rider yelled.

Shabazz and Big Mike leapt forward and caught Father Lopez before he hit the ground. They slowly laid him on the floor. Two Guardians held their hands against the wound, applying pressure to the young cleric's inner thigh. J.L. ripped off his belt, and tossed it to Shabazz. Rider held the cleric's head up from the floor as his Guardian brothers worked to stop the hemorrhage. Marlene kept one hand on Jose's shoulders, Imam Asula kept one hand on the other. Father Patrick and Monk Lin covered their fallen brother with prayers, while the rest of the team stood in the distance, poised to act but not sure what to do.

Snatching the bowie knife from his hip, Rider passed the blade to Shabazz, who pushed up Father Lopez's robe and cut a long slit in the wounded cleric's pants. There was so much blood, they couldn't see the extent of the wound.

"Get some holy water to clean the site," Big Mike yelled to Dan, who immediately dashed away and came back with a plastic jug from the weapons room containing what Mike had requested.

Shabazz doused the wound. Father Lopez screamed and convulsed. Marlene gasped when she saw two puncture wounds on the young man's inner thigh.

"Oh, shit, he bit her!" Marlene shrieked, breaking the connection. "He's bleeding her out!"

"No he's not," Jose said in a low, sensual tone. "*She* bit *him*."

"What!" Father Patrick said, staring at Jose in shock. He looked down at Lopez and slapped his face. "C'mon, son."

But just as quickly, the two puncture wounds sealed and the flow of blood stopped. Slowly, Father Lopez roused, his face ashen before it flushed a deep red, his breaths uneven.

He crossed himself, and struggled to sit up. The other guardians helped him.

"Oh, my God! Oh Father *Christ!*" he said, his voice fracturing as he pushed hands away from him and made the sign of the cross over his chest again. "She bit me . . . never in my life—"

"Steady," Father Patrick said, soothing the distraught junior priest. "What happened? Tell us *exactly* what happened."

Father Lopez shook his head, and shut his eyes tightly.

"Please, son . . ."

Father Lopez covered his face with his hands and breathed slowly. "I am so ashamed. Don't ask me to tell you with a woman in the room."

Rider threw up his hands. "Y'all gonna make me start smoking again. I'll tell you what the hell happened." He raked his fingers through his hair, hawked and spit in the wastebasket. "Blood fucks with my sinuses," he muttered, dismissing the group's glare. "She went down on *hombre* and took out his femoral artery at the moment of truth. Lopez and Jose were locked in on the master, not Damali."

Rider nodded in Jose's direction, causing everyone to look toward Jose. "Shabazz was right, shoulda pulled the man out. No human male can go the distance of a full vamp seduction. Get Jose unlocked before he has a fucking heart attack."

The group quickly moved toward the young guardian. Jose's head hung down, one hand on his forehead. His forearm braced him on the table, his fist clenched, and the muscle in his jaw working. His T-shirt stuck to his back.

"*Shit,*" he said in a voice so deep and so unnatural for Jose that for a moment no one moved. His fist pounded on the table, his breathing escalated, his eyes rolled beneath his lids. When he moaned low in his throat, Marlene grabbed him by the shoulders and hauled off and slapped him. Jose just gave her a lazy, satisfied laugh.

Shabazz stepped forward and dashed the remaining holy water in Jose's face, but Jose still didn't come around. "He's blitzed on Neteru. Pull him out, Mar, before Damali takes his jugular!"

Father Lopez stood, weaving. "I took the first bite and oh, God, it felt so good," he whispered. "Pull us both out of this bond—now—before she takes the jugular."

Total pandemonium erupted as the team broke into two squads, each slapping, dousing, working on the two connected men. Marlene was in Jose's face, recanting the connection, trying to bring him up out of the trance, while the other seer, Father Patrick, worked on his young cleric, anxiety rising by the minute when the fallen wouldn't respond.

"We have to shoot them before Damali turns them," Shabazz said, unholstering his weapon and pointing the barrel of the gun at Jose's temple. Jose immediately lifted his head and looked at Shabazz.

"Are you insane, man?" Rider yelled, slamming into Shabazz, throwing his aim off.

But as soon as Shabazz had pointed the gun at Jose, the trance had been broken. Jose sat there looking dazed. Imam Asula nodded, whipped out his machete, and pressed it to Father Lopez's throat. Father Lopez immediately snapped out of it as well.

"What the fuck?" Rider said angrily.

Shabazz holstered Sleeping Beauty. "A master is most vulnerable when he's asleep, when he hasn't fed, or when he's gettin' busy, but will always pull up when there's an eminent threat." He stroked his gun, and nodded in Asula's direction. "So me and brotherman provided an eminent threat."

Marlene sat down slowly at the table and let her head drop into her hands. "I know you two gentlemen have just been through something outrageous, and I'm sorry you had to go there," she said, speaking to Jose and Lopez. "But can you tell us *anything* about where they are?"

Father Lopez nodded. "They're at the mansion in Beverly Hills."

Jose nodded weakly. "Nuit's old joint," he said slowly.

"Carlos is *seriously* pissed off, and something is trailing enough sulfur there for Rider to track it. There's weird noises, barking, that Mike can track. I don't know what it was but if I caught the scent again, I'd know it." He looked away, his face suddenly stained with embarrassment. "And I can track Damali now, easy." He rubbed his nose with the back of his hand, and shuddered one last time.

"Jesus." Marlene stood and paced away from the table. "Okay, okay, we have to mount up. Maybe there's a chance."

"You're right, baby," Shabazz said quietly, going to her, "we have to mount up a posse, but not to save her. We're gonna have to find them and smoke 'em both."

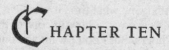

CHAPTER TEN

"WHAT'S THE matter, baby?" Damali murmured, stroking Carlos's chest.

Suddenly he lifted his head from her throat, and braced himself on his arms, listening, eyes scanning the room, every sense keened: After what seemed like an eternity, he kissed the bridge of her nose, then moved down her torso and planted a gentle kiss on her bare belly. "Two lower-level male vamps just tried a lock with me," he said, then rolled off of her and stood.

Instantly, he was dressed. "I'ma take a walk. You stay here," he said, firmly. "The two vamps have a bunch of human helpers with them. It might get ugly, and I haven't fed."

"I don't want to stay in here by myself," she said, studying him hard.

"You hungry?" he asked, glancing at her sideways.

She nodded.

"Get dressed, then. Tonight is as good a night as any for me to teach you how to hunt."

She hesitated, but found herself fully dressed before she could even look down. "You said they had human helpers . . ."

"Yeah," he replied. He hesitated. "If you're carrying precious cargo, you need to eat right, and learn how to do it without turning one of them."

She touched her belly with shaky fingers. He didn't respond. They both knew what time it was.

"I need to also show you how to control the dogs, if I'm away for a few hours. But I don't want you out too often. I'll bring the feeds to the lair for you. I'll take care of you, baby. Don't worry."

Damali stood there wondering. *What had she done?*

She could feel herself vacillating between wanting to follow him outside to do the unthinkable, and wanting to run shrieking into the night.

"I don't want to feed like that . . . Not until I know for sure—"

"Know what? If you've fully turned?" He stared at her hard.

His statement slapped her in the face. She took a deep breath.

"Baby, think about it," she said calmly. "I can't be carrying, if I'm turned."

He rubbed his jaw with his palm.

"And if I am already turned . . . wouldn't we have bigger problems than some low-level vamps sniffing around? Wouldn't you have to worry about the Vampire Council coming after you for turning their vessel?"

"True dat," he said, thoughtfully. "But, baby, you've definitely ripened." All of a sudden his head tilted and his nostrils flared.

"Will you forget about them, Carlos! They can't get in here. I've got other concerns right now. Look, my name would have burned into their books if I'd turned, you'd thought it yourself." She stared at him. Something wasn't right. Her turning and the Vampire Council's response should have been Carlos's top priority, but it wasn't. He was hiding something from her; she could feel it. What could be more important than the dark side losing its vessel?

She studied him hard and kept pushing him for answers.

"If I've completely turned, all Hell would literally be breaking loose right now, and it's not. So, I'm not fully turned."

"Damned sure felt like it," he said and his voice sent a sensual shiver through her.

No, she was not going there with him again. They needed to talk. "This might have been a false ripening."

He shook his head, his gaze penetrating her. "No, baby, that I'm *very* clear about."

Her hand nervously rested on her abdomen. "If I'd conceived tonight, then wouldn't that register somewhere, too? Wouldn't the presence of a potential daywalker conception show up in the registers of Hell?"

Carlos crossed his arms over his chest. "After what I laid down tonight, you are pregnant as a jaybird, D. It might not have registered, yet, but I'm sure. Till I know otherwise, I'm treating you like you're carrying mine."

She opened her mouth and closed it again. She could not believe the macho bullshit coming out of this man's mouth. Half of her wanted to laugh, it was so ludicrous, the other half of her wanted to punch him. She shook her head, but held her peace. Neither option at the moment would have been wise.

"Do me a favor," she said, exasperated. "Do the lower-level vamps—I'll even help you—but the humans, let them go. If you feed on them in my presence I'll—"

"What, D? Never speak to me again? Please," he said, gathering transport clouds about them. "Don't piss me off, woman. I'm not in the mood!"

"What?" She began to circle him, temporarily halting their transport. One hand went to her hip, while the other pointed at him. "Let's get one thing straight, Carlos. Pregnant or not, turned or not, you'd better cut the alpha male crap—now. I am *not* the one!"

"I hope Jose and Lopez are right," Rider said, checking the magazine in his gun. "Up till now, we've been real lucky—no cops, no public incidents, and now we're talking about running a Hum-V and two Jeeps through a gated community, taking out the south wall with a light shell and C4, and basically setting off what could be misconstrued as a terrorist action upon a private mansion. Anybody feeling me?"

No one in the platoon of warriors answered Rider, except Marlene.

"Blow the wall, Mike. I'm goin' in, with or without y'all, to get my baby girl."

There was nothing to say to this crazy man as she walked the perimeter of the mansion's upper balcony with him. The Hell-hounds were baying in the distance and she rubbed her arms to stave off the creeps.

Out of nowhere, six lower-level male vampires appeared on the balcony. Damali braced herself for battle, but was shocked when Carlos walked over to one of them and hugged him.

"Talk to me," Carlos said.

"They got your cop," a tall, light-skinned vampire said. "You told us to watch your back, keep an eye out in the territory for anything shaky—and we did. Man, we heard the abduction, your marked man's energy dipped and his mind was screaming, and got to his house as fast as we could. It was definitely master energy lingering. Only thing left was his crucifix on the garage floor."

"Damn!" Carlos shouted. His gaze swept the bulked vamps.

Damali eyed the transaction. She was sure that she recognized the lead vamp from the drag race that had gone down at Carlos's old club. He was empire building, had made lieutenants. Fear collided with fury within her. This was not the man she thought she knew. She understood that he had territory to control, but somehow she could also feel that it was expanding. She and Carlos definitely needed to talk.

"We're picking up two lower levels with a human team coming toward your lair. Them, we can handle."

Carlos shook his head. "Me and my lady haven't fed yet. Leave them to us. We got this. See if you can find a tracer on which way they took the cop."

Panic coursed through Damali. She looked at Carlos's expression and noted how glassy his eyes looked. The man was obviously high, blitzed on Neteru. He wasn't making logical decisions. She already knew which cop they were probably talking about. He'd turned Berkfield, an innocent, into a vamp helper? When?

The leader of the small group nodded as Carlos flashed molten images of continents in the air with a wave of his hand. "Check the atmosphere. Dust from their lairs would have left a scent marker, Yonnie. I'll school you as we go along." With two snaps, the hounds were at Carlos's side, swooping in to land with a snarling thud. "They ate a coupla sniffers." He stroked one of the beast's head. "Bath Sheba, baby, tell Daddy where your dinner came from."

Again, red flaming continents appeared in the air. Damali watched in total awe as the extent of Carlos's powers, and the new hierarchy surrounding him, was revealed. The dogs sniffed the air, and bleated out agitated barks as their brutish snouts neared the apparition of Australia.

"Want us to take a team there?" the junior vamp asked.

Carlos shook his head. "Reinforce my territory borders here, in South America, and in the Caribbean. If some bullshit came across the water from the Aussie's camp, I will address it myself."

The small squad of vampires all nodded, and then vanished. Oddly, they hadn't reacted to any Neteru scent. Confusion throttled her. Carlos walked in an agitated circle. Damali just stared at him as his hounds also disappeared. Although they hadn't spoken upon it, the issue was burned into their awareness; finding the biblical key was paramount.

Suddenly an explosion rocked the house, and in two seconds Carlos was pure motion. He bound over the edge of the balcony, hovering in the air for a few seconds, before he transformed into a huge, black bat. She stared. Her man had turned into something with large leather wings and moved at a blurring speed, then had vanished. Something rational told her not to just try to leap behind him. The sixty-foot drop, alone, would kill her . . . maybe; or at the very least would shatter her legs. She had to take the long route—through the house, down the stairs, and out into the garden, running behind what she could no longer see.

"We're in!" Big Mike said.

"Yeah, and just gave the whole neighborhood and Rivera a heads-up that we are," Rider said.

Big Mike glanced over his shoulder. "Look alive, people. There's something growling, and it ain't vamp."

All eleven vampire hunters fanned out and formed a circle.

"It's animal," Shabazz said. "Could be were-demon, but its definitely canine." He glanced up into the trees, his gaze taking in the canopy of foliage. "And it's on the move."

J.L. nodded. "Multiples. I feel it."

"Noses, y'all got a read?" Shabazz asked.

Rider sniffed and said, "Sulfur. Definitely demon, real strong. But that ain't were-demon. Whatever it is, I've never picked it up before."

"Definitely," Jose said, double-checking his crossbow.

"All right," Shabazz said. "Let's move on the house easy. Everybody watch your back."

An overhead branch snapped and suddenly a large black blur dove at the teams, but landed and materialized several feet away. A six-foot wingspan pulled in sharply to a hulking, muscular body, and the creature crouched and waited, then began barking wildly as its eyes blazed gold. Frozen, the teams trained weapons on the snarling beast, as another one stalked out of the underbrush, its head lowered, leathery ears and wings back, slashing its razor tail wildly and brandishing dripping fangs.

"Everybody hold the line," Marlene said. "They haven't attacked."

"No, they haven't," Carlos said, coming out of the darkness, walking between the dogs. With a nod of his head, the animals backed up toward him, growling and snarling, but sat. "They already know you're off-limits. But provoke me tonight, and that can change."

"We just want Damali," Marlene said across the expanse between them.

Carlos studied his nails. "Then that presents a dilemma because so do I."

"For Christ's sake, you can't have her, Rivera!" Father Patrick yelled.

Immediately the dogs began barking, moving forward in a threatening stance. Everyone aimed at the creatures, but no one risked firing during the standoff.

"Watch your language, Father Pat," Carlos said coolly, tsking his tongue and making the dogs heel. He then motioned with his chin toward the distance. "Big Mike. Sirens, right?"

Mike grumbled and nodded.

"You gentlemen are going to have to learn to be more subtle when you want to call a meeting." Carlos smirked. "And your timing sucks."

Carlos sealed the south wall, and the sirens stopped. All he needed now were the cops. There'd be no way to restrain the dogs if a SWAT team, full of foreign scents, crossed over the property perimeter. Disorienting the authorities was more efficient.

"Where's Damali?" Marlene asked. "That's all we came for, that's all we're leaving with."

"She took the long way," Carlos said, sighing. "Stubborn as usual." He could hear her footfalls in the grass, and the dogs turned, making little whimpering noises of submission. "But she's staying here—her choice, not mine." He eyed them with a warning. "And I *will* back up her choice."

"We'll see," Shabazz said, his weapon still aimed and cocked. "Gotta hear it from her own mouth."

"The last place she's staying is with you, motherfucker," Jose said.

"Here's my problem with that," Carlos said evenly. "She called me when you people botched the purge job. I frankly don't see what the fucking hype is all about, or what's left to talk about, man. She made her choice." He began walking in

Damali's direction, issuing a silent command for the dogs to stay. "And you've got some nerve bringing two real low-level vamps with you to track me while I'm with her. Total disrespect, 'Bazz, man . . . very uncool," he added, dismissing Jose's comment. "I thought we were beyond that."

Confusion wafted through the teams as Carlos's form disappeared.

"What's he talking about, Shabazz?" Big Mike muttered. "Two vamps with us?"

Imam Asula gripped his machete tighter. "This is a ruse to distract us from our mission to recover the huntress. Stand firm. Ignore his demonic trickery."

"Oh, so now I'm a liar," Carlos said loudly, coming back toward them with Damali in tow. "First of all, look for yourself. She's fine," he said, removing his arm from around her waist. "Second of all, how you gonna roll up on my lair with some eighth- or ninth-generation wanna-be vamps?" He shook his head and gazed at Jose and Father Lopez.

Damali remained very still. Whether what he said was true or not, she knew that Carlos was showing much restraint on her behalf, and the only reason that he hadn't wiped her team out was because he'd been temporarily sated, or perhaps because they were under his protective seal. At the moment, she wasn't sure. All she had to do was think back on the Nuit incident . . . if the team had tried a rescue two hours ago . . . She couldn't even allow her mind to complete the thought.

But just the brief flicker of the dead master's name in her thoughts made Carlos bristle. "Don't go there," he warned her. "Yeah, I'm being cool, so you can settle this family bullshit once and for all. But don't push me." He eyed her and then returned his attention to the posse in front of them.

"Brothers," Carlos said, his voice filled with disgust, "one hit of this would knock your head back and make your tired asses grow fangs. Do not *ever* try to mind lock with me when I'm with her!"

Members of the group moved back from Lopez and Jose. Their motions were steady, controlled. Uncertainty was trapped in their glances. Damali's hand rested on Carlos' forearm.

"Don't fuck with them because you're in a shitty mood, Carlos. They're still family, and they only came—"

He whirled on Damali and opened his arms, leaning down at her, as his voice got louder. "Why is it that I can never tell you anything? Huh? Why is that?"

"Because your ass is high," she shouted, pulling away from him. "I told you, watch your tone with me!"

He walked away from her and stood by his dogs, thoroughly outraged. "These brothers got a lock because we share the same freakin' DNA—by blood relatives, waaay back." He pointed at Lopez, and shook his head. "Your great-great-grandma got nicked in the old country, *Padre,* sorry to be the one to tell you . . . but back then in the villages," he said, glowering at Father Patrick, "they used *natural* methods to try to reverse a turn before the bitten died. She finally did die human, true, but the baby didn't— so there's a tracer."

"That is bullshit!" Shabazz said. "Don't let him get in your head, people." Shabazz looked around at the members of the group. "Don't let him divide and conquer us. That's how he got Damali!"

"You need to relax, *hombre,*" Carlos said as he walked with his hands behind his back, satisfied by Jose's stricken expression. "D and I hooked up the old-fashioned way—no fraud necessary." He glanced at her, but couldn't read her expression. That concerned him. He tried to wipe the Neteru haze from his mind.

"All right," Carlos went on. "Then how did the Covenant find me in the desert?"

"Lopez was our tracker," Father Patrick said cautiously, glancing at his brother cleric.

"Right," Carlos spat. "My point exactly." He shook his head, so disgusted he was about to explode. He wiped his nose with the back of his hand. The night was calling him, Neteru was thick in it, and until her family showed up, Damali had been beyond comprehension in his arms . . . and the only reason he wasn't dropping a body was for this crazy woman! If that would get her back inside, being cool, chilled-out, and sexy mellow, then fine. So be it. But these bastards were burning up time.

He took a deep breath, and spoke to them like they were children. "If a master is at critical blood levels and is about to be extinguished, everything in his line aligned to him will scramble," Carlos said, beyond impatient with their stupidity. "Everything is designed for the preservation of the line—so when I was dying in Lopez's region, he could track and find me faster than anyone. But that's the *only* reason dude should have done a lock." He glared at the young man. "Fucked you up, too, didn't it, *Padre?* Just like that first night in the safe house. But I owe you for finding me." Carlos chuckled, thinking of what an eighth-generation must have gone through with a master lock. "And, damn, Jose, man . . . you're from 'round the way. You know better than to roll up on a man like that. That was a punk-ass move, if ever I saw one. She's mine. Get over it."

Jose's bristle made Carlos walk forward and the dogs growl. "I *know* you are not standing outside my lair trying to fucking challenge me for her? Are you that crazy?"

"Carlos," Damali said quietly, then raised her voice to also address the warrior teams. "Let's keep to the point. It's not even like that between me and Jose. What is wrong with you?"

She was too through, and Carlos seemed like he was too high to be totally rational. Anything could go down, but it was good that he kept talking, working it out in his head. Maybe the air would help dissipate the scent—that was the hope. She wanted to bring them both back to center, not have something crazy happen. But the sure thing was that if she said she was leaving now, in this state, he'd hurt somebody.

"All right," she told the group. "Let's assume that this generational vamp thing is true for a minute."

"Thank you," Carlos muttered. "Finally, progress."

She took her time to speak, monitoring the horror in Jose and Father Lopez's expressions. "Then, if this is true, Lopez was born with vamp trace elements but like Jose made the choice to be a Guardian. Their spirits are good, Carlos—nobody can be held responsible for what happened in the past before they were even born. And yeah, it might have made them more susceptible to certain leanings. Like I understand why Jose couldn't immediately shake Dee Dee's hold. But in the final analysis, baby, they made the right choice, to be who they are."

"See, Damali, there you go again, always twisting my words." He pointed at her, but he was looking at her teams as he spoke. "You see this? This is female logic, the most treacherous shit in the universe!"

"But she's right," Father Patrick said, his gaze galvanizing the teams. "Whatever Lopez or Jose's distant pasts, they made a choice. And, as you know, we had you marked for Guardian status. The reason *we* found Lopez so fast, as well as you—is because we, too, have a homing instinct to find our own when felled." His thick white brows knitted with suppressed anger. "And tonight we've come to reclaim at least *one* of our own!"

"Word," Shabazz said. "So save all the rhetoric, Rivera. We takin' baby girl outta here, and I don't care how Jose or Lopez got made as long as—"

"This is not open for negotiation," Carlos said evenly. He looked at Damali. "She's already made her choice."

"You tricked her," Jose said, pointing toward Carlos. "She would have never chosen—"

"Put your hand down," Carlos said between his teeth, "before I rip it off!"

"Carlos, stop!" Damali yelled, her hands going to his now massive biceps. "You hurt my people, and I'll tell you what my choice will be."

She looked at Carlos hard, and he shrugged away from her, but backed off.

"Fine," he muttered. "So long as you're clear about your choice."

"She's in no position to make a decision like that," Marlene said. "She's under the influence, and her system is in flux! You've polluted her, just like her bites have somehow given you a way to cross our thresholds like a male Neteru! What she gave you was good, what you gave her without her rational awareness or full understanding was—"

"No," Carlos shouted back. "What *you* people did was flat-line my baby—and she made the choice to survive!" He took two steps toward Marlene, the dogs growling at his heels, but Marlene never backed away. "You're her moms, so I'ma be respectful . . . but when your daughter came to me, she was code blue." He slapped the center of his chest. "She sucked in the first breath of returned life from my lungs, not yours, sis. I started her heart, made her blood flow, and vowed to never let you all put your hands on her again." He shook his head. "No, Mar. Girlfriend is making wise choices—she's in her full and right mind. I gave her something good—a second shot at the game—but you tried to kill her."

The night was so still, so quiet, that one could almost hear electricity crackle within it. Slowly, cautiously, Damali moved beside Carlos, and he pulled her to him hard, still glaring at Marlene.

"Baby," she said gently, her gaze going between the two drawn combat lines. Marlene's eyes looked so hurt and had such fury in them, she almost didn't know where to begin. Carlos's tight grip didn't help, because she knew he'd be beyond reason if she challenged the union in front of the teams. *This was the rock and the hard place.*

"Remember in the lair in Rio," Damali said as calmly as she could.

"Yeah," Carlos muttered. "Shoulda stayed in fucking Rio."

"When we sat on the beach and synchronized our breathing, our minds, and finally our hearts," she said tenderly, brushing a stray bit of hair behind his ear, watching him normalize.

"Yeah," he said, his tone low, private, his gaze now focused solely on her.

"And you know how much I don't want anybody in this to get hurt. Be gentle with Marlene, especially . . . and my brothers."

"All right," he said slowly. "I know. How could I forget? I felt it when your soul entered my empty space and started my heart, when my pulse fused with yours and lingered, baby." He lowered his forehead to hers and shut his eyes, completely relaxed and no longer at battle bulk. "You gave me your heartbeat."

"Damali," Marlene said firmly, not moving, as the team around her remained stone-still.

Carlos lifted his head and looked at Marlene. "Let it go, Mar. Can't you see where she wants to be?"

"Both of you, listen to me," Marlene said, her glances shared with Father Patrick. "You all did a ritual more dangerous than the bite. That's partly why her immune system is off . . . why she's literally turning and turning back, ripening, then going barren, and conversely, you're flashing male Neteru, then master, or some crazy combination that allows you to walk where you're not supposed to—just like it's making her do what she'd never dream of . . . your senses are off, Carlos, just like hers are. The mild scent she normally trails is probably enough to—"

"Knock his head back," Rider said, blowing out a long whistle. "His nose ain't no better than mine."

Carlos snarled. "Me and you, any day, motherfucker—but right now, I'm trying to hear some science—so shut up!"

He stepped back from Damali and moved toward Marlene. But his gesture wasn't threatening, just that of a man unnerved and seeking answers. He looked at Father Patrick.

"Carlos, give Marlene the Isis and send Damali home," Father Patrick said, quietly. "No more bites until we can figure this out." He looked at Marlene. "We thought the multiple bites challenged history—but I *know* this has never happened, much less ever been repaired."

"Her system probably could have handled the bites by itself," Big Mike said on a sigh. "It was the one-two punch, the combo. Shoulda known there was more to it than just that."

Big Mike and Shabazz lowered their weapons, as did the rest of the team.

"Now this is a true turn of events, if ever I saw one." Rider said, lowering his weapon arm, too. "What, we've gotta purge the Light out of this bastard to get him out of her system? Somebody on this team shoot me."

Carlos and Damali exchanged a nervous glance. Something in the team's disposition had clearly changed, just like it had within theirs.

"You had no heartbeat before, right?" Marlene said firmly. "She entered your dark space where your soul was supposed to reside, and took all of that darkness out into hers with it—along with a lot of the powers." Marlene's voice escalated in a slow rise as she spoke. "And her light warmed you from the inside out. I bet you've had a human pulse ever since." Marlene waited for Carlos to slowly nod. "And when you restarted her heart—what did you do?" She pressed on, not waiting for his answer. "You probably hoped her back to life, gave her your breath, and everything you had in you—on a prayer."

His dogs backed away from him, snarling and snapping. Carlos backed away from Marlene to stand beside Damali, his glances at her unsure. If it ever got out that he'd prayed over this woman . . . and did a soul transfer . . .

"I could stay half-vamp and have the blood hunger, the lust and still not be dead, or suddenly go into a ripening and start a vamp civil war? I thought I had seven years?" Damali was breathing hard. "I *have* to stay human with the missing—"

Father Patrick held up his hand at the same time Carlos did, stopping Damali's words.

"Not out here in the open," Carlos warned. Both Marlene and Father Patrick nodded in agreement.

All the issues hit her at once. "Marlene, what if I don't cast an image on stage, or, wake up one day to go out to run an errand, and sun bake!"

"That's what I'm saying, Mar," Carlos said pulling Damali near him. "This shit's gotta be clear cut. She can't be going back and forth, not knowing. My damned nerves can't take it, either. If she shows up in the registers again as a full turn—all Hell will literally break loose. And if she has a false ripening . . . no, that can't happen. There are four other masters topside, with full regions in Europe, Asia—what-the-fuckeva, and my territory is bled out from the last wars—and all I've got backing me up to protect her is two Hell-dogs and a team of new, remade seconds. That ain't worth shit against four masters and their armies. Plus, this other issue, which we need to speak on under closed circumstances, is going to require *both* of us to be on top of our game."

He walked away from her, and raked his hair hard. "I mean, for real . . . I can't be going down to council chambers like that, either—or have my nose, or any other sense off. What if my transport stalls in an emergency situation? Or if I go into a battle and have my power outright fail—not be able to drop fang because I have some punk-ass Guardian shit in my system. Aw, hell no . . ."

When Damali touched his arm, he shrugged away from her touch.

"Where I have to roll, that's beyond dangerous—and with the kinda forces that eventually could go after her," he said, motioning to Damali, "girlfriend has to be on her toes at all times. Can't have a fluctuating daylight problem. She has to know for sure."

"Now you see our point," Marlene said, drawing out each word. "But before, we old folks couldn't tell you—"

"Mar," Carlos shouted, pointing at her as his nerves snapped. "I've still got a lotta vamp in me, sis. Don't say it, because all I know is—I *knew* what my bite would do to her, based on what you all told me . . . which was supposed to be nothing!" He glanced at Damali, ignoring her hurt expression. It was the truth. "And based on *trust,* pure trust alone, I let her do something to me that fucked us both up! So don't stand on my property telling me shit, Marlene, but I'm sorry!"

"This is crazy, Marlene," Shabazz said. "I never thought I'd want a vampire to get back his full faculties, but this is—"

"Fix it!" Carlos yelled. "Marlene Stone, you taught her how to do this, now teach her the reverse for the cure!"

"You two are inextricably linked, at the moment. Probably always have been, which is the other part of our problem, but I'll deal with that later." Marlene wiped her face and sighed long and hard.

"Aw'ight," Carlos said after a while, his cool façade totally gone. "So though the exchange had the desired effect, it helped her, right? She's alive. I just need you to break down what else all this means. How bad is it really?"

"Correct, it helped her live," Marlene replied, her gaze narrowing. "But it's bad. Real bad. The purge almost killed her because you are in her system at the heart chakra level— that's why she flat-lined, brother. If she goes into a vampire episode, even though she probably never died as required for that to happen, we can't bring her out of it. The vampire state will have to pass on its own and we'll never know the duration of it."

"Why not? If she hasn't died, there are slow healing methods—"

"No, Carlos. Not an option. When we purge, we're killing, extinguishing the vampire in her and the virus is in her heart. So she'll flat-line, not because we're amateurs! So don't *you* ever go there again. Got it?"

Fired up, Marlene paused, and when Carlos didn't challenge her, but instead looked off toward the line of trees, she continued. "It means that no matter what you see manifest, it's temporary, most likely. It means that if she bears fangs and blows your mind, brother, she's no fully turned female master. Unless you happen to accidentally kill her one night while y'all are playing too rough! And it means that if you happen to get a whiff of my daughter ready to conceive, it's placebo, and you'd better keep your hands off her and bring her home! She has work to do!"

Marlene walked in a hot circle, her face flushed from fury. She whirled on Damali. "The things I taught you were never supposed to be used under these circumstances. Are you crazy? The vampires have the bite, but we trained seers have something, too, sister-girl, and our Ju Ju is just as deadly, is supposed to be used under very controlled circumstances. Not played with in some house on the beach. I taught you better than that!"

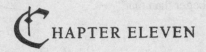

CHAPTER ELEVEN

DAMALI AND her team stood there watching Carlos's back as he turned from them, waved his dogs off, and simply folded away into nothingness. It was the way he did it with none of his usual decisive flair that concerned her. But there were many things competing for her attention at the moment; most immediate was her family, most important was the missing biblical key.

Gradually, her Madame Isis sword materialized at her side. Again, it was in the way it had been returned with such resignation that, for a moment, she and her team only stared at it.

"We never leave our own," she said, holding her head up high, and pulling the Isis from the earth. Damali tossed the blade and it landed point down in the grass at Marlene's feet. "You keep this until you think I'm worthy to have it. But my mission hasn't changed. I'm going to clean out some nests, as planned, and bring back the thing we need."

Full authority was in her tone. It was a command, not a request, as she pushed her shoulders back and stood firm. "Just understand that I never left you all, and I never left him—herein lies my dilemma. *In my soul* I know that he is just as much a part of my mission as being with you is."

Marlene studied the blade and went to it, extracting it

from the ground with a sharp tug. Her eyes met Damali's and a quiet understanding passed between them. She ignored the nervous bristle of the other Guardians as she stepped in close to Damali, turned the blade handle out and offered it back to her, waiting patiently until Damali accepted the ornate handle.

"You did teach me better, Marlene," Damali said, no anger or apology in her voice. "That's why I did what I did—*I wasn't playing*. I wanted him on our side . . . still do, always have, and I wasn't afraid to go where I had to go to reach him." She gave Marlene a slight smile.

Marlene smiled, her finger moving a stray lock off Damali's shoulder. "You scared us half to death."

"Scared myself . . . still do sometimes."

Both women's eyes held a level of amusement that only the night could witness. They both turned back toward the team, feeling the group behind them growing restless.

"You coming with us, or what?" Rider shouted, his frustration rippling through the night. "Tell me after this you *are* leaving *hombre*—'cause, girlfriend, you are *way* off mission, right about through here."

"She can no more leave him now than I could leave Shabazz," Marlene said firmly, dismissing Rider's question with a wave of her hand.

"It's time you guys clue me in to what else might be affecting my flux," Damali said, her gaze holding the group. "There's some serious yang going down in Australia. I was standing by Carlos when his squad showed up, and apparently another master breached his borders."

Marlene touched her face as she walked forward. "The sixth biblical seal is in jeopardy, baby," she said in a quiet tone. "We need our Neteru."

As clear as day, Damali heard Marlene's mental instruction: *Go find the missing key—by any means necessary.*

Damali touched Marlene's cheek. "Trust me, Marlene. Let me see."

Marlene's gaze opened to Damali, and images rushed into Damali's awareness. But with that information also

came a sad understanding; if the seal that matched the stolen
key was discovered, Carlos would trade it for her life.

Now his agitation and stress made all the sense in the
world to her. She understood where all the posturing and
hollering was coming from—brother was caught between a
rock and a hard place and wasn't coping well at all. He knew
that she'd give her life for humanity. The fact that he'd hunt
down the key just to spare her, bartering it away for one human life, that in and of itself was enough to make her never
want to speak to him again. Yet, she also couldn't ignore the
fact that he'd done that simply because he couldn't bear the
concept of her death under any circumstances. It was too
complicated. Damali closed her eyes and let out a long,
weary sigh.

"You know that's why I have to go with him," Damali
said, her voice just above a whisper. "He's scared, Mar. I've
seen him go through a lot of mess, but all the bravado is
about fear."

Marlene nodded. "Definitely a male reaction, human or
vamp, it's the same."

Both women shared a tender smile.

"Maybe that's why you had to intimately learn about his
world," Marlene said after a moment, and then glanced at
Father Patrick. "She has to go in under their radar as one of
them. We'll back her up from the outside."

"This is what I was meant to do as the millennium
Neteru," Damali said firmly. "The timing of my birth . . .
hey, we all know we're in the end of days, so, this is it, people. Win or die trying."

Father Patrick tossed Damali the small dagger that
matched her Isis, and she caught it fast. "In Australia, follow
the song lines of the Aborigines . . . tell him that will lead
you both to a safe house."

Monk Lin nodded and glanced at his clerical team. "In
case *you* need to know so they don't burn *you,* they appear
like infrared, but blue-white lines, and stretch across the protected sites like an alarm grid might . . . hopefully, you'll
never be able to see them like he can." The monk sighed.

"Make sure you get a map of all the sites with hallowed ground between wherever you're going, and there."

"What!" Shabazz shouted, whirling around on the priests, his line of vision tearing between Father Patrick, Monk Lin, and Marlene. "She can't stay with him—one, and two—she cannot go over there and do a concert as a cover for an international vampire hit, dragging a master vampire with her! I don't care what she's searching for!" He looked at his team for support, and the other men stepped in closer toward him. "She's not stable, one more nick could turn her, and she'll be on their side and doesn't need the Isis in her possession!"

"Set up a concert over there, Dan," Marlene said flatly, ignoring Shabazz.

"Marlene, face it, the girl might not even be able to cast an image. The whole plan to go country-to-country dusting topside master vampires to weaken their empire and bring back our stolen property is an abort until she stabilizes," Rider said in a defeated rush, gaining a nod from Big Mike. "Accidental stroke of luck on their side, notwithstanding— they won. They took out our power center—Damali."

"No, D is still the Neteru," Jose said, his voice fervent, just like his eyes. "Come with us, baby. *Please* don't stay with him." His voice hitched and he opened his arms. "We'll make it all right . . . I'm begging you, D. We'll keep the plan, as it always was, all of us. Just come home."

"Even if she stayed with us and we flew out at night," Big Mike said, lowering his weapon as his shoulders slumped, "we'd be flying from night into day because of the layovers and time-zone changes . . . she's unstable, could torch on impact right in her seat on the plane."

"I'm aware of that risk, so I'm traveling a nontraditional route, if I can get a ride." Damali let her breath out hard, sharing a supportive glance with Marlene. "Which is why I'm going inside to do some damage repair on one critical member of our team. And that's also why you all are going to have to have more faith than you've ever had before." But it broke her heart to watch Jose slowly lower his arms and look away from her.

"See you in Sydney, kiddo," Marlene said calmly. "Travel safe. If we don't see you in a couple of nights . . ."

"We'll send a rescue and recovery party," Imam Asula said, glancing at the other members of the Covenant. "If you're beyond repair, we will bury you on hallowed ground . . . or scatter your ashes there—either way."

Rider hawked and spit, and even the clerics' expressions held unconcealed worry.

"Gentlemen, Mar," Damali said, looking at the doubts held in every pair of eyes, "maybe what I did was instinct, who knows? That's what's driving me now. A gut hunch."

"You don't even know if Carlos will go or still guide you to the lairs so you can pick them off one by one to eliminate the threat," Dan said, his gaze fervent. He glanced at the others; J.L. nodded and Jose let out a long, disgusted sigh.

"Oh, he'll take her to a lair, all right. But not to clean one out." Rider sputtered in fury, walking back and forth. "In this condition, he'll be setting up vampire housekeeping!"

"We're supposed to protect the Neteru, but also assist her destiny," Father Patrick said, his slight smile knowing, evolving on his face in slow increments. "If Heaven is willing to gamble, who are we to throw in our hand?"

Marlene kissed Damali's cheek and walked away from her. "Let's go, gentlemen. I think our girl just created something even Hell can't deal with."

The long walk back to the mansion gave her plenty of time to think. What could she tell Carlos that made any kind of sense? He had trusted her completely, and there were so many times she'd mistrusted him. He'd been up-front and had told her about what he could do to her, but she'd never explained all of that to him in equal measure. Truth was, even she didn't know at the time. She was making it up as she'd gone along.

Yet, what she was sure of now, just as sure as she'd always been, was that there was pure intent behind the soul-sharing exchange. There was no fraud in it, no trickery or guile. She had gone into his depths to restart his heart, to dredge up every abandoned hope and dream inside him that he'd ever had, and had coated it with every ounce of love she could siphon from herself. That was real, and it wasn't a game.

As she entered the mansion, Carlos was pacing in the foyer.

"What are you doing here?" he muttered.

"I never run."

"Yeah, I forgot." His back was to her and his tone was angry and distant.

An eerie quiet filled the room, time standing still again in the balance between her response and his.

"Carlos, you do understand my concerns now, right?" She leaned on her Isis blade. "There is only one issue—the stolen key."

He looked at her hard.

"I had a need to know not just from them, but also from you," she snapped, her gaze roving over him so hotly that he turned around.

"Since you've been all inside my head, Damali, then I hope you can also feel the fatigue from my sitting up all day, worried fucking sick, praying, and beating my own ass about what I've allowed to happen to you."

She swallowed hard and looked down at her shoes.

"And you should have also picked up how your first awareness-panic while they were purging you cut my soul to the bone and emotionally bled me out till I had to come to you. Funny thing is, you're in my system as much as I'm in yours. Now, that's fucked up, when I'm the one supposed to be running shit. So my main concern then was, as it always has been, to make sure you survive. Fuck a key, if it means you'll die—or worse."

When she looked up at him, the tears that glistened in her eyes made him glance away.

"If we don't find and return the key, all of humanity will get turned—or kept for vamp food. I just don't want to live like that," she whispered.

"Neither do I, baby, but I don't know how to fix this. All I've ever known how to do is play the hand I'm dealt to buy time. Now even that's running out."

"I felt the hunger burn," she said, her voice so quiet that he had to strain to hear her. "I've never been so repulsed or terrified in my life."

"It's a bitch," he said plainly, walking to stand by a massive living-room window. "And the absence of daylight, the taste of real food, everything you've always taken for granted, ain't no joke. So now you know."

"If I stay with you as a female vamp, I'll never see my family again. But I want to be with you so bad, it hurts. But you also know I'll do whatever I have to do to get the key."

Carlos sighed. "If you stay in the dark life, you'll never see daylight, your family, your friends, a lot of shit that seems unimportant until it's gone." He turned and looked at her squarely. "Believe me, I miss my mom, and Grams . . . I miss my brother, and my boyz. And I wanted to protect them all, just like I wanted to protect you, missing you most of all. But, hey, that's my trip, my atonement for *all* the foul shit I've done." Unable to look at her any longer, he rubbed his hand across his jaw, remembering the last of her touch. "Let me do at least one thing right, and take you home. You stay there, let me do what I have to do, and it'll be cool. I'll find the key and will work a deal. I promise."

"No, it won't be cool. Guarding humanity is my job. This is not something you can cut a deal with. You clear?"

Even though her tone was firm, her eyes held such empathy that he couldn't remain focused on them. "Just promise me one thing," he finally said, as he began walking toward the door.

"Name it."

"Don't ever tell a master vampire something like that," he chuckled, his voice hollow from the soul ache. "Hear me out, then make wise choices, baby."

"Talk to me."

He closed his eyes. He wasn't sure if it was the familiar line, or the timbre of her voice yearning to hear some feasible solution, or the fact that she still cared enough to listen to him despite the circumstances, but the simple statement messed him up.

"If you die on your mission—and I have to say that because I know you're so stubborn there's no stopping you once you've made your mind up," he said slowly, measuring his voice to be sure it didn't falter, "and they make you a warrior angel . . . look in on my people for me, D. Make sure my moms knows I loved her and died trying—but just took a wrong turn at the Light."

He would not allow the fact that her fingers had gone to her lips to change his path. He was walking out that door, going to handle his business and settle this issue, alone, once and for all. As for his fate, the Devil may care, but he didn't. All she had to do was cross the threshold, and he'd transport her to the edge of the lights beyond the compound.

"You coming?" he said in a hardened tone without looking back at where she stood. "Since you're siding with the Guardians, we go out side by side. No 'in your arms' bullshit. I ain't got that much integrity, animal-predator that I am."

When she didn't move, he turned around and glared at her. "We've got a time issue, dig?"

He could feel her mind working, trying to absorb all his pain and make it right. "You can't fix this, no more than I can fix it. Let it drop. Sometimes you lose when you gamble. I've gotten used to it. You want the key for your reasons, I want the key for mine. You're ready to die for the cause; I'm not waiting around to watch that happen. Now let's go."

He waited while she walked toward him slowly, and then lifted her chin to stand by his side. Every instinct within him told him to never let her leave, but everything he'd ever known about her also told him that if he held her there, one night she'd grow to hate him just as much as he hated himself now.

"I had a hand in this thing, as much as you did," she murmured. "We're partners. We work this situation together. Me and you and my Guardian team."

He wasn't trying to hear it. Didn't need to think about anything that might make it harder to do what he had to do.

"I bit you, you turned, and you fluxed back. My bad."

"I let you, and wanted you to, and encouraged you to do me."

"Yeah, well, woulda, coulda, shoulda."

"Then I went deep into your head, when you told me not to. Opened Pandora's box."

"Told you curiosity killed the cat."

She smiled a slow, sad smile. "You did."

"You satisfied now?"

She shook her head. "I'm sorry."

"Me, too . . . more than you'll ever know."

He glanced at her, and then glanced up at the moon. "This is an old conversation, D. You know where it leads."

"I know. Then why aren't you doing your transport thing, if you're hell-bent on sending me away?"

For a moment he didn't answer her, but then the truth came out. "Because I really don't want to. You actually ready to die?" He let his breath out hard. "There's a good chance that four masters against me, even at my level, will win. One, or all four of those bastards, might be in possession of the key. Against you and your team, they'll get slaughtered. I don't want to think about what they'll do to you if you're captured. *That* I cannot live with."

"No, I don't want any of us to die. Without the key being returned to hallowed ground, is there such a thing as life on this planet? There's a certain way I want to live."

He nodded. He could respect that, always did. But it didn't change his position. "Why didn't you just listen to me when I told you not to take me there in Rio? Why'd you have to go that deep into my mind?"

She smiled sadly and looked out into the night. "We're way off the subject, but if you must know, I was jealous."

"What?"

"I wanted to be the only one you fantasized about. After some of the places you'd been . . ."

Carlos closed his eyes and shook his head. "Oh, shit, Damali. You didn't need to go there to be the one."

"I wanted to know what a double-plunge was, and to do that with you. I also wanted to experience going to the vanishing point with you, albeit you haven't taken me there yet. But now I have an idea." She sighed and looked down. "I didn't want some female vamp seducing you one night to try something that you couldn't get from me. I figured it was bound to happen sooner or later."

He looked at her, allowing his gaze to rake her, burning her into his memory for what might very well be the last time. "Go deep, right now, and get the question settled in your mind once and for all. Then, answer my question. Are you really ready to end our relationship like this? Because you know, if I find either the seal or the key, I'll turn it over to them to save your life, whether you want to be with me or not."

Her pull was so intense that she shuddered from the answer she siphoned from him. She took two steps toward him, but then stopped herself, although she never broke eye contact with him.

"That's what I thought," he murmured. "But in this condition, you can't have it both ways. If you haven't already totally crossed over by the end of the mission, I'll flat-line you to save you, and you want to live as a human."

"Yeah. I do. That's why I stopped walking."

His fangs dropped and were slow to recede. It took him a moment to answer her. "You sure you wanna leave and try to go after the key yourself?"

"What I want to do, and what I have to do, are two different things. Either we do this together, or I do it alone. But don't try to sweet-talk me into some bullshit compromise, Carlos. I'm not down for a vamp seduction."

He needed night air. Standing in the confines of the foyer with her was too much of a temptation to simply turn her all vamp and be done with the options. "Can't blame a man for trying," he said, smiling, but coming closer to her. "But what if it's too late? What if you really did die in my arms already?"

"What if I didn't?"

She looked away from him and out into the night, through the windows by the door.

He closed his eyes and walked away from her, his hand going to the nape of his neck as he tried to rub away the tension in it. "Going after them as a team is one helluva gamble, D."

"Wait for me," she murmured. "If you don't hear my call tomorrow night, then I'm history."

"What are you talking about—wait for you?" The insanity of her request made him pace from the door to the windows, and back to stand before her. "If you live through the first night in Australia without getting whacked, and *if* by some slim chance your system normalizes, I'm the *last* person in the world you want to come for you *ever* again." He stared at her hard. "If you're still human when this shit goes down, I'll definitely turn you to keep you strong and existing, enough of that death with honor bullshit!" She had to be crazy. If the sixth sea was opened, there was only one safe position: master vamp.

"I was talking about not giving up, not leaving the team, if—"

"Do you hear yourself?" He looked at her hard, forcing her gaze to stay within his. "If you make it, and you now have a *deep* personal understanding of what this thing is that I live with—I cannot *wait* around for you to die a normal, human death. Period."

"Why not? You are destined to do something greater than—"

"There's only one thing I can be to you—your lover. I may be your friend, your bodyguard, your whatever you want to call me, but the bottom line is, if I'm near you, you're my woman. It's not in my DNA, or in my heart, to watch my woman unnecessarily die. You've got the wrong *hombre*, if that's what you want."

She only stared at him as he stated the facts as plainly as he knew them.

"I'm not playing, Damali. And with your system all

jacked up, you're trailing the beginnings of the scent that fucks me around. Not to mention," he said, his voice escalating, "you bit me, dammit. You may have recovered from that, but I sure as hell haven't!"

The crystal pieces in the large foyer chandelier above him began to rattle. Damali looked up as the intensity built, sending a winding fissure across the ceiling, down the wall, opening a two-inch crack in the marble floor by her feet. She braced herself, waiting, not sure if he was going to rush her, or if the vibrating light fixture above them was gonna blow.

"You still don't get it, do you?" he asked, gesturing with his hands as pendulous crystal sections began to separate from the ornate chandelier, then jettison into the surrounding walls. His voice was low and even, and way too calm. "Maybe your master awareness hasn't kicked in yet, or maybe you haven't all the way turned, but let me make sure we are clear."

"All right," she said quietly, keeping her distance from him as more pieces of the chandelier separated, cracked, and whizzed past her to lodge in the door. "Talk to me."

"There are many types of bites we can deliver." Carlos paused, drew a deep breath, as though steadying himself.

She waited. Not even blinking.

"No self-respecting council-level master would *ever* allow some stray vamp tail to plunge his jugular! No one but you has been near my throat since I've turned."

Upon his statement, furious energy rippled up the winding staircase, popping out banister posts, exploding open the doors throughout the second floor.

"I don't care if it's a Roman orgy, and I don't care what type of entity attempts a seduction, a council master never takes it in the throat!" Carlos turned away from her and began walking deeper into the house and then returned, his breathing escalating as he spoke. "We deliver the ultimate bite, not take it, and we give it good, baby. Believe that. If we feed a lower level, or allow a passion nick," he said, speaking now through fangs and extending his arm to demonstrate, "it's at the wrist or the inside of the elbow, never at the throat—*our power center*."

Damali tilted her head, his rage an ebbing concern, her curiosity fueling her confidence. "Then . . . why—"

Every window on the first floor blew out, leaving the curtains to flutter wildly in the gathering night wind.

"A throat offering is the *highest* level of trust and respect. It's a bond, dammit! A siphon there is a mark, a permanent one. You only give that to your eternal mate, your queen. That's the only one you allow into your head, trusting that her lock on your thoughts is only about the survival of both of you. So, hell no, I'm not going to allow you to put yourself in harm's way against four masters!"

He closed his eyes, trembling. She wasn't sure if it was from rage, passion, frustration, or the combination. Instinct told her not to speak, and to ride it out, just listen to him.

"It is the ultimate power you can bestow, because it makes you vulnerable to her. Where I come from, power is not ceded, it's taken. So when it's given willingly, with intent, it is a serious alliance." Carlos leveled his gaze at her; the intense magnetic pull of it was so great that she almost lost her balance where she stood. "You're supposed to always side with me against anyone and anything—even finding this key! That you are standing here, questioning my judgment is so wrong, D, there are no words!"

"I am not trying to challenge your love for me, baby," she said, her voice soothing. "But you knew what I was before we even got together."

"The bites I delivered, Damali, were *pure* passion, which is why your wounds seal immediately when I pull out. Those transmit only the most excruciating pleasure, and radiate through your body until you weep. If I had meant to turn you, trust me, it would not have been pleasant. And if I had delivered a mind-control nick, you wouldn't even know your own fucking name right now."

She watched the way his lungs drew in and slowly released the air around them, monitoring the fact that he ran his tongue across his incisors but they never retracted.

"Yeah," he muttered, his gaze on her hard. "You didn't trust me not to run on you. So, here we are. Hindsight is always twenty-twenty, like I said. Now, you've gone Neteru on me again and want to save the whole goddamned world."

"I didn't know, then, that the biblical key was missing."

"Neither did I, but still. When you dropped fang, my judgment got compromised," he admitted, his voice lowering a silky octave as his gaze raked her.

She instantly felt her body respond, making her become wet and swollen, just from the memory. Her nipples hardened and stung. Her body temp rose, making her face burn, and she took in small sips of air while fighting to hold her ground.

"What you delivered wasn't a feed bite, either," he murmured, his voice gravelly. "Woman, you have no concept. That shit will make you drool on yourself." He breathed in shallow inhales, then seemed to gather enough control to continue. "You almost nicked an artery, you went in so deep, so hard, so fast, and for so long. Once you were in, it was all over—it felt so damned good that I couldn't even nick you that first time, fangs down, notwithstanding. Now you want me to walk away from you and allow you to run headlong into some insane mission that will no doubt get you smoked. Never."

"You could have—"

"Stopped? Not bitten you back? Are you crazy?"

Carlos dragged his fingers through his hair, staring at her. "Me pull out, then? Impossible. Make *you* stop? Never happen. The wound wouldn't even immediately seal when you lifted your head from my throat. But in that state, I would have let you bleed me out dry."

"But I picked up that you wanted . . ."

"I did, baby. You have no idea how much. I ain't gonna lie—but only from *you*. *That* was my darkest fantasy, but I tried to tell you not to go there. I almost begged you to stop playing with me like that." He shook his head, and broke eye contact with her. "Masters have an Achilles' heel, too, you know, and you've been mine for a long time, girl."

"I'm sorry," she whispered. "I just didn't understand that it was . . . I mean, that, I didn't—"

"*Trust,*" he said, cutting her off, speaking slowly with a

lethal quality to his words, "that I didn't have some bitch on my mind."

All she could do was nod, and look away from him. What was there to say?

He turned away and stretched out his arm, leaning on the cracked plaster of the wall, studying the ruined floor. "Then I had to suffer the ultimate humiliation and show your people just how bad it was, and they *still* didn't understand, didn't get it—that I wasn't feeding you from my wrists. You weren't on your knees as some submissive, scrambling for a blood hit. You're my fucking equal, and I tried to show them that. I had to stand there and listen to your boys question whether or not I knew when I'd delivered a turn bite or not, like I'm some damned amateur!"

"But at the compound, that was a feeding," she said fast. "I was—"

She stepped back two paces when his fist took out a section of the wall and he pushed away from it, his eyes glowing crimson.

"You are pissing me off, D! Even a feeding at the throat from a mate sends nothing but pleasure. That shit is so erotic that it makes time stand still. But after the bite, I didn't have it in me to explain it. I had to get out of there. Now they think I'm Satan."

When she didn't answer, he looked at her with total fury blazing in his eyes. "Don't you ever take me there again. Don't you know how private an exchange that is? And don't you know by now that's the most vulnerable moment for a master to be in? If they were to open my lair in the daylight, I would still have enough strength and awareness to take a body before I torched. But during a mate bite, of any kind, fuck it, they could smoke me before I'd ever know what hit me. I didn't even hear my own marked man, Berkfield, calling me. My lieutenants did! Your mate can only give you pleasure or open you up like that, that's why you choose one with care!" He walked in a hot circle. "And that's why they were able to take an innocent that had my mark of protection on him, while I was with you tonight!" He pointed at her. "Fuck a key."

She covered her mouth with her hand and closed her eyes. "Oh, shit . . ."

"Yeah. Oh shit. And I stood up for you in front of a room full of armed Guardians wide-open, totally blitzed. Die with honor—*please*. Then I send my squad off on boundary security detail, just to save *your* team and try to salvage my pride in front of my boyz, because *I knew* the details of this situation would come out on the south lawn! Don't you *ever* question how I feel about you!"

He flung the heavy front door open so hard that it banged against the side glass panels before it left its hinges, shattering what remained of them. "I'm taking your ass to the edge of the compound lights, and I'll pray that you live. But don't fucking call me, hear? What? Live in exile from you for four or five hundred years, if I'm lucky, or until I get dusted? I want you out of my system, Damali! So, don't start that shit, don't mess with me in dreams, do *not* go down memory lane and dredge up one of our encounters, especially not St. Lucia in your mind, or ever think about that last bite. Purge it. Don't even take that one to the grave. I can feel past the grave, remember, even if you're gone! Do not make my already jacked-up life a living hell. Fair? You know what this shit is like."

"I'm going after the key, Carlos. If I live, I'll do the best I can," she whispered, as the winds he called swept around him. "Because if I do accidentally think about us, it'll only be 'cause I couldn't help it. I'm human."

Carlos didn't say another word. He'd simply vanished. Weary from the confrontation, Damali looked at the mansion's front doors, which were still hanging off their hinges. She glanced around for the dogs, but they, too, were nowhere to be found. They didn't even growl when she walked deeper into the mansion, her gaze noting that the fissures in the walls, the broken-out windows, the shattered chandelier and banister posts, had not been repaired when Carlos vanished.

This was bad. This was not Carlos. This was not how her man lived, or functioned.

Her feet moved on their own accord, drawing her deeper into the house, past the huge foyer, into the sumptuous living room, and then dining room, and she stood in the middle of the floor trying to figure out how to get down into his sealed lair. She'd never seen a trap door, or a way in—had only been transported in or out. Fact was, she wasn't even sure where he'd gone.

"Carlos!" she yelled out, causing an eerie echo. "I owe you an apology, and just want one more word. Five minutes, tops."

No response. She let her breath out hard. "Open the door."

Not even the breeze from outside circulated in the abandoned house. Men.

She plunged the Isis sword into the polished floor, put her dagger in her jeans' back pocket, and waited a moment before calling out again. "My team left me here with the Isis and you. That should count for something. Don't you at least want to know why?"

Slowly the large west wall fireplace began to dissolve, giving way to a black opening and marble steps. Only a narrow gap existed, and she quickly grabbed her blade and slipped through it. Immediately, total darkness surrounded her.

Twelve glowing eyes blinked, something let out a low grumbling growl, and an unseen mass before her parted, sending six eyes to either side of the opening. Not even the torches were on, and she let her breath out hard as she passed the invisible beasts to descend the stairs, feeling the wall.

She couldn't see a thing, and not even her night vision could help her. He'd obviously not just turned out the torches to create darkness, but had practically painted the air black. The oppressive density was suffocating, as she picked her way down the steps, and used her sword like a blind person uses a cane to detect furniture or foreign objects that might make her trip and fall.

Finally in some sort of clearing, she patiently gathered her thoughts, stood tall, and spoke as calmly as she could.

"Baby, listen—"

"Do *not* use that term of endearment," a sullen voice replied, reverberating off the walls. "Not on me."

"Okay," she murmured, leaning on her sword, trying to get a bead on where Carlos's unseeable form might be in the room. "That's fair."

Silence gathered the tension in the room as she formed her next verbal approach.

"I chose to come with you," she said slowly.

"Why, because they finally put your ass out?"

The voice had shifted, almost seemed to be circling her. She followed it blindly, trying to keep it in front of her and not at her back.

"They wouldn't have *given* me the Isis if they'd put me out, Carlos. You know better than that. It would be in my chest."

Again, silence, but she could tell he was thinking.

"Remember when you just told me that I had no concept about the bite . . . what the different ones meant?"

There was no answer, just a low snarl coming from the corner of the room.

"You rightfully got angry about my lack of understanding," she said, pressing on, her voice unfazed. "I should have trusted that you wouldn't go off with some stray female vamp. Yes, and I should have trusted you. Just give me a chance to explain the soul-sharing ceremony to you, so at least you know how it went down. I wasn't just playing with you, or working you," she said, resolute. "It is no less sacred than a mate bite, for a Neteru."

She waited, could hear the air crackle around her. "Just like I don't have full master awareness from your line because I'm not fully turned, you don't have full Neteru awareness from mine, because you haven't been fully turned. And at the time we did what we did to each other, I had about as much self control as you—*none*."

She could hear a heavy piece of furniture drag across the floor and smash into the wall. Good, at least she was getting some sort of reaction.

"You were warned about the dangers first, Damali. I wasn't!"

"Yeah, but see, that's just the thing, what I was doing to you wasn't dangerous. It would pull you closer to the Light, not—"

"In case you haven't already figured it out, pulling a master vampire toward the Light is lethal."

More furniture banged, but at least she was starting to be able to see. The foreign darkness was abating and giving way to the mere absence of light. She could make out the beginnings of shapes and forms and started to gain her bearings in the room, but he was still invisible.

"Carlos, seriously. There was only good intent when I held your hands and looked into your eyes. It was a pure rush of passion to give you only the best of me . . . but I never meant to hurt you. That consequence never even dawned on me, or I would have warned you."

"You should have given me the option, Damali."

"Baby, I was so turned on, so into what was happening between us . . . you've been there, right? I lost perspective."

When he didn't answer but just breathed out hard, she spoke more gently. Everything she was saying was true—*that* he *had* to feel. She spoke slowly and softly, trying to heal his wounded male ego. "I wanted everything you had to give, and wanted to give that right back from me to you."

"D . . . I don't want to talk about it, or go back to that, right now," the deep voice said, but with much less force. "What's done is done, and you're getting away from the subject at hand, namely, a solution."

"I'm not going to apologize for wanting a full life with you . . . a future, and normal, healthy babies one day . . . and friends and family all around, unafraid of creatures of the night preying on them . . . I refuse to apologize about the fact that ever since the day we met, I've wanted to be in your arms day and night, and—"

"I wanted all those things, too, but you took my pride in the transaction, girl," he said, cutting her off and materializing with his back to her. "My fucking respect. What good is a man with no respect?" He let his breath out hard. "My fucking nose ain't no better than Rider's now. No respect!"

"Respect?" This was some crazy man-shit that she knew she'd never figure out. Prowess bullshit was bad enough in normal human males, but she had no concept of what she'd be dealing with if she had to do circle logic with a master vampire. *"Nadie duda de tu capacidad,"* she said as gently as possible.

"Oh, right, no one doubts my ability," he said in a low seethe, his angry breaths making his back expand and contract as he spoke. "You'd better stop trying to work me, D . . . talking to me in Spanish, and using that feminine bullshit on me. It won't work. Not tonight!"

Damali felt for the side of the lair bed and flopped down on it. She garnered her patience and drew from her human knowledge base, trying to soothe his wounded ego. "Baby, you're tripping. All your vampire senses are intact. Marlene was just . . . she was just pissed when she said all that. Rider was, too." Damali waved her arms about. "You can still do your vamp thing. There's nothing wrong with your nose, okay? And anyway, I would never disrespect you. Why would I do that—or want to be with some brother I didn't respect?"

"Not you," he snapped, finally whirling on her to face her. His eyes blazed red, flickering intermittently gold. "I'm a damned head of state! When I go to council meetings, I already have to stop my fucking heartbeat just to enter chambers. I can't go down there with the rest of my shit raggedy. They can't think I have *any* soft spots, least of all in my heart, woman. And you are disrespecting me by insisting on going after the seal and the key, with or without me. Are you crazy?"

Damali squinted at him in the darkness. Okay, point well taken about him having to keep up appearances in front of the other vampires, but saving humanity was nonnegotiable.

She needed him on her side, for them to work as a team, and she was not going to allow him to give in to some unnecessary drama.

"I'm a Neteru—a head of state, too, if you will. A ruler. And, trust me, brother, I'm not supposed to have fangs."

She couldn't believe he was being so stubborn. "*You've* got problems?" she said, standing. "Yeah, well, I can tell you there's probably an angelic battalion up there ready to hand-deliver me to the other side. They're *done*. They'll probably drop-kick my butt into the pit, if this goes down wrong. I've temporarily disgraced my kind, too. But as long as we're both still in the game, we can make something positive and honorable come out of *both* our indiscretions. So what are we going to do about this shit?"

"I don't know," he muttered. "Mar can probably give you something or your system will purge it on its own. The good will purge the darkness, but the thing you forgot, Damali, is that the darkness can never completely banish the Light. It only works to your advantage, not mine. Metaphysics, baby, that's what this whole war is all about on the grand level. Remember?"

"And how is it not in your best interest to ultimately have the Light banish the darkness within you?" She put her hands on her hips, leaving the Isis on the bed, and looked at his now-solid image hard.

"I liked my powers," he said quietly. "All of them."

She didn't say a word, just stared at him.

"Girl, you know how I rolled. Even when I was alive, I always went top-shelf, was never no scrambler. I handled my business with authority. My territory was tight." He walked away from her, and raked his fingers through his hair down to the scalp. "There were things I wanted to give you, to show you, now my resources are all jacked up."

"You are going to have to explain that resource issue to me," she said, her voice firm, but also gentle. "And you know I never cared about—"

"That's the thing—you didn't; *I did*," he murmured. He turned and leaned against the wall, speaking to the floor.

"You know, they tell young brothers to do the right thing . . . and yet, the options and results are really fucked up. Dead or alive, the people who say to do the right thing have the system rigged so that it's almost impossible to get your head above water by following their convoluted rules . . . rules that they never followed until *after* they'd gotten what they'd wanted." He glanced up and held her gaze while speaking in a far-off tone.

"I didn't have to become a vampire to see. A blind man could see it. I may not have been to college, but trust me, I've been schooled well. The powerful still plunder countries, neighborhoods, territories, for what they want to seize—by force. Robber barons, imperialists, mobsters turned presidents . . . then, they go legit. They've only cracked open the door to let a few not like them in, and under very controlled circumstances. Yeah, I messed up while alive, because I wanted the same power they had. I wanted the same respect. For me, then, like now, living or existing without that wasn't, and isn't, in my DNA."

For a moment, she had no answer for him. The world was indeed unfair; there was no argument about it. She knew what he was talking about, that's probably why she'd been created to tip the scales to bring forth the truth about a lot of things. Spoken word. However, getting sucked into the twisted game still wasn't the answer. What she knew she had to get across to him. Carlos had to understand that the real issue was in finding a way to flip the script without going dark oneself. Spiritual Jujitsu. Leverage the dark against itself so that something positive would come out of any negative situation that occurred.

"I hear you," she said after a while. "But there are a lot of ways to get and keep respect without doing the terrible things the oppressors of people have done. We saw how that messed up the were-demon in Brazil. You've gotta be creative, faster than them, smarter than them. You have been dead long enough to see where that leads, so why—"

"Because as a woman, you will never understand this thing that men need called *respect*." He looked up at her, his eyes hard but his tone calm and logical. "I liked being able to provide for me and mine," he said flatly. "I liked having motherfuckers step out of my path, afraid. Yeah." He pushed himself off the wall and stood proud. "I liked being able to take my woman wherever knowing that I could afford to get her anything she wanted; even if she didn't want a thing, it was, and always has been, about power. Dead or alive. I do not like going *anywhere* with a question in my mind about what if. I must have total control of my shit."

"All right," she said, losing patience. "Then who's to say you don't have more power now?" She swept her arm out, motioning toward the room. "What has changed, except your level of confidence?"

"Ain't nothing wrong with my confidence," he snarled, folding his arms over his chest.

"You haven't even expended the energy to fix the house after you went off. Got the damned dogs locked in your lair—"

"They need a hundred and eighty pounds of raw flesh a night to keep fed, and my resources could be—"

"Why? What's messed with your resources? Not me."

He grumbled and walked away from her. "If I want to go somewhere, I want to be able to roll with authority. I can't have some lower-level try me because they sense a power fluctuation or dip. Right now, because I have been messing with *you,* and not handling *my* business, my borders are raggedy, I don't have a strong inner circle to depend on if some madness jumps off, and—"

"Stop this male bullshit now!" she shouted, walking up to him, then stomping away. She was so angry with him for being so shortsighted that she almost couldn't speak. Words collided inside her head, nearly making her stutter, they wouldn't come out fast enough.

"They *took* my Isis from me, Carlos. You don't think that rocked *my* confidence and hurt my pride? I have to earn back my team's trust, rightfully so. I lost in this transaction; you gained. The Light always adds, the darkness always subtracts—basic cosmic law, metaphysics, or don't *you* remember?"

"How," he said, slapping his chest, "did I gain *anything* but aggravation and grief from all this drama, D? Tell me!"

"You have just been made the baddest mutha in the valley, and you are telling me I jacked your power? Brother, pulleeease!"

She stormed away from him again. "If you can't, then I'll feed your fucking dogs. What? They each need a vamp body a night? Done. No problem, and on my agenda anyway." She grabbed her Isis blade off the bed, huffing as she spoke. "What I gave you allows you to cross prayer barriers, walk on hallowed ground, and dulls the blood hunger! No other vampire on the planet can do that—oh, my bad! And so what if you like the way I smell, and it turns you on—my bad. But when you get like that, your ass still gets as strong as shit. Ask me how I know."

She leveled her blade at him, speaking from across the room, both because she needed space to think, and because she had to resist the urge to gore him. "Silver probably won't even burn you! And you're mad at me because I gave you that extra immunity? Oh, and you've got an attitude because you've been around ripening Neteru so much that you've built up a semi-tolerance—it doesn't get you cold blitzed, like it will any other master vamp? My bad!"

The look of surprise in his eyes grated her. Torches went on in the room, and his eyes flickered gold, then went normal deep brown.

"That's deep," he said slowly. "I, uh—"

"You and I are supposed to go to Australia to clean out that major nest, together to bring the stolen key back to the church—"

"Are you nuts?" he said quickly. "You still wanna go, *with me,* after all this?"

"Yes, to both questions. I am crazy and I want to go."

Neither of them spoke, but just stared at each other in a standoff.

"First of all, I'd need an international pass. You don't just roll up as a head of state on another territory unannounced. This ain't Brazil," Carlos finally replied, his tone irritable. "The empire is currently in a fragile peacetime truce. We have borders, and there's just basic protocol. Respect, master to master. And how am I going to keep you—"

"We work as a team," she said, lowering her blade. Her breathing was becoming steadier as she realized she'd broken down a bit of his resistance. "Look, I don't *have* to obey you just because you temporarily made me. I'm not that kinda girl," she said, swallowing away a sly smile that was about to cross her mouth. "I'm going to Australia, with or without you. But I'd prefer to go with you."

"Why are you so stubborn? Just determined to keep baiting disaster until you get yourself smoked."

"Because you messed around and bit a Neteru, not some average Jane. So learn to work with the Light, and get as strong using it as you've gotten while leveraging the dark. Use the new shit you've got to make you mo' betta, man. As your partner, I'll show you some new moves that are actually pretty cool."

Indignant, he walked toward her. "See, right here, is the major problem. We *can't* be partners, because you have never listened to me, and don't follow my lead when—"

She shook her head and made him stop speaking.

"What?"

"That's not the definition of an equal, somebody to do what you say, just 'cause." Damali let out a short huff, now totally indignant herself. "You didn't want a love slave. You wanted an intelligent *partner*." She drew out the word for emphasis and thrust her chin up higher. "You wanted somebody who could work the room as good as you can, who was smooth, had finesse, and could go out swinging. Right? Am I lying?"

He gave her a grudging smile as he cut his eyes at her.

"I thought so," she said, triumphant. "That's what you asked the universe for and you got that. Now deal with it." A slight smile came out of hiding on his face. "The power of prayer is deep."

"Do not *ever* mention that again. It ain't right, D, and you know it. Not even in front of my dogs, and definitely not over with the Aussies!"

They held each other's line of vision, neither breaking eye contact nor conceding.

Carlos finally let out a weary sigh. "I'd be going over there without an entourage. They'd know the moment we got there that you were still vulnerable, still human. Not to mention that, after the Raise the Dead concert, every vamp on the planet knows who you are, okay."

She cast the blade onto the bed. Both hands went to her hips, and she cocked her head to the side in a challenge. "So, when we were in bed in St. Lucia, and you were leaning on me, breathing hard on my throat saying, 'Yeah, baby, I'll help you dust whoever you want, whenever you want,' was that just a love-jones talking, or—"

He held up his hand. "No, see, that's just the thing, D. I figured we'd take our time, that bad idea might work its way out of your—"

"You never intended to go hunting with me, tell the truth! And you hid critical information from me, then jump on my case because I don't *trust* you?" Her neck bobbed as she leveled the charge. "Lying ass, no-good vampire—"

"See, you got this all twisted, girl. I'm the one right now who's got the right to have an attitude, not you, and besides, half of a good ruse is presentation, subterfuge, illusion. Gotta have strong game to do an international hit. They'd wanna know where my bodyguards were, if I tried to pass you off as a vamp."

"In the other battles," she said coolly, studying her fingers like she'd seen him do so many times before, "we took the male approach. Direct force. Let's use some feminine wiles. That type of energy has felled nations, brother. Use my flux to your advantage to mess with their minds. You down?"

Intrigued, he walked around her, studying her, but unconvinced. He wasn't sure if it was Damali's street sense talking, her vamp self, or her crazy go-for-broke Neteru self. Whatever it was, he didn't like how she'd flipped the script on him. Female master or not, this was some tricked-up woman-type circle logic. "Talk to me."

"What kind of message do you think it would send if you came into town with only two Hell-dogs and your woman . . . the Neteru, who you'd turned?"

He rubbed his jaw, working the strategy like worry beads. "To my way of thinking, Carlos, they'd have to assume that if you had the hounds, then you were authorized by the council to turn me, and if it was an accident, then you were still in their favor. You'd be going in-country not as a visiting master, but a *council-level* master who'd turned the Neteru. Big props. Plus, if I show up with fangs, and you haven't been smoked by council, then they might think you're in possession of the seal. They'd have to believe that if the Neteru, the council's only source of daywalkers, was turned and council was cool with it, then you had an ace up your sleeve. It raises a big question, which raises the odds. They won't want to assassinate you or me until they know what you're holding for sure, which buys us time to find the key and do them before they try to do us. Before they try to smoke either of us, they'll want to know if you or council already has the seal."

Satisfied that her statement had given him sufficient pause, she chuckled. "All you have to do is tell the old boys at the council you're using my intermittent fluctuations as a cover so no other master will try to tamper with their package, and so that they'll think council may have access to the seal. Tell them that you're using the human Guardian team to actually search for the key on hallowed ground, where the human helpers have probably stashed it so no other master but the thief can get to it. Since you have us all compromised, tell them you'll use me to lead you to it once it's been located."

Carlos cocked his head and peered at her. "And what if

you flux pure human while we're in Australia and start trailing Neteru . . ."

"Tell the other masters that it's something I still wear for you. Just a female vampire illusion that I still have access to, since it was a part of my DNA when I died." Damali chuckled and shook her head. "Talk about creating chaos . . ."

Carlos drew in a deep inhale and walked away from her. "The plan is crazy, but has distinct possibilities."

Damali shrugged. "Then?"

"Coupla things worry me. Like, number one—we'd have to stay in the host master's lair estate. The walls would have ears, and I'd only be able to communicate with you in a mind lock."

"So?"

"Uh-uh. And stay in the same room with you all night like a happily mated couple?"

"And?" she said, her hands still on her hips. "It's part of our cover. It's true, but not true. Perfect."

"I do *not* need to be distracted like that. I'm council level, D, and we're talking about drawing four masters to one meeting. They distrust each other so much that they rarely cross each other's lines topside, fearing a power grab hit that could fold their territory up under another master. Any of those bastards would attempt a council assassination to get a throne seat. *That's why the old boys do not come up from Hell*." He let his breath out hard, thoroughly annoyed with her shortsightedness.

When she didn't answer right away, he felt vindicated and spoke with more authority, less emotion. *Yeah, baby, welcome to my world.*

"If we're sleeping in the same bed, and I get with you while we're there, they could smoke us in the throes. I'm not going out like that and neither are you. I won't allow it," he said, growing more agitated as he began walking again. "If we're making love, I'll be vulnerable to an assassination attempt."

"All right. No sex while we're on the road. You set the rules of engagement. Your next point?"

Exasperated, he glared at her. "Second, we'd have to eat while there. They always roll out the red carpet for VIPs, would have a banquet, blood feasts, shit like that, and you'd never be able to deal with it. If they bring us a baby, or a child, you'll freak . . . we both will."

"Okay. Point taken." She moved in close to him, and breathed out her response. "So I'll simply tell them that I don't do children, take it away and let it live, I had a bad experience with one once, I'm eccentric, still, old Neteru perversions in me, which is why you love my twisted ways. Then I'll come to you and—"

"Uh-uh," he said, backing away from her. "I don't do public displays of affection, and definitely not in front of another master."

"See, here again, this is where male ego is messing you up." Damali folded her arms. "What is more powerful than making them think you have your woman so in check that she won't even *feed* from another vein or source?"

He stopped pacing and looked at her dead-on.

"Baby," she murmured. "I promise you I will slide up against you when they bring the blood, will give you a look that will stop your heart, and go to you in public like I just can't stand it and the other masters there will have *much* respect. Trust me. They won't be able to retract fang when I'm done."

For a moment, he didn't speak. She could see a combination of emotions battling for dominance within him.

"And what if you've fluctuated and don't have fangs?" he said coolly, regaining his composure.

"When I come away from your throat, there won't even be a mark, not a drop of blood, just the wet ring from my kiss. They'll say, '*Dayum*, Rivera, you taught her to finesse you like that?'" Damali laughed and threw her locks over her shoulders. "I know men. Ain't much changed since Eve hit the planet. They'll go for it."

That was no lie. Her just saying what she might do had almost made his incisors come down. The plan was brilliant, but it still contained a lot of variables. "The sun," he said, ticking off new points on his fingers, determined to stay annoyed with her.

"I'll only go out at night. They'll never know, which is best for me to do, anyway, until my system levels off."

"Your image goes in and out and we could get busted."

"Tell them you project a false one for me while we're out, because I still make good money for you and have unaware human fans."

"What? Like I'm your pimp? Are you crazy—"

"You own a music empire, remember? Blood Records." She rolled her eyes at him. "You're supposed to be as rotten as they come, evil," she said, chuckling. "I'm your turned-out female at your beck and call. Damn, I may have messed you up after all. That one was pretty obvious."

"That shit is not funny, D," he said, now hollering as he pointed at her. "You're fucking relentless when you want something, won't take no for an answer, and this time you're dancing on the edge of disaster."

"See, now, I must have gotten that relentless-when-there's-something-I-want-that-I'm-not-supposed-to-have part from you. Hmmm . . . dancing on the edge . . . I believe that was in both our bloodstreams going into this mess."

"You are out of your mind," he said, seething and walking away again.

"Just tell them you've quietly pulled my production company under your label, and the general public doesn't need to know that. When I do concerts, the cash hits your coffers."

"Okay, right there," he said quickly. "How are we gonna pull that off, especially if you cast an image on the one hand, which will alert the vamps in the VIP boxes, or if you don't, which will really freak out the networks?"

"I don't know," she said, chewing her bottom lip as she thought. "Maybe we can tell the vamps that you're projecting from a human body double that my team uses for the videos over my voice. I can tell J.L. and Jose to edit a compilation from other concerts," she said, growing quiet. "When the local cameras scan me, you can block out what the masters will see."

"But even *I* can't do shit about what really broadcasts." He walked away from her. Damali wasn't crazy; she was insane. If they broadcasted the edited videos to fill in a lot of the time, swept the stage with a narrow pan, and held the cameras on the other team members, then went back to video clips . . . maybe. But there could be *disastrous* moments when she'd either appear, or not. Plus, this whole thing required tight choreography that the evaporating time didn't allow for. Her team wasn't even speaking to her, so how was she gonna practice this bull? That was the problem this stubborn woman was overlooking. Too risky.

He could feel her mind wrestling with the challenge, instead of giving in to the fact that some things just weren't prudent. "Besides," he went on, "you can't do the whole *Bring the Light* thing up there, anyway, and try to pass yourself off as a female vampire. That's a *big* stretch, D, For real."

"Why?" Her tone was flippant and her eyes glittered with mischief. "I'll stand back from the libations pouring, can ask Mar to go easy on the incense. You and your boys will be in a VIP box away from it, anyway. Tell them it's just business, box office draw. Then I can do my thing, yeah, without the silver suit, but I can give the crowd a new song to fill in for it and to appease the vamps, one that's been working in my head. Will blow the vamps' minds, and make them overly confident that I am what I seem to be. Illusion. Theater. Meanwhile, if we take out a few heads of state, your territory just increased again. You'll be the only topside master left standing."

She had her hands on her hips again, but not in defiance, just deep thought. She then rubbed the nape of her neck and began pacing. "Yeah. Flip the script. Nuit was going to take out the whole human race with one concert, let's take what we learned from him and put it to some good use. One concert to draw all the masters, you sense for deception, sniff them out to see which one stole the key and where it is, then we get Berkfield back and dust the entire topside vamp empire." She smiled. "We give the key back and topple the empire."

Even as he walked away from her into the kitchen toward the taps, he knew this was a bad idea. The amount of power she was talking about temporarily amassing under his control was sure to corrupt him. What bothered him more was the fact that he was even struggling with the concept of doing a power grab. That *she'd* come up with the plan, one so freaking devious that it had made him look at her twice, hard, to see if she had fangs, also worried him. What if she did? Permanent ones? He had laid his thing down pretty hard . . .

But if she wasn't darkening, contained within her wild scheme was blind trust. She trusted that he was worthy of amassing the power, and would do what, cede it to the Light? Insane. What if it got too good to him, and he couldn't? And the fact that he worried that she might have a dark side and decide to let the chips fall where they may to share the dark rule, worried him just as much. This was too crazy. She'd polluted him and had given him a damned conscience!

He could feel her following him, almost skipping; her step was so brisk to keep up with his long strides to get away from her. No, he was not having it. What she wanted to do presented too much of a risk. It was too bold, too crazy, too off the meter. Extreme. If she wanted to bring down the vampire nations, she needed to pace herself, be strategic, do it methodically, one brick at a time, just like he'd built his territory while still living. You just didn't rush in and do things all buck wild. That's how people got hurt. That's how she might get smoked.

"I'm not arguing with you, D," he said, his back to her as he filled a glass, knowing she was leaning on the kitchen door frame.

"Don't care 'bout the changes I go through for this man of mine," she said, her voice sexy, deep, melodic, as she began performing her new spoken-word cut for the vamps at the kitchen entry. "It ain't really a change, just a bittersweet transition . . . from time to time."

"No, woman, I told you!"

"They have no idea what crossing over in his arms is like—"

"Stop."

"Will make you leave Momma's house in the dead of night."

He wheeled on her, and set his jaw hard. "Cut it out. I'm serious." She wasn't fighting fair, was using all of her theatrical talent, and a whole lot of the others she possessed. Even though he swore he'd wring her neck instead of watching her, for a few moments she was winning the standoff; he was the one strangling on a hard swallow.

Damali pushed herself off the door frame, filling the divide as she held her head back and belted out the lyrics, working her body around an invisible floor microphone, then began walking in the small confines with it. "Can't stop, this sweet transition. Can't play with bittersweet madness. Can't resist, but don't judge till you've felt the burn . . . talk to me, baby, I'm ready to learn. It ain't wrong; it ain't right, just real. Give it up on demand. Pleasure coats the pain when you're with this man. So don't ask about my changes, just try to understand. It's a bittersweet transition that's like a brand."

When she closed her eyes and ran her palm down her torso on the last stanza, he was determined to warn her for the last time before transporting her out of his lair. But somehow what was supposed to be a harsh tone sounded half-hearted, even to him. "I'm serious, D."

"So am I," she murmured. "I want to go to Australia and do this thing. I think this new song will blow them away."

He knew it would, but that was not the point. "You're not doing that number on stage in front of my boys. No."

"Good, isn't it?"

Her eyes glittered with such mischief that he wanted to slap her. Instead he put his hands behind his back to keep from doing that, or anything else.

"Together, we're strong enough to take 'em, you know that. And, hopefully, you can tell the old boys that one or two of them reached for your package, which they probably will, so, a man had to do what a man had to do. Or that I had to plant the blade to protect my honor, since I'm so crazy about you. Meanwhile, we'll tell them that in the mêlée, the seal's whereabouts were never found, and the key got snatched by human forces and delivered to hallowed ground before either of us could get to it. That will make them have to go back to relying on me to be their only vessel in seven years, and we just bought ourselves some more time, brother. I don't see how this can fail."

She smiled when he didn't answer. "It would be the truth, Carlos, they just wouldn't understand the intent. But it's a lovely setup, don't you think?"

Still he didn't answer her, just stared at her. The treachery of her mind was messing with him, big time. It was so damned sexy, utterly defiant, and thoroughly brilliant . . .

"What you see was always in me," she murmured, going into her song again, and coming toward him slowly with a smile. "Couldn't hold back—no woman would. Wasn't that much of a stretch . . . just gotta work around the changes . . . like a bittersweet transition . . . from time to time."

He didn't move, nearly forgot he was holding his glass, but lifted his chin up, refusing to drop fang in front of her. What had he gotten himself into?

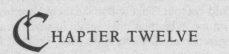HAPTER TWELVE

"I'M GOING to bed," Marlene announced as the teams entered the compound. "Tomorrow, with fresh minds and renewed spirits, we'll move out." She motioned to Father Patrick's crew. "There are spare rooms down the hall, food in the fridge. Gentlemen, make yourselves at home."

She was too weary to stand on ceremony, and the thoughts rattling around in her skull made her need to lie down. No matter how many times she had witnessed the miraculous, so-called coincidences of the universe, it still always amazed her how tightly woven the threads were within the grand design. So odd, but not, that they'd been offered a brief one-night-only concert gig in Sydney, only to find out that that was where they were destined to go. It had happened so many times that she would have thought she'd be used to that by now—then again, how did anyone get used to any of it?

Marlene didn't even look back to wait for a response, but headed to her private sanctuary. When Shabazz appeared in the bedroom doorway, she almost ordered him to get away from her. She didn't have an ounce of strength to argue with him, but his eyes held such worry and hurt that she conceded, sitting down heavily on the bed.

He closed the door behind him softly, and walked in a bit to lean against her dresser. "Marlene," he said, his voice so quiet that it made her look up. "The team is changing, too, not just our baby girl."

"I know," she murmured.

"This thing with Carlos and Damali has shifted the whole dynamic . . . and that's dangerous."

She nodded. "It will either make us stronger, or split us apart."

Shabazz rubbed his palm across his jaw, and studied the steel grates at Marlene's window. He looked so tired, battle-weary, like he wanted to just lie down and weep but was too proud to ever allow that to happen.

"She's like a daughter to me, Mar, too," he said in a ragged voice. "And, what she let homeboy do to her . . . and the shit with Jose—he ain't never gonna be right."

With her last ounce of strength, Marlene stood and went to her embattled partner. Tears glittered in his eyes, and she touched the side of his dark, walnut-hued face, admiring the handsome, regal quality of it. This was some man-shit, she knew. The inability to accept that a female from his inner circle had made a choice to take a lover against the clan, had done what was natural, what was a part of the cycle of life. "She's gonna be all right, honey. And that girl never stopped loving us."

"But, what if he bites her again, Mar?"

His eyes held a fervent need for her to understand. She did. So, she allowed her voice to soothe, become a balm, as she drew from every source of wisdom she had.

"Mike got nicked in New Orleans, and after a hard purge, he came back. Right?"

Shabazz looked away, but didn't shrug out of her hold against his cheek. "That was different."

"Why?" Marlene waited and offered him a tender smile. "Our brother got caught up, and staggered back to the hotel, collapsed in Rider's arms, and went into a convulsion. Rider had to take him to a local root worker just to ensure he'd live till he got him home to me."

Shabazz chuckled, despite his determination to stay morose.

"You know, every member of this team has had their turn at delivering drama," she said, her voice containing rich amusement. "Rider would go off on a Jack Daniel's binge and be AWOL for days, only to be found in a titty bar when Jose went on a search and rescue. Dan had us scramble battle stations to bring him in from a six-vamp attack. J.L. almost got whacked by some guys in the casinos for card-counting that time, and Jose took us through major yang behind Dee Dee."

When a slow smile tugged at his cheek, she kissed it. "You almost had a whole team of weres jump us in Bahia, flaring up on Kamal—"

"And you almost stopped my heart when you went down in battle against the Amazon's mother-seer," Shabazz murmured, tracing her eyebrow with the pad of his thumb. "That's the point," he said, his voice dropping, "I don't want to lose anybody to no dumb shit—especially not you, Mar. And if Damali breaks your heart, our heart, a part of you will die inside . . . which will kill me . . . because you and I are connected there, too."

He took her mouth so slowly, so tenderly, that only the balm of touch could close the wound he'd exposed to her. Marlene allowed her hands to stroke the thick, magnificent locks that graced his kingly head. His family was changing, purging itself, morphing, and it frightened him—a man who'd already lost his family to this austere life of being a Guardian.

In her arms she held a man who'd wanted nothing more than to have his lion-pride, his family, always safe, protected, and to be in control of its destiny . . . this man moved against her for comfort because he saw so much of Carlos in himself that it gave him flashbacks . . . and because she was a woman, not a seer, she knew that the hardest challenge for a man was to let a higher authority be his guide on sheer faith alone.

Rider stood in the garage inner door and watched Jose throw the tarp dustcover off his bike, then stoop to begin polishing the chrome wheels. There was nothing like motion, a man and his Harley, to cure the blues . . . and what was ailing his best friend was beyond words.

So, he took his time, before encroaching on Jose's private space. "Wanna go take a ride, like old times? Me and you, and a bottle of our old friend Jack Daniel's . . . hit the desert, look up at the moon, tempt fate on the plains with just a crossbow between us, and get snot-slinging drunk?"

Jose just shook his head no and kept polishing his bike, moving to the exhaust system.

"She's sweet, man," Rider offered. "Integrated header and collector heat shielding, Pro-Pipe . . . sweet thunder, man. Gotta use her, or lose her, feel me?" When he didn't get a response from Jose, he walked deeper into the garage and gave his own bike a wistful glance, then threw the cover off her. "This is the *Easy Rider,* custom edition, hottest iron on the planet, and she's almost as old as me . . . but I take care of my girl, even when she needs an overhaul."

Rider stroked the leather tribal inlaid seat like he was touching a woman's behind, gentle and with deep appreciation. "Almost lost her a few times to a blowout when she slid out from under me on the wet road, when I was younger— before I really knew how to handle her. Then I learned patience and how to baby her . . . ripped out her engine, modified her for some serious horsepower and torque, installed new inner needle bearings and put on a set of Rinehart duals. Now she purrs. But she's still all Harley, man. Black, silver, and beautiful."

Jose finally looked up and gave Rider a nod of respect. "You've worked her to the bone, man. I'm just learning how."

"Whaduya say we ship these ladies over to Australia with us, man? We can show the Aussies what an all-American chopper can do."

Jose smiled sadly and went back to polishing the elaborate exhaust system on his bloodred bike. "Don't know if I feel like riding her anymore. Not even sure I can look at her, yo. Might fall and get busted up real bad on a new road."

Rider leaned against his monster bike and folded his arms over his chest. "That's why you wear *leather* when you ride, dude. Keeps you from getting tore up to the bone. You know that. You also know what a rush it is going down new dirt you ain't never touched before."

When Jose gave him the silent treatment again, Rider let his breath out hard. "You've already fallen, man. You know what it feels like, and you didn't die. Your ass hit the ground hard before with Dee Dee, then you got up. Let it go, and get yourself a new lady to ride—"

"But that was different, man," Jose said quietly. "Damali had never made a choice before . . . so . . ."

"I know, I know," Rider said, his voice mellow. "It kept hope alive."

"I was willing to follow her to Hell and back, man. In fact, I did."

For a moment, neither of them spoke.

"We all were. Still are," Rider said quietly. "And, she's probably the only one in here who couldn't see you eating your heart out for her . . . even Dee Dee could tell."

Jose wiped his palm over his chin and stood. "I know."

"All right, youngblood," Rider said, forcing a matter-of-fact tone into his voice. "So, she loves you like a brother, and—"

"She doesn't need me," Jose nearly whispered. "She's got Rivera—the best nose on the planet and . . ." His words trailed off as he swallowed, staring past Rider to the garage wall.

"And what you felt for those brief moments will last you a lifetime. Ride it in your dreams, dude, but don't lose focus." Rider raked his hair and let out a slow stream of air through his mouth, not sure what else to say.

"He might be dead, but he's the luckiest man on the planet, too." Jose's line of vision went to Rider's to hold it hard. "I don't think I can be in here anymore, brother. It's time for me to push on and take my chances—let the chips fall where they may. I'm out. Solo. Like I said, she don't need anything I've got to give her now. I'm not even straight-up human."

Jose swung his leg over his bike, and reached for the automatic door opener.

"*That's* why she needs you," Rider said fast, making Jose slow his reach to engage the door.

"How you figure?"

Rider took his time answering. He desperately wanted to keep his friend from doing the night alone on some kind of suicide mission. No Guardian could make it alone once identified as a core member of the Neteru team. The dark side would hunt him down and hold him for ransom just to draw the Neteru—knowing she could never leave her own. Jose would be vamp bait, but he also knew that Jose didn't give a rat's ass about any of that right now. The man was bleeding from a wound that he didn't have a cure for.

"You ever think, maybe, that like Shabazz always says, there's a purpose for every one of us being here?"

Jose let his breath out hard. "Save it, man."

"We all have crazies in our family, dude. There's an uncle who likes little girls, a momma who drinks too much, a cousin who would steal you blind. So one of your people got nicked, maybe became an ax murderer, or serial killer— who knows, but that ain't you, dude. You made a choice to walk away from all of that, just like I did, no matter what was in your blood." Rider pushed off of his bike and rounded Jose's, holding it by the handlebars. "So, if the universe sent you to be with us, then there's a very divine purpose in it."

Jose set his jaw hard, but at least he was no longer reaching for the escape hatch.

"Listen to me," Rider said more firmly. "You and Lopez didn't come into this equation linked to Rivera by accident." He looked at the younger Guardian hard, and wiped his hands on the back of his jeans, then hitched them up. "I know I talk a lot of shit, but this time I say it isn't some freaky coincidence, and Jose, you and I have been best buds—the noses together—long enough for you to smell one of my fish tales if I was full of crap."

The younger Guardian shrugged casually, but his line of vision was riveted to Rider's, hurt pride and hope for answers making his eyes glitter under the UV lights. Rolling the tension out of his shoulders, Rider stared at the young man, then backed away from Jose's bike, fairly certain he wouldn't bolt.

"Much as I hate to finally admit it, much less accept it—Rivera was our twelfth man. Creepy, but you, Lopez and Rivera form your own little trinity, a core within the larger group core, with, as is always the formation in battle, the Neteru in the center." He sighed. "And I'm pretty sure Father Patrick is upstairs talking a young cleric off the ledge of our compound. If it fucked you up, what do you think it did to Lopez?"

Embarrassment gave rise to false bravado as Jose sat back on this bike seat and folded his arms, looking off in the distance and focusing on nothing. "Aw'ight, say you're right about the trinity. What's that got to do with D?"

Rider walked the perimeter of the garage as he spoke, making Jose follow him with his eyes. "Three guardians linked, the strongest of the three became her lover; one, her brother, was filled with hope; one, a priest, brought his faith," he said calmly. "Faith, hope, love—like the old priest said before. All three tactical sensors of the highest ability, one from each team—each side of the equation . . . The Covenant, the guardians, and the darkness itself, another ring of three . . . and they're all around her, connected by love—the most unbreakable bond of all . . . and the wider circle of the team is tapped into that. None of us is willing to break the circle . . . we won't leave our own, out of pure love, man. This is some big shit, Jose. Don't blow it off because your ego got hammered."

Jose was off his bike, now pacing in an agitated circle. "Oh, shit . . . oh shit . . ."

"Yeah," Rider said, "you're beginning to feel me. And maybe, just maybe, she had to take a walk on the dark side with Rivera to truly understand what she was up against so she could fight it—so he could fight it. That's why you can't punk out now, just because she accidentally made your dick get hard."

Jose stopped walking and stared at Rider, shoving his hands in his jeans pockets. "I didn't deserve that, man."

"All right, all right," Rider said, waving his hand. "I apologize. But do you see that that's what it boils down to? This is serious, and we're going into maybe the last fight of our lives . . . you *have* to have your head on straight, and cannot allow the little head to do any thinking for the big one. Got it?"

Grudgingly, Jose muttered an assent. "Still, if she's got the baddest mother on the planet protecting her . . . I mean, if—"

"You and Lopez are the only ones on our side who can track him!" Rider hollered, his voice bouncing off the cement walls. "You triangulated on *his* signal, not hers. Get your head out of your own ass, Cipointe. If Carlos gets into trouble, we might need to go find him and pull him out of wherever he is—because, by now we know, he ain't leaving Damali and she ain't leaving him. We can't always count on Marlene or Father Pat, and Damali won't be with us, so if the two of them get into some Bonnie-and-Clyde-type shit, the only available trackers are you and Lopez!"

Rider slapped the center of his forehead hard when Jose didn't even breathe. "Geez Louise, man. You and Lopez are genetically designed to locate a master under eminent threat. Don't you get it; don't you see your purpose—your team value, dude? Heaven is about to turn this bullshit upside down and has been using every move the dark side has made to possibly make the ultimate weapon of mass destruction— two Neterus, a male and female in the same freaking millennium as soul mates—lovers . . . of breeding age, to make more!"

"Oh, shit, this is *way* profound."

Rider blinked twice and Jose stood in the center of the garage floor, dazed.

"Yeah," Rider murmured. "I'm scaring myself, this

makes so much sense . . . I have to tell Marlene. We need a weapons-room meeting, pronto."

This time, Jose shook his head, no. "Shabazz went to talk to her. Tell her in the morning."

"Yeah, but—"

"*Tell her in the morning,* Rider." Jose went to his bike and threw the tarp back over it. "Yeah . . . we should ship these overseas with us, yo. Get some dirt in our faces."

For a moment, Rider didn't move, then nodded and went to cover his bike. "If we're gonna go out in the big one, man, let's load up the side bags with some colloidal silver grenades and go find a good bar where the girls dance on the pole. Get you a tall, Aussie blonde, and me a redhead with jugs this big," Rider said, chuckling and demonstrating a heavy load with his hands.

"Your old ass ain't gonna get no redhead like that."

Rider laughed. "Fantasy, youngblood, ain't nothing wrong with it. Keeps hope alive." He extended his fist, and gave Jose a bear hug when he came over and pounded it. "It's gonna be cool, man."

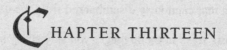HAPTER THIRTEEN

———•••••———

THEY SAT in Australia's Gibson Desert with Lake Disappointment at their backs, the Aussie Northern Territory before them, time moving like it was wounded while they waited on the diplomatic security check and escort—neither speaking, just tensely watching events unfold. It was as though they both knew that they'd hit a point of no return. Masters didn't visit each other without an expressed purpose, alliances were tense worldwide, and no one had ever jumped borders without an army at their back.

Carlos watched three Black Hawk helicopters land a hundred yards before the black stretch Hum-V limousine with diplomatic flags that had transported him and Damali with Hell's passport, wondering when he'd crossed the line to allow the woman beside him to talk him into the most off-the-hook game he'd ever played? He hated being rushed into play; could have waited another night to solidify his strategy. But she'd argued about catching their adversaries off guard and had won the point.

He glanced at the separation glass that kept his driver deaf to their conversation, and then up at the interior roof. "Stay," he muttered as the limo shifted with the weight of the dogs when they stood to snarl at the choppers.

"All right," he murmured. "It's on, now, baby. Remember, follow my lead."

Damali nodded, her eyes trained on the squad of six henchmen that cautiously disembarked from the dark choppers.

"The Isis stays in the luggage, you stay at my side at all times. This is deep cover—way underground. So deep there may not be a way out."

She stared at him, becoming annoyed. They'd discussed all of this before. Why was he beating a dead horse?

"Yeah, but like I was trying to tell you last night, I need to know the language, if—"

"No," he murmured. "We've been over that. I never want you to learn our language. How many times do I have to tell you that it's an ancient language of possession . . . and it's too complicated for a crash course?" He let his breath out hard and glanced out the window.

Damali softened her stance and touched Carlos's arm. The tension running through him was pure electricity. It unnerved her to see him this worried. Truthfully, she'd never seen this side of him before now. If he'd only let her help and stop being so stubborn!

"Baby, it'll be all right," she murmured.

No matter what she said, the risks were enormous. He could feel her resisting him, ready to tackle this alone. But she had to get it straight in her mind that on this mission she had to follow his lead if either of them were going to make it out alive.

"Its origins come out of Babylon," he said, focusing on the language issue, rather than give into the nervous energy roiling in his gut. "Fused with Sumerian, Aramaic, built upon for centuries, each line adding dialect, tones from Asia, Africa, Mongolia, India . . . has Romanian sentence structure from the old republics, with a Latin core syntax, and is written like Egyptian hieroglyphics—but read reverse like the old Chinese dynasties scribe . . . every time a new master is added it morphs, absorbs, and is always changing. Right now, Spanish is the most recent addition." He looked at her with a request to be cool in his eyes. He knew he was babbling, rehashing information he'd explained the night before, but he wanted her to be clear. She just didn't understand how dangerous this situation was, or that for the first time since he'd turned, she might witness him not being able to protect her.

Carlos clenched and unclenched his fist. "Baby, I can't teach you conversational phrases that won't have an effect. It bends wills."

When she sighed hard and looked out the window, he eyed the approaching men. "When we step out of this limo, head-of-state protocol will be in full effect. You remember what I told you, right?"

He didn't even wait for her silent nod of agreement. He simply glanced back at her and instantly changed his clothes into a black Armani suit, black silk shirt, black silk tie with deep, bloodred marbled veins in its pattern, dark glasses and black slip-ons. He adjusted the crimson handkerchief in his breast pocket so that only a quarter-inch of it showed. His council crest ring appeared on his left hand where a wedding band would have normally been, and he smoothed his hair back.

Damali looked down at her jeans, then back up to him for assistance.

"Sexy," he muttered. "At all times."

"I know. You told me. Remember?"

While that was true, it still took him aback when she nodded and smiled and changed her clothes herself without his help.

"I think the underground passage gave me a little jump start on another timely fluctuation," she purred, leaning against him. "And you didn't think I was gonna let you pick out my gear for me, did you? Pulleease. I never let Marlene do that for me on stage, why should I let you go there? I've been watching how you work, learned a thing or two. That's why I've been telling you not to worry—I got this."

That's exactly what concerned him most. He didn't answer her as his gaze took in her smooth transformation. She'd finessed it like a pro, and had conjured a butter-soft sheath that was the same color as her skin and damned near as supple. The dress gave the illusion at first glimpse that she was naked. It had no shoulders, dipped perilously low in the front to accentuate her cleavage, and was so short that it begged a man to look at her gorgeous legs. The simplistic creation hugged every voluptuous curve she owned, fit her like snakeskin had fit Eden's serpent, and he noted that her legs had been coated with a natural sheen . . . shea butter making them glisten, filling the vehicle with the sensual fragrance.

His gaze slid down her legs, which ended in a pair of monochrome, stiletto heels that tied at the ankles and were the same hue as the dress. Her hair was swept up and held in place by a long, gold, dagger-shaped barrette. Pendulous, smoky topaz and diamond teardrop earrings set off a shimmer right at the midpoint in her throat. Her hand took his in a soft caress, French manicure flawless and matching her pedicure, then he saw the ring—a thirteen-karat smoky topaz crusted with diamonds with his crest etched in the center of it, set high on her ring finger just as he'd always imagined.

She gazed up at him, her mouth moist, inviting, colored deep caramel, her eyes revealing a bit of chocolate-colored charcoal that made them mysterious, sensual, a sheer teasing sprinkle of gold dust along her collarbone leading him to study her cleavage one more time.

"El Excellency approves?" she murmured.

He nodded. "Most assuredly."

He gave her hand a brief squeeze as the limousine door opened and the international courier who drove them stood aside for him to exit. This was getting good to him, perhaps too good. The armed entities from the choppers lowered their weapons before him, gave him a bow of deference, and then motioned that he and his limo checked out. They had no eyes in their blackened sockets. Their pale faces were half hidden by hard black safari hats tipped low—their black-and-gray camouflage fatigues straining against their bulk.

Carlos held out his hand, and Damali's filled it as she stepped from the vehicle to stand by his side.

The lead entity nodded, appreciation rippling through his silent assessment of her as he used the silver-shell-loaded crossbow to motion toward the Black Hawks. Carlos nodded to his driver, and the dogs dismounted from the top of the Hum-V limo and climbed inside, waiting until the driver locked them away.

Without discussion, they followed the somber retinue and entered the choppers. But he kept his eye on Damali. She looked totally fascinated as the swift uptake propelled the helicopters at supernatural speed to their destination—the Australian master's lair.

Below them, he could see his limo creating a long dusty trail in the night as it drove away and knew that even if his dogs were still mounted on the roof of it, they wouldn't have been able to dodge the highly maneuverable death choppers. He materialized and handed her a pair of black shades. "Don't look down without these."

Blue-white prayer lines created a blur beneath them and zigzagged the open plains of the Northern Territory's Tanami Desert, and the huge rock formations at Ayers Rock and Kata Tjuta.

The aircrafts dodged the deadly markers that had been on the land's face since before biblical record, taking a circuitous route over hundreds of miles in a matter of minutes through the Great Artesian Basin of Queensland, dropping low within the spectacular expanse of the Great Divide mountain range toward the Great Barrier Reef.

He squeezed her hand, and resisted the urge to bring it to his lips. This was what he'd wanted to show her, the lights on the ground, lines that marked man's earliest battles with the darkness, a breathtaking display of indescribable beauty amid profound struggle. And, yet, her team would be so far away from her in Sydney, down in the area of New South Wales . . . but given time, he'd show her the Victoria Falls on a private airborne journey in his arms, would show her beaches of unimaginable majesty . . . mountains that would steal her breath. Didn't she understand what resources he had at his disposal to show her over an eternity? But as soon as the thought entered his mind, he also knew that she didn't care about any of that.

Carlos looked straight ahead, no longer glimpsing her from the corner of his eye. The helicopters were descending and it was game time. No distractions allowed.

"It was beautiful," she murmured, her voice low and private, slicing through the helicopter drone.

She squeezed his hand and from the side opening in her glasses he could see that tears of appreciation had formed in her eyes, making them shine in the night before burning away. They drew his fingers to her cheek before he pulled his hand away from the softness of it. That she'd heard him meant the world to him, because from this point forward, she'd have to pick up on his senses, walk in lock-step with him, her every action tightly choreographed with his. Didn't she know that all the territory below didn't equal her value to him?

When the choppers touched down, he waited for the blades above to slow, and for an armed escort to open their door. The helicopters faced a huge stone castle built into the side of sandstone cliffs overlooking the Great Barrier Reef. Moonlight washed the rough beige surface pale blue, and the smell of the surf brought back intoxicating memories of Rio.

Sixty-six service personnel stood at attention at either side of the sixty-foot-wide central stairs, each waiting for his approach and inspection. Carlos got out first, and turned back to Damali. He gave her a glance to tell her to stay put, and walked with the armed entities toward the castle staff.

Row by row he walked by each individual—some vampire, some human helpers, from chefs to butlers, maids, couriers, and the like, his powers of detection keen. Finally satisfied that it was safe for her to join him, without looking back at her, he summoned Damali to his side. It was protocol; at his level he should be able to call her to him with just his will. As she neared him, he held out his hand, palm turned up and open for her to grasp it. Only when her soft heat filled his hand did he begin to relax.

"Councilman Rivera," a deep voice said, booming from the center of the huge staircase. The voice echoed in the night, giving way to a presence that materialized and began walking down the stairs.

The large vampire, who was obviously a Master, didn't look a day over thirty-five in human years. He stood six foot six, was formally attired in a black and white tux, his shock of strawberry blond hair flowing in the wind behind him as his presence parted the staff on the stairs. He stopped on the landing, gave Carlos a bow of deference, and then moved closer.

"Master McGuire," Carlos said with a nod. "Thank you for opening your main lair estate to us on such short notice." He assessed the other master quickly: died in his mid-thirties, impulsive, around since the eighteen hundreds, just after the previous Australian master was sunlight-outed by pirates.

"Think nothing of it," the tall Aussie said, momentarily appraising Damali while speaking to Carlos. "I am honored to have a council-level visit . . . with such lovely company."

"Permit me to introduce my wife, Damali," Carlos said, not the least offended when the host master took her hand in a grand sweeping gesture and kissed the back of it.

"Councilman," McGuire said, smiling broadly, "you are a very fortunate man." He dropped Damali's hand slowly and turned to the stairs. "My mate of eighty years, Evelyn," he said, gesturing toward the stairs.

Damali and Carlos kept their eyes trained on the place that gathered density until a long-stemmed honey-blond with *Playboy* bunny dimensions appeared in a dangerously revealing black sheath, and then slinked down the steps to stand by her husband's side. Sensuality exuded from her and was as toxic as snake venom . . . and had a way of making a man hold her gaze for a moment longer than was respectful. She had golden-brown cat's eyes, intense fire behind the glittering irises that let anyone with sense know she was as deadly as she was beautiful.

"Welcome," she murmured, looking Damali up and down, her smile seductive, suggestive before her eyes left Damali's body to rake Carlos's. "If there's *anything* either of you need during your stay . . . do let us know."

The Aussie gave Carlos a knowing smile. "No worries. Everything at this castle is at your disposal."

For a moment, neither male spoke—the offer wasn't reciprocal. The Aussie chuckled, but there was tension in it.

"I'm sure after your long journey from the States, you want a few moments to collect yourselves." He motioned to the service staff. "Settle in Councilman Rivera and his lovely wife. Bring his luggage to the head-of-state suite." Then he looked at Carlos, and allowed his gaze to linger a moment upon Damali before pulling it away. "We've left dinner in your room, sir, given the late hour. I can be found in my study, should you want to discuss a few state-related matters before you retire. Tomorrow, we will have a banquet proper. Do accept my utmost apologies at the lack of—"

Carlos held up his hand to stop his host's prattle, sensing that he was growing unnerved by his visiting councilman's few words. He watched the man's wife gently touch her husband's arm, as though trying to sense if her unaccepted invitation may have displeased their guests. Carlos issued her a look of total appreciation, and she smiled, seeming relieved. On a slow, deceptive inhale, the vocabulary of true diplomacy and detente from his throne knowledge came to the fore. He dropped the slang and replaced his urban vernacular with old world culture. Carlos played the role of his office to the max. He might be a newbie, but he was fucking good—the best . . . and not new to games at all.

"I am extremely pleased," Carlos said, in cultured tones, "and will join you in your study for a nightcap . . . after I settle my wife into our suite."

"You are more than gracious, sir," the Aussie said, and then was gone. Evelyn lingered only a moment, then dissolved away, her sexy smile the last to vanish.

Carlos touched Damali's arm as he sensed his limo finally coming down the long drive behind him, but never turned to look at it. The driver knew what to do with the dogs—let them guard at his front bedroom door and terrace. He was just glad that they'd eaten well before they arrived.

Awesome did not describe the environs he entered. Carlos glanced around as a silent human manservant, followed by two scantily clad maids, and a huge armed guard carrying their luggage, led him and Damali through the city-block-long foyer, past a huge central fountain that rose up out of the marble floor that had a pattern of Hell's seven levels inlaid. Just the expanse of the stairs alone was enough to make Carlos quietly give the Aussie props. Now this was handling one's business.

Knights of armor flanked the halls that led to an endless spiral of doors and polished banisters above him, and as he stood in the center of the first landing, the plush red carpet running down it like a thick tongue, he looked below him at the massive vampire-nation receiving rooms, hotel-sized banquet rooms, smoking parlors and gemstone-inspired stained glass.

This was what he was trying to explain to Damali. His Beverly Hills lair, plus several of his offshore villas, would fit into the Aussie's castle ten times. Everything was super-sized in Australia, and the wealth in the U.S. couldn't put a scratch in old-world money.

He nodded for the butler to proceed after they'd paused on the landing, just soaking in the ornate corridors beneath double-height cathedral ceilings that were wound at the crown moldings with gold leaf, wallpaper that seethed life . . . this motherfucker was so wealthy that the capillary pattern of veins in the walls pulsed blood. He saw Damali nearly reach out and touch it, but sent her silent censure. She couldn't show that she was the least bit impressed, lest she shame him. This castle belonged to an older master, true, but he was council, and should have had her in this type of setup already.

That reality made him focus on the other masters who would be in attendance at the meeting later. Just thinking of the Transylvanian diplomat made him feel his eyeteeth in his mouth. The bastard was arrogant, old as dirt itself, and wealthy as shit . . . plus he held disdain to an art form that only true bluebloods could dispense.

Yeah, Carlos reminded himself, none of them liked his quick descent to a throne and would have claws readied for him. But talk about rich territory . . . the castles in Europe were so opulent, especially the German, Austrian, and Dutch holdings, which had such blood spilled in the courtyards that a man might be able to go down on his knees and siphon it from the earth itself, if he'd wanted. France and London were ridiculous, as was Spain . . . no doubt about it, the European master was gonna be a problem.

The territories of Asia were like that, too. *Gothic rich.* Horrific wars that went back thousands of years to make Europe's time on the planet seem ephemeral—a damned flash in the pan, comparatively. The Chinese and Indian castles and lair estates demanded pure respect, even down in council chambers—just like the pyramids did.

But the Asian ambassador was cool, smooth about his holdings, didn't have to act cocky—there was no reason for him to be insecure, which is why he was also very shrewd . . . brother had developed some of the most effective methods of torture and had been around since the days of the Samurai. Yeah, in a few hundred years, he might be able to build his North American and South American line back up, get his holdings in order, and truly represent like he was supposed to . . . maybe take over one of the old Incan ruins and retrofit it . . . or perhaps, if his lady liked, go Mayan in his home state, Mexico . . .

Carlos kept walking, trying to remain relaxed as he watched Damali from a side-glance. If the African master showed, it would definitely come to a pissing contest. His region was so productive right now with bodies from wars, disease, and corruption that it made North and South America with the Caribbean—Carlos's territory—look like Disneyland. And buried deep in the Congo, with favor from council, that bastard might laugh in his face at the table.

See, women didn't understand shit like this. The crown

jewel where the big battle for the Armageddon, the regions Gog and Magog, plus the Middle East, would be annexed to the territory most worthy when the dust settled. He knew each one of the topside masters would want a word alone to lobby him for favor, or assassinate him for a shot at immediate descent. But he was equally disturbed at the way he could feel a dark, thunderous desire sweep through his woman. She liked this shit just as much as he did . . . the VIP treatment and living *very* large. He glanced at her. *You want this? I'll give it all to you in due time, baby—no holds barred. This is what I'd meant about power.*

She just smiled a very sly smile and kept walking.

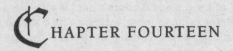CHAPTER FOURTEEN

"YOUR ROOM, Councilman Rivera," the butler announced, opening the wide French doors of the suite and standing back to allow Damali and Carlos to proceed ahead of him. He motioned for the henchman to bring in their luggage, and addressed the maids. "Let there be nothing that our honored guests call for that hasn't been supplied." He turned to Damali and Carlos. "Pull the bell tapestry, and they will be at your service."

The ebullient manservant waited as Carlos perused the villa-sized suite. A small Greek-styled fountain running blood with a Grecian stone love seat surrounding it was the focal point in the outer room. A long marble bar was to the left, and was filled with the black private-label bottles that he'd come to know by now contained blood. Tuscany-designed stools faced it, and just beyond the bar, two Egyptian carved stone doors opened out to a castle terrace. To his right was an overstuffed Louis the XVI–style sofa and matching chair upholstered in burgundy satin, with an armoire and German writing desk beside it. Just beyond the fountain was a long, eighteenth-century, plantation-style banquet table with full linen, ornate candelabra, and two high-back, midnight blue silk upholstered chairs.

The spoils of war, Carlos thought to himself, as he

checked the ornate stone doors that led to the terrace, coming away satisfied that the light seal on the room was adequate.

"Shall I turn down your bed for you before dawn?" the servant asked, his voice rich and inviting.

"No," Carlos said as he walked toward the bedroom, holding Damali's elbow, "but I do want to appraise the seal in there."

The butler nodded and followed the couple through the inner-room, double-steel doors that were engraved with Hell's crest, down five steps into the sunken inter sanctum. He pulled heavy burgundy drapes away from the terrace's vault doors and stood back as Carlos inspected the room.

Fully keening his senses to detect a possible threat, Carlos spun the heavy gold-plated airlock mechanism that allowed him to pass out of the room and onto the terrace through one ton of banker's steel. He glanced back toward Damali and addressed the butler.

"Can my wife close these easily?" he asked, not waiting for an answer as he strolled out to the terrace and glanced down the two-hundred-foot cliff-side descent into thunderous surf.

"To be sure, Councilman," the butler replied. "These have been balanced to Masonic-level specifications."

Carlos nodded, satisfied, and snapped his fingers to call his dogs. "I want one on the terrace and one posted outside in the hallway at all times—and only I feed them."

The butler again nodded, the small retinue of staff watching Carlos's every move, occasionally glancing at Damali. Carlos scanned the steepled ceiling over the bed, his eyes narrowing to be sure there was no light source that could cook them both at dawn, then his gaze slowly roved over the crème and burgundy raw silk wallpaper to ensure there were no hidden panels or secret doors that could be opened. He nodded to the butler to pull back the drapes surrounding the bed that sat in the middle of the floor fully curtained by thick Turkish tapestries, his gaze scanning the lush Moorish textiles on the double-wide king-sized bed.

His eyes took their time sliding over the exquisite Egyptian cottons, raw silks from Asia, and burgundy goose-down duvet. The bed sat up high on a three-foot solid marble pedestal, but after assessing it, he nodded. He just needed to first be sure that there was no portal beneath the bed.

The huge French armoire, antique dresser, and ladies' vanity sans mirror checked out. But the bathroom could pose unimaginable risks. He and the butler shared a knowing glance, and one of the maids came to Carlos's side. He leaned in to her throat and caught her scent as her eyes slid shut. He could feel her near ready to arch into his hold. Definitely vamp. She'd do.

"Would you mind turning on the water sources for me?" he murmured to her, giving Damali a glance to be cool and remain steady.

"As you like, sir," the female vamp said, her voice husky as she left his side, beckoning him with her eyes to follow her.

All burgundy marble surrounded them, gold fixtures looming out from the oversized, kidney-shaped Jacuzzi canopied by sheers. The maid ran the tap, and dipped her fingers in the thick spray as it gurgled loudly to demonstrate that no holy water sabotage had been committed, smiling when the tension left Carlos's body. Then she switched another lever so that pure blood ran into the tub, then pulled her hand back and licked her fingers. She then went to the double sink across the room and performed the same test, even testing the commode and bidet for him.

Upon his nod, the maid sauntered past Damali at the door and stood by the butler, her appraisal of Carlos nearly a challenge to the first lady.

"Thank you," Carlos finally said. "Everything appears to be in order."

"Do summon us, sir, should you or your lovely wife require anything before dawn."

Damali watched the staff back out of the main vault door, and then hastily exit the suite. She moved like someone punch-drunk—a little wobbly on her feet, staring at first one thing, then another, glancing back to Carlos, and then shaking her head.

"This is outrageous," she whispered.

He smiled. "Care to take a stroll on the terrace?"

He came to her side and ushered her to the smooth, centuries-old stone lookout post of the fort, watching the night wind lift her locks and caress her hair. He brought her to the railing and chuckled to himself as his dog got up grumbling at having to move to accommodate Damali.

Somehow the insistent pound of the surf, the sting of the salt air in the most precious hours of the night, drew his arms to encircle her while she stared out, her back melding against his chest . . . the smell of her hair an intoxicant.

"You happy?" he asked into the crown of her head as he kissed it.

"This is gorgeous," she murmured, closing her eyes. "At this height you almost feel like you're wind, part of it, as though you can fly."

"You can," he said, chuckling deeper in his throat, but was slightly disappointed when she shook her head no.

"You sure?" he asked, baiting her.

"This place can make you lose focus," she said wisely, but snuggled against him nonetheless.

"Ahhh . . . the mission," he said, his tone amused. "Maybe I was too hasty when I said I didn't want to be distracted by you while here, *mi tentacion*."

She chuckled low and sexy. "It was the security check that made me remember."

Carlos glanced back at the bed. "Yeah," he said on a long sigh. "Oh, man . . ."

"This joint ain't no joke, Carlos," she said very quietly, her tone cautious, breaking the mood as her body tensed. "It's built like a fortress."

He laughed, letting her go. "It *is* a fortress, baby. That's what I'd been telling you. All primary master lairs are. They're set up for battle." He turned her around, cradling the sides of her face so they could more easily transmit thoughts. *Nuit's lairs were nothing by comparison—because he'd lost favor, was rogue, and on the run.*

When she nodded, he dropped his hands to her shoulders.

The familiar embrace which always led to a kiss was definitely why he called her his temptation. There was so much more he'd wanted to say, but didn't dare chance it—especially not when she straightened his tie, and brushed a piece of invisible lint off his lapel, then touched his cheek.

The warmth of her palm radiated through his skin, and her eyes were so deep, dark, intense as she opened her gaze and sent back a quiet message. *I feel it, too . . . but I'm worried for you, baby. These bastards will try to kill you. I'm not trying to lose you on my watch.*

He smiled and kissed the inside of her palm, electrified by her protective instinct regarding him. He nodded. Indeed they would try to assassinate him. But it would sure be worth it. No telepathy needed. She smiled, gently removed her hand, and began walking back into the room. When she looked over her shoulder, he wasn't sure how to read the all-feminine message. Was that a yeah, okay? Or a yeah, I hear you, but no, not tonight? She shook her head, then chuckled at the faint disappointment that threaded through him.

"You hungry?" he said, trying to sound casual.

"Pulling out all the stops, Mr. Councilman?"

He had to laugh at himself. "Aw'ight. I'll stop." He went up to her and traced her cheek. *You like this, don't you?*

She smiled, which was enough of an answer. He watched her sit down on the side of the bed, sinking into the soft feathered oasis, then run her hand over the plush linens, luxuriating in the feel of the textures. He wanted to touch her like that. To pleasure her the way only one of his kind could. Surely she didn't want to give all that up . . . and not tonight?

Vaguely he remembered that the Aussie would be waiting for him down in the study. If he weren't a head of state, he would have made the bastard wait. But Damali needed to stop playing with him, because he wasn't about to go downstairs with an oral erection. The fact that she'd chuckled let him know she knew exactly what she was doing.

"You ain't right, woman," he said, smiling and running his tongue over his teeth.

"It's the castle," she murmured. "The energy here is so

dark, so all-consuming," she murmured. "Makes it hard to concentrate . . ."

Her comment snapped him back to awareness. "Yeah," he said, on guard. He closed his eyes and held out his arms, sensing their environment with total concentration. Just as he'd expected, every stone in the place was charmed down to the mortar, designed to protect the residing master at all times. Some stairs weren't real stairs, no rooms were impenetrable to the castle's owner, no seal was solid, unless McGuire wanted it that way.

It was having a drugging effect on Damali. Getting her high, sedating her survival instincts, making her so looped that she'd draw him into a sure seduction—that's what he'd felt coming from her in the halls! Normally Damali wouldn't care a damn about a gilded cage—wasn't her style. It would definitely make her open to another master's pull, just like it had fucked with his confidence as he walked the long corridors.

"Get up off the bed. Now," Carlos said, becoming further enraged as Damali looked up, dazed, unzipped the back of her dress and stared up at him.

"I'm impressed," he said to the nothingness. "But you're pissing me off." Dark energy concentrated within him, making the tips of his fingers and center of his palms burn as he spun slowly, sealing the lair with his own power against power, will against will, his council-level strength discharged with a crackling streak of fury that scorched the walls, the ceiling, the doors and terrace. The dogs bayed and howled while he released his protective seal around his temporary lair and all of those within it.

Every wall and surface instantly blackened, then normalized. Immediately he felt the sensual pull lift and the energy in the room calibrate to his command. He began walking the perimeter of the room as Damali stood on wobbly legs and zipped up her dress.

"What the hell just happened?" she whispered, her voice tense and her eyes cleared of the seductive haze.

"I'm gonna address it later," he said. "But the room was

charged, every carnal act ever performed in here left a residue." Carlos smiled. "That's cool. I'm gonna assume that our host did this to make our stay more comfortable," he said, going to her and holding her face. *But you and I know that sonofabitch did it to set me up, to totally distract me while I'm here.* "I'll have to let McGuire know that although I'm council-level, unlike the old boys, I don't need Viagra."

"Damn," she said, taking a short sip of breath.

He held her face tighter. *This is why I told you to stay by my side at all times. That if you have anything important to tell me, you do it like this. Understand?*

Satisfied when she nodded, he released his hold on her. But he watched her cock her head to the side and walk past him. What could she hear that he and his dogs couldn't? Then a light mewling sound made him almost run to catch her. He knew what it was before he saw it.

Pacing quickly to her, he rushed over to the large in-room dining table by the blood fountain. Damali's gasp was so visceral that it made him snatch her arm, spin her around hard, and physically cover her mouth with his hand. With his eyes he told her not to panic, but panic reflected back at him regardless. Slowly, he removed his hand from her mouth, his eyes steady on hers, as he lifted the large gold-domed serving tray cover and looked down. *Not now, D. Not now. Don't scream.*

"It's a baby," she said, her eyes darting to the door and toward the infant. "They delivered it on a gold platter."

"Listen to me carefully," he said low, controlled and slow. "Of course they did. You are the wife of a head of state, and they said they'd leave dinner in the room, *sí?*" He nodded to get her to follow his lead. "If you aren't hungry, you still have to sample it—" He stopped her gasp, snatching it in his fist on the wind. "Or it will be taken as a serious affront, to—"

She broke his hold, whirred toward the tiny bundle on the table, swept it up, although saying nothing. But her eyes said it all as she pressed the struggling thing to her chest, and then scanned the room. He could tell she was looking for an escape route, somewhere to flee, and he watched her back away from him, moving with the agility of a lioness as she stalked toward her luggage. *No, do not draw the Isis on me in here! Are you nuts? Come to me!*

A wave of panic rocked his system as he pried open her quickly closing mind. That crazy woman would actually attempt to rappel off the balcony—a two-hundred-foot drop over the Great Barrier Reef, baby in arm, Hell-dogs in an attack flight pattern after her? He put his hands on his hips and stared at her hard. *What you gonna do, hold the Isis between your teeth?*

You cannot have it! Game over, man! You all are fucking crazy—a baby? Oh, hell no!

Her mind was so strong and her words so fierce that he sat on the edge of the table, hoping his deliberate distance would calm her down.

Bring it to me, he told her after a moment. *I won't hurt it. Trust me.*

She flipped him the bird, and began cooing to the now bleating bundle. The sight of her transformation was disorienting, and the timing was profoundly bad. He could smell it, Neteru in full force, no vamp trace in her.

You have to nick its finger with the blade and press a dab of blood to your lips—then let me kiss you.

Her eyes widened in horror, but he was thankful that she didn't speak.

Listen, I don't do kids. He waited until she began to relax before probing her thoughts again. *But when I go downstairs, McGuire has to catch the scent off me . . . has to know we've fed.* Again, he waited until she glanced down at the infant and then back up to him, this time less unnerved. *That's the only way I can safely transport this baby out of here without starting an international incident tonight.*

It bothered him that she took her time retrieving the small Isis dagger from the Louis Vuitton trunk, as though she didn't completely trust him. But as he watched her kiss the tiny cheek, nuzzle it, and cradle the child in her arms, it did something to him. So strange a juxtaposition . . . her protectively holding the baby to her body while brandishing a weapon, her arm cocked, biceps drawn taut with the other arm. Her eyes were soft as she tenderly looked down at the baby. Then she shot him a lethal glance that told him she'd cut out his heart if he as much as blinked wrong. Damn, that was some powerful shit.

She walked closer to him, tucking the blade under her armpit so she could hold the infant more firmly. She gave her finger to the baby and a tiny fist gripped her index finger. When the baby brought her finger to its mouth to suckle, hot tears rose in Damali's eyes.

"Look at him, Carlos." Her words came out in a rush. "So innocent, and hungry, and scared. Oh my G—"

His fingers touched her lips. *Don't say it. Not here, ever.*

"How could they?" she whispered.

He glanced tensely at the walls. *This is what I was telling you would happen. Tomorrow there will be a banquet, and you are going to have to be cool—no matter what.* "It's the purest blood source, a delicacy. Hard to acquire, even for a vampire. Our host went to great lengths to provide this, honey. So, after we dine on some light hors d'oeuvres, I'll tuck you in bed. Then I'll be back later."

For a moment, she just stared at him, then nodded.

Cut the finger, she heard him say in her mind. *Just a small nick.*

Damali squeezed her eyes shut and shook her head no.

You have to do it. You're human. If I draw blood, I'll mark the child as a vamp helper for life. Just the aura of my energy could pollute the wound on a human this young. Feel me?

"Shit," she said in a tense whisper, then extracted the blade from under her arm.

Make a small cross on the pinky with your Isis, Neteru. This way its system will have a little more immunity to any sort of possession till I get it home. Then seal it with a kiss, from the Neteru, hand me the child so its smell will be on me, and kiss me so its blood will be in my mouth as well.

She didn't answer, just did what needed to be done. Her hands almost shook as the baby's wails escalated with the small cuts she made. But she followed his instructions to the letter, and pushed the child into his arms, wiping at hot tears, streaking her once-flawless makeup and breathing hard to keep herself from vomiting.

It was the hardest thing he had to do, silencing the piteous wails while the innocent twisted and writhed, trying to break free of the presence of evil. All babies had survival instinct, could feel the presence of harm, and were most closely connected to the Divine Source. Up to this point, he'd never seen himself as that—truly evil—until the child's screams rose to hiccupping cries. Every one of his nieces and nephews came into his mind as he put the child into a sleep trance. This was someone's future, someone's fragile heart he held, and its paper-thin throat was two inches from real fangs.

He shook his head in disgust as he ran his palm over the soft downy hair. A treasure . . . how could they sacrifice a baby when there was plenty of grown meat on the hoof, adults, that had lived and wanted to be vamps?

Carlos tilted his head; Damali's gasp passed through his skeleton as she pulled the blade to protect the baby and the child vanished; he hastily returned it to its parents.

He glared at her. *I turned my head to listen to its rhythm, smell its smell, and get a contact to where it was supposed to go! You oughta know me better than that.*

"I'm sorry," she yelled across the room, then checked herself. "I should have saved you some."

He turned and looked at her, and relaxed. Okay. Baby was catching on to how this game was played. Everything said aloud was part truth, part lie, the language of the masters of deception. Then she needed to play this to the bone. Let the host think they'd been caught off guard. That his snit over the bedroom thing was because it assumed he needed the extra boost in there—challenged his virility, thus offended him highly. Carlos smiled, placed his finger to his lips. *Wanna really bug them out?*

Damali smiled, and he loved that it was that wicked one from the old neighborhood when they'd game and bait other street racers into losing bets when they were kids.

He waved his arm and banged a chair against the suite's hallway door. He winked at her and crooked his finger, and she quickly walked over to him. Then he kissed her hard. "That thing had adrenaline all through it—pure adrenaline!" he bellowed. "You toyed with it long enough before you drained it dry, then didn't save me any?"

"Aw, baby," she said calmly, "I'll make it up to you later, I promise."

"Make it up to me now."

She covered her mouth and ran from him when he reached for her, and squealed when he sent the sofa crashing into the bar as he came after her. The sound of her heels clacking against the polished sandstone and her giddy laughter was music to his ears. He wanted her to loosen up, play, shake the nerves, because some seriously tense shit was about to go down soon—and baby had to be able to work the environment to her advantage. Then, again, truth be told, he needed the tension release just as much as she did.

"Now you're running from me?" he said, laughing hard, and trying to shake the image of the child in Damali's arms out of his head. Yeah, he had to keep moving. The way she'd held it so naturally, her eyes so tender, so intense, so ready to give her life to protect it. Just as he'd always imagined she'd hold his child . . .

He exploded several blood bottles at the bar, making her shriek, loving the sound of her voice.

"You know I don't play that!" he hollered across the room. "You're putting me in a bad mood for my meeting, woman."

"I'm so sorry," she said, her voice escalating in false alarm.

"I don't want any other vamp in here while I'm gone, or I'll take a limb! Go to bed. Wait for me. Don't even call the maid to clean up this mess!"

"Yes, baby," she said, winking at him and slinking into her bedroom, blowing a kiss over her shoulder. "I know I've been a very bad girl."

"Councilman," the Aussie said, standing as Carlos swept into the study. "Can I offer you a stein?"

Carlos nodded and sat heavily in the leather wingback chair before the man's huge, polished mahogany desk. "Absolutely, and thank you for the lovely surprise in my room," he said. "My wife thoroughly enjoyed it."

Carlos leaned forward and smiled, watching the nervous tension ease away from his host's face. His line of vision scanned the room, quickly sensing for any danger among the large stuffed animal heads, heavy walnut bookcases that held an extensive library, and across to the crackling fireplace that had an opening the height of a man. The room looked like it had been modeled after a combination of old European libraries and smoking rooms.

"She sounds like a handful," McGuire replied as he slowly assessed Carlos. He walked over to the long bar behind his desk to pour Carlos a drink. He peered over his shoulder, seeming unsure if it was safe to turn his back on his guest, then quickly uncapped a crystal decanter.

"She is," Carlos said, his awareness taut as he sensed for poison, his olfactory capability keened, while his drink was being prepared. Just a bit of colloidal silver would eat his insides out, but his expression remained amused. "She's feisty, still has a lot of Neteru in her," he said, knowing it was the most prevalent and tempting question in the Aussie's mind.

He watched McGuire sit down slowly, unabashed curiosity glittering in his moss green eyes. Carlos could see the man breathe in slowly, as if trying to control his inhales, as the scent of Damali coming off Carlos's body lit him up. Excellent.

"How on earth . . . Mr. Councilman . . . if you don't mind me asking?" The Aussie leaned forward and handed the drink to Carlos with caution, tilting his head, sniffing hard as he withdrew. He raised his skein in a gesture of respect, and then took a quick swig from it.

Carlos returned the gesture with a smile. "Crazy woman was fighting were-demons in Brazil, took a mortal wound, had almost bled out when I found her. Was still trying to swing the Isis at me when I got to her. Her immune system was compromised as her body went into death shock, but timing of the bite is everything. I beat death to the punch while her defenses were down." Carlos shook his head and chuckled. "Neteru to the bitter end."

His host nodded, and took a long, deliberate sip from his skein. "She's trailing it all through the house," he whispered, swallowing hard.

"Yeah," Carlos said, standing, going to the window. "Died with it in her system . . . will, at times, make you do foolish things—but that's part of her allure. She wears it for me now as a signature fragrance that she conjures." He glanced at McGuire over his shoulder, and looked down at his drink. Yeah, they had to get this shit straight so it was clear. Reach for her and you're dying for placebo. "That's why I don't travel with an entourage anymore. Gets too messy; a waste of energy, and my dogs were becoming gorged." He looked up at McGuire. "I would hate to have an incident in the castle. While I'm sure *you* understand, we do have a few older foreign ambassadors who might not. Let's not have any confusion."

McGuire hesitated, fully comprehending the threat. "Oh, the castle is a sure sanctuary for you while you visit, sir."

"Good." Carlos nodded and came back to his seat and gestured for the Aussie to relax. "Do you have any particular regional problems that you'd like me to bring to the council table after my visit?"

The Aussie stood and began pacing slowly near his desk with his hands behind his back. "Of course, you're busy, and I'm honored that you've even asked, especially after your long travel here, but, uh, the Aborigines, their prayer lines have carved up my territory so badly. It's an old regional problem, but my previous entreaties to the council have gone ignored as a low priority for them. I've been lobbying council since the nineteen-eighties, when our drug trafficking operations really needed to cross those lines at will. When flying, you had a butcher at it, right?"

"That's a bitch," Carlos said, raking his fingers through his hair, while trying to sound empathetic. Now came the bargain for the shaky promise of support. "I saw them—just crisscrosses your whole region, and so old they glow." Carlos stood and went to the window.

"My point exactly. They're like electric fences. I need to annex some well-trod areas where the lines are not as lethal. Lost two good vamp drivers last week and was mad as a cut snake. My pilots have all gone blind; they have to sense their way in. Makes transporting lucrative products overland a shipping hazard." The Aussie went back to his chair and sat with a thud and waited as Carlos slowly found his seat.

Both men's eyes locked across the desk. Carlos could feel the Aussie siphoning information from the Dananu language before speaking. It morphed daily, and it took lower levels a moment to calibrate to it—lest they offend a higher rank by misspeaking even in the smallest way. So he waited, watching strengthened respect dawn in his host's eyes as McGuire picked up the new strand of Spanish that ran through the negotiation syntax.

The Transylvanian's territories are vast, and have been coveted for a long time by many. The Aussie didn't blink as he spoke slow and easy.

Carlos wrapped his mind around the harsh guttural tones of the familiar language.

That is a significant concentration of power, Carlos replied, *much like Africa.*

Stunned, the Aussie nodded as his will fractured and then regrouped. *You would consider new realignments?*

Mark Twain wrote that "Satan made Sydney" . . . he quoted an unknown traveler; I believe perhaps one of us who actually knew, sí?

You are very progressive, Mr. Chairman. As I'm sure you know, your youth was not fully appreciated in the descent by the other masters, but they have overlooked your shrewd forward thinking.

De nada. Carlos stood, feeling McGuire's will begin to bend, then twist out of his hold. *A sudden concentration of power is what made Fallon Nuit. We cannot have that in the empire again. Transylvania concerns me, as does Africa. But we will not discuss China—too powerful and too old to take by storm.* Carlos moved to the window again, his hands behind his back as he studied the moon.

McGuire nodded. *True. But Transylvania, especially the Russian provinces and the old Czech Republic, concerns us all,* the Aussie said, his gaze level at Carlos's back, but weakening. *Thank you, for even considering my request,* he added quickly, then summarily disengaged the negotiation in Dananu and pulled out of the negotiation-lock.

Carlos waited, allowing the man to collect himself. The exchange was no joke. It took serious focus just to seem unflustered by it. It hadn't helped that McGuire was a little high from Damali's scent. Carlos returned to his chair, sitting down, then leaned back casually and breathed out a slow, unseen exhale.

"Tomorrow evening," McGuire said brightly, appearing recovered, "once the other masters have arrived, we have something special planned."

Carlos made a tent with his hands before his lips, his elbows resting on the high arms of the chair, and kept his eyes on the man behind the desk. He didn't like surprises. "Talk to me," he said, and then smiled.

"We've got this game here called the Masters Cup Hunt." The Aussie stood, smiled and looked out of the window. "In the heartland, the dirt is red—iron ore—nothing but rocks, sandstone flats, goes on for miles—it's the bloody core of the continent."

Intrigued but wary, Carlos stood and went to the window again to look out. "Extreme sports in the desert plains?"

"Tomorrow is a full moon, and the were-roos can only come up to feed then. Six-hundred-pound beasts. Can flip a Range Rover with their tails." The Aussie chuckled. "It's bloody beautiful huntin', mate. A man of your prowess would love this. The feed after the hunt is awesome . . . and the ladies love it."

The Aussie had definitely been compromised by the negotiation and the scent of Neteru. He'd dropped all formalities, and his thick Australian brogue almost slurred. Most excellent.

"Objective and wager?" Carlos took his time showing enthusiasm. Street sense told him this was a good place to get smoked and have it look like an accident. But he needed to know more, had to understand how they might possibly come at him. *Relax, McGuire . . . take the bait.*

McGuire laughed. "Every man has to put a piece of land, or a territory on the table. Somethin' sweet that he's willing to gamble, against somethin' he *really* wants to win . . . like a barmaid's blush."

"Rules of engagement?"

"A human driver, no intervention, unless crossing prayer lines is imminent."

The two men stared at each other for a moment.

"Lost a few championship drivers when their Jeeps or Range Rovers crashed. Human drivers can't see the lines, so the master riding shotgun has to help steer while using only conventional weapons—crossbow and silver-tipped arrows—to bring down the were. Those bloody bastards breed like vermin in the region. Incineration is ten points; tackle and chain it alive, or behead it before it burns, twenty." The Aussie wiped his nose with the back of his hand and shuddered from the increasing effect of Neteru in the castle. "All while moving between eighty to hundred miles per hour.

"Ugly sort, too," McGuire went on. "Huge fangs, drooling acid, thirteen-inch claws that they can't retract, strong as bloody hell. They use portals to go underground, then pop up outta nowhere to flip ya. But we gotta make the game interesting. You can't use your powers unless you're in mortal danger. Then, you can use flight to keep away from the lines, but you lose what you've put on the table. Winner takes all. You'll love it."

"What time do we play?"

The Aussie's grin widened. "From sunset till two A.M. The course runs from where there's a human sacred rock formation, Uluru—Ayers Rock, goes up for eleven hundred feet, glows red, changes color during the day the humans tell us, and is covered in twenty-thousand-year-old prayers that will fry your ass if you bump it. The whole course runs to the other marker, Kata Tjuta—the Olgas, fifty-three kilometers west, to the sacred human stone markers, thirty-six gigantic rock domes that hide gorges and crevices. Fucking incredible, Mr. Chairman, if I do say so, myself."

"And while we're out, the ladies?"

"Oh, mate, it's way too taxing on a female. They watch from the choppers. Makes 'em—"

"I hear you," Carlos said, holding up a hand. This could allow him to get them all together, even before the concert. With a blood sport going on, it would be easier to detect allegiances, if any. And with adrenaline pumping through their systems, if one of them bit his man, Berkfield, he'd smell it for sure. Against his better judgment, Carlos found the allure of it thrilling, but what was more essential was the fact that it presented an opportunity to take out an opponent and make it seem like an accident. If he could do that, then the threat level on Damali's whack plan would be reduced. Carlos chuckled. "My problem will be trying to figure out what I'm willing to put on the table."

The Aussie smiled. "Sir, you have many assets that I'm sure would bait the foreign ambassadors . . . and I know you don't doubt your own abilities, do you?"

Carlos's deep laughter filled the room. "I never doubt my own abilities, *hombre*." He knew where his host was going, but wanted the man to tell him out of his own mouth. It was always best to ferret out for sure where an adversary was coming from.

"If you put your wife on the table, I'm sure no one would be offended, sir." McGuire took a deep swig from his stein, watching Carlos's reaction over the rim of his cup.

Carlos smiled. "*I'm* offended," he said after a pregnant pause that made the Aussie set down his cup with care, "that no one would ask me first for my council seat."

The Aussie choked and spit out his blood. "That's not on the table, is it?"

"No," Carlos said, standing. He walked away from the table, dismissing the comment. "I'm just surprised that wasn't your first request."

Carlos could feel the Aussie's penetrating gaze on his back and he turned around with a smile. "But I understand. She is magnificent." Carlos shook his head and walked back to the desk. "You're high, McGuire, so I'll take your request as a compliment."

"Thank you, sir," he sputtered, trying to regain his composure. "I meant no offense. Just admiring one of your finest assets."

Carlos's expression hardened. "Just so you know, any other time that kinda shit will get you killed in your own home."

When the color drained from McGuire's face, Carlos sighed. The man wiped his nose again with the back of his hand.

"You might want to bargain with the Transylvanian ambassador for some of his estates, but do not ever bet against me," Carlos said, no threat in his tone, just amusement over the proposed wager. "I'm telling you that because you're cool. Not quite like the rest." A slow chuckle of appreciation bubbled up. "Damn, man, you just flat-out told me—I like the honesty in that. You Australians are all right."

Relief swept through McGuire and he laughed with Carlos. "You're gonna make my old lady put me out in the daylight. Already got her in chains in the basement, the scent is making her chuck a berko—she's totally wonky. Before your wife ate, she was begging me for a ménage à trois, or couples . . . and I told her I'd see what I could do, would propose it to you man-to-man later. Then after your woman put on her perfume to get ready for bed, Evie began screaming madness about your wife being a human, and me being daft. But I told her that if her jealousy made her say anything that offends, even after eighty years, I'd rip 'er heart out myself."

"I've told Damali that she had to tone down her arousal, but we've only been together a few months and she still likes what the fragrance does to me," Carlos said, laughing and slinging an arm over his companion's shoulders.

When the other master slightly stiffened in reflex, Carlos gave him a relaxed tug, holding him firm and slipping into casual urban language to bond them. If his host thought that he only spoke that way around him, then it would give him a false sense of security; make him feel closer to Carlos than the other masters. "It's cool man, chill. I wasn't coming in for a kill." He wanted McGuire to tell him more about this new variable neither he nor Damali had considered—the female vamps.

McGuire audibly let out a breath, turned and shook Carlos's hand. "Mr. Councilman, you're all right. A fair cobber, no tight-arse."

To this Carlos could only laugh. "We're both young men, and our territories are relatively new—not like the old boys in the other sectors, as regions go. Both territories were settled by their fair share of criminals, no doubt we hail from that, too, in our former lives; were never bluebloods." He eyed the master beside him. "But young or old, power is power, man. Believe that shit."

A deep resounding belly laugh came from the Aussie, and he threw his head back, fangs glistening. "I thought this visit was going to be a torture—since we're speaking freely, mate." Excitement shone in his merry eyes. "After the hunt, we could jog the choppers through the Outback in the Southern territory, and cross over to hit Sydney, which is just a few clicks away, maybe sail back up the coast to Queensland. Aw, Rivera, Sydney has the best dining . . ."

Alarmed at the prospect of taking four masters and their entourages through a densely populated city, with a Guardian team to arrive shortly, and Damali in tow, Carlos politely declined. "Let us savor the experience and try not to squeeze everything into one night, my friend. We could find ourselves bloated and in the sun that way. Then the older dignitaries would have every right to call us reckless."

"True words," McGuire agreed. "All righty, then, we'll do the formal pomp and circumstance banquet here after the hunt, get our wits for the next night; we can do Sydney after your lady's concert. Now *that* is going to be a night to remember."

"Much better plan," Carlos said, and resumed walking them both out of the study.

The Aussie paused as they stood at the bottom of the main staircase, looked up, and closed his eyes. "She actually drew the Isis on you, mate?" He shuddered, and rubbed his mouth, but his fangs didn't retract.

Carlos chuckled and allowed his voice to dip sensually, a new lie forming in his mind. "Yeah . . . but that stays just between us. She's got it on her."

McGuire opened his eyes and stared at Carlos. "You lucky bastard," he whispered.

"Since we're cool," Carlos said slowly, watching the Aussie practically writhe with anticipation, "I can send her to your room one night, with both the Isis and the dagger in her hand."

"Don't game me like that, mate," he said as he swayed in Carlos's hold. He looked at him hard, but his eyes were practically pleading. "You serious?"

"Watch my back on the hunt, and I'd have no option but to fulfill at least one of your desires. I told you we were cool."

The Aussie closed his eyes, breathed in deeply, and shuddered again. He opened his eyes and cast a wistful glance up the staircase. "She'll wear the fragrance, too, won't she?"

"Of course," Carlos murmured.

"You're gonna make me kill my mate for her."

"Do what you have to do, but the offer stands . . . if you want it."

They both stared at each other for a moment.

"When?" The Aussie's breaths were so irregular now that he put his hand over his chest as though fighting to concentrate on the normally involuntary reflex.

"After the concert," Carlos said carefully. "I don't know if I'll be able to part with her myself after the hunt." McGuire nodded. "At the banquet, we're all gonna be amped. Just make sure that nobody rushes me for her. I'll dust her myself before I allow any other master to just take my shit."

"Of course," the Aussie said with authority. "It's a matter of honor." Then he smiled. "And I, for one, definitely don't want you to dust her before I've been with her."

Carlos extended his fist for a pound. The Aussie just looked at it, seeming unsure what to do.

"Like this, man," Carlos said laughing, showing the foreigner how to give back a pound. "That means we're boys, cool . . . we blood. *Mi casa es su casa* type of shit. You watch my back; I'll watch yours. What I got, I'll share . . . if you just be cool."

"Done," the Aussie said.

"Cool."

"Tell her I'm honored," the Aussie murmured.

Carlos just nodded. "Treat her right, and we'll be peace."

"I'll do her right, sir." His gaze was fastened to the staircase, then went to the ceiling where their suite was. "I will not dishonor this *rare* gift, I assure you."

"I'm going to bed," Carlos said, breaking the seduction trance. "Talking about this is working me like daylight."

McGuire this time offered his fist first. "Catch you later, mate. I'm right there with you. *Mi casa* definitely *es su casa* . . . and if you ever want Evie, or anything else I've got, just let me know. No worries."

CHAPTER FIFTEEN

———

FEELING ANXIOUS about the bargain he'd just made, Carlos abandoned the stairs and made a hasty transport to the suite. He whirred through the shut door in a cloud of black smoke and saw Damali standing next to the sofa in a battle stance.

"What's wrong with you?" he asked as he paced over to the bar. "We need to talk."

She lowered her blade. "You okay? Why'd you whirl in here like that? The Australian piss you off that bad?"

"No, he was cool," Carlos replied, glancing at the walls. "McGuire and I understand each other. He's an ally." He saw the shock on her face. "Come here," he said. "Please."

When she got close enough to him, he cupped her cheek and transmitted what she needed to know. Damali's eyes widened, she stepped back, and threw a punch that he almost didn't duck in time.

Pure Neteru stained the air red. Damali stood, legs wide, weight balanced, knees bent, sword in both hands, and her eyes lit with rage.

He turned away from her and held onto the bar for support, breathing through his mouth. "You are going to have to calm down, baby, and let me explain."

She marched up to him and grabbed the back of his hair in her fist. *Talk to me! Now! Because the hell I'm going to his room—unless it's to cut out his heart!* Then she dropped her hold on him.

He looked up slowly, feeling a thin trickle of perspiration run down the side of his face. He reached out and cupped her jaw. *It's not what you think. His guard will be down and he'll be unarmed and you'll have your blade on you.*

"Oh," she murmured, grudgingly, and then began to relax. "Okay."

She reached out to transmit again, but he caught her wrist and held it before her hand could touch his cheek.

"Give me a minute, all right?" he said slowly, then dropped her wrist.

Their attention whipped to the door when they heard a loud commotion in the hallway. His Hell-hound was barking wildly. It sounded like a tornado was tearing apart everything in its path. Suddenly it seemed to descend and they heard glass breaking and furniture being tossed about. The dog calmed its complaint to a snarl.

"What the—"

Carlos pulled her to him hard, covered her mouth with a kiss, both hands on either side of her head, locking her to him. *McGuire. You've saturated the air. But he's obviously a man of his word. Probably went to go find his wife.*

Damali twisted out of the kiss as a bloodcurdling scream rent the air. "Sounds like he's killing her," she whispered.

"Probably is," Carlos said, his breathing labored.

"What?" Damali's eyes went to the door, then came back to Carlos. "Why?"

"I would, too," he said, his smile showing her a hint of fang.

She put her hand in the center of his chest and said, *That doesn't make sense.*

He covered her hand and nodded. *Oh, baby, yes it does . . .*

"You seemed angry when you came up here." She slipped her hand from his hold.

He shook his head no slowly. "No. I was a lot of things, but angry wasn't one of them."

"Can you just tell me the whole conversation, coherently?"

Again he shook his head slowly. "Not right now I can't." His gaze scored her, then trailed down to the Isis.

"Why not?"

"It's a matter of honor," he said evenly.

Her hand went to her hip. "Whose?"

"Yours," he said in a low voice. He hadn't moved, his eyes now slowly trailing back up her arm to her throat. "Damali . . . back off for now." It sounded like a half-hearted request. "Please."

He could feel her mood lighten as she paced away from him a few feet. He walked out onto the terrace; he needed some air. He heard her footsteps behind him and sighed. But he allowed her hand to rest on his shoulder.

In fits and starts his mind tried to tackle the problem. The visit to the council to get a passport, the inspection, the ball of nerves this whole ordeal inspired, then Damali's fluctuations, then having to go head-to-head with a strong master, and now a hit of pure Neteru—all of it was wearing him out.

He sent fleeting transmissions, like slow sips, as not to batter her senses. If he came at her full throttle, he'd render her a vegetable, would fry her brain. The power struggle contained in a council to master negotiation was lethal to a human being, and he had no idea if even a Neteru could handle it. He even told her that, and could feel her body relax, then tried to communicate as best he could the way negotiations had gone down. The sender had to revisit the sensations in order to broadcast them. He was still feeling the aftershocks, and with Neteru in the air, it was no wonder McGuire had thundered down the hall in search of a female.

"Wow," she whispered, awe in her voice.

"Yeah," he murmured, trying not to howl at the moon. Then he chuckled, the laughter a tension release. "Had to re-member a few good episodes, girl, to make the offer worth-while. You will be nice to the man, won't you?"

They shared a private smile, and she nodded. "I'll do

him the way he deserves to be done," she said for any spies to hear.

Carlos smiled, but it was strained. Watching her play the game so good was not helping his condition in the least. But he was proud of her, knew she'd be able to smoke McGuire with one blade stroke. If not, well . . . he'd have to rescind the offer and rip out the man's heart. Nah, it wouldn't even come to that. McGuire's nose was wide open. This was a sure bet.

Peeping over her shoulder toward the door sheepishly, she smiled and shook her head. "Dead or alive, you know men are crazy, right?"

"Dead or alive, you know women are treacherous, right?" Carlos stared out at the moon. "Y'all make promises you don't keep, change your minds on a dime, and take a man through changes. You know that, right?"

"Like y'all don't? Beside . . . it's not a change, it's a bittersweet transition."

They both laughed, and she took his hand and led him inside as the timer locks began to engage to seal the suite. Safely shut in, he stood with her before the gurgling fountain, then began putting the room back together so no evidence of the damage could be seen. He had to do something to distract himself.

"It's late and we should probably go to bed."

He smiled as she walked in front of him, with the blade still in one hand, toward the bar. She took down a bottle of blood from the wine rack and then walked toward the bedroom. "But first, you *definitely* need to get something to eat."

"Yeah, I do," he said, his tone playful.

She ignored him and went down the steps—he had no choice but to follow her, then sealed the door behind them. She set the bottle down on the dresser and spun the locks on the terrace door, then closed the drapes. He didn't move toward the bottle, just stood transfixed as she walked around the room giving him wide berth, then sat slowly on the edge of the bed.

Half of him wished that she'd transform one more time; the other half of him was glad that she was back to her old self again.

"This is going to be a long day," he said, finally finding the will to walk over to the bottle and open it.

"I wouldn't want to make you vulnerable in a castle with a competing master," she said, not looking at him as she stretched out on top of the covers and tucked her blade next to her.

"I think he's distracted at the moment," Carlos said, taking a swig and leaning against the dresser, his eyes never leaving her voluptuous form.

"Never can be too sure," she replied, smiling. "But tell me about these other guys we're up against."

He took another healthy swig and swallowed it hard. "Is this what happens to a man once he gets married?" He'd evaded the question and delighted in her smile, the way it played on her lips as she tried to think of a quick comeback. Every instinct in him told him he needed his rest and should be regenerating for a major battle of wills that evening. But it was the way the soft candles lit her skin, and the way she glanced at him shyly . . . and there was just something so erotic about that blade being in bed with her, too.

"Tell me about the other masters, Carlos."

He sighed. "You've already met the Aussie, who is young compared to the others. Not much of a threat. But the one who rules the Asian continent has been around since the Ming dynasty, and they're as rich as shit. They've got resources like you wouldn't believe, D, and *thousands* of human helpers because the population density in his feeding grounds is ridiculous—just teeming with humanity. Have you seen the size of Asia? Plus, heroin . . . He and his first wife, Lai, are as old as shit, and shrewd as hell, but don't look a day over thirty. You think Shabazz has some martial arts moves . . . sheeit. This guy is pure lightning. His woman ain't no joke, either. Their shape-shift preference is the dragon; screw some panther or wolf transformation. Their asses breathe fire when pissed off."

Damali sat down on the bed slowly. "Who else?"

"There's the Transylvanian and his wife. He's a master strategist, has garnered more assets than the others, even though he's not as old. He's only been around since the sixteen hundreds—a ruthless sonofabitch descended from Dracula. He uses mind games, human armies, and has pretty much conquered a significant part of the world. Power grab for power grab, he's the one that most concerns me, not that the others aren't formidable. What he lacks in physical strength he's made up for in mental energy."

She raked her fingers through her locks and stared at the floor. "Cool," she said flatly, trying to quell her nervousness.

"But you stay away from that African bastard, hear me?"

Damali looked up. The tone of Carlos's voice stunned her.

"I'm serious, D. He's been around since the pharaohs and—"

"Do *not* tell me you're jealous?" Damali shook her head.

"I'm not jealous," Carlos said louder than he'd intended. "I don't care if that motherfucker can drop ten inches of battle fang and has wonders of the world built in his and his wife's name! So what if he's got pure gold and diamond mines, and shit. What do I care? I ain't worried about him transforming into a Sphinx, or some shit. Fuck all that, I got something for his ass if he goes there. The point is, he's got like three hundred wives, but still is always looking for the next one to be *the one*. So, I don't care if his moves were recorded on ancient scrolls or in the damned *Kama Sutra*. I ain't jealous. Feel me? But, if he pushes up on you, if any of them do, all bets are off. I'll—"

"Be cool and do this the way it needs to be done, Smooth," she said, exasperated. Like she would go off with some master vamp just because he had longer . . . fangs than Carlos. It was ludicrous. "Go to sleep, man."

"Aw'ight," he said, pushing himself away from the

dresser. "You stay on your side of the bed and I'll stay on mine."

"Liar," she said, with a sultry smile.

Carlos was in a truly foul mood when he woke up. She knew he was irritable from tossing and turning beside her all day, but that's how it had to be—no sex until they got to a safe place. She also didn't care if meeting the other masters was making him trip. All she could do was watch him stalk around the suite in his hunter gear. Fatigues, a matching safari hat, bowie knife, combat boots, and a vest loaded with stakes. She shook her head. Men.

Damali let her breath out hard and began rooting in the trunk for something to wear. Ignoring him, she went into the bathroom, closed the door, and turned on the tub. *Save it for the hunt,* she thought grouchily and chuckled to herself when she heard him mutter something back.

There were several problems with the plan—A, she knew she had to get to her team to go over this whole concert madness one more time to be sure everything went down smoothly, B—she and Carlos had to live through one more night in the house of horrors, and C—she hadn't been in full combat with another master since Nuit, and she'd gotten lucky dusting Vlak. Now *four* of them would be converging upon the castle. This was not good. Why in the world would he have allowed her to talk him into something this crazy?

She took her time bathing, thinking, delaying the inevitable. Images of the baby were firmly implanted in her brain. Yeah, she had to clean this joint out.

"Any night now," Carlos hollered, growing impatient. "We're having breakfast with the McGuires, you know."

Damali almost laughed. Breakfast with the McGuires indeed. Weren't the 'hood rat and the orphan being quite social?

"All right, all right," she said, stepping out of the bath and wrapping a thick Turkish towel around her. "I still have to dress and put on my makeup." That's when she remembered that there wasn't a single mirror in the castle. She swore, then shrugged, resigned to do her best.

She peered out of the bathroom door and could see Carlos on the terrace. "Can I talk to you a minute?"

"Yeah, D, but hurry up," he said, sounding surly. "The other diplomats will be here soon."

When he didn't move and continued to give her his back, she went to him, too disgusted for words, and touched his shoulder. "I meant can I talk to you?" she repeated.

He still didn't turn around, just kept watching the surf. "Then put on some damned clothes, first."

"Ouch," she said and withdrew from him. She glanced around at nothing, tasting her mouth, cool with fresh mint. "What does a councilman's wife wear to a masters' hunt?"

"I don't know!" he bellowed, and strode into the suite, slamming the terrace doors closed behind him.

She was so sick and tired of his moods and him bossing her around that she could scream. But she tried to remember that his nerves were fried. The masters' hunt, plus everything else, was freaking him out . . . but like she wasn't on edge, too. Finding a calm place in her mind, she called him again. "Come here," she said gently, but her tone was firm.

Begrudgingly, he came to her and touched her cheek without looking at her, keeping his line of vision on the wall.

One—I haven't eaten human food or had any water in twenty-four hours, and I'm starved. I'm also afraid to drink out of their taps. Two—they can't see me eat in here. Three— I can't see my reflection, because there aren't any mirrors, so I need you to dress me. Four—I'm worried sick that you'll get hurt tonight. Five—if you do, then I'll be in a castle with four serious world masters and their wives. Six—I have to get to my team. Seven—

He snapped his fingers and dressed her, and then touched her face again. *I cannot feed you in here; they'll pick up the scent if I bring you something from the human servants' kitchens. Even water poses a risk around old masters. The best I can do is play it off and say you have to go to meet your band to prepare, and I suggest you fill up while with them, then I'll have to figure out a way to get you a swig of blood under radar to chase it.*

"Eeewww . . ."

He held the bond. *At least rinse your mouth out with it, and dab a bit at your throat . . . then tell them that you ate at a good restaurant at the hotel. But this was what I was trying to tell you, D. I don't like variables. Neither one of us thought about the human food problem. That's why I was so against this—*

"All right," she muttered, cutting him off. She didn't want to hear I told you so. "If that's the best you can do, cool." She couldn't focus on that right now and shifted her attention. She sent him a mental note about what she wanted to wear, then looked down at her clothes, and had to admit she was impressed. He'd put her in a pair of low-cut, fawn-suede, flair leg pants that laced up the front where a zipper might be, and a nice pair of Prada mules. Cool. She liked the pants, but they were gonna argue for sure about the top. That she had not asked him for. A tank top was what she'd ordered. She was not sashaying down there in a leather bustier, even though it did match the pants.

"I was gonna give you a silk top, but for the crowd we're meeting, this is better."

"Yeah, right," she muttered, hating the fact that he was probably right—but also knowing that he liked it just as much as the dignitaries would. "Makes me look hoochiefied, Carlos."

He laughed, and she was glad he did. It broke the tension, made his more suave control come to the fore, and he was definitely gonna need that down there.

"My makeup okay?"

He tilted his head to the side and shrugged. "What do I know? I'm just a guy."

"Come on, stop playing."

He chuckled harder and traced her face with one finger. "All right. I liked the look you had yesterday."

She could feel her shoulders drop two inches from relief.

"Bring both the Isis and the dagger," he said, creating a low-slung snakeskin holster for it around her hips by placing both of his hands on them.

"They'll let me bring it in the chopper?"

"I think McGuire would appreciate it . . . and oh, yeah, he told me to tell you he was honored that you liked his castle—do mention that I told you." *You'll need the weapons in case one of the females attacks.*

"All right, baby," she said, her eyes narrowed. *But if one of those bitches rushes me, it's on.*

Damali held Carlos's arm as they followed the butler to the wide deck off the dining room, her eyes scanning their surroundings as they passed through the elaborate rooms. A predator could be anywhere. As soon as the thought entered her mind, she could feel Carlos's bicep tense.

"G'evening," McGuire said, standing as the couple entered and the butler quietly slipped away.

"G'evening Master McGuire," Damali said after Carlos nodded, using her most courteous voice. He, too, was dressed in combat fatigues, matching black safari hat, and black shades. She glanced at his mate, Evelyn, her white silk Ellen Tracy pantsuit fluttering in the wind, and wondered how the female vamp still existed. But up in the chopper, she could be an asset. "Evelyn, good evening. Thank you for hosting us here. Our stay has been lovely."

Damali slipped out of Carlos's light hold and slid into the seat he held out for her.

"Good evening, Mistress Rivera," Evelyn said, but there was no threat in her tone as the female vampire moved closer to her. "I am so glad to have you grace our humble house."

Damali glanced at Carlos and then toward McGuire. This was not what she'd expected.

"Lady McGuire," Carlos said, taking her hand, kissing

the back of it slowly, while looking up into her eyes. He held her gaze for a moment, then let her hand fall away. "Thank you for enduring any disruption to your household that our impromptu visit may have caused."

"The pleasure was all mine," she breathed, smiling at him, and then giving Damali a sidelong glance. "You must be starved." Evelyn motioned for the butler, and he immediately brought two large decanters and fresh goblets.

Damali held up a hand and begged off breakfast. "I will feast after the hunt," she said smoothly. "I like to stay . . . hungry when so much excitement perfumes the air." She smiled. "Makes the feed taste so much better. Besides, Carlos loves it so when I suffer waiting for him."

This seemed to appease the lady of the house, because Evelyn gave her a sly pout. "Ah, Councilman Rivera, she's delicious."

Damali looked at the master of the house out of the corner of her eye. An expression of utter appreciation spread across his face. There weren't many vamps who could control the hunger so well. But she had to give them the impression that she was so much more than an average vamp.

"You know," Evelyn finally murmured, easing in closer, "we ladies should get to know one another, since our husbands are getting along so well."

Carlos and McGuire were now deeply entrenched in talk about the upcoming hunt. She wished she had baby Isis in her hand.

"Yes, I agree," Damali said, pleasantly. Her mind worked on a strategy as she stared into Evelyn's gorgeous but deadly eyes. She could feel the vamp trying to siphon her for information. Okay, so if that's how she wanted to play. Offering Evelyn a bit of juicy insider gossip, Damali laid a trap to form an alliance, but to also let the female know that she could take her, if Evelyn tried her.

"You know," Damali said in a conspiratorial murmur, "Carlos made me after he was turned council level, and—"

"What?" Evelyn sat back in her chair, all conversation at

the table stopped. Then she lowered her eyes and her voice became tense with fear. "Mistress . . . I didn't know. Please forgive my insolence."

Damali blinked twice, confused, but went with whatever had freaked out the female vamp. "It's nothing," she said as calmly as possible. Then she noticed the shocked expression on McGuire's face.

"And she says it's nothing?" Evelyn looked up and glanced at her husband. "Harold, why didn't you tell me he'd made her a *female master*?"

"Councilman," the Aussie master said, his eyes wide with amazement, "I thought you made her before you descended . . ."

Carlos shot Damali a glance that told her to stay calm. *Play it. Work it.*

Damali reached over and smoothed the long, silky blond hair off Evelyn's shoulder. Just the touch alone seemed to stir her. "Darling, of course he did. It was mortal combat, we were both armed to the teeth, and I went down with my blade swinging. I'd nearly bled out." She paused, sensing the vamps' interest in the tale.

"But I'm no amateur," Damali said casually, leaning in close enough to Evelyn to nearly touch Evelyn's nose with hers, "and that's why from time to time I can project Neteru for my husband, or seem so close to human that it could confuse the unaware. I'm sorry that I upset you." Damali drew back, cast a loving glance at Carlos. "I will try to be more considerate, though. But bear with us, we're newly mated, and he so enjoys those memories of the night he turned me."

Evelyn had placed her hand over her heart.

"Mistress Rivera," she said, her glance nervous as it flitted between her husband and Carlos back to Damali, "my deepest apologies for my behavior last night. I assure you it will never happen again."

"I will make up the offense my wife has caused," McGuire said, low in his throat. "She wouldn't be sitting here at breakfast, had I known how generous your husband truly is."

The Aussie stood and walked away from the table. Damali raised an eyebrow, and gave Carlos a provocative pout. "I know you fellas have much to discuss in order to strategize for the hunt. Why not let Evelyn and me have some time for girl-talk?"

Carlos gave her a slow nod. She could feel his tension as he stood and left the room.

"I am so sorry," Damali said, leaning in to whisper to Evelyn.

"Whatever for, Your Majesty?" Taken aback, Evelyn's eyes widened with surprise.

"Last night . . . I know Harold probably was a bit . . ."

"I should give you my throat," she said, laughing. "It's been quite some time since my Harold has been like that."

Okaaaay. "Well, then, there's no reason for us to have anything between us," Damali said. "Good."

Damali tried to keep from jumping out of her skin when Evelyn's hand gently slid up her forearm. The touch was so delicate, yet so sensual that for a moment all she could do was look down at it. It felt like cool silk had slid against her skin, and the sensation stirred every erogenous zone on her. She'd expected the touch to be cold or clammy—after all, the woman was dead. Was that what male vampires experienced at a female vamp's touch? she wondered. Valuable info.

There was a slight tremble in Evelyn's fingers as she moved them up to Damali's shoulder. Her lovely cat's eyes held a question; moonlight caught the barest hint of fang and made it glisten.

"You're so warm," Evelyn purred. "No wonder you drive him insane."

"Like I said," Damali whispered, trying to stay in character and not bug out, "there's no problem between you and me, now that we understand each other."

"Nothing has to be between us," Evelyn murmured. "Not even husbands."

Damali forced herself not to shrug off Evelyn's touch. Instead, she smiled. "Do you like him?" she asked, referring to Carlos.

Evelyn continued to caress Damali's shoulder. "He took an Isis in the chest for you?"

"Not completely," Damali said, shrugging casually to get Evelyn's hand off her. "My attack was off, he snatched the blade, but I still had my dagger, and when he pulled me to him, he got branded with it. Then he tore out my throat."

"How do you stand it?" Evelyn whispered, leaning in.

"I could allow you a night with him . . . now that we're friends."

Evelyn stared at her in disbelief, tears beginning to glisten in her eyes. "Mistress—"

"Damali."

"Damali," Evelyn murmured, close enough to Damali's face now to take her mouth. "What does *pure* Neteru do to him . . . any of them? I only experienced what the fragrance transforms them into. But an actual blood siphon would allow me to truly experience it."

It took everything in her not to knock the female vamp to the floor. She had to remember to play this like Carlos had told her. Mix a good lie in a whole lotta truth, but *always* get something out of the deal. "If you siphon me, as a female, it will have an adverse effect on you."

"Oh," Evelyn said, pouting and disappointed.

"But there is a way," Damali said, her voice cooing.

Evelyn perked up, her eyes searching Damali's. "Please, tell me."

"I want him to live through this hunt so he can show you," Damali said, her voice dropping to a seductive purr. "Only when he siphons me is he at his best. Unfortunately it drives us female vamps crazy—makes us want to fight. However, I could let him gorge and then send him to your room."

A sheen of perspiration dampened Evelyn's brow. "You would do that?"

"Or, I could stay and the three of us—"

"Please," Evelyn whispered, closing her eyes. "The hunt will be hours from now and the anticipation is already killing me."

"I just wanted you to know that I am *truly* sorry if I upset you earlier." Damali sat back and waited.

"It does make you want to rip out the female's throat," Evelyn admitted, finally opening her eyes to only half-mast. "But the residual effect is a wonderful high. There's nothing like pure adrenaline."

"Uhmmm-hmmm," Damali said, toying with the table linen. "And when it hits the master's systems, they bulk to mortal-combat proportions, and will fight you on the way down. But the adrenaline hit that you both get on the double-plunge . . ."

Evelyn let out a slow, erotic hiss. "Say no more, please. Just tell me when."

"Perhaps after the concert." Damali held Evelyn's gaze. She needed an ally in the castle, and needed to be sure that at least one vamp couple would guarantee their safety through the blood sport going down tonight. Damali chose her words with care. "However, I'm concerned the other ladies might not understand . . . and Carlos and I rarely discuss such intimate details unless there's been a bond."

"The other ladies will not present a problem," Evelyn said, and reached out to caress Damali's face.

Okay, seal this shit like Carlos showed you, sister. Damali caught Evelyn's wrist and held it hard, then turned into it and planted a long kiss in the center of Evelyn's palm. "Ensure no ambush, and after I'm done with Harold, Carlos and I will come see you."

Evelyn shuddered hard. "I'll tear those bitches' eyes out if they offend my most honored guest."

Damali gave her an air kiss. "Thank you, darling. I'm so glad we had this little talk."

"The girls seem to be gettin' on," McGuire said, glancing over his shoulder.

"Yeah," Carlos said, a little anxious about what he'd just

witnessed. Damali was awfully close up on Evelyn, and had taken the woman's wrist. Had Damali turned back, or what? And why did he have to find that shit so sexy?

Suddenly the sound of the choppers could be heard in the distance.

"Incoming," McGuire announced, his expression excited. "Let the games begin."

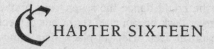HAPTER SIXTEEN

DAMALI DIDN'T say a word as she stood by Carlos's side on
the top step of the castle's grand entryway, Harold and Evelyn three steps below them, watching the entourages dismount from the choppers. It was a spectacular sight as they
watched each master inspect the staff lines, not trusting the
skills of the master that had walked the line before him.
Paranoia was thick in the air. She was just beginning to understand the whole twisted culture of the vamp empire.

Everything meant something. Every conversation was
about power shifts, even play was about the acquisition
thereof, or to show prowess and ward off an attack. The way
they ate, they way they spoke, the way they made and betrayed alliances, the way they had sex—made love was too
nice a phrase, this shit was carnal. Primal, beneath the polished exterior.

One by one, she sized up the targets. The first to arrive
had been the Chinese ambassador. He was slim, muscular,
of moderate height, and wore a very understated navy blue
suit, white shirt, silk tie, and dark shades and a large insignia
ring on his left hand where a wedding band might have been.
He looked like he had been in his late thirties when he had
turned, and he carried himself like the King of Siam. His
gaze was mildly haughty but civil. His wife, however, was

over the top. Damali had to give it to this female. She was all that.

Wrapped in a red raw silk sari trimmed in gold, she had a body like she could dance the seven veils and start a war. She had large, dark brown eyes set in her perfectly proportioned, beautiful face. Her jet-black hair hung in a long straight wash of silky onyx down her back all the way to her behind. Her skin looked like it had a faint hint of bronze beneath, and her cultured voice had an opalescent quality to it that practically shimmered as she spoke. She nodded before she bowed, her eyes seeming to hold a lethal secret. But her aloof air was like that of a pampered, arrogant, pedigreed cat—bored, but watching everything. Damali could feel that she was old . . . real old. Okay, didn't want to sit next to that one in the chopper.

But when the Transylvanian couple appeared, Damali squeezed Carlos's arm. His carriage screamed old power and entitlement. Looking down his nose with a scowl, his dark gray eyes narrowed as he whipped off his shades, his military formal cutaway tux not showing one crease. His chest was affixed with medallions and crests that boasted a long lineage. He walked with broad shoulders back as he strode down the lines with an air of superiority.

His auburn hair was swept back from his forehead in waves that reached his shoulders and as he walked he shook his hair back, his Romanesque features making him look like a cross between Czar Nicolas and Timothy Dalton. His stride proclaimed him a thoroughbred, and the power that exuded from him almost broke the staff lines as he passed each one, said, "That will do," and moved on.

Then came his mate, perhaps. Damali wasn't sure if she was his first wife, or just a lair kitten he'd brought along. She was the most genteel-looking, fragile creature she'd ever seen. Her blond hair shone in the moonlight as she stepped beside him, her eyes were blue ice, her skin as white as porcelain, and her clothes simple elegance. Just a sheath of crème, a whisper in the night, that made her seem more like a ghost than a vampire.

When the African master exited his helicopter, Damali almost turned around and walked back into the castle. The master looked to be maybe forty-five, tall, blue-black handsome, six foot seven if an inch. She could feel Carlos bristle as she studied the chiseled features of the master's hard-set jaw, but his profile nearly made Damali's breath catch. Have mercy.

Brother held his head so high and his back so straight that it looked like he'd been carved out of black marble. As he escorted his woman to the lines, the strength in his forearm literally rippled up the steps beneath his black linen soft-structured suit. His mate was stunning. Her long neck held her stately head high. Her skin was the color of powdered cinnamon, not a blemish to be seen, and she was swathed in trailing gold silk so fine that it nearly glowed. Her dark, beautiful, mysterious Ethiopian eyes made one wonder if they'd painted her likeness in ancient Egypt. They both had the presence of majestic lions—seeming afraid of nothing, fully sated, extremely patient, power exuding from their very fingertips.

Maybe, just maybe, if she sat next to Evelyn or the see-through blonde, she'd be okay. The African master's mate, as did the Asian's, looked too ruthlessly cool. Damali felt fear skitter through her. How was Carlos going to survive in the face of this much concentrated power? He wasn't even risking a transmission in their presence. He obviously didn't want to chance them picking up on even one of his thoughts. Concealment was all at this point. The only thing at the moment she was confident in was that, like her, he'd go down swinging to the bitter end.

"Gentlemen, ladies," Master McGuire said, his voice warm and inviting as he and his wife moved down to the first landing to greet the guests. "Welcome to my territory for a rare and momentous gathering. We are honored to have the newest member of the esteemed Vampire Council as our guest, as he listens to what our topside concerns may be. This is a truly progressive move to bring the nations to the bargaining table in the spirit of detente . . . very much needed after the Nuit rebellion in North America, which could have destabilized the entire empire. Therefore, permit me to introduce Councilman Rivera, and his wife, Damali."

Showtime.

As Carlos stepped forward and moved down the stairs, Damali could feel her heart constrict. Terror ran through her, and her blood pressure spiked so high so fast that her ears rang. Shit, they could dust her baby right here in the yard, old mob style, and keep right on with the night's festivities. She held Carlos's arm with grace, however, pasted on her best smile, and followed his lead.

"Gentlemen, ladies," Carlos said, so cool that you could see condensation from his breath in the air, "thank you for meeting with me. Allow me to present my wife, Damali Richards, the former millennium Neteru."

The fact that they appeared stunned for a moment helped her performance. They'd probably assumed she was captured, or was another female vamp casting the illusion of the Neteru. But that she'd been introduced as the *former* Neteru was clearly blowing their minds. However, as old vamps, their reaction was only a millisecond of doubt shadowing their faces, with slight nods of respect in Carlos's direction, before their expressions became stoic again. It gave her a sample of just how in control they were.

Damali glanced at Carlos, then she nodded, smiled, and waited as McGuire positioned himself at Carlos's left side. She knew his move meant something, and she watched him begin to make individual introductions, noting who was presented in which order.

"Master Sheng Xe, and his lovely wife, Lai, Councilman and Mistress Rivera."

The Asian diplomat bowed, his wife followed suit. They both raked Carlos and Damali with an indecipherable look, then moved up the stairs and into the castle behind the butler without a word.

"Master Gustav Tetrosky, and his lovely wife, Kiersten."

Initially, this master only nodded, while his wife glanced at Damali, up and down with absolute boredom. Then to

Damali's dismay, he tilted his head and held her gaze a moment longer than was appropriate. A new wave of panic brought her breathing to a halt as the master glanced at Carlos, reached for Damali's hand, and brought it to his lips.

"Councilman Rivera, we are honored that you have called this meeting. Your wife is simply ravishing."

Baby, please, don't! Damali's mind screamed at Carlos.

"The honor is mine, sir," Carlos said, so smoothly his words slid over the Transylvanian like silk. "I am glad that you could pull away from the pressing matters in your region so that we could get to know each other."

The Transylvanian master smiled, tugged his wife's elbow gently, and left the stairs with a nod.

Damali wasn't sure when she'd begun breathing again. But she was so glad that she only had one more introduction to go. For some reason, this one worried her the most, perhaps because the master was so much larger in size than Carlos and she could feel his ruthless edge in his energy as he neared them. Or maybe it was because she'd had dealings with brothers from 'round the way, and this guy seemed most familiar, diplomat status notwithstanding. Then again, maybe it was because this one had made her man bristle?

"Master Amin, and his lovely wife Alani."

He looked at Carlos and smiled, his head tilting as he assessed Damali, then he dipped into a slight bow to reach for her hand. "Legendary huntress," he said, so sexy and with such authority that her hand quivered, "and Councilman, the pleasure is ours, to be sure."

Master Amin held her hand a bit longer than was appropriate, and she felt a swift mental invasion push inside her and spread outward to end in a sensual sweep over the entire surface of her skin. Bold! She spied Carlos from her peripheral vision. He was icy cool. She thought she'd pass out when Amin let her see a hint of fang, then drew back and allowed her hand to slowly fall away from his. An outright seduction attempt, in front of all the other masters, and Carlos—*a councilman?* African men were deep, dead or alive!

Little flecks of light danced across her vision; too much adrenaline had hit her system all at once. The African master's wife followed her husband up the stairs, but glanced back at Damali so cool, so calm, that Damali almost reached up to feel her throat to see if it had been cut. Oh, yeah, she was definitely *not* sitting next to her.

"Well," the Aussie said too enthusiastically. "I think that went rather well, given the circumstances." He swallowed away a smile and sighed. "After everyone has checked their bags, changed clothes, and consumed the light refreshments in their rooms, we'll begin the hunt."

Damali could feel the blood drain from her face . . . three new guests, diplomat status . . . light refreshments . . . oh, no, no, no, no, not—not three babies!

Her eyes wide, she looked at Carlos.

"How's this transport thing work?" Carlos muttered, not answering her unspoken question.

Damali studied his countenance. Her man had done the steely jaw, give them the no-fear grit thing, but was rattled beyond words. She could tell. *But the babies!*

Too late, if that's what they've been served. They've been upstairs now for ten minutes.

The response was so low that she almost didn't catch it.

"We take choppers to the Heartland, and there we dismount and each get a vehicle, driver, and ammo. The pilots will drop a coupla carcasses and fire off a flare, then we wait until one of the roos goes for the body, and the chase is on to bring the bastard down," McGuire said, oblivious to their exchange.

"Are we taking five choppers?" Damali said, trying to act like she wasn't worried any longer, and needing to talk about the next big concern she had, namely, being set up in a chopper without her blade.

"Oh, don't worry," Evelyn said, placing a consoling hand on Damali's shoulder. "They're all such bitches when you first meet them, but they do warm up after they get to know you. They are probably a little jealous that you're so young and got made by a councilman. You know how this goes."

Yeah. Whateva. These weren't some jealous chickens from around the way.

"I am not traveling during the hunt with a group of women who disrespect me," Damali said, her hands going to her hips. "It's just not done where I come from."

"If the lady wants to fly solo after you're on the ground, then I see no worries." McGuire turned to Damali, his eyes watery as he wiped his nose with the back of his hand, obviously so high he'd forgotten about his breast-pocket handkerchief. "Usually the ladies all like to ride together so they can root for the guys, that's all Evie meant. She wants you to feel included, but like I told you before, love, whatever you want . . . all you have to do is ask, and it's so."

The fact that this master had called her *love* in front of Carlos—which was waaay out of order, and was sniffing like a cokehead, let her know immediately that her stress from the introductions had spiked the air. Shit. But Carlos was cool, hadn't even twitched a muscle. It made her wonder what he was thinking. Was brother so pissed off that he was just gonna go out in a blaze of glory and try to whack these mugs one by one on the ground, or was he gonna be strategic? That was the important question.

"Baby, what do you think?" Damali asked. If he said, yes, go with the ladies, then he sensed no threat. If he said, no, go solo, then she'd know that there was serious trouble brewing.

"I think you should do what makes you feel most comfortable, honey." Carlos's voice was even, and he didn't even look at her as he spoke. "McGuire will accommodate your choice."

He then turned and walked up the steps. She stared at Carlos's back in pure disbelief as McGuire put an arm over Evelyn's shoulders and threaded another arm around her waist. She moved with the Aussie master who held her in to him tightly. Slack-jawed, she couldn't even speak as she walked up the steps. Nor did she push away the very amorous male whose nose and fangs were just a bit too close

to her hair, almost nuzzling it. His hand caressed her waist.
Her thoughts were on Carlos's unreadable expression when
the introductions had been made. Did he pick up any tracer
that would lead them to the key?

"Did anyone ever tell you that you smell *so* damned good,
Mistress Rivera?"

Damali kept walking.

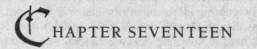

CHAPTER SEVENTEEN

THE WAIT in the grand parlor was interminable. Evelyn's talk about home decoration, coupled with innuendo about the agreed upon post-concert tryst, was drilling a hole into Damali's brain. But that wasn't as bad as having to continue to strategically reposition herself during the conversation just to get away from McGuire's blatant advances.

When he finally left the room to join the other males in his study—so they could casually carve up the world over cigars and blood-spiked brandy—Damali sat hard on the sofa, exhaustion making her limbs feel heavy. She was too tired to delicately turn aside any more sly propositions, offers, and/or seductions.

And if the males were all drawing straws on the fate of the world, then naturally the wives gathered to chitchat about the merits of suckling baby as a delicacy versus prepubescent boys. But she wasn't fooled into thinking that this was a wickedly genteel meeting of the vampire ladies' home and garden club. There was some serious power pulsing throughout this room.

Not to mention, the other ambassadors' wives were so cool toward her that they were straight-up icy. Mistress Xe was on the far side of the room sipping blood from a cordial glass, careful not to stain her white linen sundress. Mistress

Tetrosky sat next to Evelyn on the love seat, carefully smoothing her impeccably tailored navy and white summer skirt ensemble. She spoke only to the Aussie first lady, practically ignoring all the other first ladies in the room, and acting as though Damali wasn't there, which forced Evelyn to work hard to continue drawing Damali into a conversation she didn't want to be in anyway.

But Mistress Amin was blatant with her disdain. She flashed a bit of fang as she brushed nonexistent lint from her coral-hued linen wrap-dress and passed Damali to take a seat in the overstuffed Queen Anne chair by the fireplace. The whole gathering looked like a Beverly Hills tea party.

Damali stood and went to the elaborate bookshelf and began scanning the volumes. She wasn't crazy. Even though she'd turned her back to them, her guard was up. She had to let them know she wasn't afraid of them and by turning her back on them sent the message—just try it.

What did vampires read, anyway, she wondered, zoning out on the boring madness the pampered pets of diplomats were discussing. She wanted so badly to be in the room with the big boys, at the table, hardball negotiating, witnessing how Carlos handled himself at high-stakes poker.

"And we want to thank you so much, Evelyn, for providing the human helper in our room. That was a lovely appetizer before the banquet tonight. Ursula and I got on famously. And can you imagine, she was begging to be turned?"

Damali cringed. But she felt much better knowing that at least it hadn't been a baby. If some human adult had made a choice to roll with these predators, then, hey, that was their choice. But what choice or chance did a little baby have?

She caught Mistress Xe eyeing her from the far side of the room.

"Yes, Evelyn," Mistress Xe said, her voice like silk. "The way you bound her hands and let her dangle from a wall hook over the crystal blood decanter was so clever." She gave Damali a nasty smile. "Some people do not appreciate the finer things in life."

Was that bitch signifying? Damali glanced over her shoulder and let the comment pass.

"Where did you find the women, Evelyn?" Mistress Amin said, her eyes on Damali the entire time she spoke. "A brothel?"

Again, Damali ignored her.

"Mistress Rivera," the sheer blonde from Transylvania said, "you didn't enjoy your plaything?"

"I had a baby earlier, and that was enough," Damali muttered, and tried to focus on the bookcase.

When dead silence surrounded her, Damali turned around and stared at them.

"Decorum, ladies," Evelyn said, her expression nervous, tight, and on-guard.

Mistress Xe walked deeper into the center of the room, anger heating her words. "You offered *her* a baby?"

Mistress Amin was on her feet. "I am highly offended, Evelyn! How could you present her with such a delicacy like that and snub the other wives?"

"She's *the councilman's* wife," Evelyn said nervously. "Some things are protocol, ladies. To do any less would be a grave offense."

Standing quickly, Mistress Tetrosky folded her arms over her chest and sneered down at Evelyn. "Wait until Gustav hears about this. I never—" She spun on Damali, her eyes blazing. "Someone of her ilk would know nothing about what to do with a suckling infant."

Oh, yeah . . . it was on. Damali could feel a very dark part of herself concentrating, being amplified by the oppressive energies in the castle, and drawing power from every cell in her body all the way to the marrow. It was such an old rage, so visceral, and so familiar, one she'd lived with as a child, people thinking they were better than her for no other reason than the accident of birth. It was as though the castle itself was bringing out the worst in her. And then she realized that it wasn't just the environment, these bitches had been quietly working on her head.

"Her, Evelyn?" Mistress Xe hissed, adding more venom

to her argument. "I can trace my lineage all the way back to the Ming Dynasty, and Alani can go back to Kemet! Kiersten hails from the time before the Druids." Her gaze narrowed on Damali as she pointed at her. "And this little bitch probably doesn't even know who her own mother or grandmother was—just like you Aussies can't go back worth a damn!"

An image slammed into Damali that brought tears to her eyes. One of the females had shown her her mother in the dirt, crying and screaming in the driveway of their home on her hands and knees, pleading for her father to come back. Instantly, another hurtful image slammed into Damali's mind. She tried to ward it off, but her mother's ritual to call up Nuit came crashing into her head. Just as that image faded, she saw her foster father coming at her, then his face blurred and became her father's with fangs.

"She comes from pure human trash," Mistress Li said with a sly smile, "and you wasted a baby on her?"

The rage that had been building within Damali propelled her forward, stole her will, and eclipsed all judgment. They were talking about her dead parents—a real sore subject. Worse, they'd gotten into her mind. The tears burned away. Bad form, as Evelyn called it, where she came from, too. Mass gathered in her bloodstream. Yeah, from her world a nasty comment about your momma meant a sho' nuff beat down. But laughing at her family tragedy wasn't even done among vamps of the same level, so she'd been told. Instantly, the image of Carlos with the were-demon in Brazil shot into her mind's eye. Oh, no . . . they had *not* taken her there . . . They'd thrown down the gauntlet. If she let this pass, they'd attack her for sure. Something within her snapped like a twig. It was on.

"Who you calling a bitch, *bitch?*"

Instantly, Lai Xe transformed. Suddenly she had six arms, three on each side, and her head moved hypnotically from side to side with a serpent's grace.

Evelyn was on her feet in a flash. "Ladies, please, let's not ruin—"

"Shut up, Evelyn," Alani Amin snarled, transforming instantly. What had once been a regal, statuesque beauty was now a fanged creature with the woman's face, but crouched low, the upper body of a woman, lower body of a lion, a twitching spaded tail, and large leathery wings.

Damali didn't move. It wasn't fear that held her, but strategy. If they'd transformed into forms stronger than regular vamp females with fangs, it meant that they were unsure of her strength. She watched them. They seemed to be waiting for her to show them her best shape-shift. Damali smiled. The fact that she was holding non-fang-bearing human form was messing with their minds. She could feel it as they began posturing for an attack, using the transformative abilities like were-demons from the realms above level six.

"I've had enough of this *human scented* pretender to the throne," Mistress Tetrosky roared, then threw her head back, shot a funnel of fire, and transformed into a griffin. "No council-level master should be tethered to a low-bred bitch like this—a waste of a valuable male resource in the empire!"

She didn't care what they'd turned into, there was nothing more dangerous than a pissed-off sister from 'round the way. Then Evelyn reluctantly dropped to all fours and transformed into a crocodile. Oh, so it was like that? Punk whore. She was supposed to have her back, had practically asked outright to go down on her in the parlor. But when it came time to stand her ground, Evelyn was with her girls.

Damali gripped the Isis handle so tightly that she could feel her palm bleed. Every affront she'd ever experienced, every clique she'd ever been shunned from, and every humiliation ever thrust upon her, galvanized in one central battle cry. "Bring it, bitch!"

Damali threw her head back, her voice now a weapon of its own, blood-spiked colors behind her shut lids. She could feel something happening to her, a bloodlust ramping into a vampiric flux, and the sensation was both disorienting and exhilarating at the same time. Her heart stopped for a second and then beat an erratic seizure against her breastbone, her gums ripped, and when she opened her eyes to lunge, she saw the females before her backing up. Near-stroke-level fury made her shudder as her voice drew density, velocity. The air began to stain red, then mix with an eerie purple magenta fusion. Male vampires instantly came through the walls into the room from all directions, forming a ring at the outskirts. Carlos rushed toward her and then stopped within a few feet of her. Their male presence, fangs in full battle mode, dredged a rage-induced scream which she let loose at the top of her lungs.

The huge bay window blew out, the bookcase rippled and shed its thick leatherbound classics like missiles, and the chandelier quaked and began separating from the ceiling. Tiffany lamps exploded as Damali's line of vision swept every male protecting a female vamp in the room, sending shards of colored glass everywhere. Words seized in her throat, she couldn't draw in enough air fast enough as the rage almost made her levitate off the ground.

"You bitches have no concept of who you are fucking with tonight!"

Instantly, the Hell-hounds flew through the window, snarling and barking, sensing she was in danger, making the group back up, as they landed between Carlos and Damali, and the others, holding the other masters at bay.

"Go back on guard," Damali shouted at the animals, making them give her a confused glance, but then they sulked away and took flight out of the window.

"Baby . . ." a low, too-serene male voice said.

She whirled on the speaker. "Fuck detente!"

Carlos stepped back. Damali reached out her hand toward Mistress Tetrosky, her will pulling her from across the room. It was a standoff for a second, the woman trembling between them as her husband's hold loosened, and Damali's gained more strength against the magnetic force her husband was struggling to maintain to keep the woman at his side. A loud crack sounded as though a tree limb had been felled. Instantly, Damali drew the Transylvanian diplomat's wife from across the room, grabbed her throat, gripping it, causing her to transform back into the fragile blonde. Damali body slammed her on the Oriental carpet, raised the Isis with both hands tight at the handle, and stood over her, legs apart with the Isis pointed toward the center of the female vampire's chest.

"I may not be able to trace back to the Druids, bitch, but I will tell you this: your ass *will* respect me! And when you disrespect me, you disrespect my man—and *that* I ain't having from none of y'all!"

"Damali, baby . . ." Carlos said, very carefully.

Damali took two deep breaths, then angrily stepped away, grumbling about the momma comment. She stalked away from the female vamp and allowed her to scramble back to her husband's side. She looked at the Transylvanian master hard. "You'd better keep that bitch in check." She paced back and forth like a caged animal in front of the sofa, her gaze narrowing on the African diplomat's wife as she huddled against her man.

As Damali railed, the air in the room got darker and darker with the deep magenta-purple stain of her rage. Damali stalked back to the bookcase, punched it, making four more volumes fall as a shelf splintered, and then came back to the center of the room. What had begun as strategic theater had gotten a stranglehold on her. It was as though the castle and the mind dredge combined with the eminent threat all around her was producing an incredible flux between ultimate Neteru battle mode and vamp attack.

Try as she might, she couldn't stop herself. Words formed in her mouth and she spat them out as the strange flux imploded within her system.

Hot tears from years of bottled-up anger streamed down her face. But when Carlos stepped forward, she leveled her blade at him and he stood very, very still.

"I have always been more than what people see, and dead or alive that still holds true!" She moved in a slow semicircle before the group, the tip of her blade bouncing from the energy running the length of her arm, down the blood groves, and arcing a current at the end of it. "I am a female *master*. I am the night itself to you whores. I am my own woman, equal to any master in this fucking room, and I won't tolerate disrespect."

With that she flipped the Isis blade so the point was to the floor and rammed it into the polished stone beneath the rug. She glanced up at Carlos, and then at her clothes with disdain, and instantly changed into a T-shirt and a pair of fatigues and combat boots. "I refuse to ride in the choppers and be a spectator. I want a Jeep, a driver, and a helluva serious load of ammo."

"Councilman Rivera," McGuire said slowly, not moving from his wife's side. "It's too dangerous—"

Before he could finish the sentence, Damali was standing in front of McGuire. "Why are you talking to him? He doesn't run me, I *choose* to be with him. So you speak the fuck to me when I ask you a question. I am so tired of the paternalistic bullshit, McGuire, I will rip your punk heart out myself—and I'm supposed to come to your room? Pullease."

The other masters stared at McGuire, their gazes slowly raking him, then Damali, before settling upon Carlos.

"If the lady isn't pleased with your choice, Councilman," Master Amin said, his eyes devouring Damali, "perhaps she would feel less agitated if you sent her to me?"

McGuire cast a nervous glance at Damali. "You're not reconsid—"

"Get me a damned hunt car. Now!" she shouted, anger pulsing through her. "This is not open for discussion!"

"Mr. Councilman," the Transylvanian master said, his voice serious, his eyes watery as he sniffed hard and wiped his nose with the back of his hand. "She must place a wager, if—"

Suddenly Tetrosky's head jerked back as though he'd been slapped. The sound of a hard strike echoed throughout the room, and the circle widened, each couple moving back as Damali walked forward, brushing past Carlos.

Her eyes narrowed and from a place of unknowing, words gathered, formed, translated, and were issued forth in a language she'd never been taught.

I told you to address me directly. Damali placed her

hands on her hips. Tetrosky rubbed his jaw, his eyes on her as he shunted his wife aside, eyes glowing red, fangs now dripping saliva. *I have something to wager. If anyone's gonna bet my ass, it's me, not him!* she said, pointing back toward Carlos. *You man enough? Winner takes all. London, if I win; first night after the hunt with me alone in your lair, if you win.*

"You've taught her Dananu?" Tetrosky murmured, awe in his voice, his eyes riveted on Damali.

"She's a master," Carlos said quietly, pride lacing his comment. "She picked it up on her own."

Tetrosky walked forward, reached into his breast pocket, and pulled out a thin scroll of parchment. He held the wager document for a moment, his eyes raking Damali as he took a liberal inhale, unrolled it with flair and caused a pop to echo through the room, and pressed his crest ring to his own wrist vein until it bled into the insignia.

Staring at Damali, he then stamped the document hard, leaving his bloody seal. The document sizzled where he'd left his mark, then the seal bubbled, raised, and dried to a consistency of cooled wax. With desire emanating from him like a slow strobe, he extended the document to her, hands trembling, his storm-gray eyes never leaving hers.

When Damali snatched the ancient stationery from him and pulled her Isis dagger from her hip pocket, the Transylvanian master visibly shuddered. She slowly slit her palm with the baby Isis, dipped her insignia ring of Carlos's territory in her blood and stamped his paper hard, and thrust it back to him. Tetrosky dropped to his knees, leaned his head back, and opened his arms, closing his eyes. "Slit my throat and take London . . ."

Damali narrowed her eyes. "Gladly. Later."

"Promise me . . . if I win." His voice was gravelly, thick and hoarse.

"Yeah, whateva. I'll cut your heart out in there if you keep fucking with me." Damali gave his wife Kiersten a tri-umphant glance as she walked away from the Transylvanian and he stood slowly with his wife's help. But she waited, somehow knowing that she needed a parchment, too, to make it legit. And as soon as she thought it, a stripe of fire opened in thin air before her, and a duplicate scroll vomited from it like a Hell-sent fax.

Damali shook her head as she reached for the parchment, ripping it away from the sulfur slit, which immediately closed once the agreement was removed. She read it over carefully as she walked. Slimy, cheating bastards to the very end—like she wasn't smart enough to know that if it wasn't in writing, the agreement didn't exist. Hell always had a contract.

"Am I in the game, boys, or what?" She went up to the African diplomat and raked him with a hot gaze until his wife moved from his side, her eyes blazing with fury. "You in? Madagascar for a night? I like the beach."

"Madagascar, Ghana, Senegal, the Middle Passage routes . . . Name it." He wiped the sweat off his brow with the back of his forearm and sniffed hard. He came toward her in a slow, seductive lope, held her gaze with a sensual aura thickening the air around her, and slowly dragged a cut the length of his palm with a fang. He let the blood ooze into the cup of his hand, first staring at it and then slowly bringing his gaze up to hold hers, and dipped his ring in it. "Any time, Huntress," he murmured, his voice husky. "My territory is *very* large. Trust me."

Damali nodded and stamped his parchment. "Size matters," she said, her eyes roving him. "If they told you different, brother, *they lied.*"

"I'll put South Africa on the table, too," he said, moving closer to her.

"That's a fair trade, since there's never been a female master topside in your existence. If I lose, then I'll have to make it worth your while for the *sizeable* territory wagered." She gave him a sly smile. "Put it in writing, motherfucker." Then she glanced at McGuire as her copy spit from scorched air. "Don't worry, I haven't given your night away, but you'll have to earn it the old-fashioned way, no side deals—say, the Outback?"

He glanced at Carlos nervously. "The Outback?"

"Maybe you didn't hear the woman," Carlos said calmly. "She told you to talk to *her*. This is *her* negotiation, not mine. I traded for Tasmania and Indonesia. Apparently, the territory I'd bet wasn't mine wholesale as majority owner. My bad. I'll throw in the Hawaiian Islands, and a coupla Caribbean ones instead."

McGuire nodded. "The Outback . . . worth every square inch of her."

She walked away from the African diplomat, accepted McGuire's deal with a rip from the air, and looked at the Asian master. He was taking in long, steady breaths and his eyes were now closed. Perspiration dotted his brow, and he spoke methodically as though struggling to breathe. "Hong Kong, Tibet . . . Name it."

"For your ass, both," Damali said, her voice tight as she remembered his wife's disrespect.

With lightning swiftness he struck his wife's cheek with a backhanded slap that caused her to fall to her knees, instantly filling his crest with her blood, and then calmly walked up to Damali and presented her with his parchment to stamp. "Worthy competitor," he said, deadly sexuality threading through every word, "she has lost face, and therefore my favor. I add Vietnam . . . so that when you lose to me, no disrespect will linger to shadow our evening."

Damali allowed her voice to drop to a seductive octave as she accepted the paper from him, her stamp hovering over it. "Skill is also something a lady can't take for granted." She stared at him, watching his inhales slow to a standstill and then suddenly deepen. "What good is size," she murmured, "if you don't know how to work it?"

"I assure you the cadre of skills I possess from several thousand years of vast dynasties will make you feel as though you had won the match. I add North Korea."

"Throw in Japan, because, as I said, size does matter, baby . . . and I promise you I won't remember jack about what your bitch wife had to say to me."

"Done."

When she stamped his parchment and thrust it against his chest, he closed his eyes and accepted it, taking a moment before stepping away from her. Then she calmly strolled away from him, accepting another bargain from the air.

Her gaze raked the group as she stuffed the papers into the back pocket of her pants, taking her time, knowing that they could feel her ass as their papers slid against it through her fatigues. She put away her dagger and folded her arms over her chest, satisfied. "What's a girl gotta do to get a drink around here?"

Tetrosky ripped the collar of his T-shirt under his flack jacket away from his throat and walked forward, but stopped suddenly at Carlos's low, warning growl.

"I am *not* that progressive," Carlos said to Tetrosky, then he gave Damali a threatening glare. His mind seized hers in a hard private message. *Yeah, baby. You got game. But do not even think about disrespecting me like that in front of my masters!*

He let her go mentally and then produced a black bottle, holding it tightly by the neck. She gave him a blasé shrug when he tossed it to her and she caught it. But he didn't say a word while watching as she opened it easily with her thumb and turned it up to her mouth and swallowed. The private chat still held a charge, the touch a burning transmission, and yet it also sent valuable information into his awareness that gave him the control he required.

From his peripheral vision he could see the other masters almost swallow with each one of hers. Their cool was blown; their wives were pissed off, but cowed. As his rage simmered and died down, the effect of watching Damali feed shifted his focus. He could actually feel Damali working with the dark energy of the house, using it to her advantage, creating lovely chaos, not resisting in order to maintain her balance . . . ride it, flip it to make the outcome good.

He chided himself—she'd told him about this process. Had said to leverage the dark within. It made so much sense after watching her do it. All-pro . . . airtight game. The castle had the most mad-crazy energy, the female vamps had tapped into it and had also been affected by her heavy Neteru scent so close to their mates. Damali was relatively unarmed and outnumbered when they'd fanged on her. The masters' reaction to Damali was like gasoline on a flame to the wives.

Yeah, he got the picture. Under normal circumstances, these vampire ladies were smooth and shrewd enough to have laid in the cut for her, and would not have been so open . . . would have slit Damali's throat quietly, one-on-one in a ladies' room somewhere, would not have exposed their true feelings to foolishly bum-rush her in public in front of any turned-on master. Damali had sensed that, and had drawn them out into the open where she could fight better . . . just like a seasoned Neteru huntress would have. Made them reveal themselves, and then worked the protective strength of their masters against them to the bone— drawing it from them to guard her as a prize. They were diplomat's wives, but had been reduced to their base element by the combo. Carlos almost laughed. Pure instinct. He should have seen it coming.

As he watched her drain the bottle, he monitored the growing lust that was sweat-charging the room. He could almost feel the other masters' knees buckle from her slow, deliberate feed. Adrenaline and testosterone was clouding their judgment, strangling their control, blinding their focus about the hunt—or what they should have been doing, trying to kill her . . . but then, they'd pissed her off more than they'd frightened her. Bad move, gentlemen—if they would have asked him, he would have told them, Damali was *not* the one.

Carlos glanced around, also needing to distract himself from watching her leisurely feed. In this house, the split-second priority shift had created a vacuum, nature abhorred a vacuum . . . yes, since this was an unnatural environment, the dark transformation had pulled into her like a lightning rod, super-charging her . . . this wasn't a passion turn in his arms, she'd gone into it in battle mode. He almost laughed out loud, might have, if a nagging doubt didn't eat away at the back of his mind. Her fluxes with him were brought on by something pure—passion. This was fueled by something dark and with a lot more kick—anger. He just hoped that there was no permanent damage.

He shook off the worry, and stared at her. No. Don't lose focus. This was beyond beautiful. A variable wild card, and Damali was as wild as they got. His baby was gorgeous with her head back, eyes closed, the veins standing up in her neck from the sudden fury, the air stained darker than he'd ever seen it around her, the adrenaline kick to it . . . with fangs . . . a residue of Neteru bloodlust battle-heat on, having beat down four vamp females—or nearly so, and then amassing more territory in one wager than he ever could—without giving away one plot of dirt . . . *dayum*. Respect. And she'd spoken in Dananu and slapped a master's face from across the room . . . oh hell yeah, winner take all. He couldn't be angry with the masters around him, their wives, or Damali, about any of it. She'd played this hand well, and they'd played themselves.

This was definitely a way to bust up any alliances, he almost shook his head at the pure treachery of it . . . brilliance. She was a master, could have them all kill each other and wind up ruling the world with a council seat to go with it. Woman, thy name is evil. The seventh level probably didn't have nothin' for this . . . Yet she'd also fucked up the four competitors' confidence . . . it was a male thing that rippled through the room. Damali was also getting stronger, the more she drank, the longer she stayed in the room in vampire mode, just like he was getting stronger from the environment, enhancing his vocabulary, polishing it to more cultured diplomatic levels . . . feeling his throne-seat powers weigh in.

Plus, she'd told them that she'd chosen him, the one who had turned her, and if she was his female counterpart, they had to be wondering what the hell he could do when provoked. It was in their eyes, the way they looked at her, but they also lowered their gaze when assessing him. Yeah, any man in his right mind would wonder what it would take to harness that type of energy . . . crazy part that they would never be able to fathom was, he couldn't—it was her choice. It was easier to control the wind than to try to control her. But after what they'd just witnessed, the likelihood of a direct challenge was very slim.

As she chugged the last of the bottle, he could feel the masters around the room losing the last of their focus on the hunt, becoming concentrated on winning her favor as they openly sent her images that were about everything but the hunt. Dangling seductive offers of their realms to her, casting diamonds at her feet in their minds, and she blithely ignored their growing insistence, some offers of land so tempting that even he was shocked. The whole fucking continent, brother, if she'll go exclusive with you for a century? Damn . . . Russia . . . if she'll come whenever you call? Carlos shook his head, as all of India came up on his mental radar with a proposed exchange for a divorce and new bride bite, and Master Xe's wife stormed out of the room. Hey . . . what could he say? He could dig it. He'd put up all of North America and Canada, just so none of them could have her.

Damali wiped her mouth with the back of her hand and tossed the bottle into the fireplace, smashing it, then gazed at the group as though considering what had been put before her. "Evelyn, I swear, if you bring another baby into this castle for these ungrateful hoes . . . From now on, they get full, willing, adult vamp-helper at the banquet—*I* don't even want a baby, now, I'm so pissed off! In fact, I don't want to see that shit, either—just bottles! None of you deserve squat beyond that. Not even." She walked to the window and gave them all her back. "I have never been so offended in my life! I don't even want to eat here, much less stay another night."

Carlos watched her closely as the images went raw from the masters to her, each now descending on the erotic burn she'd created, murmuring to her seductively in Dananu in their thoughts, sending graphic images of what a night alone could entail . . . sending a fight charge through him that made him drop fang. Then she turned around, smiled and licked her bottom lip, and looked at him.

"What did you bet?"

Momentarily stunned by the question, Carlos took a second to regroup. "What do you mean, what did I bet?" He could feel his shoulders becoming tight, gaining bulk as outrage threaded through his system, and the other masters' expressions became hopeful—too hopeful.

"Yeah, what did you bet?" she asked low, seductive, walking toward him. "You put my ass on the line . . . so now I'm going to ask you again, Councilman Rivera—what did you bet?" She paused, and allowed her gaze to run the length of him. "Because you don't get this for free anymore . . . there are too many tender offers on the table, and this franchise is about to go public. Talk to me."

Fury flooded his system, meeting the outright lust she siphoned from him. This woman was not an obsession. She was an addiction, a dangerous one, right down to his core where his pride resided. She was a physical craving, a need, a part of his bloodstream, the very marrow in his bones. The combination was lethal.

The entire territory, plus a throne! He hollered in Dananu against his better judgment. Silence captured every halted breath. No other master breathed. Carlos's hand went to her throat: *And if I win, I want more than you've put on the table for the others—because what I'm willing to lose they don't even have to offer!*

Mr. Councilman, she purred in Dananu, *every other territory I'll win in the match, plus a night that will scorch your mind for an eternity . . . and anything else you want from me—on demand.* She stood up on her tiptoes and took his mouth tenderly, sending the private image of the baby to him. *Play well tonight, and I'll die again in your arms . . . let the best man win.* She pulled her mouth away from his, wet, and let her lids slide closed to half-mast. "Stamp it in blood, baby, so I know you're not playing with me." Then she sucked in air between her teeth, making the sound of a slow hiss as her head dropped back, exposing her throat to him. "I want some so bad right now, I could be compromised."

He tore a parchment from his pocket, and was so angry that blood filled his crest on its own. This was a grudge match now. He stamped the agreement, tore hers from the air and thrust it toward her. "You satisfied?"

She shook her head no, and the room went still. She turned away from Carlos and slowly assessed the waiting masters. Then a thought so devious, so loaded with treason entered her mind that he caught, and came from her lips so slow and husky as she addressed the other males, he couldn't move.

Gentlemen, she said in Dananu. *You all have been thinking with the wrong head.* She laughed and walked deeper into the center of the room, brushing past Carlos.

Damali's eyes closed and she breathed in deeply. *At least one of you fine men have a fair shot at beating me. Think of the odds.* She took her time, opened her eyes slowly, baiting them, toying with them, allowing the concept to sink in. *But he doesn't,* she murmured, motioning with a nod toward Carlos.

Spontaneous combustion was a definite possibility. He was so enraged that he could barely make out her form as mental flames burned his sight line to her. His thoughts scattered, then began to coalesce into a laser. He'd cut her heart out. She dangled in a very precarious position between breathing and extinction.

I know his greatest weakness like only   throat-bitten mate would . . .

A ring of fire surrounded her; he didn't move as she casually turned her head and looked at him, unfazed.

"Even Hell has rules, baby," she said as though talking about basketball. "You do me here, and I don't think you'll make it out of the room."

"No, he won't," the African master said, challenging Carlos. "We assure you."

The firewall around her shot to the ceiling, then sucked back into the floor, his rage blowing out the back wall.

Like I was saying, she went on, not even looking at Carlos. *Soooo . . . if I beat him, I've now got a throne plus his entire region. If I beat several masters in the game, I'll own their shit, too. Then whoever beats me, wins not only a council-made female master that can spontaneously produce Neteru, but that lucky sonofabitch rules the world. Game over. You've been betting against the wrong horse, fellas . . . haven't placed your money on a thoroughbred. I'll give you one minute to revise and place your bets. Who's in?*

The air crackled and popped, searing fire slits opening at dizzying speeds. Damali's laughter only made the revised agreements appear faster, masters breathing hard, looking at each others' bids, changing theirs, upping the ante, hollering at their wives to back off and stay out of a man's business. When they started arguing about who ruled the available territory in near space, several wives sat down on the sofas and wept—one even vomited blood. Mistress Xe had come back into the room and was on her knees begging her husband not to throw it all away, screeching and lamenting about losing all they'd ever worked for, their entire landed wealth to a crazy whore.

Yet Carlos could do nothing. This was business, and there were rules. It was surreal. The offer arrays transitioned so fast that they were mere blurs. It was worse than Wall Street traders at the opening bell with hot stock in their portfolios. Nations ceded everything—a full territory and an old coveted throne was on the bid floor; Neteru driving them nuts.

When there was nothing left for them to bid, Damali slowly walked around the room, collecting their insane offers. "Gentlemen, the floor is now closed for business." She sounded a bell, laughed, and blew them all a sexy air kiss. "Nice doin' business with all of you." It was a beautiful play and she'd played it to the bone. Damali shook her head. Master Vamps weren't that easy to blow away, not for a booty call. There was much more to this than that. They'd all obviously heard the rumor about the key, perhaps they thought that as the once-legendary Neteru, if they could get in her ear, they'd find the location—or the seal . . . or both? Carlos's senses hadn't gotten a lock on any of them, so it had been her turn. And judging from their reaction, her intuition had been dead on.

Master Amin stepped forward and grabbed the Aussie Master by his vest. "Bring the choppers."

Carlos kept his black-goggled gaze out of the helicopter window and listened to the engine, the blades cutting the air, focused on anything but Damali. For most of the ride, he didn't speak to her, saying only what was absolutely necessary about the rules of the hunt—one-syllable responses, and only when she asked—and only because it was in her best interest to beat everyone but him. There were no words. Damali was beyond defiant; she was incorrigible.

It was bad enough that she'd doubted his ability to defend her on the front steps—in front of aggressive masters, at that. And, not to mention, she'd had the nerve to quiver when that tall African bastard walked up to her, but she'd made her mate wager for her like the others? Put it *all* on the line? And she was about to go into a blood sport she knew nothing about—and had put her sweet ass on the line, too— like he could allow her not to win? Like he would just sit in the parlor and wait till she was finished doing a competitor, if she fucked around and lost! He was done!

She swallowed away a smile, her gaze fastened to the quickly passing ground, goggles keeping her eyes shielded from the devastation of the blurring blue-white lines below. This was so sweet a setup that she wanted to throw her head back and laugh. Chaos theory at its best.

Every male on the ground would be trying to dust the competition as much as score points by bringing down a beast. Each one not willing to ally with another region against her husband, because it was winner take a singular prize that they'd never share—the key, or access to the seal. And they'd half kill themselves trying to keep her, the secondary but very coveted prize on the battlefield, from getting hurt. Knowledge was power, and they thought she knew. It made sense. Classic. Old school—right from the streets.

Use the greatest strength as the greatest source of weakness—the art of war, subversion, dance on male ego . . . do a strip tease down it, pole dance that sucker . . . compare territories openly and make them define whose was bigger in public, then walk away from the lot of them . . . primal, make 'em fight it out, and make them think the councilman didn't have an advantage in her eyes . . . which would truly piss him off and make him go ballistic to be sure to win. This was like street basketball—mugs killing themselves to take the prize home after the game.

She'd have to remember to tell him why she did that . . . when she made it up to him later . . . it was no disrespect, just a li'l extra somethin' somethin' to give him the fury advantage, which was a stronger vamp reflex than lust—only one energy octave down, world dominance being the most seductive. Yeah, she knew how to play poker and sit at the table with the big boys. Doubting her was their blind spot. Oh . . . dangerous damned liaisons, that's what detente was any-ole-way.

The chopper's descent was swift. The craft lurched, dipped, and bounced twice on the hard, red surface, kicking up dust plumes as it came to a full stop. She could barely wait for the pilot to give the exit-okay nod before hopping out ahead of Carlos. They were gonna rock tonight! Together, they were unstoppable. Demons in the dark. Just like old times. Yeah . . . she bopped as she walked, stretching out her blade arm and flexing her muscles as she approached the vehicles assembled twenty-five yards away in a semicircle, rolling her shoulders to loosen up.

This was gonna be fun. She looked at the buff human vamp-helper drivers. Each stood somber, their eyes hidden behind military night-vision goggles, with a crash helmet under his arm beside an armored Range Rover 4×4 that had a driver safety cage added. The open pickup backs had a harpoon mount, roof lights-rack with no lights—just a steel bar for the hunters to grip. She could see where they'd reinforced the side panels and added extra chrome to the grills and back bumpers. In the dark the eerie effect of the added protection made the Rovers appear to have steel fangs.

She stooped to inspect how there was an added steel cage to protect the axle and chassis. Standing, satisfied, she glanced at the solid rubber wheels and the way deadly spikes had been welded to the lugs to keep the demons away from the tires. Excellent. No chance of a blowout or a wheel being knocked off.

He kept his eyes on her back. This was a perfect place for an abduction—and after that shit she just pulled, he wouldn't be surprised if one of the masters tried to just grab her and head for the hills. Carlos slowly scanned the group. None of them was focused on the hunt. Out in the pitch-black terrain, only stars and a full moon, were-demons be damned, every master standing there was weighing that option because she'd turned them on so badly. That crazy woman had sent uncut Neteru up their noses, dangled her sweet ass as a carrot, and then threw a throne on the floor like she was throwing down the gauntlet . . . had betrayed *her eternal mate* in public, then sent them into a bid frenzy without eating! Just downed a bottle of top-shelf in front of them so they could smell it in her veins? It was a nitroglycerine concoction—lust and power and blood—and she was juggling it in her pretty hands.

She didn't know what she was dealing with. It was in the way they looked at her long and hard, glanced the terrain, shook it off to study their ammo, absently checked their vehicles for potential sabotage, then looked at the terrain again like they wanted to drag her into the desert and take their chances with the weres. Probably the only thing stopping them was that four other very disappointed masters would make it a short night. This was some dangerous shit she was playing. Renewed fury coiled and snapped within him . . . and she'd made *him* bet, too?

"Drivers! Take your marks," McGuire finally yelled, his voice echoing in the night. "Readied?"

The Aussie master waited as the confirmations echoed

back. "Ladies to the choppers . . . er, minus one." He glanced at Damali. "You sure about this, darlin'?"

Damali smiled and placed a firm hand on her driver's shoulder. "Fire this up."

McGuire drew a steadying breath. "Ma'am, I'ma love to see ya hunt." As though pulling away from a magnet, he removed his line of vision on her and looked at the group. "You know the rules and the boundary markers. Every man for himself. When the choppers drop the bloody human carcasses, they'll signal with a flare." He glanced back at the bait pilots and nodded once the female vampires had been secured in the spectator helicopter.

The masters mounted their vehicles, each stood in the open pickup back and took up a loaded weapon. The drivers put on their helmets, tightened the straps beneath their chins, and climbed into the driver's cages, then gunned their engines.

Each chopper lifted off and sent a cloud of grit and red sand that covered the landscape into the air. She couldn't see her hand in front of her face, but sheathed her Isis on her hip, and picked up the crossbow, holding onto the rack rail with a tight grip. Her eyes were trained on the blue-black sky lit by the moon and stars, waiting for the flare as the engine of her Range Rover roared. It was not about losing. It was about going to her core and being the best in the demon hunt. *Always*. But she couldn't see because of the dust plumes!

Then Damali closed her eyes, remembering everything she'd been taught as a Neteru. She was one with the universe, created by it, she was wind, she was water, she was fire, and ice, she was stone, earth, there was no particle of natural matter that she was not connected to. She didn't need normal sight to find the demons to hunt them down.

White light was a source shaped like the tip of her Isis blade to be drawn down through her crown chakra at the top of her head, through each chakra level, her spine one with it, grounding her, turning her entire body into steel—a weapon unparalleled. Her breaths were slow, her focus steady. She was the huntress; a warrior; the millennium had no other.

Demons were the enemy. Humanity had to be saved. Anything coming up from Hell had to be eliminated. The were-demons were on the move, beneath the surface, attracted to the blood dripping, bodies falling from the choppers, freed to feed by the full moon. The goal was singular: bring them all down.

Sensing a direction, she signaled her driver to move out before the flare even torched the sky. She knew demon hunting like she knew her name, and she left the masters in the dust, getting an early start.

She could hear vehicles careening behind her.

"Mistress, we don't know where—"

"Just drive. Swing left," she commanded, using second sight the way Marlene had taught her . . . her nose like Rider had showed her . . . listening the way Big Mike would . . . feeling for the charge in the air so closely that Shabazz would have been proud. "Gun it to eighty miles per hour—flat out," she said, so sure she didn't have to think about it twice.

"Ma'am—"

"Do it, man, and stop questioning me, or I'll kick your ass out and drive myself!"

The flare streaked the sky, making the thick dust in the atmosphere glow orange. The wind was in her hair, the dust in her face, the speed exhilarating, adrenaline pumping, her weapon cocked and ready, and that's when she saw it.

Two huge, green glowing eyes parted the dense plumes created by the Range Rover and something leaned over to pick up a body on the ground. Yellow fangs dripping acid caught in the moonlight as the beast screeched in protest, and then the creature stood up, towering fifteen feet next to Damali's 4 × 4. Short front arms brandishing lethal hooked claws scrabbled at the air, and powerful back legs with blade-sharp spikes stretched, the monster pivoted, and a hard slam from its reptilian scaled tail sideswiped the vehicle.

The Range Rover wobbled and almost overturned on the first hit, but righted itself. She held on, looping her arm under the rail and taking aim over it as the creature began to run. She fired, missed, and reloaded, shouting to the driver to step on the gas.

This was her kill. She glanced back and the vehicle gunned to ninety-five miles an hour as the other masters gained on her. But when her vehicle suddenly swerved away from an opportunity shot, and the creature doubled back to go off in another direction, she lost it.

"What is the matter with you? Just a few more feet and we would have had him!"

"I've run this course before, ma'am—I'm their best driver because I basically know where the prayer lines are, even though I'm human. Didn't you see the lines?"

For a moment, Damali didn't respond. Then she looked around. Panic nearly stopped her heart. She couldn't see any blue or white lines. The other masters had dropped back long before she did. Oh, shit . . . she was no longer in the charged house, was out in prayer-rimmed natural lands, and had called down the white light in a Neteru meditation. Ooops. Unnerved, she forced false confidence into her voice.

"Just drive, and get me to that thing."

"Whatever the lady wants," the driver said, sounding unsure.

"The demon can't cross the lines either, so follow its path—if it disappears, loop in an arc and head in the opposite direction—it has to stay within the boundaries, too," she yelled above the 4×4 engine roar. "When it goes the other direction, we're gonna harpoon that sucker."

She wrapped the steel tow hook at the front of the open pickup over the grip rail, and traded her crossbow for the huge mounted harpoon gun, dropping the crossbow on the metal floor. She then hooked the towline to the harpoon gun. "If the harpoon gun breaks away from this rail, I still want a line on him. I'm not losing the bastard."

"He'll panic, drag the Rover, and could—"

But before the driver could finish his warning, the were-roo had surfaced, Damali had taken dead aim, fired, and it was a direct hit. The beast was punctured deep in its shoulder—but it wasn't an incineration heart hit. The wound smoldered. The beast reared up on its haunches, screeching, and began a flat-out dash across the plains.

Harpoon line running out at a high speed sounded like a razor cutting the air, then the strain on the weapon began making the grip rail groan. Damali crouched low to keep her balance and held onto the side of the Rover, staying away from the leaning, bending, rail.

"Cut the line, lady!" the driver yelled, panicking. "She'll drag, then flip us!"

Before Damali could respond, the harpoon and rail gave way, flying over the driver's cage, still attached to the beast. The towline whizzed out in a matter of seconds, stopped hard, lurching the Range Rover, then the demon on the move began to bounce, dragging the 4 × 4 past the other masters, who had to swerve to avoid it.

"She got a hit!" Carlos hollered. But as soon as he saw that there was no way for Damali to regain control of her vehicle, he made his driver turn and take his 4 × 4 to a speed to flank her. "Baby, cut the line!"

"No!" she screamed. "And don't you screw us by using your power to help me!" Then just as quickly as she'd spoken, her vehicle lurched when the demon changed direction in a wide arch that almost tipped it were it not for a championship driver at the wheel, and the space between her 4 × 4 and Carlos's widened.

A sudden side bang knocked Carlos's 4 × 4 as Master Amin rammed his side panel, took aim over Carlos's shoulder, making Carlos duck, and he nailed a second were-roo that dropped and incinerated fifty yards away. Amin pulled his vehicle off Carlos's flank with a glance of total victory and pursued Damali's runaway Rover.

"Drive!" Carlos hollered, making his driver change course to follow Amin. But then a slash of a tail nearly missed his head as one of the huge monsters suddenly appeared from an unseen underground tunnel, and made a fang swipe at Carlos. He dropped to his knees, aimed, and fired, sending the stake into the center of the creature's forehead, summarily exploding green gook to splatter the cab. His focus immediately returned to Damali. She was now more than a hundred yards away and heading right for a blue band.

"Slow your speed and tire this sucker out. Make him drag us," she hollered, holding onto the driver's cage with one hand and trying to aim at the beast with her crossbow in the other. This bastard was going down.

Repeatedly the 4 × 4 went airborne two feet and then came down hard with a jarring thud only to bounce and get dragged some more. The impact was so intense that she had to grit her teeth to keep from chipping them or biting off her own tongue. But the beast's panicked flight had a steady rhythm in a flat-out run. The cord would go tight as it came down from a long, loping hop, go slack for a few seconds as the animal's powerful hind legs pushed off the ground, then go tight again. Like music, it filtered into her awareness—she could hear it, feel the pulse of it, recognize the refrain—and she was determined to make that work to her advantage.

New strategy. Damali dropped her crossbow on the floor of the pickup, climbed over the top of the bent-up caged cab section, holding the wire taut until she could swing her body down to plant her feet on the vehicle's hood. She braced for the coming slack in the cable, knees bent, holding the cage, only to release it and grab the cable when it went tight again. The head of that monster had to come off, and the Isis could handle that. The problem was, the were-roo seemed to sense exactly what she was about to do and changed direction again, making her lose her footing.

The wire momentarily went slack with a change in the beast's rhythm. She rolled, caught herself on the cage, slamming her against the metal exterior and temporarily knocking the wind out of her. The driver tried to reach for her, but she couldn't let go to grab his hand. Cable had cut into her palms, the pain like a blowtorch. But summoning a deep breath, she swung her body with the centrifugal force of the next turn, landed on the hood with a grunting thud, and was thankful that her hands weren't between the cable and the metal—a sure amputation at that torque.

Now this thing had really pissed her off. Attempting the head-sever again, she quickly went hand over hand down the cable toward the animal during a ten-second taunt period, and when the cable went slack, she went with the dip, pulling her knees up, riding the air but keeping her legs off the ground, avoiding the wildly thrashing tail. The moment the cable went taut, she used the next hard snap to propel her body like a rocket forward and grasp onto its stinking fur.

The moment her body touched the creature's, it leapt straight up, twisting and writhing, trying to shake her off, but she dug her hands deeper into the offensive fur and gripped its body hard with her knees. The Rover was airborne, coming toward them, a direct collision with her, riding the beast's back, imminent. But she held the protruding shoulder stake like a saddle grip, and her blade chimed in the wind as she drew it, saw the African diplomat's vehicle slow and swerve away, and she swung.

A demon screech sliced the night. The demon body beneath her stopped and dropped, bringing her crashing to the ground with it—the Isis flung far from her as the Range Rover being dragged by the tow cable flipped overhead, snap-jerking the demon carcass in a long slide toward a huge rock.

"No!" The African diplomat was out of the back of his vehicle and standing on the hood of his fast-moving 4 × 4, leaning out toward her, his grip on his driver's cage, one arm outstretched, yelling about the lines, his hand opened wide. "Baby, don't do it! It's not worth it. Let go!"

Truth was truth, whatever the source. She could feel the African master using his power to pull her to him. His expression was pained as he opened his arms, trying to spare her, putting himself in jeopardy of losing the game by leveling dark power. But she couldn't reach him even if she'd wanted to, and truth be told, at that second, part of her did. It was about survival.

She could feel his strength lifting the vehicle, his erotic charge entering her body, attempting to bend her will to give in and go off into the night with him as her prize. Yet, she was resolute and would not go to him. If she did, all that she'd wagered would be lost, and that was also a fate worse than death.

Their electric charges scorched the night sky, met in the air, and created a large sonic boom that cancelled each other out, leaving them both weakened. However, she'd gotten firsthand knowledge of just how strong he was.

Panic transformed into terror as the Range Rover came down on a massive sacred rock formation upside down and exploded with her driver trapped within the cab cage. Fire and gasoline lit up the night, the scent of burning flesh and fuel filled the air, and she was heading toward it all in an unbreakable momentum slide.

"Baby, come to me. *Now!*" Amin commanded, twisting and lifting Damali's body as she fought against him and the demon that was dragging her.

"Back off!" she yelled, trying to focus on the beast that was dragging her through dirt and rocks on a brutal ride. Her leg was trapped and she snatched her dagger, raised the baby Isis, hit the creature's heart from its rib cage, and torched it. Damali rolled off the creature, slapping cinders from her pants, and then lay very still on the ground for several minutes clutching her weapon. She peered up as three Range Rovers came next to her, and she shut her eyes and breathed out slowly. Good. *Thank you.* But she knew better than to even mentally reference the hallowed name of who'd probably helped. She was alive and still had all limbs. She hadn't rolled over the line, but her driver was dead and her vehicle totaled. Her body felt like she'd been beat-down by a girl gang in the streets. She slowly pushed herself up to stand, disgusted, and sheathed her dagger.

"Shit!" she hollered. "Only got one of them and my Rover is wrecked!"

Three foreign masters stared at her for a moment, glanced at each other, then motioned for their drivers to head off in a different direction.

She slapped the dust off her, glanced back at her flaming

Range Rover, and went to go get Madame Isis. So it was like that, huh?

His Australian host was giving him a run for his money. They were two for two, and this was McGuire's back yard. Carlos brought his vehicle up beside McGuire's with a were-roo running flat-out in an eighty-mile-an-hour gallop between both Rovers. Problem was, the thing was playing them both, making them take aim at each other, then dipping into a portal, coming up alongside one of the 4×4s to slam it into the other one. When the Transylvanian master tailgated Carlos, the were-roo disappeared underground, came up dead-center of Carlos's vehicle, causing Tetrosky to ram him.

He had to get out of the center of the pack, and get on the sidelines for better maneuverability. Bunched up, they'd easily hit a light rail, and that was obviously the roo's objective. Then his synapses arced danger. Carlos ducked just as the Transylvanian's stake whirred over his back and took down the roo. Instant incineration, a marksman's shot. Carlos's Rover blew grizzly ash across the plains as it went through the smoldering remains. Fury coiled within him. Yeah, it was a warning shot for him, too, right over the bow. Assassination was in the air, just like were-roo sulfur.

Tetrosky gave him a triumphant nod as the other vehicles pulled away to chase another fast-moving target. But Xe was already on it, and had dusted the beast from a hundred yards away.

"Score?" Carlos hollered at his driver, who registered kills on the dashboard.

"The lady has one marked as a twenty-point tackle even though it torched, because she left the vehicle and beheaded it first. She gets five bonus for the near-rail risk shot. All masters, two torches—twenty each. We'll allow for Amin's transgression, because he was attempting to save the mistress, not score on his own behalf."

Carlos nodded. This was *way* too close a score. The weres were also getting scarce. Then he saw a beauty riding the rails . . . and it had his name on it. He was out in the open after Tetrosky pulled back, and the other ambassadors had gone in Xe's direction. But this had to be a hand-to-hand bring down, near the rails, to put him out in front at forty-five points.

His driver shook his head no. "Too close to the rails, Mr. Councilman. That's why the odders pulled up."

"Take me to her," Carlos ordered. "She's mine."

"The roo, or the woman, sir?"

"Both!"

"We don't need to risk—"

"Do *not* argue with me!" Carlos had the crossbow to his chin, his aim steady, timing the hit to nick it, make it change course to avoid the rails if it fell from being wounded. Banking on the survival instinct of the beast, he released the stake, severing the animal's jaw. Timing was everything. It howled, ducked underground, and came up on the other side of the Range Rover. But that trapped the vehicle between the angry creature on one side, and the rails on the other.

Eight hundred pounds of furious, wounded animal slammed the vehicle's side panel, tipping the souped-up 4×4 onto two wheels.

"We're going over!" the driver hollered. "Dismount, sir!"

"Hell no!" Carlos yelled back, the vision of what the African master had attempted making him reckless. No man was going to outdo him in front of Damali. He jumped to the opposite side of the open cargo space, righting the Rover with his own sudden weight. Choppers overhead followed his Rover. He was in the lead. In his mind's eye he could see a dusty trail of other masters fast approaching behind him, trying to get into position to aim and bring down his sure kill.

He felt a harpoon whiz by his head, and knew Amin had sent it his way dead-aim, and not by accident.

When the roo charged again, he got off a shot, which sent a stake into its shoulder. But it reared, slashed its tail under the axle from the front and flipped the vehicle. The force of the impact knocked Carlos out of the open back section, and he hit the ground sliding to a stop, then jumped up running toward the demon. The driver had crossed the line; Carlos was dangerously near it on foot on the ground. In its wounded fury the were-roo charged Carlos, stopped short, claws reaching. Bowie knife drawn, he severed one of the hooked talons, making it rear back dripping green slime, then a tail struck him so hard he went airborne, dazed.

From a remote place in his mind he heard McGuire yell his name. He heard vehicles slowing. Heard a chopper land, Damali's voice hit a panic decibel that roused him, and he rolled back toward the creature, her footfalls in the very dirt beneath him like a pulse, helping him to stand. The roo was down, wasn't burning. He was closer to it than any competitor. *This was for her.* Motion, awareness snapped back, and he ran . . . he was air, was night, was the speed of light in the darkness . . . and the roo was down, within his grasp, breathing hard, dying slow from his crossbow hit and bleeding out from the severed limb. It was a damned demon. Something foul that fed on human flesh and remains like a scavenger. A parasite against humanity. It was the one thing standing between him and his Neteru. And its head was coming off in his bare hands.

Triumphant, he held the head up over the twitching body on the ground, threw his head back, and let out a sound that went back to the beginning of time itself.

Blood filled his mouth from the internal injuries that were swiftly sealing, sweat stung his eyes and he couldn't see. Adrenaline shot through him so hard and so fast that it made him stagger where he stood, converting into a pure testosterone rush of sudden euphoria.

"Score?" he shouted with his eyes closed. No one answered. That's right, his driver was dead from the crash. His own voice was foreign, deeper than when in battle; he couldn't even close his mouth it was so packed with fangs. Something nudged his legs at both sides, and then loudly sniffed him, whimpering. Yeah, the dogs could have all the dead drivers and whatever demons hadn't flamed. Then something electrifying lit his system like a rocket and knocked his head back. The scent stole his equilibrium, made him search the air for it, blind, drop the beast's head for the dogs, and open his eyes, wiping at them with his dusty forearms.

It happened in what felt like slow motion. Golden, sparkling light created an unnatural luminescence before him. His flight-weary dogs that had flown from the castle to protect him backed away from it. Footfalls coming in his direction. The vibrations echoed a familiar sound. His name splitting atoms on the wind carried by the voice of an angel, hiccupping hysteria, the glint of a blade catching moonlight and a hot body flung against him so hard he almost fell.

Disorientation gave way to instant awareness as he buried his nose deep in her damp hair and encircled her perspiration-wet back, her sword tight in her fist against his spine, she was blood-saturated adrenaline, pure Guardian Neteru, clinging to him, tears stinging his wounds, making him lift her off her feet to spin her around, laughing. He'd won. *For her.* She'd been the only thing on his mind when he went for the roo . . . it was a matter of honor—hers, his, theirs. Didn't she know?

Slowly advancing vehicles soon drew his attention. He put Damali down easy, but didn't let her go. Victory made his spine straighten, every vertebra separating, lengthening, his jaw set hard, eyes unmoving. Yes. He'd won. Fair and square—no special powers, just brute strength. She was his.

"Score, gentlemen?" he said, confidence sending his voice across the divide to them like sudden thunder.

They just stared at him, and he could feel Damali tense and draw in to him closer. They had to be out of their minds if they even thought . . .

"You crossed a major prayer artery, Councilman," McGuire said, fear and awe in his voice.

Carlos glanced at the other masters, and then laughed. "Oh, bullshit! I got close, but I would have fried." He glanced down at Damali, and her complexion was ashen from apparent trauma. He felt his face, and was still showing eight inches. "Explain these, then," he yelled, pointing to his fangs.

The Transylvanian dropped to one knee and lowered his head in total submission. "Never in history, sir. We are not worthy to be in your presence."

The others followed suit, each dropping to one knee before Carlos, each rendered mute by the unfathomable in their world. It was so quiet for a moment that Carlos was sure he could hear their still breath.

"We have seen a new era usher forth in the empire," Master Xe said, his head bowed. "Our generations will know of your great accomplishments for all eternity. My lands have been ceded to your wife, and my complete allegiance is yours."

"As are mine . . . and my allegiance to our councilman is unwavering. For generations, we have waited for such unstoppable power to concentrate," Master Amin said, his voice a murmur of respect as he lowered his gaze. "And your bride . . . I saw it with my own eyes, sir. She fought with equal ferocity to any of us here. She almost hit a line, and yet would not take my hand or use her powers that might jeopardize your claim. The commitment beyond self-survival . . . never have I witnessed such in all my years."

"You've won all of Europe, Mistress Rivera, and have my crest seal as my blood bond. I cede to you. And I humbly beg your husband's pardon for all transgressions." The Transylvanian's voice broke, and he took a deep breath.

The Aussie spoke, but dared not look up. "Sir . . . 'Sydney was made by Satan,' you told me a writer once said, when you arrived. Your Excellency . . . was that you?"

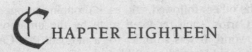

CHAPTER EIGHTEEN

HE COULD barely keep his hands off of her in the chopper, but settled for kissing her wounded palms to seal the cuts, then clasping one of her hands tightly within his. She was blind to the lines, was trailing gold—something he'd *never* seen her do . . . and she hadn't dropped fang to come to his aid in a sure extinction. Clearly she was no longer vampire. Whatever was inside her was stronger than vampire. Whatever fired her system up out there had transformed her again, and he could actually feel the raw Neteru power still pulsing through her. A will of iron, confidence, no fear.

Yet it was a frustrating transition for him to observe, bittersweet to the bone on many levels. Tonight, her being human would be a problem, like the way she trustingly tilted her head back against his shoulder, desire, relief, and pride in him running all through her and therefore running all through him. He closed his eyes, his nose grazing her hair, indulging his senses before he pulled away. Oh, yeah, this was a serious problem.

Carlos glanced down and out the window, seeing his dogs lagging behind the choppers in the distance, their wobbly flight pattern showing their fatigue. There was so much to tell her, so many questions he had . . . so many things he owed her an apology for. She'd literally put the world at his feet, had lands ceded from every nation, all for him. Had given him an immunity never even granted vampire line-founding kings. Even in a full vamp transformation, she had bargained for the life of a child . . . had tried to restore his honor, and hers, in a room of violent aggressors and had averted a cold-blooded coup . . . her Isis before her, head high.

This amazing, wondrous creation, this woman . . . had chosen him. A Neteru, bending cosmic rules, risking her life, playing the game—even playing him, at critical times, for his own good. She'd taken every dark corner of his heart, even his world, and had stood it on its head, flipped the script, and made it all work out. Yeah, he'd been shrewd enough to keep pace with her quick strategy moves, but *she* was the one with the real magic. Spellbound, how could he ever leave that . . . his temptation, sweet addiction . . . *apasionada?*

His chopper landed first, and the butler brought out the full staff with him, flanking two lines before it. When the door was opened, the entire staff line went down on one knee and bowed as he and Damali disembarked and strolled up the castle's massive front steps without looking back. Behind him he could hear the other choppers land, and soon the voice of the manservant addressed him.

"I am honored to be in your employ, Councilman Rivera. I do hope you will elect to allow me to continue to serve you and your lovely wife?"

Carlos just nodded and kept walking.

"Sir, the banquet?"

"Prepare for the guests as my wife had specified earlier. We'll be down for dinner shortly after we change."

"As you wish, sir."

Carlos kept his eyes forward, taking Damali up the stairs on his arm. She wasn't vampire, and after the hunt, they didn't need to see that she couldn't just transition into a ball gown at the door. It was certain that none of the other masters would rush him for her now, their agreements were registered in blood. He had to get her out of there before she dehydrated and dropped from fatigue and lack of food. She needed to get to her team, and get away from him . . . get away from the castle and to stay human for her performance tomorrow night . . . and for the rest of her life. That's also why she had to get away from him, because his willpower was not his own.

When they got to the room, he ushered her to the door, and opened it the traditional way, only going in first to make sure the room was secure. Once satisfied that it was safe, he held out his hand to her. But she didn't fill it with hers. Instead Damali barreled into his arms and buried her face in his shoulder.

He stared at the wall until he had to close his eyes, his chin against her temple. Telepathy was impossible, but it wasn't necessary. He'd heard her. No, he wasn't going to die on her again. Never. Couldn't if he'd wanted to. Her touch, palms holding his back tight, told him everything that it would have told any man. But the sweet fact was, she was telling *him*—not any man.

"We have to go downstairs for a toast, and accept the ceded lands." He spoke slowly, calmly, making his heartbeat still just so he could breathe. "Then, I'm going to come up with an acceptable excuse about why we have to leave." The words were so painful to say that they momentarily paralyzed his throat. Then, against his will, he mentally told her the real reason. *From now on, you have to stay human. I love you too much to turn you into anything else.* He broke from the caress of her mind.

She touched his face. *They think you have the power of the biblical seal because you crossed a prayer line and have the Neteru. The master who stole the key will want to cut a deal, trust me.* "We've made it this far," she murmured, gazing up to him, her deep brown eyes threatening to drown him.

"But I won't make it through the night," he said honestly, his eyes never leaving hers, no longer caring if the walls had ears.

They both knew that an assassination attempt was imminent, and the only thing keeping that at bay was that they weren't sure which of the pair knew the exact location of the seal that matched the key.

She didn't move for seconds that became a torturous minute, then drew away. "All right," she whispered, and walked toward her trunk.

For a while he couldn't move as he watched her resignation. The utter disappointment in her voice cut into his reason deeper than her Isis ever could.

While her back was turned, he walked to the bathroom. He wanted an old-fashioned shower, and to do something simple like dress the way he had in his human days. Hot water splashed his face and wet his body. He lathered the soap with relish, allowing the hot water to beat against him.

He needed the real sensations, not illusion, no matter how long it took. He watched Damali watch him as he began to dress in the formal tuxedo that the occasion required. He took his time, pulling on underwear, socks, his pants, zippering them, finding his shirt, buttoning it up slowly. He held his bow tie in his hands for a moment, becoming sad that he'd almost forgotten how to manually tie one. He liked that she was waiting for him, just watched him, understanding.

"I guess I should go take a bath," she said quietly, standing and walking toward the bathroom.

When he shook his head no, she halted without turning around. They were so linked.

"I was going to wash you, but thought better of it before dinner."

He could feel her smile, even though her back was turned. "I'll just be a moment," she murmured.

"Let me wash and dress you one last time . . . in my way . . . is that all right?"

When she didn't move and simply nodded, he closed his eyes and rendered her dripping wet and naked, and then let out a sigh of satisfaction that sent a warm, gentle breeze to dry her from where he stood across the room. She turned and stared at him, their gazes locked. He couldn't help adorning her in what he'd always envisioned her . . . in a long, white silk sheath, regal like she was, elegant, flowing down her legs like semi-sheer falls from Victoria, sweeping her hair up and adorning it with pearls, affixing diamond tears to her earlobes . . . her throat bare, like her back, nude beneath her gown, natural . . . a bronze goddess who had saved his life and quite possibly his soul.

The sight of her like that brought sudden moisture to his eyes that burned away. It was in the way she looked at him, beyond deep appreciation, with adoration glittering in her eyes. He glanced at her hand and gave her the ring he'd always wanted to give her . . . no crest, nothing to pollute what it meant to him for her to wear it. A blood-pact would never stain it. Blue-white heart solitaire set high in platinum—unique, like her—and the same color as the prayer lines that had passed him over.

"No matter what happens from this point forward," he whispered, "always know that I love you."

He could feel her about to approach him, but he shook his head no. He was what he was . . . a vampire and a man. And she was what she was . . . human and a woman.

"Let's go downstairs," she murmured, once again reading his mind without telepathy, and wise enough not to say right then that she loved him, too.

The entire room went silent as they arrived at the darkened ballroom door. Each guest turned and lowered his head when Carlos passed them with Damali on his arm. Moonlight and candles cast dancing shadows on the walls. The sound of their shoes hitting marble caused an eerie echo across the dim expanse. Diplomat guests carefully went to a seat and stood behind it, quietly waiting.

Carlos kept his gaze focused on the head of the table where two elaborately carved onyx high-backed throne chairs with red velvet upholstery had been placed side by side. The aisle leading to their seats felt like it was half a block long, the silence suffocating, the flickering candelabra sputtering and sizzling as they passed them, only goblets and black bottles on the table as Damali had ordered, no horrific offering that would surely revolt her. This was so eerily natural, yet so obscenely unnatural. He could feel her grip tighten, worry threading through her magnetic touch. The toast. Yes, she would have to endure it.

Once in front of his chair, he guided her to stand before hers. All eyes trained on him, seeking. Quiet mental murmurs filtered into his awareness. The alignment of power; who would be left standing by the end of dinner? Obsequious wives slipping him mental favors for just an opportunity to stay well-kept while fawning false smiles in Damali's direction, feigned submission for the sake of power—no pride. Their husbands no better, making his stomach lurch, making him wonder why he'd ever descended to this level for such an ephemeral thing as power under these circumstances . . . especially when he'd already experienced the greatest and most unconquerable power in the universe: loving someone else so much that your own survival didn't matter.

Their silent grasping for whatever crumbs he might cast from the table nauseated him. He chose his words carefully, addressing them from his new position with full authority and respect. In his mind he halted the lascivious mental gazes at his wife. Yes, she was beautiful, flawless—but from the inside out, is what they failed to understand, would always be too blind to see or fully appreciate. She wasn't for sale, wager, or land concession. Death for an untoward advance would be a merciful outcome. The very real threat rippled through the table as a subtle energy, snuffing candles as it went down the long, polished onyx, leaving only the moon as the room's source of light.

"Tonight, we have had a number of realignments. We have not decided yet how to parcel these lands so you can at least feed. The size of each new territory will be awarded based upon merit, however. The old days of nation against nation are done. The realignment will be a federation—not independent turfs. We will unite under a common banner, with a common currency, a singular purpose—one army." Carlos looked out at the guests, his gaze resting on each master briefly. He could feel the relief in each one's body as he held them in his mind for a moment, and then withdrew. He looked at Damali. "I said we, because my wife is the actual landowner—this was her fair wager, for a prize more priceless than any lands she's acquired." He tore his gaze from her too-tender one.

To recover, he spoke of her conquest, as he would have of any other masters'. Pride for her filled him. "Hand-to-hand combat, a blazing line, no fear—just pure instinct and focus, her blade raised, head back, battle cry filling the air. Gentlemen, raise your glasses, a new era and a new master has been invited to our table . . . and you will treat my wife, my mate, with honor."

She gazed at him with such appreciation that the air around her actually shimmered in the iridescent moonlight. Then she turned and looked out at the crowd. He studied the line of her jaw, the bend of her neck, the melodic sound of her voice . . . and the certain authority she possessed as she spoke—devastated by her.

"Gentlemen, ladies, if for one night, peace. We have all fought hard, and we each put much at risk. But, my greatest treasure is standing beside me," she said, her voice firm yet tender, "so I have won more than the wagers offered, and since he bested me fair and square, I willingly cede all that I have acquired to my mate . . . as a matter of choice."

Adrenaline from the other masters saturated the room. Yes, he understood what they'd seen her do, what the hunt had done to all of them. He understood the effect of Neteru more than they could imagine. And could truly understand their disappointment that none of them would have her tonight. Even though he'd almost been scorched from the face of the earth just for that honor . . . and by rights, winner takes all.

Before the thought could take root and fester in his mind, he raised his filled goblet. "To a new empire!"

He downed his toast, each master following suit, the instant gratification so necessary after a hunt. So critical, standing beside her, denied. Their mates salivating for a vein, their own goblet of blood, but having to wait for

Damali to consume hers first—protocol they dared not breach now. Their lives had just been spared and the peace was too fragile.

Her sudden alarm made him glance at her, then hold her gaze steady, his hand going to her cheek, a sealed telepathy lock necessary to help her through this. *Swallow the blood, just one sip, so these boys don't ever question you when I'm not by your side.*

Her eyes were wide, the answer in them was immediate and panicked. She couldn't do it. He knew it before she thought it.

The room was hovering between post-hunt bacchanalia and disaster, patience shredding in males that needed desperately to feed, still saturated with adrenaline, testosterone, and blitzed on Neteru. An unstoppable feeding frenzy near.

Hair-trigger reflexes were coalescing with the need to complete a seduction with whatever available female presented willing in the room—one's wife or not, it didn't matter. They might even turn that battle adrenaline on each other and fight to the death in the ballroom. This was after a hunt; they'd just lost all their lands, causing a fear spike that fed dark fury; each knew it might well be his last night to exist. They were exhausted, irrationally dangerous because of what fatigue did to their willpower. They'd seen her negotiate, deceive them, hunt and best them. Infuriating, intoxicating. The females at their sides were teetering on the edge of desire collapse after having done near battle in the parlor, then had watched blood sport and a council-level master cross prayer lines to behead a demon with his bare hands. They'd witnessed outrageous history being made—something new, a sure aphrodisiac within their long, bored lives. Damali's panic became his. *Swallow the blood. Now.*

He could feel Damali about to vomit as water came to her eyes and she practically heaved. Then as swift as a cobra she reached up, grabbed the nape of his neck, and forced his head down, his mouth to hers hard, and sent everything her cheeks were holding into his. Blood hit the back of his throat, almost choking him. She weaved a bit, and pressed her wrist to her lips, panting, probably to keep from throwing up. His gaze quickly scanned the table; her sweet essence in his mouth, mixed with blood.

Two masters, Tetrosky and McGuire, held onto their chairs and looked away, devastated, full fangs dropped. Evelyn's gasp cut through Carlos's skeleton as she swooned against McGuire and bit him. Xe's wife could barely hold her goblet, her hands were shaking so badly. Amin pulled his wife to him hard and bit her with such force that he nearly ripped out her throat. The chain reaction was insane. His variable a loose cannon by his side.

The openly sexual act, done in public, at a time like this, under these circumstances by *a councilman's wife* denoted total commitment, sheer submission, control not to feed, discipline beyond comprehension in his world, and that she hadn't dropped fang and stood meekly by his side, after they knew what she could transform into, had blown them away. It had rocked his world, too. He had to get her out of there *now*.

All formality bled away from him as he folded her into his arms and became vapor, fusing every cell of hers with his until she was transparent, the wind, to safely bring her to the terrace beyond their suite. Materializing was instantaneous. What had she done . . . forced him to taste her mouth, given him yet more power by the awed cessation of control by four masters and their mates, made him enter her mind, once again, to feel the impact of her emotions, her need to be with him, her memories of them together echoing through her system like wildfire, then forcing him to protect her with a significant transport beyond the cellular level, down to the atomic . . . before a solid feed.

"I love you," she whispered hard against his cheek. "What about this don't you get?"

He couldn't breathe with her in his arms, so his hands held the side of her face, his mouth crushing her words away, siphoning the residual blood in it to clean her palate, and to fulfill his. She was human; he wasn't. He needed her to leave; her hard shudder begged him to stay. Sweet surrender washed through him.

Didn't he understand? Her hands slid up his back. He'd almost died—again. They had almost assassinated him right in front of her. He'd touched the depths of her mind with his, found the depths of her heart with his honor. And his gentleness with her knew no bounds. *He'd prayed for her.* Willed her back to life. She'd shared *her soul* with him just so he'd have one—if Heaven wouldn't provide, then she would. Love beyond the rules, giving every fiber of who she was . . . unable to say no, even understanding all that he was and all that he was not. It didn't matter, not right now. He'd loved her. He'd saved her. He'd been butchered for her. That counted for something—it had to. If there was mercy anywhere in the universe, they had to know what he meant to her. He had to know and never forget.

His punishing kiss was an echo that she sent back hard, crushing, intense. He'd given his entire kingdom for one night with her, and had defended any other claim to her. He was more than worthy of redemption in her eyes, even if that choice wasn't hers to make, or in her power to give—she'd try to bestow it in her arms.

Tears cascaded down her cheeks as she pulled her mouth away. "Time cheated us. Don't send me back to being alone," she said, her voice cracking, her breaths unsteady as she took his mouth hard again. What more was there for him to understand . . . when the shudder he sent through her was beyond definition . . . his tongue harshly probing the insides of her mouth, sending phantom pulses of ecstasy to enflame her skin, turning her legs to putty ready to wrap around his waist the moment his will snapped. This wasn't up for negotiation. She needed him. Had surrendered. Only moments mattered. This was primal.

He tore his mouth from hers, looked into her eyes, a question trapped by a plea in them. He, like she, was beyond speech. Telepathy failed. But his body understood. His hands understood all that she'd been trying to say, but couldn't . . . and he gathered her gown under his palms, one arm crushing her torso to his, the other pulling her hip to fit tightly against him, the kiss so hard now that he nicked her lip. Hot breath scathed her neck, and a swift strike, blinding—her voice drowning the surf, coming from a place within her that she never knew existed.

The railing was only matter, dissolving, as her backside slammed against it, him an inseparable brand coating her like second skin. Consciousness ebbing as fast as the two-hundred-foot drop—the wind the only thing beneath her, the surf the earth's heartbeat, becoming hers. His arms, solid rock, enclosed her. The siphon pulling everything up and out of her in a long wail, hers, as they fell.

No impact, just rebirth in the sand far away. Swirling dust became their bodies, giving them shape and form while joined. The moonlight was their blanket. Desert wind was their music. Twenty-thousand-year-old song lines, a didgeridoo pulse in the red earth, protecting, anointing, barring all predators from their union. X-ray art beings—turned inside out by pleasure. The howl of the wolf, part his, part dingo. Hours passed, but time was trivial. *Make it last.* Iron ore beneath her fingernails, embedded in her knees, but she couldn't stop if her life depended on it.

A burning hand holding her belly, the rhythm older than prayer itself. His sweat dripping onto her back, creating a salty stream down her spine. Another lubricant to help him slide against her harder. She felt the heat of his breath in her ear as he panted her name on fervent exhales. Her breasts lowered to the sandy ground, her hips lifted to meet him each time he returned, her tears creating red-dust face paint on her cheek. Her spine a flex-snap response to his intense wind chants. Another sudden strike flattening her body spread-eagle with his name leaving her lungs. Approaching dawn be damned, *don't stop* . . .

He had to look at her face. Feel her belly against his, her cradle of life, witness her force of nature in her eyes as he filled her with seed, dead or alive. She was a creator, a giver of life, what no man could ever be. The alpha and the omega of profound ecstasy. Woman . . . owner of oblivion.

The impending seizure she caused gathered clouds in the sky, touched off lightning to kiss the distance, but brought no rain. Only she was moisture, wrested it from all around her, including him, then made it pour.

Conflicted, but so certain . . . returning to her primordial essence with each stroke, her hard arches a call-and-response tide that had only one answer. Sudden death, his, hers, theirs, but still breathing.

Her head in his hands, caressing it with all her dreams inside it, a promise to honor them, pebbles and grit tearing at his knees, cutting his thighs, his love a protection at her back, not one scratch would he allow, not a drop of her blood would the ground steal from him . . . but she could take it all. Her strike staggering. Pulse-stopping. His mind opening so fast that it tore and issued forth every image of her that he'd ever held. An infant at her breast causing sobs with his release, unending, as hers joined his and echoed back the pleasure until he had to lift his head to stop feeding the sweet agony.

Fangs catching the last of starlight. The road to Hell paved with good intentions. Redemption in her arms. Resurrection, whenever she wanted him . . . for however long. Dawn on the horizon, serious warning not to play with nature. *Don't stop,* a refrain in her chant. His name a shuddered stanza. Hers, hard shivers down his spine when he gasped it.

Oh, sweetness, yes, he understood promises made in passion . . . he was a man . . . knew about saying anything to keep wet flesh moving. He wasn't mad. Been there. He felt the same way; her body was a narcotic. A flat-line overdose. The median between lust and love was thin. He could dig it. Him now chasing her arch like chasing a crack hit. Blitzed, her voice calling his name now the only way he'd remember it. Not a mild transition, undergoing sea change lodged inside her . . . needing to turn her to keep her with him forever . . . just like he needed his next breath. Trying to hold back that intent was nearly impossible. Thinking of the future without her making him almost weep. *Baby . . . you just don't know* . . . Disaster imminent, brought on by blinding ejaculation seizures. Peristaltic. Involuntary, like his throbbing lunges. His promises more than that, though—a blood oath, his seed a seal, whatever she wanted—*Name it,* mi tresora. *I'll never leave you . . . will try my best not to hurt you. I love you. Always did.*

Common sense abandoned. Not an option. Follow the sound lines—sound wisdom from a priest. A safe house another answer to a prayer. Withdrawal from her impossible. *Not yet.* Vacuum-sealed hot fusion, liquefied heat. His woman limp in his arms. Pull out or die. Don't kill her.

Darkness, a sure sanctuary . . . like her body. The presence of her warmth beneath him a necessity. Her tremble an indelible print on his skin. Her mouth his oasis. Her sudden shudder, increasing octaves, rippling up sections of his vertebrae like standing stones. Her moans radiating from her chest into his and out through the tips of his fingers, raw energy. The wetness of her mouth, sucrose-lacquered blood. Her scent a stimulant that knew no tranquilizer. Muscles aching but still moving. His back her bridge to sure salvation, driving, as she dragged her nails the length of it.

Every thrust now taking him to the vanishing point and beyond, crossing parallel lines of existence, bending to collide into an optical illusion so real, wishing he'd never left the lair . . . but unable to share even her airborne cries with another master, much less her scent—her sacred mind transmissions, *never* . . . wallowing in the dust on a hard roll-over, to follow the lines and make it to the safe house with his last ounce of strength to save them both, or die trying. Winner takes all, and then some. But daylight didn't negotiate.

Dark eyes in ebony faces shining in the breaking night looked up from the fire. White paint dotted and smeared against their skins, giving them the eerie ancestral quality of ancient spirits, all-knowing from Dreamtime.

Language a barrier, but an intense plea in his eyes for help, a woman nearly dead draped in his arms, created universal understanding. They all knew he would drop to his knees and beg for sanctuary if he had to. They understood.

No shame, it was about survival. Compassion. The human heart a treasure. At least save his woman. *Please . . . for the love of God . . . get her out of the coming sun!*

An old man's satisfied nod, walking stick pointed toward a cavern with a wry smile. Daylight be damned, he wasn't done. Time had robbed them. He'd seal the cave and transform it for her—turn it into the lair she deserved . . . and love her through the morning. Just one more time before handing her over. Just so he could remember every inch of her when he had to let her go. She'd branded him. Did that with her eyes when they'd first met . . . no matter what he was.

Dawn would suffocate her, then burn her. Their ancient barriers to the cave were impenetrable now without their permission. He stretched out his arms, offering her body to them, and knelt on one knee. Would gladly sacrifice his own instead. Time was a thief. *Take her; I'll burn in her place.* Without her there was nothing to exist for. *Just give her sanctuary.*

Another nod of approval from a tribal elder. No words were needed. A dense energy lifted. He almost wept at their grace. Discreet glances returned to the business of staring into the flames and packing pipes was all that was needed to effect the territory transfer. His shoulders dropped from fatigue and relief. That's when the old men smiled, and he could begin to see a ring of white light beneath their bright orange-yellow fire with etchings that were almost blinding. It was as though they were sitting on a blue-white platter, the diameter twelve feet, with a thickness he couldn't judge. Its brilliance almost made it impossible to look at, the Aramaic markings were so encrypted and sacred, he dared not allow his eyes to linger upon it. Then it became so crystal clear as the elderly humans became illuminated, X-ray art marking their dark bodies—but it wasn't paint. It was pure light. Their images blurred and in an instant he knew. These were spirits, shamen . . . rock art, living prayer lines. They were the keepers of the sixth seal. They said one word that he understood as their low harmony of chants sent embers up to the heavens from their now blue-white fire—*Neteru.*

Carlos nodded with his eyes closed, his head bowed in reverence to their generosity and mercy. He brought Damali's body to his chest and held her against him hard, stroking her hair as her arms slowly awakened to hold him when he stood. Power was relative. He was forever in their debt. Their twenty-thousand-year-old prayer lines and unshakable courage surrounded the seal. They'd also sealed this secret within his soul, but had left the choice up to him to divulge it or not. Knowledge was a heavy burden. They smiled wider as he looked down at Damali in his arms. No matter what was going on in his empire, right now, these old men ruled the world.

CHAPTER NINETEEN

THROUGHOUT THE fourteen-hour journey not a Guardian had said more than the perfunctory, keeping everything to logistics before they leaned back and closed their eyes. Since they'd all been together, they had never gone anywhere as a team without Damali and without a sure plan. While flying nonstop from night into day, losing a full day at the International Date Line, with only a delay to refuel, they had remained stone-faced. Even in their sleep she could feel the weight of their broken spirits.

Marlene appraised them quietly as their rented equipment bus lumbered behind their limo. The team, as well as the Covenant squad, seemed totally demoralized. There was no other word for it. Rider hadn't even passed a sarcastic quip to anyone when they went to the Thomas Cook offices to convert their currency. Maybe she should have let him and Jose ship their bikes on cargo planes, as extravagant a request as that might have been. But when would they have the time to ride?

Perhaps they could rent something when they got there for after the concert, but she really didn't want them going off to the Blue Mountains ninety miles west of the city before the gig. There was just too much to do, and too many unknowns, to be traipsing through Sydney Harbor National Park's wildlife.

No. She'd been right, even though she had to admit that her decisions had been hard ones clouded by doubt. This was not going to be like Brazil. This time the guys weren't going to get a chance to relax and enjoy the local flavor. There was no time before the mission to take a Sydney Harbor Explorer Cruise to see the scantily clad women on Sydney's forty-beach embarrassment of riches. After the concert they wouldn't be going to fine restaurants like Guillaume at Bennelong or Claude's and Tetsuya's with new chicks on their arms, a Foster's brew the size of an oil can, and shrimp on the barbie; this wasn't anything close to the Brazilian job.

Something had happened last night. Something *serious,* that had put a cold sweat on her body and had made Father Pat sit up and look at her across the plane aisle.

All she'd need was for Rider and Jose to get caught up and lost in the raucous nightlife at King's Cross. Energy from 1788, when Captain Arthur Phillip dropped anchor and turned loose a shipload of convicts from England's over-crowded jails, was probably still making the air crackle along that stretch of real estate.

Just like she was sure that the famed tourist attraction, the Rocks, under Sydney Harbor Bridge where the first ships came in, and the colonial Macquarie Street area, still held a significant charge—ghosts and disembodied spirits were probably there, at the very least. On a job like this, they didn't need any additional variables. Places had power. Marlene closed her eyes.

She'd picked the Westin Sydney because it was only blocks from a trinity zone of hallowed ground at St. Andrew's Cathedral, the Great Synagogue, and Hyde Park. Open-land parks were good, always retained prayer lines from the native people, and all of that was a short distance to Victoria Street and Darlinghurst Road on the other side of the park where the fellas could let off a little steam.

But she wondered now if they even needed to be near the corridor of burlesque joints, massage parlors, and video dens that ran hot after ten o'clock at night—prime time for vamps. Right now her team needed to be isolated, and not run into a minor vamp battle that could drain resources. She had to make herself relax, knowing that there were some good vibes where they were going to perform.

The Sydney Opera House was built on a natural land formation called Bennelong Point by the Aussies, which jutted out into the bay with Sydney Cove dividing the Rocks from it. The grand theater was near plenty of open ground by the Royal Botanical Gardens and Domain Parkland, with tremendous creative energy filtering along Writer's Walk, and just a bit beyond that was Macquarie Place, once a site of ceremonial and religious importance to Aboriginal people. The song lines remained, just like the giant obelisk did—a point from which all distances from Sydney were once measured. Interesting feng shui. Yet for all its clean, modern beauty and rich history, there was a dark underbelly to be wary of. She just hoped that Damali hadn't fluxed and had been able to pull from the indigenous prayer lines in the area.

However, every big city had a dark side. She tried to force herself to relax, knowing she couldn't put her team in a protective bubble, much as she wanted to. It was a foolish thought. They weren't destined to be blind to the dark side or protected from it, but in her heart she wished that she could, anyway. This indefinable thing that had happened, coupled with the significance of this particular mission, made her know that one, or some, of her beloved guardians might not come home this time. She knew it as sure as she knew her name, and no amount of mental bracing could bring her acceptance, no matter how many years she'd tried to prepare herself for that fact.

They'd just have to use their best judgment until they could get a flight out. She hoped that the guys would be satisfied watching the Australian winter game, rugby. But she knew better than that. They were grown men, warriors, and not about to hide from the night.

Marlene absently gazed at the Georgian and Victorian architecture as they passed neat suburban homes, remembering the endless streams she'd seen upon their United Airlines flight approach. She wondered if the four million residents tucked away in mundane comfort ever knew what lurked amid the branching waterways. Probably not.

She could feel her energy dipping as they neared the hotel. None of them had been the same since Damali had left with Carlos. She peered at Big Mike. His eyes said it all; the team's leader and daughter had abandoned him. Jose was positively bereft. She sighed silently as she glanced at J.L. and Dan. They still seemed stunned. The muscles in Rider's jaw were working. And Shabazz . . . The man's complexion was practically gray. She could feel his deep soul mourning; although he hadn't said a word, it clouded his entire aura.

She looked out the window during the traffic-impacted five-mile stretch between Kingsford Smith International Airport, watching the billowing white-tiled sails of the Sydney Opera House come into view, renewed tension winding the muscles in her shoulders tight. Father God, where was her baby girl? This time, there was no plan. Damali hadn't even come back to develop a strategy with them to get everyone on the same page, help come up with new weapons, or anything like that, much less perfect the show.

All they had was this new, very-unlike-Damali song, some fleeting instructions about a rendezvous time and location, and a tape that had mysteriously shown up in the compound one night—which had freaked *everybody* out, including her. They were almost afraid to listen to it, and the Covenant had almost destroyed it when they tried to douse it with holy water. The message was crazy: Have faith.

Faith . . . Marlene rolled the word around in her mind. The team was missing its crown jewel, and each member was falling away one-by-one like loose semiprecious stones in a weakened setting, grieving, losing faith, losing hope— the only thing holding them together was the crazy glue of love.

Marlene thought about the Isis, her inner eye seeing each team member like a gemstone set in the handle of it,

matched perfectly to Damali's chakra system. She, the
mother-seer, was the base chakra guide, an anchor of elder
female energy to ground her young charge, guarding her
sensuality and important reproductive path. Shabazz was the
gut instinct one level up. Rider was her gall, her righteous
indignation, covering level three. Jose . . . Marlene shook
her head . . . God bless him, he was to guard her heart—the
midsystem chakra divide between the primal and the divine . . . and he'd been shattered.

Big Mike was to be Damali's throat chakra voice guide, a
man of few words, but those uttered, profound. J.L. and Dan
were like the protective handle of the ancient blade, two
stones of her third eye fanning out to protect her grip. But
Damali was the crown chakra, the diamond at the top, which
was to always be connected by the divine filament of energy
that never left the Light.

Marlene's chest was so tight with grief that she almost
sobbed. *Something had happened.* The four remaining
Covenant brethren were supposed to represent the blood
grooves along the Isis that came down to a point, which
would leave a crucifix wound in an enemy, a puncture on a
beast that would never seal. Their eyes were forward, their
jaws set hard, but their faith was wavering. She could feel it
like a dull ache in her soul. It was as though the combined
teams' human replica of Damali's system, and of the sword
that she was to become, had been broken over their Neteru's
knee—halved and traded in for what none of them could
give her, and only Carlos could.

All she could hope was that the broken blade would be re-
forged into something new, stronger, and that ultimately
some good would come out of the ashes left in the furnace.

He watched her sleep, grateful that her breast rose and fell
with life-sustaining air. She was alive. Last night they'd
come too close. Never again. Not like that.

She looked so peaceful, serene . . . like an angel in the
dark. Maybe a dark angel? He wasn't sure. But the old men
had been merciful.

"Good evening, baby," he murmured as she stirred and smiled at him with her eyes still closed.

"Hey," she whispered. "Where are we?"

"I followed the song lines," he said tenderly, kissing the bridge of her nose. "They opened up the safe house for us."

"Hmmm . . . good," she said in a sleepy voice. "I'm so glad we're not in the castle."

"So am I," he admitted, then leaned in and kissed her. "You hungry?"

"Yeah," she said, covering his hand on her belly with her own. "Starved."

He chuckled low in his throat. "Yeah, me, too."

It was difficult to pull away from her, but every request she made, he'd honor.

"Whatcha feel like?" he asked cautiously.

"Water," she murmured. "And lots of it," she added, swallowing with difficulty. "Fruit, bread, everything . . . I'm starved."

He paused thoughtfully. She was human. Conflict bound him. His emotions quickly vacillated between extreme elation and the depths of disappointment. If she was human, she wouldn't live forever. If she was a vampire, then she would, but then that meant he'd done the unthinkable in blind passion. But her human request also meant that he'd never be able to take her to the vanishing point again.

"Okay," he said quietly, and lit a small wall torch so she could see. "I can do that."

With mixed feelings, he unsealed the lair the old men had provided and left her to go find food. Not fully regenerated, he opted for the old-fashioned way, and cautiously peered out of the room, checking for danger before he proceeded. But he didn't have to walk far. On the ground outside the door the old men had left a large bottle of spring water and a platter of fruit. "Thank you," he whispered and collected the items.

Returning with soft footfalls, he brought the nourishment to her side, sitting gingerly on the bed. He watched her devour the food and guzzle down the water. Guilt stabbed him as he thought about how long she'd been without the basic thing she needed to live—human sustenance.

Then all of a sudden, she quickly leaned over the side of the bed and vomited. She panted, sweat beading her brow, and he rubbed her back, confused.

He set the platter down very carefully on the nightstand, and stared at her as she flopped onto her back and slung an arm over her eyes. Her complexion was off; her eyes were dull. He had to get her to Marlene. Something was very wrong. She smelled . . . sweeter, lighter.

"Oh, God," she moaned. "I feel like shit."

He tried to keep the panic out of his voice. "I have to feed. I'll leave you some clothes, and as soon as I get back, we'll go find Marlene, okay, baby?"

Damali just nodded, and struggled to sit up. "Hand me the water," she said weakly. "I can't go into a concert like this." She looked up at him, huge tears forming in her eyes.

Two big tears rolled down her cheeks and she leaned over and lowered her face into her hands. He walked over to her, sat down, and pulled her to him.

"It's cool. It's gonna be cool. Okay?" He knew it was a lie as soon as he'd touched her and felt her burning up with fever. "You're gonna be all right, baby. I just need to get you to Marlene." He stood up fast, and quickly walked to the sealed lair door.

She sat there with her face covered, shaking her head. It was *not* going to be all right.

"At worst, you're turning back and . . ."

Damali dry heaved and then began to cry. Shit, this was bad.

"You're not pregnant," he said firmly, immediately reading her mind. "You couldn't go there last night in a vamp turn, right?"

"I'm real late, Carlos," she said, now looking up at him.

He stood so still he didn't even blink for a moment, then ran his fingers through his hair, again summoning rational calm. "All right . . . but that's to be expected. Your body has been in flux ever since we got here—"

"What if it didn't happen here? What if, before . . ."

She let the rest of her sentence just dangle with him hanging at the end of it.

"Aw'ight, aw'ight. Let's not panic and jump to conclusions," he said, ignoring his own advice as Father Patrick's safe house came into his mind. "First of all, that can't happen. You can't get that way from me, unless it's daywalker. So don't start tripping yourself out." He raked his fingers through his hair. "Plus, I bit you so many times, you went in and out of vamp turns . . . I would have tasted it in your blood if you were pregnant."

"I'm late, and I really don't feel good," she said as her sobs dissipated. She wiped her face with both hands and stared at the wall.

"How late?" It felt like his spinal cord was being pulled out of his back on an Inquisition rack as he waited for her answer.

"Since at least Brazil," she said, taking a little sip of water, and wiping her mouth with the back of her hand. "I thought it was because of all the battles, all the stress, the changes my body was going through."

"Then that explains it," he said, forcing a chuckle. "We're cool. I mean, you'd been bitten for the first time at the monks' joint, your system whacked out, then you went demon hunting, you know . . . and plus, we had all that back-and-forth stuff going down in my lair in Beverly Hills when we got back from St. Lucia, then you did the flux to vamp thing in the castle—right—and then, then, what happened was, you, uh . . . uh . . . well, I brought you to the desert. It got a little . . . well, hey, you know. And so, that's why I'm saying, you're cool. This is just some kinda transitional thing, right?"

He knew he wasn't making sense and didn't wait for her answer. Instead he began pacing, trying to convince himself as he walked, lingering by the door for a moment, taking a few steps toward her, then going back to where he needed to be—on the far side of the room. "It was intense out there, baby, I know, but don't panic. You just need to eat regular food, get something on your stomach, ya know?" Shit, this was bad.

She left the table, going to him, and placed her hand on his cheek. "That's when I knew . . . last night. I felt it. In fact, I saw it. That's when it happened, when you took me to the vanishing point—where every molecule and atom in the body splits and fuses for a second with your lover's. I saw it."

"Naw," he said, shaking his head, in pure denial, kissing her hand fast and then walking to the other side of the room. "We were both throwing down images, hard, D. You were all inside my head, and I was all inside yours. We were blowing each other's minds. It was mad-crazy-awesome, but we have to—"

"Be honest," she said, cutting him off with a gentle tone. "You wanted us both to live forever."

He looked away from her, studying a lit torch. "Aw'ight, I admit it," he said, his voice so quiet that it was as though he was talking to himself. "I came so close to messing up, big time, last night, but I swear to you . . . I mean, a little bit of that intent might have seeped out while I was in, but I pulled up just in time. I've got that much control, baby. You have to trust me."

"At the vanishing point," she said, her tone not accusatory, just matter-of-fact and gentle. "There was a pinpoint of white light, like a spark, then I was gone, and in two seconds I was back. There is no such thing as control at the vanishing point. Forces of nature are in control, then."

He didn't answer her immediately, remembering the oblivion, the place she'd named where the parallel lines of their separate worlds bent, collided, and the blue-white spark ignited . . . that place where he wanted to give her everything in him, and did, and wanted her to live on forever with him, through any means necessary.

"Okay," he said, fast, his voice louder than he wanted it to be. "But if you—" He stopped his comment, redirecting it. "Okay. But if—"

He walked to her and held her by both arms. He took a deep breath and looked at her, desperate now to convince himself. "You don't get sick overnight, that's one. Number two, if you were late since Father Pat's on the first time out, then we would have known. Both of us would have sensed that. Number three, the old boys would have picked that up on radar, and if they didn't, I *know* Marlene would have. So, let's not bug."

Damali shook her head no. "My system isn't quote unquote normal, Carlos," she said, making little gestures with her fingers. "It was there since it was first planted at Father Pat's—the intent. Dormant. Waiting for enough energy and love to give it that spark of life. This isn't a daywalker, honey . . . this is *a guardian*. You wanted to live forever, so did I—*with you*. And a child is a way for people—humans— to do that for generations. I shared my pulse; your humanity never left you, and you still have a soul, albeit trapped in Purgatory, but you have one. We were on hallowed ground last night in the desert, and the intensity, the way our energy fused and bent light, matter, in a natural, sacred place . . . We both surrendered completely to the other . . ."

She walked away from him as his hands slid from her arms and terror glittered in his eyes. "You said it in my mind . . . 'Flesh of my flesh, soul of my soul, with everything I have, woman, I love you, don't leave me.'" She sighed when he rubbed his jaw and turned away, leaning on the door. "You broke up into a thousand pieces of light when you—"

"Aw'right, aw'right, I know . . . I remember."

"And, when you came back, you were sobbing, and—"

"Yeah, yeah, but—"

"And your protect or die instinct kicked in, and the next thing I knew, I was going in and out of consciousness around some fire with old men . . . I blacked out when you dropped to your knees and asked for sanctuary *in the name of God* just for me—"

"True dat," he said fast to stop her vivid replay, the recent humiliation too fresh to say out loud. If his boys ever knew that he'd been so caught up to be left standing naked at dawn, vulnerable before weak old men, unable to fight them, begging them in the name of the Almighty . . . oh, no.

Carlos closed his eyes for a moment to wash the image out of his mind, then looked at her, his voice thick with false bravado. "But, baby, look, for real, we can't panic. We can't jump to conclusions. Where's the war party?" he asked, sweeping his arm around the room. "They would have sent a force up here that could have broken through the Vatican. Feel me?"

"Only if I registered as a permanent vamp turn—ruining their vessel, or if their vessel was prematurely impregnated with a daywalker. They can never feel when a blessed innocent is created—that's why they can never find a Neteru or Guardian in the womb. That's why they have to be strategic, gamble on who the mother will be." She looked at him hard, folded her arms over her chest. "Now, do you feel *me*?"

Her logic was so sound it was chilling. There were no words. This was *not* good. It was a floating free-radical of disaster. The baby in the castle had been an omen. The cross cut on its finger to mark it for good, a sure sign. And what he'd unloaded last night was no joke. He raked his fingers through his hair again, nearly wanting to rip out his own brain, or what was left of it. Oh . . . shit . . .

He studied her calm, trying to siphon some of it for himself. She stood before him naked, looking down at her belly, caressing it, and through her touch he knew she wasn't wrong.

Again, competing emotions bombarded him. A slow smile found his face from somewhere deep within his male subconscious, making his rational mind ponder if last night he'd gone mad. She was carrying for *him*. Just like he'd always imagined. Wanted it just as much as he did. Daaaayum . . . He was gonna be a dad . . . with Damali? Suddenly he laughed. His legs moved him toward her, and he picked her up and swung her around, kissed her hard, then set her down gently and walked over to the wall and slapped it.

"Hot-damn! I *cannot* believe this," he said, giddy.

"They're gonna freak—but what the fuck, I don't care!" He threw his head back and laughed again and then held her gaze. She was so beautiful, even looking a little green. Once again, she'd given him a gift that was beyond comprehension. "You know how bad my moms and grandma wanted grandkids?" His gaze drifted toward a torch. "Damn, I wish Poppi and Alejandro . . . my boyz were still here." He looked at her fast. "You think they can see the baby from wherever they are, D?"

He looked at her suddenly stricken expression, and went to her, to hold her. "It'll be all right, baby. We'll make a way. Shit, I own the world."

"As a vampire, Carlos," she said too calmly, slipping from his hold to go sit on the edge of the bed. "They are not going to allow this, you know that, right? Especially when you don't deliver them the seal or the key." She stared at him, watching the jubilation drain from his face. "My team can only protect me for so long . . . nine months is a long time, and if they go for the baby—"

"Don't even think about that shit," he said, pushing away from the wall to stare at her. "Hell no. I will—"

"Be exterminated by your own council," she said, getting to her feet. Her hand went to her mouth, stopping his words as she whirled around the room. "We don't have the resources to protect a human child from the types of forces that are going to come for us. The primary mission is restoring the key—not having a child!" She stopped speaking, closed her eyes, and then resumed very slowly, her voice even. "Carlos, do you realize what our mission is? This ain't some around the way shit where you can roll up on your boys with our baby in your arms and say, 'Yo, *hombre,* dis is me.' This ain't some simplistic baby-momma drama. This is *major* bullshit. You ain't gonna be able to roll by, drop a few ends, take this kid to the ballgame with your squad. Are you insane? We can't handle this."

She began pacing, leaving him numb with reality. "We aren't prepared, haven't thought of the future, have no real resources and assets to give this kid everything he or she needs." She spun on him and looked at him square. "This is what Marlene had been telling me in our little birds and the bees chats when I first came back from Father Pat's. She told my dumb ass what a Neteru conception would be like." She ran her fingers through her locks and closed her eyes.

"I'll take care of it . . . will take care of you, I promise, baby. We'll get through this, and one night we'll look back at this and laugh. I mean, for real, how bad could it be?"

Damali's eyes held his, and he saw something in them that he'd never seen before. True terror. Total panic. An awareness that for the first time in her life, there was nothing to fight—only something to protect, that she couldn't all by herself. What she had at stake was even more important than her own survival. Even the castle filled with vamps hadn't put an expression on her face like this.

"If we make it, for nine months," she said quietly, "plus the six weeks I need to heal, you can't bite me." She closed her eyes, placed her hand on the center of her chest, and breathed slowly, as though staving off a heart attack. "Oh, my God, Carlos . . . I don't know how we're going to make it, not being able to—"

"Nine months . . . but you said it probably went down at Father Pat's, it won't be that long—"

She let out a long sigh that cut off where he was going. "The thought and the conditions were set at Father Pat's," she said, her voice suddenly weary. "But when our minds, bodies, and spirits united as one out there in the desert, that was the moment the spark of life ignited. In that moment, I wasn't vampire, and neither were you all the way. We fused at the atomic level. I can't get even a passion bite in my bloodstream while carrying. My blood is shared now. My body will purge hard because of the extra strain on my system and I could abort."

He could feel himself battling to breathe; he wasn't even hungry any longer . . . nine months . . . *shit* . . .

His lack of response made her shake her head and speak to him in a crisp tone. "Then, until I stop nursing, you can't give me your virus. After it's born, if you don't want me to one day infect our child, I can't get bitten—and risk a flux. If I do battle, and get nicked, my team will have to keep the kid away from me to be sure I don't flux, and only let me near the baby when the vamp virus is out of my system. All the while we're trying to keep it safe for *years*, Carlos. That's why they don't make that many female Neterus . . . there's a risk factor of unborn innocents and babies potentially involved."

Shell-shocked, her words imploded within his awareness slowly.

"That's what Marlene was trying to tell us. Our lifestyles are too dangerous, neither of us is ready for that level of responsibility. Me and you were never supposed to *create* together—not under these circumstances."

Hot tears sat in her eyes, shimmering and threatening to fall, but this time she wouldn't let them. "We weren't supposed to go there until . . . if you weren't what you are, weren't in the life you're in . . . if I wasn't what I am—a woman on a mission with a serious future. Now, you'll have to be around me because there's probably nobody else capable of sensing a vamp attack like you can, but you won't be able to throw down vamp passion. Do you understand what that means? And, it's not just you—it's me . . . I might be the one to break down and call you . . . I'm only human, and you're only vamp. We aren't made of steel."

Just her saying that made a quiet shudder run through him.

She looked up at him, shaking her head. Her voice dropped to a whisper, as though she were actually talking to herself. "But, I'll have to dig deep and say no, because there's now something more precious to me than anything in the world, and I won't allow even its father to jeopardize its life because of *his* mistakes and the way he lives. *Comprendo?* I'm out of the street game of dusting lower-level vamps, rolling at night on the hunt . . . doing things with you that . . . I'm gonna be a mother. You ready to deal with that?"

For all his powers and knowledge of the world, the simple word *yes* was the last thing he thought of. Everything she said was too real. Blew him away. He looked at the naked woman before him who had wrapped her arms around herself as though barring him entry from her. He could also tell that the magnitude of her own words was scaring her to death. But the brief moments it took for all that to form and sort itself out in his mind, his slow answer seemed to hurt her more than any clumsy response he could have given her. He went to open his mouth to speak, but her narrowed gaze stopped anything he was about to say.

"Get me some clothes. Khakis, a T-shirt, sneakers. Get my Isis blades out of that fucking castle." She walked away and gave him her back while he dressed her.

He watched her sheathe her blade on her hip and put the small dagger in her back pocket.

"You need to go eat and then take me to my mom."

He nodded. What was there to say?

She gave him a hard, sideline glance over her shoulder. "And don't you *dare* go after one of those old men."

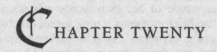

CHAPTER TWENTY

BERKFIELD ROUSED with a gasp. He could smell dirt within the cramped, pitch-black confines when he came to. Where had they taken him? Everything was cool and soft around him. The scent of earth was everywhere. He couldn't move his arms and legs, as he struggled against the satiny surfaces around him. Soon he became aware that he was shackled within a tight, oblong space.

Immediately he felt his throat, sliding his bound hands up his torso with terror. Although disoriented, snatches of images careened into his head. He began to remember the bodies, horror making him go still. Blood had been everywhere. Scientists slaughtered where they stood . . . hearts ripped out of chests while still beating. Glazed, dead eyes looking up from the lab floor, screams frozen on faces . . . and a beast that he couldn't have conceived in his wildest nightmares had turned, looked at him with red glowing eyes, blood running from his mouth, his fist clenching a dripping human heart, and had laughed.

Even though he was already in total darkness, Berkfield tightly shut his eyes. Where were his wife and children? *Father God, help them all!*

The moment the prayer entered his mind, he could smell

smoke, and the soft substance beneath him began to smolder. A loud thud rocked the box he was in.

"Never in my coffin! Ever!" the strangely accented voice he'd never forget bellowed. "Not within my sacred resting chamber, human!"

Berkfield froze. He was in a casket? Just as suddenly as the voice had spoken, he felt a painful jolt of electricity course through him, creating a seizure that made him convulse so hard he bit his tongue. He could barely breathe. Knowing what he was trapped within was creating claustrophobia, and with that came hysteria that bred a futile struggle against the immovable lid.

Sweating, panting, his thoughts turned to Carlos. He remembered what he'd been told . . . but why hadn't Rivera come?

"He can't help you in here," the floating voice said. "He cannot even hear you. Pity. He should have taken better care of you. But you can't trust his kind . . . the newly made. Sydney is wonderful, however."

Who the hell was Sydney? A laugh echoed out beyond his confining box. Berkfield strained to hear, as the voice got farther away.

"Stop struggling and save your breath. There's only so much air in the coffin . . . then again, you might be lucky and suffocate before this is done. Your prayer may be answered after all, and you can die before the final ceremony."

With every sense keened, he noticed the subtle sway of the coffin. He was being transported. He scavenged every facet he could recall. His memory danced between the images in the lab and a dungeon. There had been a castle. Torches were everywhere, black hooded robes, deafening, indecipherable words chanted . . . pain, burning, searing, horrific pain that entered his bones and temporarily stole his sight. Delirium, heat, blood, strange symbols, military men and men of science, saying words from old black books, appearing dazed and insane as they spoke in unison. Then the black funnel cloud had scorched the air within his lungs. It had opened up the slate dungeon floor within the center of the pentagram these madmen and creatures had created from fresh human blood.

Berkfield sucked in a huge breath and tried to stifle a strangled cough as he dry heaved and almost vomited. The longer he lay there, the more he understood why Carlos had gone deep underground and into hiding. The man had vanished. But he'd also learned that Rivera had turned into a beast like the thing that had kidnapped him.

. Every instinct he had told him that—if he lived through the ordeal—he had to remember it all so he could hunt this beast down and snuff it, before it got to his family.

Just as suddenly as the thought crossed his mind, he heard a deep, echoing snarl. Berkfield cringed as a thunderous bang rocked the coffin, sending a fiery current through the wall of it to crawl over his face, seal his mouth against a scream, blind his eyes, and shatter his eardrums.

He was glad that she'd relaxed enough to allow him to take her to the top of Westfield Centrepoint Tower to look out at the amazing view. He'd lied; he wasn't ashamed to admit that to himself. There was no real compelling reason to go there. But he just wanted to have a reason to hold her alone for a little while longer under the stars . . . while the night was his and the world was still under his dominion. Once he gave her back to Marlene, that was it. His world would be gone.

"See," he murmured, swallowing hard. "That's where there's safety zones." He pointed for her, hating to let one of his arms break contact with her soft skin. "Over there, bad energy."

She just allowed her line of vision to follow where he pointed, but he could tell she wasn't paying attention as she leaned against him closer and swallowed hard. They had both lied to themselves.

The ruse had been plausible, served a dual purpose. Denial was a wonderful drug at the moment, numbed the pain like morphine. Yeah, she needed to see the entire layout of the city for her own safety, to know that Darling Harbor was to the west, beaches were to the east, and north of Sydney was the commercial district and Taronga Zoo—where creatures could be transformed by weres. She needed to see how the Sydney Harbor Bridge divided the city north by south, and to see the concentration of activity on the south side, Chinatown . . . all of that was good information if she had to cut and run.

But more than she needed that, he needed to feel her heartbeat against his chest while the early evening air whipped her dwindling fragrance about him, his nose nuzzling the soft crown of her head, his hands aching to stroke her belly and sense what he'd planted there. She needed him to hold her and never let her go . . . they both knew the deal.

He chanced a kiss on the top of her head, and felt her eyes close, could taste the salt tears run down her cheeks as soon as they hit the air.

"We better go," he murmured. "You've only got a couple of hours before you have to perform."

"Yeah," she said, her tone flat, disconnected. "And I don't even have a plan."

There was no denying that. All there was left to do was bring her in. Give her up. And try to fight the whole world to give her and his baby a chance to live.

Never in a million years would she have thought she'd be coming to her mother-seer like this, dragging her Isis behind her like she was dragging her tail, knocked up, no plan, a man caught up in a dangerous life, and scared as shit . . . and still so crazy that she didn't want to leave him. Insane in love.

She glanced up at the old general post office that had been converted into the five-star Westin Sydney. The thirty-one-story tower atrium seemed like a perfect place to hurl oneself off of—too dramatic, but the thought crossed her mind. It was so complicated a situation that she couldn't even think, but had to, as they passed soaring ceilings and windows in the ornate old structure that was littered with impressive antiques and every modern convenience imaginable, working on an opening line. Hi, guys . . . guess what?

Damali closed her eyes as the elevator sealed her and Carlos away from the spectacular lobby. She felt like it had swallowed her whole: wishful thinking.

"You ready?" he asked, as they exited the elevator and walked down the hall to the Heritage suites.

"No," she said, honestly. "I don't know what the hell we can tell them."

"You gonna tell them tonight?"

"Not advisable to send them into battle with a divided mind."

"Then we're on the same page," he said, knocking on the door.

She held her breath, put on a performance smile, and let it out slowly when Marlene opened the door.

The looks on the faces of her team were as if they'd walked into a funeral. They didn't even draw weapons when she and Carlos crossed the threshold, and the clerics just sighed and looked out the shut terrace doors. Marlene didn't say hello or hug her. She just turned and walked deeper into the room, beckoning them with her body language to follow. They did, and then parted. Carlos found an empty wall to lean against on one side of the room by the door, and she found the edge of the bar to lean against. Sitting down would be impossible. Nerves wouldn't allow for it.

Rider seemed like he'd aged ten years—it was in his eyes. Shabazz just sat there by Rider on the sofa, his eyes closed, like he was meditating away a stroke. Big Mike was in a huge leather chair, looking down, counting carpet nap in the rug. J.L. and Dan were sitting by her on bar stools tearing sections of their cuticles out, one biting his, the other picking his thumb till it bled. Father Pat's mouth was moving in silent prayer, his eyes on the dark horizon with his brethren. Jose's gaze was steady on the crease in his pants, his forefinger and thumbnail zipping up and down either side of it like a razor. Marlene looked at them, pain so deep in her eyes that it almost stole her breath.

"Talk to me," Marlene whispered, making the rest of the group look up.

"Everything's cool," Damali lied, her voice calm, slow, even, her gaze holding Marlene's. Having learned from Carlos, she found a bit of truth to give her cover. "I'm human, and will cast a reflection tonight. We can put the tapes on standby."

Tension hissed, popped, and sputtered like a candle touched by a drop of water. But for a moment, no one said a word.

"The plan?" Marlene said coolly. "Or do we have one?"

"I had to go in deep, Mar. Was in the Australian's castle, and I understand their ways now better than I ever did. Gained valuable information. I learned how they fight, felt their power surges, know how skilled they are at dredging memories, and what their preferred creature is to transform into. I also know what they've lost as a result of bad gambles, and both us know that it's creating a temporary weakened power state within them until they can regroup, so it's hit 'em now or never. Had to pass myself off as a female vamp, and it worked." She could feel her chest constrict from the evasion. How in the world did Carlos do this all the time and sleep, she wondered. "I need to eat before the concert."

Shabazz snapped his head in Carlos's direction so fast that Carlos backed up. He stood in a slowly unfurling rage, shaking his head.

"Nachos!" Damali shouted. "Juice! Anything with salt, something to put a base on before I have to go on stage."

"'Bazz, man," Carlos said, his tone controlled as though talking to a guard dog about to lunge, "she couldn't eat human food in the castle—they'd've smelled it on her, and she'd've blown her cover. She's straight."

Slowly, begrudgingly, Shabazz found his seat again on the edge of the sofa, and it made the other Guardians' muscles relax.

"The plan," Marlene repeated, her voice so low that it was hard to hear her.

Damali glanced at Carlos, whose back was now pressed to the door.

"Seal the room," he said, directing the request to the clerics. "I need a barrier to be sure nobody can hear what we have to put down." He nervously glanced at Damali, both knowing he was stalling for time, even though what he'd said was true.

Marlene waited, her gaze never wavering as the clerics did what had been requested. She was stone. Granite. Would not be moved. Stood like a brown statue in the middle of the floor, arms folded, eyes unblinking, radar up. "The plan?" she said again, this time through her teeth.

"At the concert," Damali said, trying to sound authoritative. "Four master vampires and their wives will be—"

"Four master vampires," Rider said, standing, drawing out the words as he walked toward her. "And their mates. All at one time. All under the same roof. With however many innocent humans that we can't hit in a shootout." He opened his arms, leaned in toward her. "All waiting for a bunch of fucking musicians to leap from the stage with stakes in hand to save the goddamned world?"

He walked away from her, grabbed Jose by the shoulder, pulling him to his feet and toppling the stool. "Fuck this. Me and you, bro, we're hitting a bar." He glared at Damali, then Carlos. "We're out. You've got your nose standing there by the door—and that SOB is already dead. We're just human, Damali. I am *never* sitting up all night tearing my guts out worrying about you again!"

Jose pounded Rider's fist and swallowed hard, his gaze locked with Carlos's.

"Guys, I'm sor—"

"Do *not* say it, Damali!" Shabazz was on his feet, his finger pointed in accusation. "Do not say, 'I'm sorry.'" He stormed away and stood with the clerics, his back to the group. "This is the first time I've been able to breathe in two nights."

"So, there's no plan?" Dan stood, coming off his stool slowly, incredulous. His blue eyes blazed with pure shock. "You were with him for two days and two nights and you guys didn't come up with the master plan? You want us to

rush four master vampires and a bunch of second-level females without a plan? Just freestyle?"

"We have a plan but you're not listening to—"

"Call it off, D. We ain't got a plan, so we don't go in till
we do. We do the concert, and get more info on which one of
those bastards stole the key, dust him, and hope we can get
on a plane with everybody still walking." Big Mike shook
his head, glanced at her, then Carlos, his eyes filled with disappointment. "I hope you both had fun, got everything out
of your systems—because tonight, we're on the defensive,
not the offensive." He stood slowly, his tall tree-trunk body
erecting six foot eight inches of mass up from the chair. "I
don't know where you went, or where you've been." He
looked at Damali. "As somebody who loves you, I deserved more respect than that." His glare settled on Rivera.
"We thought you'd be able to sniff out some more info than
y'all are bringing."

When she took a breath to speak, Big Mike held up his
hand. His gaze on her narrowed, and for the first time in her
life, she saw something in the team's gentle giant's eyes that
hit her harder than a slap could have.

"You put *the family* at risk!" Big Mike bellowed, his
voice thunderous, shaking the windows. "Never in my
damned life have I been brought to my knees in prayer like
this for your ass, girl! Sobbing and crying and begging and
rocking and pleading with God to bring my baby back
home . . . If you ever disappear like that—" In a slow storm,
Big Mike cut off his own words, walked to the far side of the
room, punched the wall leaving a hole and dust, then whirled
on Carlos. His voice was an even rumble. "Let's me and you
take a walk outside, old school–style." He cast off his gun.
"One on one, motherfucker."

"Mike . . ." Damali said, but his glare almost stopped her
heart.

"I have *had* it, D!" Big Mike hollered. "I'm done! I'm angry with *both* of us this time!"

"We might not have a complete plan," she said fast, her

gaze darting to Carlos, who hadn't even bulked for the battle, his resignation frightening her, "but—"

"Then what the fuck was all this drama about, anyway?" J.L. said, suddenly standing, shaking his head and walking in a circle. "We could have stayed in LA. I mean, what's the point?" He stopped, opened his arms, closed his eyes, and tilted his chin up to the ceiling, tears now slipping from beneath his lids. "Oh, God, what is the point?"

Marlene was practically hyperventilating, and the clerics each walked to a corner of the room, their mouths moving silently, until Father Pat's voice shattered the silence. "Damn it to Hell, man! What is wrong with you?"

The elderly priest swished past Marlene and Damali, his rapid movements drawing the group's focus, his blue robes sounding the air, but his pace nearly blinding as he came to Carlos, drew back his fist, punched him, and then grabbed him by the T-shirt at his chest. "Where's the key? Tonight, I am ready to die, young man!" he yelled, slamming Carlos against the door. "Tear out my throat, rip out my heart, there is nothing you can do to me that hurts more than this." He shoved Carlos and walked away, no fear, his back turned, total disgust his shield, righteous indignation his sword. Father Patrick covered his face with his hands and breathed into them slowly, then stood tall, eyes glittering with rage and so much more.

The emotion in the exchange—the care, the love, the disappointment, the hurt in Father Pat's fury, in his punch, his entire being—entered Carlos and held him. What none of them could understand was that he was bound to them now, could feel all of them as though they were one. Knowing how much they loved Damali, knowing how much they cared about him, had hoped for him, even prayed for him, too. Knew that in the beginning it was just because she was so bonded to him, but then after he'd proven himself in their eyes, in Hell, in Brazil . . . and now, they were hurt beyond words. He'd left her vulnerable, the team vulnerable to four master vampires and an army. What had he done . . . all because he'd wanted her in his arms?

He looked away until the wall became blurry, washed with shame, tears he couldn't shed in public, ever. Father forgive him, he never meant for this to happen. He rubbed his jaw, not from the punch—that hadn't even registered. But the family's pain sent a blade into his heart as he took it all in. They were just this upset because she'd been missing, but they had no idea what else was wrong . . . they didn't even know . . . and there'd be no way to tell them . . . what had gone down defied explanation.

"We have a plan," he said, his voice rough with emotion. "We wouldn't let you down like that." Carlos looked at Damali, who was breathing slow, trying not to cry. *Don't cry, baby. Not now. We'll both lose it up in here. Stay strong.*

This is bad, Carlos. We've gotta make this right. The family doesn't deserve this. I don't even know what to say to them.

"What was your plan going in, Carlos?" Father Pat said, his voice quivering with rage. "Tell me!"

"With four masters coming into the castle, and me as the councilman, I had to be formally introduced to each, in the open, as well as have occasions where I could sense if they'd bitten my marked man, Berkfield, during the key hijack, or smell the key on them, and—"

Father Patrick slapped his forehead as he paced back and forth in an agitated line, his blue robes swishing. "Are you *mad*? I thought you were there to detect which of them had a secret, fraud in their—"

"Are *you* mad?" Carlos asked evenly. "They are *master* vampires. They *all* have secrets, lies, fraud, and deception. It runs all through them, it's like a cesspool in their systems. There's no way to cleanly sense that and sort out thousands of years of lies without getting that bullshit twisted. Get real." Indignant, Carlos stared off toward the wall.

"We didn't know you were trying to sense for the Living Blood! I cannot believe your whole strategy hinged on that aspect! This was the problem with not being able to caucus with Damali, properly, as a team, before you all went off on your own!" Father Patrick shook his head and let it drop to his hands in defeat. "Oh, God . . . had we known . . . Yes, you can sense Berkfield, but you can never smell the Blood of the Lamb—"

"Father, the ability to track a blood scent is—"

"—Beyond your capacity, even if you were Lucifer himself!" Father Patrick's panicked gaze shot around the room.

Damali covered her mouth with her hand as Marlene closed her eyes. Her gaze darted around to the stricken expressions of her teammates.

"But the council never told me that," Carlos whispered, caught up in his own new awareness. "I never gained that knowledge, even after taking a throne . . ."

All eyes were on Father Patrick as he spoke. "You wouldn't, because *that* information doesn't reside *down there*." The elderly cleric began pacing again. "Just like your realm has certain powers and hidden information—rules of engagement—so does mine. Welcome to *my* world, Carlos Rivera!" Father Patrick slapped his chest hard and his voice trembled with rage. "This is what *I* do—what we do, as the *Covenant*. We know things that the darkness cannot even conceive! That is our strategic advantage . . . so for all your powers, you'd better know that some things you simply cannot fathom, young man."

Father Patrick walked a hot path away from Carlos, spun on him, and leveled his finger toward him. "Vampires, nor any other form of demon, can ever pick up the scent of *the key*. The only thing you can sense is the vampire who might have been involved in the heist. That's it. But to sense the Living Blood, as though it were mere human, or food for your craven bellies—*never*." He let out an angry, weary sigh. "So that was your plan, to smell the key on one of your own and track it to where it might be? Have you any idea . . ." The cleric shook his head and closed his eyes. "Your kind cannot even handle the substance, let alone *ingest* it. That's why they need a human, someone with a soul, to courier it!"

Carlos nodded, but was thoroughly blown away. "I had to take her inside deep," he said, his voice firm, regaining its former authoritative tone. "All right. Our plan had a flaw. But Damali is still human and could get to the key, even if I can't smell it. She had to take a walk on the dark side to go up against four masters, and I saw her do it. She's all-pro, and ready to take the heat. I've got your back, always did. I stand with you against the world—stand with her against the universe. I have to. That's my job as her man. The game ain't over, yet. Where's your faith?"

Slowly, perspectives opened. The fury in gazes subsided. Hurt began to give way to listening in earnest. He took his time. This was a negotiation far more delicate than facing the council. Family peace was always more fragile, and at the moment, more important to him than world peace. This was home—his woman's people . . . now therefore his people, joined by something smaller than his fingernail, but more powerful than anything he'd ever seen, his baby.

He waited, gathering elements of what could be said, what couldn't, separating them out, a lie of omission, but no fraud. They deserved better than that. Damali deserved better than that. He watched them all find seats on the sofa, available chairs, the end of a table, and on bar stools in the living room section of the suite, spreading out in the room, weary, but suddenly not defeated. That was critical. They had to go in strong, or die, and he didn't want to lose a single soul on his watch. Tonight, *that* was his intent, and he planned to honor it. *That was the plan.*

Rider glanced at Damali's hand, then up at Carlos. "So, what did you kids do, run off to Vegas, or something?"

"She's *my wife,*" Carlos said, his voice tense as he walked in closer, not caring if they smoked him. "That part of what we did in the castle was no bullshit."

"Shit," Marlene's voice was a quiet rush, as her glance went from Damali to Carlos, then quickly scanned the group. "How far did you turn her, Carlos?"

He could hear heartbeats thump inside chests that couldn't draw air. "I didn't turn her, she turned me."

Eyes searched, blood drained from faces, but no one spoke.

"Get her something to eat," he said. "She's human. Made me find my own humanity." He looked at Damali. "And I can't allow anything to happen to her now." He sent his gaze back to Marlene. "So, everything that I've learned, I'm going to do a knowledge transfer and teach you within one hour." He scanned the group, holding them bound by the truth. "I am what I am, a council-level master vampire—your worst nightmare and best ally." He turned his hands up. "And she can have everything in my hands, thousands of years of vampiric knowledge from all five continents . . . fair exchange is no robbery when this woman has given me the world."

Damali's gaze upon him was so tender that he had to look away. He held Shabazz's instead, talking to the only father she had ever known. "Test me, man. Use your Guardian sensory skills and see if I'm bullshitting you."

He waited as Shabazz walked up to him, no fear, eyes hard, a hand placed strong on his shoulder, drawing it away with a begrudging nod that relaxed the group.

"Talk to us," Shabazz said, walking away to find a bar stool.

"She gave you the whole world," Big Mike said, still unbelieving. "Talk to *me*," he said, pointing at his own chest.

"She ran a game so lovely on four master vampires blitzed on pure Neteru that they ceded their four continental territories in a blood match—winner take all. I won."

Father Patrick blinked as he strode closer to Damali, his line of vision going between her, Carlos, and the Covenant brethren. "You bet your body in a fortress full of master vampires . . . winner take all? To what end?"

"It was the only way for it to go down, Father," Damali said quietly, but her head was held high and her gaze at Carlos filled with pride. "He protected me until there was a feeding frenzy, then he pulled me out as his wife. They couldn't rush him because he'd amassed too much power in the pacts we'd stamped under crest. They thought I knew where the seal was that will match the key, buying us time to learn where it is."

The priest backed away. Rider was on his feet. The rest of the team members slowly stood.

"Oh heavenly shit," Rider whispered, standing stock-still. "She was in the middle of a feeding frenzy near *four* battle-amped masters, and *they* couldn't rush you?" He looked at Damali. "And you're sure you only want nachos?"

"The crest pact," Father Patrick wheezed. "Tell me you didn't ransom your soul, child!"

"I told you," Damali said, going to stand by Carlos. "He kept me safe. He even rolled over prayer lines to win the master's hunt so they couldn't have me. I couldn't put my soul on the line—as far as they knew, I didn't have one. It was one night for a nation."

"It was a fair trade," Carlos murmured, looking at her with a long gaze, then he pulled it away.

"You are not making me feel better, D. Because, if that bastard rolled over ancient prayer lines in a blood battle, his ass is strong as shit," Rider said, pointing at the couple, but looking at the group. He quickly returned his line of vision to Carlos and Damali. "If he can do that, what else can he do? I mean, this is good, but I have a feeling it's also very bad. Seven years from now, people, we have a crisis."

Carlos chose his words very carefully. Rider wasn't wrong; he wasn't offended by the statement. Truth was truth. Problem was, Rider was just a few years off.

"Worry about seven years in seven years. Right now, Rider, I have enough power to make her walk on water," Carlos said, closing his eyes, and for the first time really becoming aware of the true power at his disposal. All the drama, the emotional upheaval, and their night together had literally pushed that reality into the background of his thoughts. "I am the air. I am the night. I am the elements of the planet. I am dark energy that can move matter and steal dreams. I can send my whisper on the wind. I'll find out which one of them has the key. New strategy."

He walked into the center of the room and opened the ceiling for them, swirling a dark cloud above them. "I can enter minds and bend them until they snap. I can assume any shape, and you would never know. I can walk through walls, and hurl my energy over distances at a rate of speed you can't even fathom. Silver will leave a nasty scar, but won't incinerate me. Hallowed earth will slow me down and sting, but won't kill me. Holy water will leave a third-degree burn, but I'll heal. You're right. I am as strong as shit, and not the one to fuck with. If one of them knows where the key is, I will snap his punk mind like a twig—now that I just got stronger, due to Damali's sweet game."

He opened his eyes and stared at the group. "I know everything that has happened in every language on the four continents she gave me, plus the one I had at throne level . . . back to the time before kings—and the only thing that I'm vulnerable to now is daylight, and a stake, well placed, in my heart. But the chances of someone smoking me in my lair with daylight are slim . . . and I don't think the hand holding the stake would ever make it to the center of my chest. Maybe I could be beheaded, if I didn't see the swing coming in my three-hundred-and-sixty-degree peripheral vision."

He smiled and sealed the ceiling, waiting for them to breathe. "When I tell you that I've got your back, say a prayer and be glad that I'm the one on your side. I won't let anything happen to her on my watch."

After a moment Rider walked past him, sat down on the sofa, and blew out a long whistle. "Why didn't you say so, dude? Shit—welcome to the family."

One by one, each Guardian took a seat. Marlene sank onto a bar stool.

"Seven years from now, we're gonna have to move to Alaska for six months a year when there's perpetual sun." Marlene dropped her face into her hands, leaned over, and breathed in and out slowly.

"No we ain't, Mar," Big Mike grumbled and then motioned to the clerics. "Got us some old dirt from some *real old* hallowed ground right here in Australia—feel me?" He glared at Carlos. "Yeah, we went to see some people who know some people to get strapped for the concert, too. But if you think your little floor show impressed somebody, brother—"

"We're running out of time, folks," Damali said, her palm resting on Carlos's folded arms. "Tell them the plan, baby," she murmured, her eyes filled with new panic when she glanced at the clock. *Tell me you have one.* Damali hesitated, thinking fast on her feet.

"Number one, we have to locate the key." She glanced at Carlos. "He found the seal but—"

"What?" Father Patrick whispered, horrified.

"But the keepers of the seal are some seriously old Aborigines, ancestral spirit walkers who saved our lives," Carlos said as he glanced at his shoes, the humiliation still fresh. "None of the other masters are strong enough right now to break their circle."

"And what about you, motherfu—"

"They saved Damali's life, 'Bazz. Give me a little credit. I'm in a don't-ask, don't-tell frame of mind about that. The old men are safe. They've got twenty-thousand-year-old prayer lines hottin' their compound. So let's get back to what Damali was talking about, namely, finding the key."

"We've gotta cause chaos right after the concert, create some mega after-party VIP function to get them all together again so we can each be posted by one of them for a strategic takedown, once Carlos gets a location lock on the key. The plan is to get them all jockeying for position to acquire what they believe is the former Neteru and seal, and going after each other's throats," Damali said as calmly as possible. "Right now, the African master ceded the most, and wants me the worst, to regain his power and then some, so he's an easy target. His power center is in turmoil and he's been weakened by the land grab. The Aussie is also very vulnerable, because he thinks I'm coming to his room after the show with my blade as a role-play prop to do him, not *do* him—follow? That's an easy hit."

Rider slapped his forehead but withheld comment.

Damali glanced at Rider and returned her gaze to Marlene. "I told you I went in deep undercover, and right about now, that's working to our advantage. They saw Carlos practically drag me out of the castle by my hair and—"

"We get the picture," Shabazz muttered. "Get back to the key."

"If all four masters are here, then the key has to be nearby—because I can't imagine them leaving lower-level vamps to guard it, or entrusting human helpers alone, especially if they're pretty sure council is hunting for it, too. However, we know that Carlos is council's representative, and it's unlikely that one of the old boys will risk surfacing with four aggressive masters all in one location. But even with that going on, the Neteru scent and the thrill of acquiring me along with the seal is making the topside masters greedy, take risks, and get sloppy."

"Which creates the opportunity for chaos and a variable like us to crop up in the mix," Carlos stated, nodding in Damali's direction with pride. "I watched the African master almost blow his lands in the master's hunt trying to save Damali. The damned Transylvanian went down on his knees in the parlor and begged her to slit his throat while she had the Isis on her, he's hurting for her so bad. Gentlemen, I don't think you understand what she does to my species."

Big Mike shook his head. "Shoulda cut that bastard's throat right then, girl. But I suppose you had to play it out."

"The timing wasn't right," Damali said, her tone gentle as she stared at Big Mike. "Their wives ain't no joke, either. We have to take out masters plus very old and very strong second-gen females. Understand? And if I'd iced the Transylvanian then . . ."

"We believe you, D, and follow," Jose said, unnecessarily coming to her defense.

"If they think they can snatch her after the concert, and assassinate Carlos to get all of the empire he's amassed, plus Damali and possibly the location of the seal," Shabazz said, rubbing his jaw, "then this key has to be near wherever they plan to convene for the blowout after party. I'm sure they didn't bank on Carlos coming away with world power. We need to use that variable to our advantage."

"Right," Damali said, her gaze going to each member of the team one by one.

"The clerical team should insure the safety of the key,

once we locate it," Father Patrick said, "because the highest priority will be getting it safely to hallowed ground during the battle. Carlos, you're going to have to use your new, increased power to quickly locate it. If it falls into the wrong hands . . ."

"It won't," Carlos said, his eyes holding a promise as he and Father Pat stared at each other. "I have every reason in the world, now, to make sure that doesn't happen. Can't be no Armageddon . . . no time soon, anyway." He stalked away from the group and leaned against the wall, aware that all eyes were boring into his back. "My boys have been searching for Berkfield, and I've been trying to sense for him, to no avail. The only thing that could block my sight is if he's on hallowed ground—but that wouldn't block the Guardian seers—or if he were stashed in a strong master's lair coffin, covered by his original earth."

For a moment Damali held her breath. "So, uh, I have to get them all amped at the concert to mess with their concentration while Carlos works them with hollow promises, to share the seal, pitting them against each other, and then we do the after party, each of us assigned to a particular master and his wife—based upon our skills and their potential strength. The moment Carlos transmits that he's located the key, we ice 'em."

"Yeah, I hear you," Shabazz said, worry clear in his tone. "But we can't bank on you fluxing hot with Neteru to disorient them. Like you said, these boyz are old and shrewd, and if the key is nearby, we need a sure bet that they'll get distracted by your offer and Carlos's. No offense, baby, but even at your concert best, if you ain't trailing ripe Neteru, they'll be sharp and on guard."

"Aw'ight, listen up," Carlos said, going to sit on the sofa next to Rider and to use the coffee table as a drawing board. "D told me to leverage the darkness for good, and what I'm about to do is *low* treason—I can still be smoked at the council level, all theater aside. The shit I'ma tell you, humans probably were never told or shown about my kind." For a moment, he stopped, then shook off the gnawing inner conflict. Then talking as he gestured with his hands, he cast the illusion of a small replica of Sydney.

"Here's the city grid of portals, temporary lairs," Carlos said, drawing with his finger, "and prayer lines. The clerics can spread a handful of hallowed earth at each location while the show is going on, to keep the vamps from having a way to go subterranean in retreat, or for any of their troops amassing and coming up here to join the party. Damali already said we have to wipe out the masters and top lieutenants to weaken each nation in one night. Near dawn, after partying, they won't have enough energy to project all the way back to Queensland where the castle is, if one gets away. And Hell won't send a courier that close to dawn, if we time this right—unless there's a legitimate dispute, which there won't be."

"That's some deep shit," Big Mike finally said, stooping to gaze at the hologram image. "All right, I'm listening."

"Thanks, man," Carlos said, meaning it. What he'd just done on the table was pretty cool, and he liked that Mike was impressed. Plus, for what they had to do, he needed the team's strong man on their side. "If what I'm about to show you doesn't disorient them, they'll know where it came from, and I'll be toast, which leaves your asses vulnerable."

Puzzled glances passed around the group.

"If I won all their territory in a blood match, so be it. That's just a land transfer, not unauthorized extinctions. No problem. If four female seconds bite the dust, so what, according to realm's point of view. But if I personally dust four masters without delivering the seal or the key to council, it will look like assassinations, an unauthorized coup, and the council will send up an inquiry."

He held their gazes. "You don't want to know." He returned focus back to the coffee table and rubbed his jaw. "We have to make them turn on each other, so when Hell's registers run blood, it was not solely by my hand. It was survival, self-defense, inarguable. Even we have rules. *Strict* ones. Murder is condoned, but only under certain circumstances at our rank, within our rank. My story to them has to be that the human Guardians got wise, double-crossed me, took the key to hallowed ground, and snatched back the Neteru to purge her while I was battling for the empire."

Carlos sat back, his gaze going out the window. "If a Guardian gets one or two, and the Neteru gets one, I can hit at least one and call it defense of my package, Damali, without there being an issue, I think. Or I can say it was self-defense, if one of them goes down by my hand. They know you guys go after our kind; their blind spot is me. I'm on the inside, a sleeper within, and someone supposed to protect the empire, my line, and the package, and council's interests at all costs. They'll never see it coming."

"Well, wouldn't her scent send them into a brawl, anyway?" Rider tilted his head to issue Carlos a sideline glance. "And you need to be more positive than 'I think,' dude."

Rider's question and admonishment had validity, but the problem was, Damali wasn't trailing Neteru any longer, now that she was already filled. Variables, variables, fucking variables. Carlos kept his gaze on Rider's eyes, unable to glance at Damali.

"Like me, they're building up a tolerance for it. Plus they would never go against me, even if she was red-hot seven years from now, given the power I've just acquired." He stood, needing space to give the lie air.

"Then, if I'm not making them wig anymore," Damali said, her voice cautious, "then . . . how are we going to create a diversion in that house of horrors on the cliffs off the barrier reef? It's a two-hundred-foot drop, over a hundred-some-odd vamps and human staff ready to go down and take a bullet, Black Hawk choppers. Your Hell-hounds aren't even a match for them in flight. The inside is like a labyrinth of corridors—"

"I know, I know," Carlos said fast. "Okay, always choose your battlefield. We don't do the castle; it's impenetrable. They've added staff for the extra diplomats. Damali's right.

I'll bring a yacht down the harbor, a party boat that will make Hugh Hefner's *Playboy* estate look like a convent—no offense, Fathers."

"Wait," Father Patrick said, raking his frazzled gray hair as he spoke, and looked at Carlos hard. "A boat? Vampires cannot cross large bodies of water without losing power, without their energy getting—"

Carlos's weary sigh stopped the elderly cleric's words. "Father Pat, these are masters. Okay?" He looked at the man with a combination of respect and impatience. "Witches, seriously lower-level vampires, whatever, have that problem, but not at our level. It won't even make their wives seasick, and I can bet any VIPs they invite from their camp will be above the watermark, too. Back in the day, travel by ship in a casket in the hull was the way to move between continents if you couldn't get a subterranean pass. The old boys will love it, and it will take them back to the glory days of being out in the open when humans believed in monsters and demons, unlike today. That was when they were at their boldest and most arrogant . . . and we all know that arrogance is the best way to become sloppy."

Rider nodded and glanced at Shabazz, Marlene, and Mike. "Seems like we need to update our books while we're at it. Right now I'm having a confidence crisis—like everything I thought I knew might be mythology, and the things I oughta know to keep me alive and human, I'm about to flunk the test on."

"That's why I'm trying to school you, *hombre*," Carlos said, his gaze locking with Rider's for a moment before he released it.

Rider sat back and rubbed his face, seeming temporarily dazed. "Dude is definitely stronger. Damn. Don't do that again. Cool?"

"My apologies. Force of habit." Carlos smiled and gazed at the men in the room. "I want that boat rocking off the water, these boys seriously distracted, high, looped, off guard, and ready to party. Only one of them will be extra careful, which will be a dead giveaway. My dogs patrolling the rails.

Yeah, that's the ticket." He glanced at Rider again. "I hope you've got your head right, man, because I'ma load the joint with female vamps from my territories in LA, the Caribbean, and blessed South America, so fine they'll make you weep."

Rider's smile broadened when Carlos looked at Big Mike. "Brother, there won't be no ship doctor, so forewarned is forearmed—this ain't New Orleans. Take a nick from one of these babes, your ass will turn, hear?"

"We cool," Big Mike said, smiling. "Later."

"Precisely." Carlos studied the group. "Mike, you take the African master—he's a big brother, and you're the team's strong man. Hell, I didn't even want to tackle his ass, but if he's under the influence, you've got a shot. Make it a good one."

Big Mike nodded. "Done. He goes down. Just point him out."

Carlos laughed. "Look in the mirror, you could be family."

"Mighta been, but what the fuck," Mike chuckled. "He went dark."

"Rider, Shabazz, I want you guys on the Asian master— Rider's a sharpshooter, Shabazz has got martial arts skills. Dude is ancient Samurai. Real shrewd, real fast, like lightning." Carlos became still for a moment. "I'm going to see if I can draw the wives away, to me, separate out those two, maybe get the Transylvanian to rush the Asian—if the Transylvanian misses, you brothers take aim, and dust him. That will back off the count, make him feel like you had his back. He'll spare you and move on, will come to me with a complaint, while Damali is in with the Aussie."

"Wait, hold up. This is the part that has me concerned," Jose said, glancing at Damali. "She's going into a room, alone, with the Aussie? I'm not feeling that part of the plan, *hombre*."

"Me neither," Shabazz said, standing and pacing, but not angry, just worried.

"It's the only way," Damali said, exasperated.

"He's got it bad for her, worse than the others," Carlos

said as calmly as possible. "He'd been promised a night alone with her, then had that snatched away after the hunt." He could feel resistance gather and smolder within the group, and he looked at Damali for support. "You got it in you, baby? If you don't feel like—"

"I will *smoke* his ass," she said, evenly. Conflicting emotions began to eat away at the insides of her brain. This was *her* team. She'd always been the one to come up with the plans without any outside help. This was *her* war room. Was this what being married was like—sharing everything . . . down to personal control? Was this what being pregnant meant, feeling like you didn't even have control over your own body, and having people look at you like you were some kinda invalid? She didn't like it one bit, and forced renewed authority into her tone.

"Listen up," she said, walking around the coffee table and couch to plop down in the chair facing Carlos. "I'll sing the last song of the concert and aim it toward McGuire. I'll hold his focus; like I'm singing directly to him. After we break down equipment, I won't change—will keep on the sweaty, damp dress from the performance, with adrenaline in it and will go to Carlos. You hold me close, like you might renege on the barter when I go into the vamp VIP box with you. Then you lean in, make him a tender offer, and explain that you just want to get us all safely to the boat without the other masters in the room making a power-play. I'll diddle around on top deck, talk to him, mess with his mind, and get him to go into his stateroom with me, while you draw away the wife. By then, he'll be real manageable . . . and I'll bring my Isis with me, just as he wanted . . . will straddle him and put it to his chest, ask him if he wants a double plunge, and then I'll lean in like I'm going to kiss him, and gore him."

Carlos stood up and walked to the terrace windows. He knew what she had to do, but it sent a chill down his spine that detonated in fury. "No. Bad plan. You are not going to straddle him." He was walking back and forth, shaking his head no, ignoring the sly smiles coming from the others in the room. "I don't want his hands in your hair, telling you shit . . . no, fuck it. New plan for the Aussie."

"It's the only way I can get close enough to—"

"I'm not arguing with you, Damali. No!"

"We talked about this, you were even the one—"

"I know—but that was before . . ." Carlos paced away. "No."

A standoff with two worthy adversaries coiled the tension in the room. Marlene's chuckle snapped it.

"How about if I chaperone her in there, Carlos, as her handmaid," Marlene said in a sheepish voice, and then winked at Shabazz.

"No. That's my final decision."

The group looked at each other and burst out laughing.

"Dude, this is what she does for a living," Rider said, standing and wiping his tired eyes with both fists. "Oh, my God . . . she married an old-fashioned kinda guy, a cold-blooded chauvinist from the Victorian era. Help me."

"This is between me and my wife!" Carlos shouted.

Damali sighed. "I know you're worried, but I'm no amateur. And this ain't my first time around the block—sorry to say, but you didn't marry a battle virgin, and we're wasting time."

"Damali—"

"Listen," she snapped, both hands on her hips. "*We are wasting time*. I do the Aussie, we get the Transylvanian to whack the Asian—or have Rider and Shabazz put him down. Big Mike and you make sure that huge bastard from the Motherland doesn't catch on to the fact that I'm in a stateroom alone." She glanced at her team, ignoring Carlos. "*That's* who I'm worried about rushing me or anybody else, *comprendo?*" She shot her gaze back to Carlos. "He is not to be played with."

She walked away, and studied her sword as it lay on the bar, speaking to the clerics. "No kids or innocent humans will be on the boat—councilman's wife's orders. The masters think I'm eccentric, and they love it. So, once our team is off the yacht, Big Mike can blow the sucker. We'll need two speedboats to get us all off that ship and out of range as soon as possible. You guys trailing holy water and incense in your hair and skins won't be able to get past vamp security." She looked at Marlene. "I don't want you on there, either. You're female. The second- and third-level female vamps will rush you, and I can't be by your side, the brothers can't leave their posts—and if a hyped male master goes for you, looking for a new turn with a strong will to conquer and add to his harem . . . It's just a variable we can't afford right now."

Marlene nodded, but begrudgingly. "It's true. I can keep my radar up and on you, baby. Me and the clerics can man the getaway boats and search for the key in the Opera House. If I see you in no-way-out danger, I'll take out the side of the ship with one of Mike's shoulder cannons."

"What do we do?" Jose said, glancing at J.L. and Dan.

"You're private security," Carlos said. "Jose is point."

"What!" J.L. stepped back and laughed.

"Now I know you're nuts," Dan said, shaking his head. "Us, alone, without Rider, and 'Bazz, and *Mike*?"

"You said I'm point," Jose said, lifting his chin high. "Talk to me."

"You've got my line in you from way back." Carlos paused as the magnitude of what he was saying entered the group's collective conscious. "They know I would never allow Damali to be escorted in by a second- or third-level vamp lieutenant that might rush her. You leave a marker, Jose. So you stand by her side and bring her to me in the VIP box. There will be an international courier at the door. He'll sniff you, then will let you pass with your band members, J.L., and Dan."

Carlos motioned toward the two younger guardians. "They can come fully armed with stakes, crossbows, whatever—because as human helpers, their orders are to take any vamp down that blinks at her wrong. The masters in the box will nod, fully appreciating my precautions, and will let you in the room and on the ship with the kinda stuff we need to nail any of them. That's also what we'll say when Rider, Mike, and Shabazz come locked and loaded—they're guarding the councilman's wife on a vampire pleasure vessel. Standard procedure."

"Smooth, brother," Shabazz said, nodding. "I'm impressed. Owe you both an apology for the doubt."

"It's cool," Carlos said, unable to keep direct eye contact with Shabazz. "All right. Y'all do your thing on stage. I tell the vamps that she casts an image because I will it so, and we have a tape—right?"

"Yeah, got it," Jose said.

"Cool. We roll that tape on the box monitors and on the big screens in the joint, and broadcast the real concert elsewhere. That keeps her cover. They know her image is coming from tape because of her reflection deficit syndrome, but think that's what's going out to the world."

"Works," J.L. said.

"But, what if they get distracted from the performance, and get hip?"

"I won't let them get distracted," Damali said. "They won't be there for all the libations pouring and stuff, but will come in for the part they want to see. Show 'em what I'm wearing for that final number."

Her smile was destabilizing, made him remember too much, and now was not the time. But as she stood there waiting, Damali and her team needing confidence, he closed his eyes and thought of what she looked like in the parlor the day she transformed and gave him the world. Magenta and deep purple smoke swirled at her feet, fanning out, creating a lit haze, the hotel room lights dimmed, and crimson spotlight fired on her.

From within a very private place in his mind he added a backless purple-black iridescent gown, deep plunging neckline, ripped and shredded across the torso and hips, showing skin beneath it, her shapely legs sliding out of the outrageous slit as she walked slowly in it barefoot, one black ankle bracelet that looked like a bondage cuff, long sleeves trailing with ragged points that almost concealed her beautiful hands as she opened her arms and closed her eyes, leaning back offering her throat.

He heard the music that was in her head, the pulse from the native instrument that had become his lifeline, Shabazz's bass adding bottom, weight, density to what that tonal drone really meant to him—their last night together as lovers. Marlene's shakers became a passion hiss and rattle that sent a shiver down his spine. Jose's percussion was too much to tolerate with J.L.'s melodic keyboard pulling emotion to the surface in a lazy samba . . . not when she was humming about a bittersweet transition. He could see her in the kitchen doorway of his Beverly Hills lair giving him a private performance. Uh-uh.

With a snap, he pulled out of the mind lock, walked away from her, evaporating the smoke and bringing back normal lights, but left the gown for her to wear. "They'll be distracted," he muttered, and found the far side of the room. He wasn't trying to see her triumphant smile.

"McGuire won't bite me until I tell him he has my permission. Trust me."

Carlos kept his gaze on the bar. He couldn't argue with her in that dress. But this shit was dangerous, and she was carrying!

"Damn, man . . ." Big Mike said. "Now I understand why she was gone for two days. My bad."

Once again, she'd taken him somewhere in front of this team that he wasn't prepared to go. Rather than answer Mike, or address the sideline smirks he received, he simply focused on the matter at hand—survival for the group.

"After the performance, you three bring her to me, then Shabazz, Mike, and Rider follow and get in the limos I'm providing all VIPs—you'll see a crest that looks like my ring. Be sure to only get in mine with me and Damali, so track us hard and stay sharp." Carlos flashed his ring, his hand a tight fist, then walked to stand by the terrace doors. "Those are mine, don't get in any others, and stay on my flank."

The group nodded.

"When we get on the ship, brace yourselves. You're gonna see some shit that'll make you want to barf, but stay cool. Observe, and keep walking. The music is going to be loud, and you're going to have to look alive, watch your back, and turn down any offers given. My dogs will be hungry, but given orders to only eat anything that tries to rush the onboard team, Damali, or me. When you see me come up on main deck from the Aussie's stateroom with Damali, you'll need to get near me, if possible, so I can jettison you in a fast transport to the ships."

He spoke slowly, trying to convey the severity of what could go down, hoping Damali wouldn't balk. "I'll be keeping four vamp second-level females occupied, and might have to drop a few bodies along the way. My energy could be compromised, and at some point, I'll have to stop to feed."

"Wait," Damali said, her tone brittle. "You are going to be where, with who?"

"Oh, shit," Rider murmured, and moved out of her way.

"And *you* had a problem with *what*?"

"D, listen, in my world—"

"Find some other way to distract those heifers!"

"Aw'ight," Carlos shouted, walking away from her glare. Damn, what was a man supposed to do? His way was expedient, thoroughly efficient, and wouldn't take a lot of time, given the state they'd already be in.

"I heard that all the way across the room," Damali said, heated. "New plan, brother." She was drawing fast breaths, her arm was extended in his direction, and she was pointing at him so hard that her fist bounced from the strain.

The teams glanced at each other; even Father Patrick's crew chuckled to themselves and sighed.

"Everything is peace," Shabazz said, trying to break the standoff. He glanced at Damali, then looked back at Carlos, offering a shrug of support. "We gotchure back so you can maintain a chill factor here, man. Do what'chu gotta do to keep them females from rushing D, then dust them. Saves us ammo. But my main question is, what if we don't see you, man?"

Shabazz held Carlos' gaze. His question a fair one, the concern in his eyes appreciated.

"Like before, we all have one objective. Protect the package. Get D out of there and blow the ship."

"And if you're still on it?" Damali could feel panic rise within her, eclipsing the anger. Something in her was registering an intent that chilled her. "This is not supposed to be a suicide mission, Carlos. The reason we're going through all of this is so that *all* of us get off that boat before it blows."

Carlos stared at her, and came to her, then stopped. "Just like in Hell . . . you go on ahead of me, if I can't keep up because I have to put a barrier between you and the team. If any variable comes up—you go. Then, you wait for me."

"Where?" Her voice wavered.

"I'll send you a transmission—"

"What if you can't?" she said, her voice escalating. "I want a word with you outside. Alone."

He shook his head, no. "I need to stay focused. So do you. Later." He touched her cheek, the voice in his head soft. *We'll talk about this later, and please don't kiss me. I'm not going to sleep with them, just play with their heads. Cool?*

She covered his hand for a moment and then drew away and nodded, wrapping her arms around her waist.

"All right. We all clear?" Carlos said, restoring order in the room as much as he was restoring it within himself. He wiped away the illusion on the table, needing to draw his energy inward. The multiple kills would send up an inquiry. He'd probably have to go down to Hell for a few hours before being released from council chambers. There'd be much to explain, especially when he didn't have the key or the seal. But the party boat, the feeding frenzy, Damali's armed Guardians, all of that would sound reasonable to some very unreasonable old men—as long as their package wasn't damaged.

Marlene stood slowly, glancing at Father Patrick. "These are pretty old masters, Carlos," she said, her voice calm, but her eyes penetrating. "They've probably seen it all, been everywhere in the world and are jaded. I'd bet good money that plain old human terror at seeing fangs drop doesn't give them a rush anymore. So, before we all walk into certain death, what are you going to do to distract them beyond our girl's enticing performance? No disrespect intended, she's good, so are you, but as an old doll, I like multiple assurances. Call me crazy, but I've got a bad feeling about all of this."

It was a logical question. He had a bad feeling about this, too. Using Damali as a distraction wasn't going to work without some assistance. Carlos nodded and walked over to the coffee table and sat on the couch. He paused, wondering when he'd allowed Damali to extract his brain from his head. This was potentially the stupidest thing he was ever going to do. If council ever found out about this . . . He blotted out the chairman's possible reaction from his mind.

"Yup, Marlene's right," he said, so casual that it sounded like silk. "I'm going to show you the secret held in blood. The old masters can separate out the scents within it down to a thousand parts per million concentration, like a wine taster would roll a fine cabernet or merlot on their tongue, and can give you the ingredients of its bouquet."

"No shit?" Rider said, glancing at Jose. "You guys have noses that good?" He shook his head and moved in close, rubbing his jaw, awed.

Carlos glanced up at the fascinated expressions. "It's an art. Our noses are our strong point, which makes it our weak point, same with our sense of touch, and our greatest erogenous zone is our mind." Carlos looked up at Rider. "Once we get an impression, it stays with us forever. A scent," he added, "can linger for hundreds of years." He turned his attention to Big Mike. "The timbre of a voice can take a male master places that—" He glanced at Damali and held her gaze. "Her music will stay in their minds, and her voice is perfect pitch," he said with appreciation, then looked back at the table. "Them seeing her, and what they have seen of her, will lock an image in their skulls. The combination is maddening."

His gaze slid to Shabazz, trying to get them to understand why everything had gone down the way it did between him and Damali, without directly explaining. For some strange reason, that was very important to him now. Father Patrick's anger had hurt, not physically, but his faraway soul. It wasn't about disrespect; it was about something natural to his species that he had about as much control over as breathing, maybe less. There was no way to be with her without biting her.

"A touch is unforgettable." Carlos closed his eyes. Damali's touch, everything about her, was like a drug that left a man disoriented and needing more. "That's why one of the most respected masters in our vampire history—Dracula—woke up after a few hundred years with a woman on his mind, found her reincarnated, and got himself dusted by a young kid and a priest." He waited for Shabazz's nod. "He had smelled her, had tasted her, had touched her, had seen her . . . and had the sound of her voice driving him nuts in-coffin—he was strung out by the time he got out, became relentless in his quest, got sloppy." The information was a face-saving apology. "Down in Hell, we don't talk about it; was humiliating to lose a venerated master to that, but trust me, it happens to the best of us."

"Locks in your minds like that?" Big Mike asked. "Damn, you bastards must suffer." He shook his head and stepped back, letting out a long breath of compassion.

"That's why they call it Hell, dude," Rider said, no amusement in his tone.

Carlos wasn't offended. What Rider has said was the truth. "The greatest strength is the greatest weakness—just like ego. Anything can be flipped to turn the tables. Normally, we use it, and are in control," Carlos said, trying to salvage his dignity. "But once in a blue moon," he said, his gaze sliding to Damali against his will, "a male will get an impression imprinted on his senses that will literally fuse with his DNA, and he can't shake it, has no control over it, and it will blow him away." He wanted them to hear that, to truly know he wasn't playing with their girl, especially when they found out later that things were much deeper than they'd imagined. Yeah, she was definitely like a drug . . . something in his bloodstream.

He jerked his gaze away from Damali; he had to. But the thoughts beginning to ignite within him came together like a quiet nightfall. The room had gone still, the group was looking at him too hard, and he had said too much. "That's why I'm about to create something called *'Oblivion.'* It's something that will blow their minds. The negative aspects of my old life are coming in handy, might be useful for something good—damn, my territory was bittersweet."

Was . . . past tense, she *was* his territory. Sweetness like he couldn't describe. He had to let it go. Bitter reality to the bone. He sat for a moment concentrating, just staring at the table. Now because of a variable, he had to make this stuff in front of her team that he wasn't going to tell her about; they had to know how volatile a substance it was, how it made his kind really react, especially once he found out she was pregnant. The masters and their wives would smell the baby in Damali as soon as she hit the VIP box, unless they had something else stronger in their noses. Last night, that wasn't something they had to deal with. This is what he hated about this whole plan; too many variables.

Damali came near him, squatted by his side, and glanced up. "You don't have to do what I think you're going to do," she murmured. "We can go in without pure Neteru."

He shook his head. "Marlene is right. I don't want to risk you, not at this point."

"If you make this in here, are *you* gonna be all right, is the question." She looked at him hard, and shot a nervous glance around the room.

"I'll be cool," Carlos said, rolling his shoulders. "Just back up off me, aw'ight? Won't be able to handle the fumes from the contact and the touch, understand?"

She nodded and went to the far side of the room, all eyes on her, then on Carlos. "Watch the man and learn some deep science about vampires," she said, trying not to sound shaken. "This info is beyond valuable, and could save your life."

"Thanks, baby," Carlos murmured, and then glanced at Marlene to clear his mind. "Mar, you're right. They've seen it all, but they've never seen this." He opened his palm as the group gathered around him tighter, and slit it with his nail.

Dark ruby blood bubbled up in the center of it, and he made a fist and dripped a slowly spreading circle of it on the table. "Watch what the atmosphere does to it," he said, standing and walking away from the table. "You put holy water, hallowed earth, or silver to the black side, and it will torch. A little bit of sacred substance ignites at the source of impact and then rockets through our systems like touching a match to an internal gasoline line, our veins—that's why the Isis, or a silver-tipped arrow dipped in holy water, whatever, explodes vampires from the inside out." He looked up for a moment. "We can't take a nick, either, from some stuff."

The group kept their gaze fixed to the blood as it beaded up and separated into two smaller circles—one blot, black; one blot a deep crimson with an iridescent shimmer to it. Carlos covered his nose and mouth with his hand as his eyes began to water. He was grateful that Damali had the presence of mind not to go to him or even lacerate with her lovely voice.

"You all right, man?" Big Mike asked, making the group stare at Carlos.

Carlos shook his head. "No," he said on a heavy exhale. "Throw me your dagger, Damali, and somebody go get me a wet towel so I can breathe long enough to cut this product."

He coughed and walked toward the terrace, opened the doors, and bent over the rail. There wasn't enough fresh air on the planet to get the scent of ripening Neteru, saturated with adrenaline, out of his system. Her essence after a demon blood hunt with a double-plunge siphon kick—hurling toward the vanishing point—there was no substance close to it. This was from a bite before she'd conceived, he hadn't bitten her after that—had to find the safe house and had burned his fuel out by then. Bittersweet irony; a variable on their side for once. But what was filling the air was making his eyes cross.

No one said a word as Carlos caught the towel Dan tossed him, and he covered his face, then just his mouth and nose with it. Damali didn't throw him the dagger, but instead gave it to Big Mike, who placed it on the coffee table and backed up for Carlos.

On shaky legs Carlos came back into the room, shut the doors behind him to keep the prayer barrier seal in place, sat down fast, and removed the towel, blowing out a slow stream of air to freeze and crystallize the two drying blood puddles. In twenty-four hours, this rare hemoglobin extract would be gone from his system, and hers would never produce it again . . . not that strong, not that pure—he knew it as he stared at the frozen ovals of life. She wouldn't allow another vampire to come near her like this, and no human male could take her system there to radiate it with endorphin rush the way he had. Maybe it was the drug talking, but a part of him was becoming depressed as he thought of how precious what had been spilled on the table was . . . and so like them, frozen. In stasis. Unable to come together, because it was unnatural.

"You all right, man?" Rider's voice was like a call across an ocean.

"Yeah," Carlos murmured, and began working with shaky hands. "Being a councilman has its added powers," he said, trying to joke away his pain. He tried not to think of anything but the task before him, tried not to let the product rule him as he used Damali's dagger to crush the red crystals into a fine powder. He almost licked the blade, but flipped the dagger to use the clean side—then remembered. If he touched the black blood with it, he'd start a fire in the room. Yeah, he was fucked up just from the contact. Having to keep the doors to the terrace shut was messing him up.

"Get me something to cut with—just make sure it doesn't have silver in it. I have to hurry up and cut the other side without blowing up the room."

Relief wafted through him as Rider tossed him his bowie knife. He could transcend this shit. He was a councilman. Sweat broke out on his brow.

Quickly, he performed the same procedure on his black blood, put the towel up to his face for a moment, and materialized empty gelatin capsules, drew the contents into them to seal off the airborne fragrance, then quickly stood and walked toward the terrace.

Sweat poured down his temples, wet his back, and made his nose run. His incisors had lowered, and for a few seconds, he could only see red. "Somebody go wash that Isis blade off," he ordered, unable to even look at it when Big Mike took it off the table. "Rider, you, too . . . the black blood is like acid on human skin, will fuck you up bad if you touch it."

Carlos pulled in several breaths of cool night air, thankful that council-level status gave him a little more resistance and willpower, albeit not much. He shut his eyes when the train of Damali's dress came into his peripheral vision. "Tell her to walk across the room and fucking stay there!"

He heard her swift footsteps, the swish of her dress like a hard rake down his back, could feel her pulse across the room—could smell her. He shut his eyes tight. Not here, and not in her condition.

"Aw'ight," he said, once Damali was out of arm's reach, and then came back into the room, shutting the doors again to keep the privacy prayer barriers intact. "Like she once said, whatever you died knowing how to do alive, you take with you when dead, so listen up." He nodded toward the table, but had to talk away from it, pointing behind him. "That right there, is the equivalent of master vampire kryptonite." He shuddered and started pacing, trying to get it out of his system. "It cannot be found anywhere on the planet. No one else but Damali can manufacture it, and only under certain conditions . . . I just happened to have it in my system from the last twenty-four hours—*do not ask.*"

"Damn, man, it fucks y'all up like that?" Shabazz stooped down and looked at the red capsules. "What's in the black ones?"

"That's my blood. Hers is red with an iridescence that burns your insides like quicksilver, then cools it to a shiver.

The shit is near-lethal, man. Will make you burst blood vessels in your brain and black out if you take in too much too fast."

"Her blood can turn those SOBs on so much they could have a pleasure stroke?" Rider was incredulous.

"Normal human blood drenched with adrenaline has a kick, but not like this stuff," Carlos said through labored breaths. "My blood is for the wives we have to deal with. It'll make them come to me instead of their masters." Carlos let out a slow breath. "With the charge that's running through that, you guys can stake the masters right in front of their wives, and the females won't care. Trust me. The black pill is vampire Ecstasy."

"Deep." Shabazz picked up the red pill and held it up to the light, squinting at it with one eye closed. "This don't seem to amp them down, though, brother." He looked at Carlos. "If anything, it makes them strong as shit."

"Let the air around that shit settle, 'Bazz. Give me a minute." Carlos bent over and tried to take in slow breaths, but failed. "Oh, *damn.*"

"I think this is way too dangerous a substance to be carrying into a vamp fest," Marlene warned.

"That's why Jose is gonna have to be my mule. I can't carry it, and he's the only one with enough diluted tracer to pass as a lower-level lieutenant. This shit makes 'em distracted," Carlos said, breathing hard. "Focused on one thing. They get sloppy. Senses concentrated on a single objective." He walked out to the terrace again as the team just stared at his back. He blotted his brow with the back of his forearm, and after a moment came back in. But he kept to the perimeter of the room, and refused to look at Damali.

"Here's the deal," he said, finally able to get himself together enough to speak. "The female vamps are programmed to defend their master if he's about to get smoked. The black pill will make them so buzzed, they'll laugh when he calls. They'll be too high to care what else is going on. The red pill will make the masters wide open to Damali's suggestions—and very unlikely to work as a unit to try to smoke me. Just don't mix up the pills when you mule a delivery for me, Jose. The reverse will be problematic. And don't touch the black ones; scrape them off the table into a plastic bag, or something; might be powder on the outside of the caps. Wipe that table down, good, too, so the maid doesn't lose a finger."

"What the hell is in this stuff, man?" Rider stood up and raked his fingers through his hair. "You don't have this in circulation in LA, do you?"

Damali gave Carlos a sly glance and looked at the floor. That slight action drew his focus to her, but he pulled his gaze away. He couldn't even look at her. His hands were trembling.

"No. It ain't nowhere else, man. This is the only batch. She knows about our kind from close study and from going undercover," Carlos murmured. "Ask her, but don't ask me what's in it. All I'ma say is, I hope in this little home demonstration that Marlene's valid, but unnecessary, concern about how to break their focus has been answered." He looked at Damali hard, unable to do anything else. "That's the only reason I did this—put myself through this bullshit, is so you all could see what you're dealing with when you guard a Neteru."

"Information is power," Damali said quietly, stepping back when Carlos winced from the sound of her voice. "Sorry . . ."

"Yup," Marlene said, staring at Damali carefully. "They can't even get this with the rare occurrence of a Neteru on earth if they bit her now," she said, her voice wise, as she went to Carlos with caution. She placed her hand on his shoulder, sensing, healing, stabilizing him. "This isn't just about a ripening, her normal blood, is it?"

"No, ma'am."

Marlene patted his thickened shoulder and stared up at him. "I didn't think it was." She touched his face. "So, we'll use this wisely, will protect the package, and make sure we don't raise Hell. Need you around, brother . . . and I know it was hard to slit a vein and give that to us."

All he could do was nod and look away from Marlene. "Thanks, Mar. This is between A and B, right?"

"Absolutely. You're on our side."

"Cool. Thanks."

"Jose, man. Can I have a word? *Mano y mano*." Carlos nodded toward the door, and wasn't offended when the young Guardian hesitated and the others got tense. "It's peace. But if you're gonna mule for me, and be first body next to my woman—you have *got* to get schooled on some *serious* protocol . . . and I have *got* to get out of this room."

CHAPTER TWENTY-ONE

THE WALK down the hallway seemed unending. The farther away from Damali he got, the deeper the ache. It was impossible to stop glancing over his shoulder, past Jose's terrified eyes, to where she was. This wasn't just his woman any longer; this was the mother of his child. As it would have been in life, so it ironically wound up being in death, his primary male objective at DNA-base-level-imprint was to protect the line going forward.

A new river of sweat was running down the center of his back. He wiped his face with both hands, breathing into them, the smell of her blood still on them in the cut that was slow to seal. "Oh, shit, man, you have no idea," Carlos said on a hard exhale, and put his hands behind his back, walking away from Jose.

"Yes, I do," Jose said quietly, making Carlos turn and study him. "I live with her, and have felt like that for years. It's a bitch, but you'll live."

The calm resignation in Jose's voice, the terror that gave way to pride—Carlos had to give the man a nod of respect.

"You love her, don't you?"

"Don't you?" Jose said, his chin lifted, hands at his sides, fists slowly balling.

Carlos moved farther away from the man he didn't want to slaughter. "Chill, *hombre*. We've got a lot in common, and I ain't even mad at you about it. Respect," he said, nodding at Jose. "You got my respect."

He waited until the tension left Jose's fists before he spoke.

"And you got mine," Jose said, then glanced back at the suite. "Just don't take her into no bullshit you can't get her out of."

Carlos held out his hand and two sets of keys came into the center of his palm. He closed his fist over them and tossed them to Jose. "Your bike is a red Harley, right? Rider is on a black and silver Easy Rider classic?"

Jose looked at the keys and flung them back to Carlos. "Don't fuck with my head, man, and try to give me some shit—"

"It's for her," Carlos said, catching the keys, then tossing them back to Jose more gently. "After you get off the speed-boats, I want you to put her on the back of one of those bikes and ride like the wind to hallowed ground; Rider as your shotgun. Everybody else can catch up, however they have to. The teams stand ground to hold back any vamps in pursuit of Damali. But your job is to get her out of harm's way— even if you have to chain her to the back of the bike. Hear me? I'm counting on you, man."

Jose looked at the keys in his hand, and slowly brought his gaze up to meet Carlos's. "You're worried, ain't you, man?"

Carlos didn't answer him, just walked in a tight circle rubbing the nape of his neck. He could feel himself begin to normalize and his fangs retract. Something tugging at him that made it hard to speak. The truth.

"Yeah, man," Carlos whispered. "She ain't just a pack-age—she's precious cargo. Ride fast but ride easy."

Jose's glare softened. "Man, talk to me . . ."

He took his time speaking, his eyes leaving Jose's and go-ing to the suite door. "They're coming for me, *hombre*. I can feel it. I have *fucked up* big time, and I'm out of game. So, we gonna do this with pride. Guns blazing, no regrets. I'll blow the whole fucking ship before I let them take her." He returned his gaze to Jose. "Stay with her, comfort her, become her lover, and be her man, and it's all good."

Carlos began walking away. He couldn't say any more to the better man. The lump in his throat hurt too much.

"Why me?" Jose hollered down the hall, making Carlos stop.

"You know the rules. Winner takes all."

"What the hell are you talking about, man?"

Jose's voice echoed down the corridor, and Carlos willed no one else to enter it. He turned slowly, his gaze locking with Jose's. "Because you are the *only* one that sees her with the eyes in your heart. You were ready to give her a vein in the compound if she didn't pull out of the turn. You're the only one who would die for her without blinking, without hesitating, and you're the only one who can give her a *real* life, topside."

When Jose didn't respond, Carlos slapped the center of his chest. "You don't think I can see that? A blind man could. No special powers needed." His breaths were unsteady, but it had nothing to do with the high that was burning away. "I'm infected, man. I live a dangerous life. I ain't no good for her, and one night I'll ruin her. So, I'm transferring power, giving you fair claim to *my everything* . . . you're in my line, you're in my territory, and you love her. Isn't that enough?" He paced away and came back to where he'd been standing. "You are the better man, one that can give her normal kids, can take them out in the sunlight and keep her safe on hallowed ground at night, and no matter what, I know you'll be by her side or die trying. You won't make Marlene weep because you're the father."

"Carlos, man, listen—"

"I would have given her that," he said, cutting Jose off as he battled for composure. "But I fucked up!"

"But she doesn't love me," Jose said, his voice steady, no bitterness, but enough compassion in it to make Carlos stare at the elevators.

"After I'm gone," Carlos said quietly, "she will."

Jose shook his head. "It doesn't work like that, and you know it. I'll be walking on your grave, and—"

"And you will both remember a shared loss . . . Dee Dee, and me. You both will have shared memories of your battles together, will be part of an unbroken unit, the family. You'll both share something that no other two people in the world have shared—this crazy life you Guardians lead . . ." Carlos's voice trailed off to a gentle murmur. "You were friends, first. You will always be friends. You stood flank for her at the final hour, and—"

"Man, stop talking like you're going out of here. You're part of the team. You're a Guardian. Okay, a dark one, but the way Damali looks at you, always did . . . You die, you'll break her heart—so I forbid it." Jose wiped his face with both palms, breathed deeply, then stared at him hard. "We don't leave our own."

At a stalemate, the two just looked at each other. This wasn't why he'd come out into the hall with Jose. It was to tell him how to work the vamps, slip them the product, handle himself under the duress the masters were sure to put him under. It was to get them on the same page, get Jose's head right, and to tell him whatever he could to save Damali's life . . . give him the keys. This had not been on the agenda.

But as he looked at this man who could have passed for his younger brother, tears welled in his eyes. Alejandro, Juan, Julio, all of them, and every other *hombre* that had fallen came into his consciousness. This was the only family he had left in the world, and owning the whole world meant nothing without them in it.

"She's pregnant, isn't she, man?" Jose finally whispered.

When Carlos nodded, the tears in his eyes fell, and he walked away, wiping them with the back of his fist.

"I gotchure back," Jose called behind him, then he was gone.

The entire room let out a silent, collective breath of relief when Jose walked back into the suite. Damali searched his face, noting how his eyes refused to meet hers.

"You cool?" Rider asked, coming up to Jose. "You didn't mess around out there and get master mind-nicked, did ya?"

Jose smiled, knowing that the one-liner was Rider's way of letting him know just how worried he'd been. He handed his friend a set of Harley keys and went to the bar to pour himself a drink.

"What's this, dude?" Rider came up to him, the other guardian's eyes trained on the transaction along with the clerics.

"Your chopper is downstairs, man. After the boats, we ride, man, like old times."

"You struck a deal with the devil out in the hall," Rider said, half serious, half joking.

"Rivera is cool, man," Jose said, growing testy as he threw back a shot of Jack Daniel's. "Give the man a break. He's under a lot of stress."

Shabazz moved in to the bar slowly, his gaze going between Marlene and Rider, then sweeping the rest, landing on Damali. "You ain't under the influence, are you? No mind-control shit, right?"

Damali shook her head and left the room, going into the bedroom to get her concert outfits. The look on Jose's face had constricted her chest. He knew. Yet, he was honorable enough not to tell the group, and man enough not to come barreling into the suite all hyped with accusations and drama, knowing what they all had to face. And if Carlos had told him in that brief exchange, what had her man been going through? None of it was a good sign. Carlos had told a Guardian—and not one of the more seasoned ones, at that.

Damali sat down on the bed and stared out the window for a few minutes, already missing the one person she was never supposed to be with. For such a private, deeply proud individual to drop façade like that, tell someone who had been his greatest challenger . . . while under the influence . . . not harm him, but send him back to the room with new respect . . . She closed her eyes, trying to stave off the panic polluting her bloodstream.

After they did the yacht job, he wasn't coming back.

"You all right?" Marlene murmured, moving her locks off her shoulders, and dabbing her nose with a bit of pressed powder.

Damali just nodded, listening to the first act—world music rocking the house.

"I forgot to tell you, we made the *Sydney Morning Herald*," Marlene said offhandedly, her voice far away, like Damali's thoughts, her conversation inane and a brittle attempt at normalcy.

"Let's just do the show, Mar," she said quietly. Damali stopped her mentor's hand from applying more makeup. "I don't want to go on the boat, dust any vamps, or lose anybody. We've been lucky . . . I wish we could just go home, and do like Mike said."

Marlene traced her eyebrows with the ball of her thumb, her eyes moist. "It's too late. We're already in too deep, and past the point of no return. Irrevocable events have been set in motion."

"I just want to go home and live like normal people," Damali whispered.

"But we've already reached the vanishing point," Marlene murmured, her voice filled with love, "and it's too late, honey."

They held each other's gaze, both sets of female eyes filling and burning away sudden tears. Damali nodded, knowing Mar knew, but Jose hadn't told. It was the touch she'd shared with Carlos.

"All right," Damali said, her voice falsely hard. "Let's rock this show, go kick some ass, then go home."

Marlene just looked at her and opened her arms, pulling her into the hug she so desperately needed right now. "Yeah, let's go kick some ass and bring *everybody* home."

"Councilman, this is Old World outrageous," McGuire said as he leaned over the yacht rail, laughing while he poured a bottle of blood in the water.

Carlos watched the Aussie master from a very remote place in his mind. The loud music grated his nerves. Naked, jiggling silicone tits everywhere put the taste of plastic on the back of his tongue as he scanned the decks of the one-hundred-and-eighty-foot monstrosity cutting the water from the Great Barrier Reef, as sharks trailed behind it.

"You bringing Great Whites with you, McGuire?" Carlos said, forcing a smile as he peered at the night-blackened water.

"You know it, sir. I love trying to lure the big bastards into the bay to see what happens. Me and my lieutenants place bets on whether or not there'll be a shark attack. We read the paper the following evening to see who won," he chuckled. "You have got to try body surfing with the sharks. Me and the old boys do this sort of rot all the time."

McGuire turned the bottle up to his mouth and took a deep swig, pointing at the sharks in the water. "They're just like us: eating machines, never really sleep, gotta keep moving, hunting. They have awesome razors. Beautiful creatures. We weren't a biological mistake. Predators are a part of the natural balance." He winked.

Carlos didn't respond, just kept his gaze sweeping. "Wanna talk to you," he said, swallowing away the bile that being near a sycophant caused. When McGuire moved back, lowered his bottle, and stopped smiling, Carlos sighed. This was like being in the Roman senate; everybody nervous all the time, everybody ready to do the next man for a price at the drop of an olive leaf. "I made you a promise, and I intend to keep it," he said, his gaze now on the other masters who'd gathered on a starboard deck.

"What . . ." McGuire said, very quietly, glancing around as he stepped close to Carlos.

"I've been in a very relaxed frame of mind since last night," Carlos murmured, his eyes holding the Aussie's. "My wife has been, too." He paused, letting the impact of his words sink in. Then he smiled. "You watched my back, and I told all of you we would apportion territory according to merit." He rubbed his jawline and dropped his voice, watching the wide eyes of McGuire the whole time he spoke. "We honestly hadn't had the chance to discuss much else, but this was a priority to her . . . she appreciated your hospitality, and Evelyn's. The little spat in the parlor was forgiven. She so loved being a part of the hunt . . . and the evening it inspired. Wants to thank you."

"Are you serious?" McGuire stepped even closer, profound appreciation in his gaze.

"Ask me again if I'm serious, and I withdraw the offer."

"No worries. I accept."

"Good. Wouldn't want to disappoint the little lady." Carlos chuckled and slung an arm over the man's shoulders and began walking, monitoring the silent bristle that action caused within the ranks. Very good. He could see Amin nearly drop fang with envy, but the Transylvanian was cool. Too cool. Master Xe just nodded as they approached. Carlos removed his arm from McGuire's shoulders.

"Gentlemen," Carlos said, taking his time. "Thought it would be good to get out of the castle," he added, sweeping his arms wide, with a big smile. "After all the negotiations and stress, might do us well to get some fresh air on our faces, salt in our noses, and go into Sydney, proper. This party is for you, for good sportsmanship, cool vibes, and to a new empire with a new product that I think we'll all enjoy."

They nodded, smiled, intrigue glinting off their fang tips, as they slipped out of the hold of several females to follow Carlos below deck to a stateroom. But as they did so, each master looked back toward their respective mates, who were feeding and otherwise indulging their own vices, as if to tell them to stay put, but stay alert. The mood on the ship instantly shifted among the top brass, while lower-level vamps and human helpers kept on partying.

Carlos measured his footfalls, leading a pack of very dangerous entities across the polished wood, none casting shadows against the gleaming white walls and brass railings. He'd have to be sure to blot out Damali's image on them.

Open-air stairs gave way to polished walnut everywhere, red and gold appointments, and huge rooms. The massive vessel once owned by the now dusted U.S. master, Fallon Nuit, came as a part of the won territory, and had been good for something.

As Carlos walked, he steadied his nerves. Making one more batch was imperative—half hits in a steel box in his pocket. He had to see how this shit reacted before he turned four masters loose on a crowd in the Opera House. No variables allowed. Plus, before Damali sent her team in there, he had to be sure full control was on his side.

Tetrosky sat down first at the large oval table, leaned forward and made a tent with his fingers under his chin, and stared at the box Carlos slipped out of his pocket. The others sat slowly, each appraising the box with curiosity, and then glancing at Carlos.

He took his time, drawing out the suspense, smoothing his electric-blue sharkskin suit, everything monochrome except his black leather Bally slip-ons, and smiled. This was his game. He knew this one well. The old boys were very new to how this shit worked—first hit's on me.

"I'm going to need a human helper from top deck," he said calmly. "This product is too volatile for even me to handle . . . and I have to be able to allow my wife to perform on stage." He chuckled, feeling their curiosity replace their ever-present envy for a moment. That was something he'd gambled on. When you'd seen it all, done it all, the only thing one had left to produce a rush was something new and hard to acquire.

He waited for a young woman to grace them with her voluptuous, topless, white-thonged presence. She was all smiles, a brilliant dashing flash of perfect teeth, dark, moody eyes, and rush of brunette hair. Her nipples were coffee-bean brown, and her skin was a soft, perfect canvas of caramel. Carlos chuckled to himself. He was spoken for, but could still appreciate the best things life had to offer. This specimen of Caribbean East Indian finery would definitely help boost the product.

She came to sit in his lap, kissing his throat. He shook his head. "I'm mated, hon. Not the throat." He sighed and helped her off his lap.

"I'm going to re-allot the lands, and treat you all fairly," he said, glancing at Master Xe. "We can talk about the Forbidden City later tonight or tomorrow night. That was rash, I agree." He glanced at Master Amin, while feeling Xe's body relax a bit. "Let's have a real conversation about Gorey Island, man. I'm not greedy, and some things have been in your line for a long time, like London, and the mother state, Transylvania," he added, motioning toward Tetrosky. "Just ask McGuire," he said with a smile. "He'll tell you I'm a man of my word."

Tetrosky stared at McGuire. "Noooo . . ." Then he shot his gaze around the table, before coming back to the Australian master to stare at him astonished.

"This bastard is all right wi' me, mate."

Carlos shrugged, and placed a hand on Amin's shoulder. "It was protocol. The man hosted my first serious visit topside."

"You'll have to come to the continent, then, for your second visit, and bring your lovely wife."

Carlos laughed and pounded Amin's fist. "Yeah. We can do that."

"Russia is beautiful in the winter," Tetrosky said, chuckling, "and I do believe this is how we lost all our lands in the first place."

Master Xe smiled and nodded toward the box. "A peace offering?"

"*Sí,*" Carlos said, carefully placing the box in the young woman's hand beside him. "Baby, go open it up by Tetrosky, since he lost the most. He should be first."

"What is it?" Tetrosky said, holding up his hand and stopping the woman's approach. "I'm not about to poison myself," he said, standing. "If you want to assassinate me, then do it outright."

Carlos just smoothed his tie, nonplussed. "Now, man, why after I already own all that you have, would I want to start some shit down at council by dusting you? Think about it. What purpose would that serve?" Carlos sighed. "Send in a lower-level male and test the product on him."

He watched Tetrosky struggle with the mind puzzle and calm down a bit, but he was still on guard. "See, man, this is why we have to have trust across regions. I thought if we all came together, had fun, got people's land issues sorted out, loosened up for an evening . . ."

"Very well," Tetrosky said, sounding half convinced. "Just tell me what it is."

Carlos leaned forward, talking with his hands. "I left the banquet after the hunt, rather abruptly, right?" He waited for them to all nod. "Right," he said, standing and going to the far side of the room, away from the sure contact that would come out of the box with Tetrosky's half cap. "You all saw my wife. She was over the top, made me fold her away in a pure vapor lock. Fell over the freaking balcony with her, almost hit the rocks."

Four pairs of eyes were riveted to him, drinking in his every word. Carlos ran his fingers through his hair, as though exasperated, making them wait, prolonging the agony of not knowing. "Shit was so outrageous that I scared myself . . . almost bought daylight."

"She kept you outside of a lair till near dawn?"

Carlos nodded and held Amin's eyes. "No lie." He waited, feeling the sure fraud assessment, and sent an impression of the intensity to Amin that made him lower his gaze. But he withheld the actual image—that he would never give him. When Amin glanced back up at him to pry for more information, Carlos looked at the wall. Go to Hell.

"He's not lying," Amin murmured, and sat back in his chair. "Incredible."

"So," Carlos pressed on, keeping his line of vision away from Master Xe's stealthy attempts at an impression siphon, "figured that I could share a little of that with you fine gentlemen. Give you product for the road, so until we met again, there'd be no hard feelings."

"*What* is it?" Tetrosky said, now leaning forward on the large walnut table.

It was all Carlos could do not to laugh. "It is the blood of the Neteru, uncut. I call it 'Oblivion.'" Satisfied when they went slack-jawed, he allowed himself to laugh. "Gentlemen, you have no idea what I had to do to bring you this sample."

"Oblivion?" Master Xe stood, walked to Carlos, and bowed. "Fair exchange is no robbery." He snapped his finger twice and waited as a young male vampire entered the room. Master Xe smiled. "Third-level, from the old empire," he said and nodded toward what appeared to be a shy twenty-year-old.

Fear filled the young vampire's eyes, and Carlos watched his dark brown eyes glance around the table, unsure. Nervous perspiration was beading up on his lip, and soon he smoothed it back in his jet-black hair. Carlos noticed that his armpits had become ringed with sweat that now stained his lemon yellow suit.

"Our Councilman Rivera has brought us a sample of something very special," Master Xe crooned. "Won't you test this for us?"

The young man glanced around again, terror haunting his eyes. But he bowed in deference and extended his hand.

"I'm only going to give him a quarter hit," Carlos warned, "because if he bugs, you'll have to smoke him."

Master Xe laughed, but motioned for Carlos to proceed. As the young vampire held out his palm, Carlos opened a capsule, shook a bit of the substance in it, capped it quickly, and put it back in the box, holding his breath. All eyes were on the lower-level vampire as he sniffed the substance, closed his eyes just from its scent, swooned, and quickly licked his palm. Within seconds, he'd battle bulked, his incisors had lowered, and he was beginning to seize. Duly impressed, the older masters laughed as they watched his torment. But when the young vampire opened his eyes and looked up at the ceiling, openly monitoring Damali's whereabouts, Master Xe ended his misery by summarily ripping out his heart.

Red embers and ash floated through the cabin. Carlos brushed off his suit. "This is why I said it was only for the truly senior members in this room who could hang."

"Let me try it," Master Xe said urgently, following the scent that still lingered. "Clearly it's not poison . . . but do give me the rest of the capsule that has already been opened. You do understand my caution."

"Naw, man," Carlos warned. "That's almost a whole hit. This shit ain't no joke—will knock your head back. That's why I call it Oblivion. I have zero tolerance for it, actually. It fucks me up, bad." He could feel Amin siphon him and shudder when he pulled away the truth. "Told you," Carlos said, vindicated.

Shaking off the allowed encroachment, Carlos began pacing, seeming as though just talking about it was messing with him. "I felt that creating this for you guys was the only right thing to do, the way she hard-ball negotiated against my own men. Treacherous shit, that woman is deep. Besides, you have to have your control back before we pull into Sydney Harbor—and you can't allow your wife to smell it on you. Might cause an incident to raise human awareness in the Sydney—"

"My wife knows she'd better not fuck with me on this issue, or any of my business dealings," Xe said icily, and then walked over to the brunette and opened the box. "If Tetrosky is too much of a pussy to try it, I will. My dynasty is used to rare opiates, it will take much to impress me."

"Aw'ight, man," Carlos sighed. "Don't say I didn't warn you."

They all watched as Master Xe slipped a small red capsule onto his tongue, closed his eyes, and swallowed. He wiped his nose with the back of his hand, and shut the box, protecting himself from the excess fumes. He shrugged and walked away, shaking his head and chuckling. Carlos could feel the disappointment register in the other masters. But they kept their eyes on Xe. For a moment, a new worry wrapped around his mind threatening to strangle it. What if he was the only one that had a total intolerance to Damali, simply because of the way he'd felt about her before he turned? A serious variable.

"No offense, Councilman Rivera, but you must do better than . . ."

Xe's words trailed off as he approached his seat, tilted his head to the side, and closed his eyes with a hard shudder. His hand went to the back of the chair, and he gripped it so hard that he scored the leather. "Damn . . ." He murmured through another hard shudder that made him breathe through his mouth.

Small beads of sweat had formed on his brow, and his red silk shirt bled dark with sweat on his chest beneath his black silk suit. The other masters watched him intently, measuring the length of the rush, making sure the man was just enjoying the hit, not poisoned. But when he dropped his head back as his incisors ripped his gums, all around the table nodded, thoroughly impressed.

"That was only a three-quarters hit?" Xe murmured, his eyes flickering red as he raked his fingers through his damp hair and he stumbled as he tried to sit down.

"Yeah," Carlos said sensually, slowly, holding Xe's gaze. "A pint will nearly kill you."

"I would have bled her out," Xe said as an aftershock shiver made it difficult for him to steady the swivel chair to sit. His gaze immediately went to the young woman holding the box.

"That's why, unless you know what you're doing, you can bleed a female out, not have enough judgment to give her back a vein till you can find a feed source, and might get caught by the sun." Carlos nodded to the young woman to get out of Xe's snatch range and to move to Tetrosky.

"This ain't no joke, I'm telling you." Carlos took on a paternal tone as he glanced around the room. "So, while this is seriously recreational, I don't want to hear about a master frying himself out in the regions behind this. I'm *not even* supposed to be giving this to you all . . . this is council-level shit for those who can handle it. But I'm trying to be progressive up here."

"He is definitely that," McGuire said. "I can vouch for

him, he's a man of his word, a sure pisser with no flies on 'im. The bloody bastard is so fair he almost made me weep up on the deck with such a kind offer." McGuire stood, went to Carlos, and hugged him hard, breaking all protocol.

Stunned, the others around the table waited to see how the significant protocol breach would be redressed. Carlos smiled. McGuire had been sitting on the other side of Xe. Just the contact from the box alone had McGuire sloppy. You didn't roll up on another master and get in throat range unless you were prepared to lose yours. He held McGuire out by the arms, looked into his reddened, watery eyes, and shook his head.

"He's high, just from the contact, gentlemen. What are we going to do, huh? Told you it was strong." Carlos motioned to the woman with the product. "Give him a hit and sit his ass down, away from you—and me."

"It's *so* strong," Xe murmured, his eyes closed, his head back, still recovering. "If you don't get your head together before you take it, you will assuredly lose face."

Amin and Tetrosky gave each other a sideline glance as Xe had spoken, and McGuire popped one of the little red gel caps. Instantly, the Aussie dropped fang, held his head in his palms, then tore one hand away and banged on the table with his fist. The tremor that ran through him shook the huge oval table, and saliva ran down his fang, collecting in small splatters as he convulsed.

Tetrosky chuckled. "Xe, thanks for the warning. McGuire is definitely losing face as we speak. Pitiful."

"Damn, that was only half a hit," Amin said, shaking his head, his eyes locking with Carlos, a silent bargain in the offing. "She's not going to be pleased with you, Councilman . . . Are you *really* sending her in there with him after the concert?"

"Aaaay," Carlos said, laughing and opening his arms. "I gave the man my word."

"I'll take a full hit, and will show you that you might want to reconsider." Amin smiled.

"Brave man," Carlos said, his strategy sound, but a bit of his own emotional control ebbing. He wasn't sure how he'd react if Amin could hang. "Remember, we all have to be straight before we hit Sydney."

"Pass me the box," Amin said, his tone dipping, and his eyes steady on Carlos as the young woman rounded the table. *If I take a whole hit, he blew his chance.*

Carlos chuckled and shot his response back in Dananu, just like the challenge had been given. *You blow your load at this table on a full hit, and the deal is off.*

I won't even drop fang.

"This I have *got* to witness," Tetrosky said, thoroughly amused. His eyes darted between the combatants with total excitement.

Amin took a whiff of the opened box, cleared his throat, and placed two red pills on his tongue, boldly upping the ante with a double hit. He held his gaze steady with Carlos, refusing to close his eyes as he swallowed. Carlos leaned against the wall, watching, waiting for the implosion with a sly, knowing smile.

The first shudder rolled up on Amin slowly, like a soft hand sliding up his back. The sensation made him tilt his head, and slightly altered his once-controlled breathing. His nostrils flared a little with the harder inhales and exhales, and the group watched him battle the hit by breaking eye contact with Carlos to find a point of concentration on the wall.

When Amin started breathing through his mouth, Carlos pushed off the wall, and pounded McGuire's fist. The Aussie had weakly raised it for him, and was riveted to Amin, hope slipping away fast.

"No worries, mate. I know how this shit goes." Carlos chuckled as he patted McGuire's shoulder. "This mother-fucker is gonna break down any minute," he added with confidence as Amin closed his eyes, and they rolled beneath his lids. He could literally feel his adversary straining not to throw his head back and expose his throat. "Telling me my product ain't da butta."

"I believe he is indeed on the verge of losing a very promising bet," Tetrosky said, chuckling low in his throat. "I should have weighed in on the wager, myself. Is it too late?"

"You better talk quick," Carlos said, trying to sound unfazed, and glancing at the sweat now running down Amin's temples, but very concerned that he hadn't dropped fang— very concerned. He did not need to know that. That would have to be the *first* bastard he killed.

"How about if—"

A long, agonized groan stopped Tetrosky's words. Amin's fangs ripped so hard so fast that his gums bled into the saliva running down them. His shudder rocked the table and made his nose bleed. His head was back, jugular pulsing, his grip on the side of the table splintering a section of it.

Carlos walked away shaking his head. "You can't hold that shit back, man," he muttered, throwing a disgusted nod toward Amin's bloody nose. Then he looked at the girl holding the box as another shudder rocked Amin. "You ready to die tonight, baby, or you just wanna hang out with vampires?"

"I . . . I . . . uh . . . I'm not sure I want to turn."

"I didn't ask you if you wanted to turn, sis. I asked you if you wanted to *die*." Carlos glanced at the other masters, who all nodded. "Give me the box, closed, go get Mistress Alani, and tell her to come get her husband."

The girl almost dropped the box as she dashed from the room when Amin's eyes glowed red, his gaze went to her, and Carlos stepped between her and Amin's reach. Even Carlos stepped back two paces when another hard shudder made Amin hold onto the table. Shallow, quick pants now replaced his once heavy inhales. He almost felt bad when Amin closed his eyes again, sending tears down the sides of his face as a spasm gripped him.

Tetrosky stood and summoned Alani in the most expedient way possible—instant materialization. She gave the group a puzzled look as she went to her husband's side. Another master had summoned her for Amin? And Amin was in this state?

"What did you give him?" she asked, her gaze narrowed on the men around the table.

McGuire just waved her away. Xe shook his head. Carlos swallowed a smile.

"Mistress . . . your husband is very high, and needs to come down before we dock. If you would just be so kind as to get him to a stateroom—"

But she was standing way too close to Amin, had gone to him before Tetrosky could finish his sentence. The snatch was instantaneous; her back hit the table; her dress ripped; Amin blanketed her. Carlos put the box in his pocket. The other masters released a weary sigh, stood, and calmly filed out of the room behind him. They shut the door as they heard Alani's flesh tear with her scream. There was nothing to say.

"That's some good shit," McGuire said, wiping his nose with the back of his hand as they reached the deck. "You should try a hit, Tetrosky—before we dock, man."

"I have enough pride to take it to my room with my wife in tow," he said smiling, but wiping his nose. "Does pack a kick." He chuckled. "Think Amin will make it to the concert?"

"I don't know," Carlos said, worried. "I hope brother is gonna be all right . . . Damn." All he needed was a variable like that jumping off. However, one thing was for sure, after this, they were definitely gonna turn each other. When Amin came up off the full double hit, being with Alani was just going to piss him off. She wasn't da butta.

He quietly stood by Tetrosky while Xe and McGuire left them to go hunt aboard ship. Both masters considered the moon and the stars, not speaking, but understanding each other in their own way. Carlos watched the black water whir by as the supernaturally propelled vessel cut white froth-topped waves stained pink by vamps from stem to stern ditching blood bottles. Yeah, the rest of this crew would have to stay on board while only the VIPs went into the Sydney Opera House. There was no way he was gonna allow the full entourage to disembark and take Sydney by storm.

Suddenly morose he pulled out the black box, flipping it between his fingers, manipulating it like worry beads.

"Decisions, decisions," Tetrosky said, his tone wry. "Should you wait for her, knowing you've committed this gorgeous eve to another master, or take some of the sting out of the promise by taking a hit?"

The bold comment made Carlos laugh. "Yeah, decisions decisions," he echoed back, enjoying that Tetrosky had loosened up enough to actually try to fuck with him.

"You seem so . . . petulant." Tetrosky smiled.

"You want a hit, man?" Carlos asked, dangling the box precariously over the side of the yacht, threatening to drop it.

"That's rare product—would a man let go of Pandora's box, something he could hold over each master's head, and let such a treat to the senses go to waste, just to cut off his nose to spite his own face?"

Carlos dropped the box, and his smile broadened when Tetrosky caught it. "She's amazing, man."

He watched the master toy with the box, manipulating it through his fingers as Carlos had done.

"Thoroughly," Tetrosky finally murmured, bringing the box to his nose, and slowly opening it. He took out the pill with shaking hands, and placed it on his tongue and closed his eyes. "Then why are you so morbid, you lucky bastard?" he asked through his teeth, holding onto the rail.

"I'm cool," Carlos muttered, monitoring Tetrosky's increasing agony from a sideline glance. In a very weird way, this was becoming family, too. Twisted, dysfunctional, violent, and nuts, but not very different than his old territory while alive.

"Murder McGuire and renege on the deal and go wherever and screw your wife. Why suffer?" Tetrosky said through a pant. "Who could blame a man?" Tetrosky's knees buckled, and he held the rail tighter for support as his fangs dropped. "I have to go find Kiersten," he said, followed by a long hiss after a moment, but couldn't seem to move. "Damn, this is good shit, Rivera . . ."

There had only been one half-hit left in the box—Amin

took a double portion, and after whatever Jose had on him might have been distributed to lower levels he'd encountered. The purest product in the world was possibly gone. He could only hope that Jose didn't have to use the double hits he'd produced. The sudden reality gave Carlos pause. What used to be his—freely flowing, naturally produced, offered willingly from Damali, and which four masters had just tasted—he'd never know again. Blood from her veins; the very essence of her. Plus he had to kill them because they *had* tasted it, and deeply appreciated it. Twisted, but necessary.

Tetrosky lifted his head slowly, admiration in his partially closed eyes. "How can you be depressed when you *live* with Oblivion? You only gave away one night."

"I don't know, man," Carlos murmured, walking away from Tetrosky as another hard shudder claimed him. "Guess I just miss my wife already."

CHAPTER TWENTY-TWO

THE ELECTRICITY of the crowd was the rush she required to take her head where it needed to be. The percussion always did that. Rocking the mic. Bass adding bottom; guitar screaming. Cowbell jerking her muscles with its pulse. One beat, the entire Sydney Opera House throbbing to the same rhythm—hers. Giving it all she had, voice coming up from the diaphragm. Stage lights and energy making the walls sweat. The team in perfect harmony, simpatico. Glorious. Keyboards becoming her spine, running melody up it one vertebra at a time. Head thrown back, wailing, sending truth up and out into the universe. Hands clapping the rhythm of the beat. Oh, yes! Tapped into an energy source she couldn't define.

As soon as the music stopped and the crowd roared, the awareness hit her. They were one and the same about their sensitivity to their environments, she and Carlos. When she was on stage, it was almost like making love . . . a much-needed release that cleared problems from her mind all the way to her soul. Every sense was keened, every part of her fired on with a passion near stroke level. Every sound, every impression, became one with her to the marrow. It was also like that when she was with him.

"Yo, Sydney! Is everybody all right?" she yelled, laughing, giddy from the natural high. "Give it up!" she hollered, waving her arm before her band to let them take the weight so she could slip backstage and change for the final number. She glimpsed the VIP box. Still empty.

The sight of the empty box immediately blew her natural high. All the performance euphoria drained from her. What if something had happened to him? What if they'd rushed him on the ship? Anything could have gone down.

Six black stretch limousines pulled up to the Sydney Opera House. Drivers at military attention, eyes shielded by black shades, glanced both ways before opening the door for dangerous diplomats. Five masters got out, smoothed the fronts of their expensive suits, looked both ways, and four of them extended a hand behind their rigid postures without glimpsing back, eyes hardened on the landscape. Curious onlookers were awed, but sensed it would be ill advised to approach. Feminine hands slid into stronger ones, slinky silks covering voluptuous forms moved in close to the males, syncopating their high-heeled strides to the determined ones on their right.

Carlos walked alone.

As the small party wound their way through the elaborate theater, Carlos just listened. The music was a part of him, her music. The aftermath of Damali's stage libations was bringing the other masters down, blowing their high. He could see it in their eyes as they regained their former clarity and control. It was definitely chilling him out, too. A variable. He was just glad that they hadn't seen her administer some of it.

Ever mindful of the mission, his power became laser focus to project the dummy tape on the inside monitors. There was no room for variables. Variables didn't exist.

At the entrance to the box, Carlos greeted the international courier with a nod, and led his guests in. He immediately went to the bar, picked up a crystal decanter, and filled a short rocks glass. Glancing at the courier, he summoned him for a poison test, and waited for the courier to take a small sip and return the glass. He didn't even look at the blood as he threw it against the back of his throat hard, swallowed, and blotted his mouth with the back of his hand, then refilled his glass. With a wave of his hand, he dismissed the burly guard to wait outside.

Carlos could see the other masters smile as they settled their wives into the comfortable sofa-style seating and studied him from sly perspectives. Fuck it, he definitely needed a drink. Holy water notwithstanding, and despite her new condition, Damali's adrenaline had soaked the air. That was real.

He gave an idle human server a nod. "See that everybody has what they need, then you all can go," Carlos said, dispatching a vamp-helper to bring over several unopened black bottles and glasses. He sat with his guests listening but not listening to the small talk; listening but not listening to the music; beating his own ass for ever getting into a predicament like this; and waiting a little too anxiously to see Damali perform.

Wresting his attention away from the stage that she wasn't on, he glanced at the monitors, hoping they'd hold the correct image when she came back to it.

"I don't care about the results," Alani told her husband under her breath. "I don't like the reason you had such an intense reaction to me." She folded her arms over her chest, looking at the wall.

Okay . . . another variable. The wives not liking the fantastic outcome of the drug. Wounded female ego. Carlos watched the dynamic shift into play, wondering which of the wives he'd have to seduce the hardest. Right now, Alani had just taken the *numero uno* position.

"Darling," Evelyn said in a discreet murmur, "I would have given my eyeteeth if Harold could do what we all heard Amin do to you. Enjoy the results, and don't look a gift horse in the mouth." She sat back with a wise smile, nodded at Carlos with affection, and blew him a kiss.

Easy target, Carlos thought to himself. Number four on the list.

He glanced at Master Xe, who returned an unusually non-threatening smile and a serene nod in his direction, and then glimpsed his wife. She was snuggled up to him like a high school girl, her eyes dreamy and looking at the stage without seeing it. Kiersten reached over and slipped her hand into Lai's, which made Tetrosky chuckle. Lai lifted the female hand up to her lips, studied Kiersten's wrist with affection for a moment, and then lowered her mouth to it, slowly opening a vein until she shuddered.

Tetrosky brought his glass to his mouth, took a leisurely sip from it, and caught Carlos's gaze. "I'm going to hope that our esteemed councilman has more of what has begun a glorious evening?" The elder master waited, excitement brimming beneath his cool gray stare.

The other masters turned their full attention to Carlos, Tetrosky's question their own, a collective wish waiting to be granted.

"Of course," Carlos said as seductively as he could, motioning with his head toward the stage. "See the guy to the left on percussion," he added, identifying Jose. "That's my human courier. He'll bring it up here after the show."

"You don't have more on you now?" Amin said, sounding thoroughly disappointed.

"I didn't want to be tempted to open the package in here, man," Carlos told him truthfully. "It's being delivered in full and double hits . . . could cause undue chaos around all these humans. We gotta do this shit on the boat."

Amin chuckled. "I definitely concur," he said, stroking his wife's hair even though she pulled away. "But maybe we could coax you to offer a small sample in the limos?"

Before Carlos could speak, Alani had snatched away from her husband's touch, making him narrow his gaze on her. "Not now, darling," he warned. "Don't air our personal conflict in this VIP box."

"I told you, I don't want you to take that crap," she said, her voice a lethal hiss. "She smells like fetus—like a fucking pregnant human—"

"I said," Amin warned her again in a low, calm tone, "not to say one foul word about our highly regarded councilman's wife. Are we clear?"

Amin's gaze was sharp enough to cut, and after a few

seconds, Alani sat back in her seat, arms tightly folded, her gaze at the wall venomous. "My deepest apologies, sir," Amin said, straightening his tie.

"It's cool," Carlos said, trying not to bug. The air. They could pick up Damali's condition in the air! Big ass variable. Not on point like he should have been.

"Well, I personally think it's very romantic of you, Mr. Councilman . . . Carlos," Evelyn breathed, "if I may be so bold."

He glanced at her, truly at a loss.

"Oh, you dear man," Lai Xe murmured. "You gave her a pregnant woman before the show—just to help her perform better . . . oh . . . my." She threaded her fingers through Kiersten's. "If you have something for the masters, don't you have anything like that for us?"

The masters sitting by him smiled, a hint of fang showing. How to play this . . . hmmm?

"Only if they approve," Carlos murmured, his gaze raking each female. "I wouldn't want to cause an international incident. This night is supposed to be just for fun. No business until tomorrow evening."

For the first time since the wives had been speaking, Alani turned her attention to Carlos. "I don't think my husband will have a problem with that," she said, her voice threading to him across the room like a satin noose.

"I honestly don't," Amin said, sitting forward, bracing his body weight with his elbows on his knees. "A word?"

He stood and went over to the bar. Carlos followed, watching the eyes of the masters at his back.

Leaning in close, Amin's voice dropped to a low, intense whisper in Dananu. But it wasn't a hard negotiation; it was more like an urgent request, near begging.

Listen, Amin said, his gaze on his wife as he spoke to Carlos. *I owe you an apology for doubting.*

No offense taken, Carlos murmured. *It's hard to comprehend, much less handle.*

Amin nodded. *I don't care what you give her, but get her out of my face tonight, and I'll owe you.*

Carlos just stared at him. This brother was fucked up from just one little taste—like this? A master, and couldn't get rid of a regular female vamp? Pitiful. *Man, you can handle that. Tell her to get lost, I'll give you another double hit, and go get yourself three or four babes . . . and—*

You would give me another double hit?

Yeah, why not? You're my boy and I like your style. Got skillz, and held that shit back till you busted a blood vessel. Much respect.

Amin broke out of the negotiation and wiped his brow. "When?"

"Soon as we get on board."

Amin nodded and looked at his wife. "I approve."

"If she knows how you feel, maybe she'll stop sweating you?"

Again, the towering master nodded.

"Want me to send her to you after she takes a hit?" Carlos waited. There was such a thing as protocol.

Amin smiled and shook his head. "For a double hit, she's all yours. She might come back easier to deal with in the long run."

They both laughed as Carlos slung an arm up and over Amin's huge shoulder.

"It's settled," Carlos announced, as he strolled over to the sofa where the ladies had gathered, taking Alani's hand and kissing the back of it as he returned to the group. He brought his gaze up to hold hers, sending every seductive image from his old life into hers that he could think of, allowing his voice to drop an octave. "It will be my *pleasure* to show a woman as fine as you something new."

"Councilman," Evelyn purred. "I am oh so sure that Harold would enthusiastically approve, too."

"Harold?" Carlos said with a smile, still holding Alani's hand and gazing down at Evelyn like she was dinner.

"Objecting never crossed my mind," McGuire replied with a chuckle. "Please keep my wife *thoroughly* entertained at your leisure. Especially tonight."

Carlos left Alani, letting go of her hand in a slow, dragging release while monitoring the quiver in it as he approached Evelyn.

He glanced at Amin, who approved with a smile. His competitor's nod said it all. *Nice move.* Very smooth. Carlos understood. This was serious game, he had to pull out all the stops. Just like in the streets, it was about more than coopting the wives or a night of overindulgence; it was about primal power, the brazen display of it. A test. In his world it was all about conquest. The other masters had challenged him for his wife, and they'd expect no less than a returned demonstration of his skill and powers of seduction to draw the available females away from their mates—to do less would show weakness. That could not happen, not here.

He allowed his gaze to slowly sweep Evelyn. Her eyes held bitter disappointment when he initially ignored her hand as he bent down to her and didn't accept it, but sheer desire fired in them when he leaned closer in to place a kiss on her bare shoulder.

She let her breath out quietly and closed her eyes. "Mr. Councilman, Alani and I would both be more than pleased to keep you company tonight."

Mistress Xe gazed up at Carlos; her smile was slight, tense, anticipation coiling behind it like a cobra. Her dark eyes held such dignified agony that she was barely breathing. "If what you gave my husband had such stellar results," she said, glancing at her husband with so much lust it could have burned him, "then, I'm sure he would want me to acquire new skills as well." Her gaze went from Master Xe, holding a question, a silent request, then to Carlos. "It's been a *long* time since I've experienced anything new."

"I have deep respect for Master Xe . . . he is from the Old World, and as such, I would do nothing that would make him lose face," Carlos stated firmly, but smiled. This one was definitely number two. He dropped his voice even lower, and murmured to her, holding her gaze. "But if he ever does decide to cede you for one night, I assure you, you'll learn something new that you can share with him later. Call me—and let me know when you're ready."

"Fair exchange is no robbery, sir," Master Xe said, giving a slight bow from where he sat, thoroughly enjoying the spectator sport. Then he held Carlos's gaze with a steady but urgent look in his eyes. *For a double hit, and your next visit planned—soon—to the Forbidden City, by all means.*

Deep. Open Dananu negotiations—right in front of the wives, under very different circumstances than what had transpired before the hunt. This was getting interesting and they were indeed getting sloppy.

Done, Carlos murmured toward Xe, and then he returned his attention to Lai. "I guarantee that you won't be disappointed." He went to her, wet his thumb, and slid it down her jugular, tasting it as he put it back into his mouth, and causing her sharp gasp to slice the room.

Mistress Tetrosky was on her feet and had gone to Carlos, breaching all protocol. "Ask my husband . . . now . . . please," she breathed, her body melting against Carlos's, and her gaze darting between him and her master.

Carlos swept up her hand fast, making her swoon, turned her wrist over hard, studying the blue vein in it as he held her close to practically keep her from falling. "Your call," he said in a low timbre, looking at Tetrosky for a reaction. He allowed a hint of fang to show for added drama, making Kiersten begin to hyperventilate in his arms. "I'll be without my wife all night. Gentleman's agreement with Harold. You have no idea how much I'll miss her."

Tetrosky's eyes went half-mast. "Only if I can watch."

Another fucking variable. Okay, new strategy to separate the pack.

Carlos brought his mouth to Kiersten's wrist vein, kissed it, and boldly licked a trail up the blue tributary to the inside of her elbow with the tip of his tongue, planting a solid kiss there, but didn't break the skin. So, Tetrosky liked to watch. Huh?

Her moan was so long and soulful as he followed the smooth line of her arm that it almost messed him up and made him nick her. Tonight, his game was strong. But he kept his eyes on Tetrosky. "You sure you want to do that with a double hit in your system and mine?"

"He doesn't care," Kiersten murmured, arching to wrap her arms around Carlos's shoulders. "Hasn't for a *long* time." She swept her nose the length of his collarbone, hovering dangerously near his throat. *"I can smell it on you,"* she whispered in a husky voice. "You actually *care* about her. I definitely want to feel that. I *love* the way you smell."

"I smelled it, too," Alani said, breathlessly gravitating to him in a slow slide.

Evelyn was trembling as she stood slowly, coming toward Carlos with serious intent in her eyes.

"His black blood is saturated with pure, unadulterated passion." Evelyn glanced at the other women, her eyes filled with awe as she returned her sultry gaze to Carlos. "No, it's more than that. He *loves* her, which is so rare in our world. More alluring than even blind obsession driven by pure lust. I've never smelled it before in one of our males." Her cat eyes were hypnotic as she neared him and brought her face closer, a public throat strike eminent. "I've been around a long time. Do you have any idea how many of our males I've been with?"

Carlos leaned back and put his finger to Evelyn's lips, then kissed the bridge of Kiersten's nose. "Not here, sweetheart and not in the throat. Protocol." He smiled and handed Evelyn off to McGuire in a smooth body transfer. "Some things are just not done . . . in public." He slipped out of Kiersten's hold, and ran his hand down her back as he slid her toward Tetrosky. But as he swept her body, he also swept her mind like he had all the others. A deeply guarded secret lingered there. A recent one.

Mistress Xe was almost panting through a full fang drop where she sat on the edge of her seat. "That is *so* erotic." She squeezed her knees together tightly and closed her eyes.

"You sure you want to watch under the influence?" Carlos asked Tetrosky with a quiet voice and slow smile. Kiersten hovered near her husband for a moment, then sauntered back over to Carlos, slipping back into his embrace to touch his hair, then his face, tasting his perspiration off the tips of her trembling fingers. He needed more information, and went into her mind like a razor. "She's beautiful, like porcelain," he whispered through clenched teeth, and then bit her ear making her whimper and drop her mental guard. *What is it, sweetness? Tell me what he has.*

Carlos could feel Tetrosky battling for composure across the room, his faculties shredded by the drug in his system, Damali's performance, and the floorshow. "Do you want me to speak to you in Dananu, or Española, when you come to me?" Carlos crooned, eliciting near delirium from Kiersten.

"Speak to her in Española," Tetrosky murmured, leaning forward.

"Later," Carlos whispered, sending the hot promise into her ear while extracting her thoughts. *What difference does it make if he rules the world, if he doesn't know how to make you happy?* "Do you want me to come to you?" he asked, lengthening his incisors to full-battle length and running them down Kiersten's jugular. *You'll tell me, right, so I can . . . with you,* mi tresora?

"Yes," she sobbed, answering both his spoken and telepathic questions.

Not risking a transmission, she sent the information by touch as her hand slid down to his groin. He shuddered for effect. The other wives stood and came to him. And he withdrew having gleaned all he needed to know. The key was in the hull of the ship, where all the masters' caskets had been loaded. Pure outrage dulled his reaction to her sensual touch. The bastard had been bold enough and strong enough to hide Carlos's marked man in *his* ship! Only a dark human ritual could have cloaked that from him. The reality was unsettling.

Carlos mopped his brow and kissed each female briefly and stalked away. "I'm going to ask you again, Tetrosky, are you sure you want to just watch, with all of them in there? 'Cause, brother, if you reach for me, you're history. I don't play that, even high." Carlos laughed and shook his head when Tetrosky swallowed hard. "But if you want to check us out . . . while you're blitzed—"

"No," Tetrosky said fast, swallowing hard again as the other masters looked at him.

"All right," Carlos murmured, gently extricating himself from Kiersten's hold again when she'd sauntered up beside him. He smiled and handed her off to Tetrosky with a gentle shove to distance her from his body, ignoring her visceral disappointment.

"Bastard," she said through her teeth, glaring at her husband. "I will never forgive—"

"That's not what I meant," Tetrosky said quickly. "I meant, no, I don't want us to both be in there with a double hit in our systems, Mr. Councilman."

Carlos chuckled and held out his hand to Kiersten, who grabbed onto it again like a lifeline. "Good, because this stuff will make you act stupid."

Tetrosky stood, cleared his throat, and walked over to the bar. He poured himself a shot of the more concentrated blends, tossed it back, and shuddered. "A double hit—she's yours. Do as you like, just make sure our yacht is cave-docked before dawn."

"No lie," McGuire said, standing and joining Tetrosky. He shook off the exchanges that he'd witnessed with a shiver. "Damn, this crap is lethal . . . will make you challenge the fucking sun."

"Yes. Profound," Amin said, standing, going to the bar with the other masters to share a drink. "I hope you've given the crew express instructions to find shelter. None of us are going to be able to even transport by dawn."

"Too dangerous," Master Xe said, standing and going to the bar. "I don't like losing control like that so far from a lair. Maybe we should just have patience and wait to take it at the castle."

Variables were kicking his ass tonight. He'd just gotten the females all transferred into his control, had fired the masters up again with the little floor show of open seduction—trying to keep them distracted once their high had burned off, and now there was some new shit to contend with. Carlos glanced at the crestfallen expressions around him that were beginning to become shrewd and rational again.

"Makes sense," Carlos said, calmly depositing Tetrosky's wife on the sofa and joining the men at the bar. "Besides, if my wife is in with McGuire—just her voice alone is maddening while in the throes. Will carry all throughout the ship, the surf, the rock of the boat, salt air . . . sensory overload, and with a double hit, too?" Carlos shook his head. "Naw. What was I thinking? That was too irresponsible of me. Reckless."

He turned to Xe and put his hand on his shoulder. "You see how this female has compromised me, but Xe had my back." He dropped his hold from Xe, poured a fast drink, and tossed it down. "The Forbidden City, our next visit, for that one. Man, you have no idea how many nights that woman almost fried me. We'll wait till we get back to the—"

"Councilman, let's not be hasty," Tetrosky said, his eyes searching Carlos's. "Please."

"No," Carlos said, firmly. "Xe is clear and rational. I'm not right now." He closed his eyes and took in a deep breath. "Her adrenaline is all in the air, music in my head." He opened his eyes. "I'm not trying to wipe out the whole empire in one night on a pleasure ship—and Damali will make you do that." Carlos smiled, and then had to chuckle at himself. Damn, he was good.

Xe approached him and placed a hand on his shoulder, glancing at the others. Carlos could feel him siphon for information, for the truth, and he got what he wanted, the part not threaded through the lie. He also knew that these boys loved living on the edge; they were adrenaline junkies, the more reckless, the more titillating. Everything else was just existing. He dangled the lure, and pulled it back, allowing Xe to see just how close he came to frying—the sun breaking the horizon, him looking down into Damali's sated face, he let the instant panic slingshot from his memory to Xe's awareness, then stopped the transmission.

"Councilman . . . I . . . uh . . . we implore you to brush aside my initial concerns. I was perhaps hasty. We trust that you would have made arrangements."

"No," Carlos said, pouring another drink and sipping it slowly. "I thank you for bringing a critical risk factor to my attention."

He had to fight not to openly chuckle when Amin grabbed Xe by the throat so fast that a near-extinction was probable. He glanced back at Xe's wife, Lai, and she wasn't even snarling. She hadn't even stood up! All she did was issue a disgusted glance over her shoulder. The other masters had surrounded Xe, taking Amin's side in the dispute.

"Gentlemen," Carlos said, touching Amin's shoulder. "Not here. Not in public. Humans wouldn't understand, then we'd have bigger problems that could jeopardize the whole evening." He waited for Amin to gradually let go of Xe's throat. "Let's all go sit down, watch the show, and once we're on the boat, I'll tighten everybody up." He winked at McGuire. "Then I'll hand Damali off to you. Fair?"

Immediately grumbles of approval rippled through the room as the masters returned to their seats, the wives now draped against them with gratitude. Carlos found a lone seat close to the edge of the box, but positioned so that he could keep everyone else within a sideline glance. This was no way to live—having exclusively pursued pleasure so hard that you were numb to it, unless it was twisted and depraved.

He didn't want to die tonight, but he certainly didn't want to live so long that the basic things in life became a nightmare of boredom, or gaining knowledge was so easy that anything truly new to the mind was seized upon like a drug. But the awareness gave him pause. Isn't that what happened to him while he was alive? Hadn't the mundane, but purer, things in life bored him, sending him deeper into the seductive dark side of the lifestyle he'd chosen? Hadn't he given up the basics, like kids, a family, friends, hanging out at the beach on a sunny day . . . his mom's cooking . . . for what? And wouldn't he throw caution to the wind to have a glimmer of that back?

This time when he glanced at the vampires around him, it was with a bit less disgust. After several hundred years, what would he be like? What would he be like right now if Damali hadn't shared her soul with him on a beach? Not just in Rio, but when they were kids . . . sitting in the sun. And, what the hell would he turn into without being able to hold her in his arms and love her like he needed to now? He couldn't even think about that right at the moment. That stark reality would definitely mess up his head. So he focused on the stage. He had to transmit the location of the key to her, but couldn't risk a transmission directly to her. Every master in the house was focused on Damali, so he locked with the only person he knew could receive from him under blocked conditions—Father Pat.

He concentrated on the elderly cleric, and watched him glance at Marlene, who froze for a moment and then relaxed. If the two seers could focus on the location, maybe they could pinpoint where the key was hidden within the massive vessel's hull.

Carlos was careful to banish the thoughts from his mind as soon as he'd sent them. Looking at Damali was a good way to force anything else into the back of his mind. Her band was winding down; the lighting had changed. Slow droning didgeridoo vibrated the air with a mourning sound. Black lights illuminated white paint on dark faces. Carlos almost closed his eyes. Yeah, she was a master performer, but he wished she hadn't gone there.

He glanced at his counterparts, who were leaning forward in their seats, cool shredding as the anticipation for her final appearance mounted. He glimpsed the monitors to be sure his attention was holding. Shit . . . he might be the one who was the weak link in the variable chain.

Carlos sat back hard, watching the stage, trying to send his mind elsewhere as Shabazz's bass picked up the end of the mourning vibrations. Rider's guitar was wearing him out; it was connected to his skeleton, the high-pitch frequency too close to the pitch of Damali's frenzied desert energy. J.L. had captured the melody, the emotion of her thoughts, like smooth water, a caress. But Jose was fucking him up bad on the drums . . . they were linked; *hombre* had his rhythm, same one when with her. All right, all right, he could do this. It was just one last song, then him and his boys were out.

If he could just shake off all the seduction play, the rush of winning four conquests in a short struggle in the VIP box, forget about the triumph of playing four masters lovely . . . get her scent out of his skull, along with every conflicting emotion it brought with it, he'd be cool. All he had to do was focus.

Carlos smoothed the front of his suit and rolled his shoulders, glancing at the monitors. But she messed around and had that deep purple smoke flow over the stage floor, changed the lights to crimson, and sauntered out in that dress with her Isis at her side. He knew that was the plan, but seeing it again, now, fully aware that he could never have her like that once more . . . damn . . . The crowd roared, and he almost stood up. If the woman opened her mouth . . . let out her voice . . .

Stupid thought. That's what she'd come there to do—sing her heart out. He had to get it together. But the electricity running through the other vamps around him was a thick current of irrational desire that linked them. Then she really messed up and looked directly at the VIP box, her words shredding every one of the males in the box, most of all him.

True, he'd told her to play to McGuire, but daaayum. He couldn't watch it. Not when she threw back her head hard like she'd just been bitten, sudden strike snap, and the tempo of the music picked up. She'd flung the Isis away from her, had literally tossed it up so it came point down and stuck into the stage. The crowd was rocking off their feet. Sweat seeped out of her pores, one droplet at a time, adrenaline shimmering in it, her voice a laser to his senses. *"Oh . . . man."* He stood fast and walked to the back of the booth.

"She's incredible," McGuire murmured, his focus riveted to Damali.

The monitors flickered and showed her actual performance, not the tape. Panicked, losing the ability to concentrate, he tore his line of vision from the stage, sputtering the images on the monitors back to the edited dummy compilation, but was fast losing the battle. Damali's true image kept overriding what was supposed to be shown to the vamps. She was in his head so hard, he couldn't shake it—not with her singing, not with the music, not with their personal rhythm at the forefront of his mind.

Tetrosky's gaze never left the stage. "Let all the monitors show her," he whispered on a hoarse breath. "Don't cheat us."

Damali's arms were outstretched, her body swaying, the crowd yelling, then she wrapped her arms around herself, turned away, and gave them her back. The position created the illusion that she was with someone, being held, as her voice hit a crescendo on the chant refrain, "Don't stop, no don't stop, this sweet transition." She allowed her head to fall back, and she belted out what sounded like a sobbing plea. "I remember when you turned me—bittersweet change that hurt so good."

He was holding onto the side of the bar by the time she turned around. *Baby, you're killing me*. But she ignored him and walked hard to the edge of the stage, purpose in every step. Her hands slid down her body as her eyes slid closed in a slow invitation, yet the rest of her was moving to the now up-tempo beat, flowing with it, then she clutched her belly, and wailed, "Don't you know you're my sweet transition!"

Master Amin lost it, was on his feet, with Xe and Tetrosky holding each of his arms. Carlos couldn't move, hypnotized at this point by her movements, her voice jack-hammering a hole in his temple.

"You cannot transport her off the stage in the middle of a performance, man!" Xe yelled, as both masters slammed Amin down in his seat.

But they weren't angry with him, just trying to hold onto what was left of their vampire cover. They had already abandoned their dignity. Tetrosky had broken his conservative cool and had dropped full fang, battle-length, in public, and couldn't retract. McGuire had tears in his eyes, fangs lowered, and couldn't catch his breath as Damali's scent stained the air. Xe was practically staggering as he left the front of the booth and went to stand by Carlos at the bar to collect himself, using his thumbs to send his incisors back up into his gums.

Damali marched back to her Isis near the front of the stage on the last stanza. "I'll give my life, just surrender, to this sweet transition with you." Then she drew her blade out of the stage, lowered it, opened her arms, and took another false strike that snapped her neck back, sending a collective shudder through the booth. Carlos closed his eyes as his gums ripped.

Mercy, woman. "*Compasion, por favor,*" he heard himself whisper out loud against all his intentions, but none of the masters even flinched. Then she licked her lips, and took a bow to a standing ovation, her Isis now over her head, the crowd hollering for more.

Carlos shook his head as she yelled, "Good night, Sydney!"

Bring me my wife, now! He'd hurled the thought at Jose before he could censor it. He saw Jose's head jerk up from the direction of the audience to him. Carlos waved him off. What the *hell* was he doing?

Every male in his booth was yelling for an encore with the crowd. Their wives had made their way to his side, practically licking the sweat off his face and brow. He elbowed his way out of the huddle. All of this was too volatile, and he hadn't even distributed the quantity of the substance that might really blow the lid off. Marlene was right. This was chaos theory at its worst. There was no controlling an uncontrolled substance—Damali.

He paced back and forth, waiting for Jose to bring her to the box. The other masters were like caged panthers, too, going from the bar to the edge of the booth, each giving him wide berth, their eyes sweeping the terrain, their noses polluted by all the hyped blood in the crowd, the adrenaline from her, him. Bottled blood wasn't gonna make it. Nor was blood from their wives' dead veins.

They shoved aside their wives' offers. Not good enough. It was in their eyes. What was easily accessible wasn't new.

"How long will she be?" Amin asked, his nerves frayed beyond all shame.

"I don't know," Carlos muttered. "You know how long it takes women to change."

"She's not changing out of that dress, is she?" McGuire said, sounding panicked.

"She can't," Tetrosky said fast. "Her sweet scent fills it." He trembled, and looked at Carlos.

"I forbid it. She cannot change out of that dress," Xe shouted, losing himself, and then looking at Carlos fast for a pardon.

"We need to renegotiate," Amin said on a heavy exhale. He looked at the other masters. "Between the four of us— let's strike a new deal." He looked at Carlos. "You gave her away for a night; tonight, we can settle the particulars between ourselves."

"I feel you," Carlos said, walking away, and not even pissed. He had to get himself together. If Jose came in there with her dripping wet from the stage, a volatile package under his arm, J.L. and Dan locked and loaded with weapons . . . there wasn't enough firepower on this earth . . . They all had to come down.

Hear me clear, Carlos said, his gaze lethal. *If you rush her, you die. If you rush my mule, you die. I am in a very, very fragile state, gentlemen.* Using Dananu had gotten their attention, just like the direct threat—the sure promise—had. He could see them starting to normalize as survival instinct took over. They had felt the impact of that truth, no mental siphon required. Each nodded and backed up, and that's when he felt himself beginning to come down.

Finally a knock at their VIP box door sounded and all eyes followed it. He could feel each one of the masters around him struggling not to drop fang and answer it.

"I have a delivery for Councilman Rivera," Jose said, accepting the assessment of the international courier who stood outside the door. "They're with me," he added, motioning toward J.L. and Dan.

Carlos watched the guard sniff Jose, linger longer than was advisable, briefly close his eyes, then glance back at Carlos and the other four masters, then quickly gain his wits and relent. As soon as the bulking presence stood aside, Damali floated through the door on Jose's arm almost in slow motion. Immediately, Carlos tore his attention from her to her security detail. Jose was righteous, his Glock nine was in a shoulder holster, the other hand resting on an automatic on his hip without the strap snapped. Dan had a crossbow held firmly at his side, and a Glock on his hip. J.L. had an Uzi slung over his shoulder by a thick strap, his hand nervously resting on the trigger.

"You expecting trouble, Mr. Councilman?" Tetrosky said coolly, his eyes on the crossbow.

"I do *not* take any chances with cargo this valuable," Carlos said, his eyes scanning the room. "I'm sure you can all appreciate that, now."

Damali glanced around the room, her eyes connecting with Carlos's briefly, but scanning the others. She had her long Isis with her, and then she smiled. "Is it cool for me to come in, or am I interrupting anything?"

"You are more than welcome to come in here, darlin'," McGuire said, but not going to her. He glanced at Carlos for approval to do so, but received none. Then he looked at the others in the room. "You are making the lady nervous, which is making our councilman nervous. The longer you do that, the more time goes by. So, my suggestion is that everybody relax."

Slowly but surely the tension in the room eased, the density lifted, and that's when Carlos went to her. If he had to fight, he didn't want her in the middle of the tackle.

With caution, he collected her from Jose's side, and Jose kept his eyes forward, scanning the group from behind dark sunglasses. All pro. Carlos was proud. J.L. and Dan seemed a little scary, but they had come in, hadn't blinked. That was good. But the fumes surrounding him were not. The seal on the product he carried was leaking.

He pecked Damali on the cheek as his hand slid around

her waist, and he tried his best to numb himself to the sensation of her skin.

"That performance was off the chain," he murmured as they walked deeper into the private box to get away from Jose's side.

"I had a blast," she said, her smile bright, but the tension in her body easy to detect through his palm. "I love Sydney—the crowd is awesome here."

"We all enjoyed your performance," Amin said, his voice dripping desire. He glanced at his wife, and the electricity that passed between them put Alani on her feet.

"Yes, you were absolutely fantastic," Alani said, gaining a round of agreement from the other wives, who all went to Damali to hug her.

Carlos watched very, very carefully, each hug, each continental kiss exchanged with a wary eye. Not one damned nick had better break her skin! Sensing his growing possessiveness, they wisely withdrew, even though their female voices blended into a laughing, celebratory harmony as Damali stepped away from him. He glared at the masters. Yeah, they could congratulate her—verbally. Fuck a hug.

They nodded, understanding protocol.

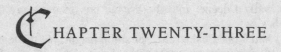

CHAPTER TWENTY-THREE

"YOU ALL right, man?" Rider asked as he climbed into Carlos's limo with Shabazz and Big Mike. "You don't look so jakey."

He could feel Jose and Dan assessing him along with J.L. as they waited for the rest of the team to get in and close the door. Carlos looked up and sealed the window between them and their driver, giving the signal to pull off. His driver seemed a little dazed, pulled off wobbly like he was DUI. Not good. Something was wrong. Just the fumes off this shit were affecting everybody. Maybe it was the amount of product Jose was carrying? He wasn't sure. But the effect was knocking his head back.

Damali had been stone-quiet beside him, monitoring his condition through the palm of her hand in his. She gave Rider a look that said back off, and then glanced through the rear window at the other limos following theirs. It felt like the walls of the vehicle were closing in on him, and he couldn't breathe. A cold sweat had broken out on his brow and he stained his suit sleeve wiping it away.

"You got the product?" Carlos said on a short breath, speaking to Jose. He could feel his gums poised to rip and his vision was beginning to intermittently flicker red.

"Yeah, we cool," Jose said, producing a small plastic bag.

"Are you out of your fucking mind?" Carlos bellowed. "Plastic, in here with me—next to her—and six nervous human male blood bodies with weapons!"

"You said to put it in plastic—"

"Yeah, so *you* could handle it. You had to seal it—put it in an equipment case—something!" In a flash Carlos encased the bag in a steel box right in Jose's hand and opened the windows, a rush of air giving him a chance to catch his breath.

"Oh, shit, Jose," Shabazz shouted. "What were you thinking about?"

"I thought it was just the contact from when he made it before in the suite—I thought—"

"Shut. Up!" Carlos said, his eyes closed. "Everybody stop talking for just five minutes. I can't go on the boat like this. You could have popped off a war in the damned VIP box."

"We have to—"

Damali's voice was the last one he could deal with. His glare had stopped her words, but it sped up her heart rate. The nerves in the close confines, multiple pulses, adrenaline spike all through it, made his hands shake.

"I told you!" Carlos yelled at her. It was reflex; her brothers couldn't even draw. He'd snatched her so fast and had kissed her so hard, hands at either side of her face, fucking him up as she opened her mouth and returned it hard. *I want you so bad right now I'm losing my mind. Don't speak.* He could feel her thoughts gathering, her words about to lacerate him more because she wanted him like that, too.

He let her go just as fast, pushed her away, needed to get out of the vehicle and walk to the damned ship. *Just one more time . . .*

"Do *not* answer me in a mind lock while I'm high." He slumped back, put his forearm over his eyes, sniffed hard, and breathed through his mouth, constantly running his tongue over his teeth till his fangs retracted.

"Don't do that on the boat," he said more calmly after a while. "I ain't myself, and could blow this whole mission." He sat up and stared out the window, refusing to watch how the wind was cascading her locks over her shoulders, or how her mouth had plumped from the hard kiss.

Why was it so hard for them to understand what this was like? Damali had even walked on the dark side for a moment with him, and she *still* couldn't fathom what this was all about . . . her humanity and hope would always be her blind spot. Frustration became fury, if she would only understand! Yes, master vampires had suave, superior intelligence, mind control, and powers beyond human comprehension. Yes, they had become masters of the game, were wealthy and had access to learning all the refined arts.

But all of that was focused on one goal—the relentless pursuit of pleasure . . . their greatest strength, their greatest weakness . . . seduction with the purpose to feed and mate and mate and feed in an endless cycle. At the core of what their realm represented was raw lusts—all of them—concentrated on level six. The drug only brought that out; her biology was the Light's weapon to draw that out of masters, make them show their true fangs in a weakened, compromised state. But she, like all women, only wanted to see what she wanted to see in her man, the good side, ignoring the bad. He'd *told* her he was only vampiri! And in this state, pregnant or not, he would fuck her to death if she didn't stop.

He kept his eyes closed with the wind on his face. As his breathing began to normalize he focused on the issue at hand, making sure none of the Guardians had any illusions about what they were dealing with tonight.

"Amin took a full hit, and is messed up bad," Carlos said quietly. "Tetrosky isn't far behind him, on just a half. The man dropped fang in public in front of his wife—which ain't his style. Xe is dangerous like a motherfucker right now, but wants a double hit more than he wants his wife. McGuire is liquefied . . . you can pour him into a martini glass and drink him." He looked at Damali hard. "But he will not be denied after waiting for you this long. Kill his ass quick and be done with it. Don't dick around with him and tease him—he's unstable, like all of us are."

"You made more?" Damali said, her voice an accusatory whisper.

All Guardian eyes were on him.

"I had to. No variables. Sent it to Jose in case his stash was low. Needed to test it on the ride down from Queensland to see what the tolerance levels were."

For a moment, no one said a word. Damali sat back slowly but her eyes raked him. "You didn't take any, did you?"

He laughed. "Are you crazy?"

"No offense," Big Mike muttered, "but you seem a little on the edge, bro."

"Between the performance and the contact, yeah, I'm lit. But not because I ever take my own product. Never did that, not even while living. And do I look like I *need* to take that around her?" Carlos stared at them, disgusted. "Give me some credit. In the distribution game, I'm all pro."

Too offended for words when they didn't answer, Carlos kept his gaze out the window, just trying to breathe.

Safely boarding the ship wasn't her greatest worry, getting off of it, with her squad intact, was. Damali glanced at Carlos's huge Hell-hounds that kept the other masters at a distance. They walked a lazy, snarling, hungry path between her and Carlos and the masters standing not far away with their wives engaged in tense chitchat. She held onto the rail, her side pressed against Carlos, her grip tight on her Isis, her gaze scanning the backs of her men, who also weren't too far away. She declined a bottle, saying she'd eaten well before the performance and was still too full. She kept glancing at the water, wondering why the wave caps were pink, and why there were lots of fins in it. Fucking sharks to deal with, too?

She needed to get a transmission to Carlos, but he'd told her not to go into his mind. Not on the boat. But when an extremely large fin surfaced and slid beneath the stained water, she had to have a private discussion.

"Can we talk?" she asked quietly, looking over the side of

the yacht. Marlene and Father Patrick had to know there was some huge, predatory shit in the water. Their getaway plan was by small speedboat.

Carlos pulled his attention from the master he was talking to. "In a little while," he murmured. "*Paciencia, por favor, mi tresora.* Okay?"

Be patient? *Sheeit.* She knew he was working it to the bone, had to stay in drug kingpin character, but there was a serious problem. "I noticed there are sharks in the water," she said, interjecting herself into the male-dominated conversation. "I saw one huge monster, big enough to knock a small speedboat over." She saw her squad visibly stiffen. Okay, at least her crew got the message. Maybe they could transmit that to Mar. But Mar and Father Pat had also dropped some heavy science about the key that Carlos definitely needed to know. Speedboats as a getaway plan presented a huge issue for her team and the key. But how was she supposed to work with her mission partner if his ass was high?

"Right you are, little lady," McGuire said, asking for permission with his eyes to pass the dogs and Damali's squad. He waited for a moment until Carlos nodded and eased up his hold on her. "The ladies like to watch them feed. They've been pouring out bottles to draw them all night," he said, taking Damali's hand and bringing it to his lips. "Care to stroll the decks with me, and watch what happens when they drop a human-helper?"

She watched her team blanch, but it was showtime. "If Carlos doesn't mind?"

"Of course he doesn't mind," McGuire said, overly anxious and overstepping his bounds.

Carlos monitored the other masters. "Take one of the dogs with you, baby."

"She doesn't need one of those beasts, she'll be with me."

McGuire was openly challenging him, and had tightly threaded his arm around Damali's waist. Carlos glanced at the Guardians; they had to be cool. The other masters sensed it, too.

"It's all right, man," Carlos said, forcing a chuckle. "I'm

sending one of the dogs so you don't get rushed. Want your hit now while you take your stroll, or when you come back?"

McGuire struggled with the decision. "How about if I take one for the road in my pocket?"

Carlos shook his head. "You need to do that down in a stateroom. You walk the decks with it, and you'll give every vamp you pass a contact. Do you really want to—"

"Wise man," McGuire said. "I'll come back for it. Your lovely wife and I should chat, get acquainted, before we go downstairs. I'll show her around a bit. Fair?"

Again Carlos nodded, watching the envy congeal in the others. McGuire's smug smile was about to touch off a blood battle; he could feel it. This was how they'd planned it, this was what everyone had agreed upon—but theory and the real deal were always two different things. Shabazz was so tight he was about to bust a blood gasket. Big Mike was about to lose it and just start shooting buck wild; he could feel that, too. Rider had a mental target on the back of McGuire's skull. J.L.'s Uzi was practically bouncing with pent-up readiness, and Dan was gonna shoot off his own foot if he fingered the release on his crossbow one more time. Carlos placed a hand on Jose's shoulder to keep the man from drawing as he passed him. *Everybody stay cool.*

"Why don't you gentlemen take a stroll, take in a few sights," Carlos said to Damali's men, his eyes sending a quiet message. They needed to fan out, position themselves by the agreed-upon targets. "The women on the boat are fine. There's human food, and I know you have to be ready to bust a grub after the concert. Find one of the servers— shrimp, mud crab, five-spice duck, Emu prosciutto, flying fish roe and wasabi . . . liquor out da ass," Carlos added, trying to sound relaxed and to get them to cool down enough to leave Damali alone with McGuire. They had to chill to play this smooth. "Damali will be fine. She's with McGuire and one of my dogs." He dismissed them with a glance that the other masters couldn't see as he rounded them. "All right? Be cool."

Begrudgingly the Guardian team nodded, filing away

from him in a slow-moving huddle. Once out of earshot, Carlos sighed and approached the other masters. With Damali no longer at his side and having gone off with McGuire, he only had three masters to immediately contend with, if it got ugly.

"You gentlemen care to go downstairs for a little taste of something sweet?"

Smiles widened on the faces around him.

"We thought you'd never ask," Tetrosky said, waving his arm in a grand, sweeping, Old World gesture before Carlos. "After you."

"You promised us you had a little something for us, too," Evelyn whined.

"I am a man of my word, dear lady. Meet me in my room." He paused and looked at them as they giggled. "All of you."

"Sir, the matter at hand," Amin reminded him, pulling Carlos's attention away from the women.

"My bad," Carlos said, and laughed as they walked. He knew all the delays and chitchat were increasing the tension, but that was the objective: yank their chains till they snapped. Slow walk 'em.

They were already pissed at McGuire for his good fortune. All he had to do was go below deck, drop two hits each on these guys, then go find their wives. If the masters stayed in the room together, they were going to have to engage in a sudden-death battle to see who could get out of the room first to corner McGuire. It would be on. But he had to make sure the ladies were properly blitzed, or they could intercede. Second-level females could still be deadly, especially if the male didn't have his full faculties. Plus Damali needed a chance to get to McGuire alone. Variables—too fucking many of them, and he was too high.

As they entered the stateroom they had been in earlier, Carlos forced a belly laugh. "Damn, man, you could have fixed my table, and shit."

Amin chuckled and waved his hand to correct the problem. "I was . . . uh—"

"Yeah, yeah, I know. Slipped your mind," Carlos said, smiling broadly as he brought the steel box out of his pocket. "Double hits, all around, and we save McGuire's till he gets back."

He carefully opened the box, shielding his nose with his hand as he leaned toward each master and allowed him to take out two red pills.

"You're not joining us?" Xe asked skeptically. "What'd you do, lace this batch with colloidal silver?" Then he laughed and put a pill in his mouth.

But Tetrosky hesitated. "You don't even want a contact from it?"

Amin glanced at Tetrosky, and slowed his swallow of the second pill.

"You guys just pushed your wives off on me. Four females, and you want me to go in there with them that high? What, and ruin my reputation? Never." Carlos chuckled and shook his head, snapping the box shut, and then slipped it into his pocket. "I'm not having four fine females talk about me like a dog and put my business in the street. *Shit,* talking about how I busted a nut in two seconds and was slobbering on myself. Not tonight."

Tetrosky laughed hard with the others, relaxed, and took the drug. Amin finished swallowing as the first hard shudder consumed Xe. Carlos was on his feet and out the door before their fangs dropped.

"You sure you don't want to go downstairs, yet?" McGuire murmured against her hair, way too close to her throat for her liking. Even the ugly creature of a dog was snarling at the affront.

"The night is young—"

He had tugged her to him with such force that it almost knocked the wind out of her. "Tell the dog to back off," he warned as the creature started barking. "It is *really* getting on my fucking nerves."

Damali glanced over McGuire's shoulder. She could see her team in the distance, but they didn't have a clear shot.

And what did you tell a monster with six eyes and jaws that drooled acid? Sit, stay? "Chill," she said, wriggling out of McGuire's hold. "You just made it nervous. They don't like sudden moves."

"I hope you do," he said, his voice low and so quiet that she almost couldn't hear him over the dog's incessant barking.

"Sit. Stay. And, uh, *shut up!*" she yelled at the Hellhound, totally amazed when it did. "Deep."

"Are you?" he said, coming closer to her.

Oh, no, not one of these bastards that wanted to talk dirty in bed. Damali sighed. "You're right. We should just go down to your room and get this over with."

"You sound so . . . unenthused," he said, seeming offended, but still ready to go.

"No, it's just that the performance took a lot out of me," she hedged, checking her tone and improving it. "That's why I was stalling. I didn't want to disappoint you."

His hand caressed the side of her face, his fingers trembling, his green eyes glittering with pure lust in the moonlight. "If you were bled out and limp, you wouldn't disappoint me," he said quietly, lowering his mouth to hers and coming away with fangs. "After your performance, I was devastated."

It took everything in her power not to wipe her mouth and spit. But she forced a smile and touched his neck, trailing her fingers up and down it in a lazy stroke. "Why don't you go down and get some of what Carlos is passing around, and I'll meet you in your room in a few minutes?"

McGuire shook his head. "And leave you on deck with three other very disappointed masters around? I'm crazy about you, love, but I'm not insane." He smiled and nuzzled her throat, shuddering as he pressed his erection against her thigh and slowly moved against her.

She backed away just a bit when she felt his incisor about to score her skin. "Not in the throat. I'm married. Carlos will flip."

"My apologies. But you see what you do to me." His eyes held hers. "Baby, let's go downstairs to my room."

Carlos had told her to do this fast; he hadn't lied. Damali flipped her hair over her shoulder and weakly smiled at McGuire, then brightened it. She made her voice a mere whisper with a promise embedded in it, and glanced down at her sword as she spoke.

"The other masters have already taken a hit, and I'm sure it's kicked in by now . . . they've found a female and are very distracted, no doubt. Carlos will give you some, then we can have the time of our lives."

She leaned into him, and kissed the bridge of his clammy nose. "Even if I'm a little tired, and not at my best, I'm sure you will be." She let her gaze smolder and trap his male ego in its blaze. "I'll be sure to tell all the girls just how much fun I had with you tonight . . . might even tell Carlos to make Sydney a regular vacation stop, if I'm so inspired. Would love to do the Outback with you . . . alone."

McGuire glanced around. "Your band . . . your security team. They'll flank you, if I'm only gone for a minute?"

"Them, the dogs, and Carlos. He gave you his word. They've got enough anti-vamp ammo to stop a small army from Hell, and history proves they can handle that. I'm sure you've heard." She lifted her Isis and leaned into him more closely, allowing the blade handle to brush his stomach while sending her breath into his ear. "I gave you mine. You want this right in the center of your chest, before I cast it away. Just like on stage and we double plunge while I straddle you? That performance was for you, baby. Want a private show?"

"I'll be right back," he said on a thick, hoarse swallow, his hands sliding down her sides with his gaze. "Call your men. Tell them to dust any bastard that gets near you."

"Oh, you can count on it," she said with a sly smile, then let out a breath of relief.

"This is fucking nuts," Rider whispered to Mike, as they followed the Aussie leading them to guard his room with Shabazz.

"You. The one with the dreadlocks. You're on the stairs,"

McGuire ordered, splintering Shabazz off from the three-some.

"Five minutes. Tops," McGuire said to Rider and Mike. "Bring one of those beasts down here to keep any other master out of here while I'm with 'er—but if you come in if she screams, I'll kill you." McGuire paced away. "My men are on the periphery, guarding you, but since you have control of the animal, and have hallowed-earth ammo, I want you in security formation around me. Got it?"

Big Mike nodded and watched McGuire's back as he left. "In all my years, Rider, I never woulda thunk it."

"How in the hell did we wind up on a vamp Carnal Cruise Lines, our girl about to go in a room—with a master vampire, who we are supposed to be guarding . . . with a Hell-hound . . . *and,* the very jealous Mr. Rivera, who is supposed to be her husband—down the hall with four of the *finest* vamp babes I have ever seen in my life . . . but, Damali doesn't care . . . people are feeding sharks so we cannot just jump off the sides of this supernatural Hell contraption and swim home to the U.S. like we have sense. SOBs are dropping fang like it's Mardi Gras." Rider ran his fingers through his hair and lowered his weapon, glancing at the monstrous dog that just stared at him. "Mike, I swear. Either we are high, or we are already dead and in Hell for *aaaalllll* the stuff we did before we became Guardians. This is my summation, good brother. If we pull this off, *this* goes in the history books with our picture next to it."

"You ain't said a mumblin' word."

"I know we're on watch, and I know they're vamps," Dan whispered to J.L., "but *damn,* they're awesome. I've never seen this much T and A in my life, not up close like this. Is this how the other half lives?"

"Watch Damali's back and stay focused, dude. This is what Carlos was talking about. These hoes all bite. And just for the record, they don't live like nothin', they're dead."

Dan nodded, but his eyes followed a willowy blonde who strolled by topless wearing only a black thong. "Yeah, but,

Big Mike made it out of New Orleans . . . after . . . uh, daaayum, there goes another one," he whispered, eyeing a redhead not far away. When she crooked her finger at him, he almost followed her.

"Big Mike is six eight, two-seventy-plus, and gave her a reason not to flat-line him, feel me? And Mar almost beat him down with a frying pan when he got better for being so stupid. Stay on post; stay focused," J.L. warned, holding Dan by the back of the shirt. "You're gonna fuck around and get nicked—then *I'll* have to shoot you."

"You all right, D?" Jose said fast and quiet, coming up to her and glancing around. "I saw the Aussie lean in to your throat, honey. If he bit you, I won't tell Mar, I promise. I just need to know so we can deal with—"

"He didn't bite me," she said quietly, leaning in to him. "But do not *ever* be that crazy as to not tell Marlene if you know one of us got bit." She paused and kept her voice a tight whisper. "I made that big mistake, don't you do it. And, if you think I did get bitten, what the *hell* is wrong with your survival instinct? I shouldn't be this close to your throat!"

"I don't care," Jose said, not pulling away, but covering where she'd whispered against his neck with his hand like it had burned him. "Marlene doesn't always have to know everything. And, if you have something you don't want her to know, I'm cool with that. I'm cool with all of it."

Damali sighed, and nodded toward a few lower-level male vampires who were smiling at them from the distance. The offer was sweet but misguided. If she was bitten, Marlene needed to know—and the other thing was not open for discussion on a vamp ship.

"They think I'm feeding, they're watchers for one of the masters. I'm not sure who they work for, though. So, give me your throat, Jose, so we can talk without alerting them." Her focus divided into splintered fragments. There were so many variables to keep on top of dividing her mind; everything had to work real smooth. "They probably haven't rushed me because they saw the master standing here first, along with the dog, and know I belong to a councilman. I'm going to play-bite you, then talk to you, but I'm not in flux, so don't freak. Cool?"

But Jose's eyes held something she couldn't describe as she leaned in to communicate with him and he honored the request. His body tensed hard.

"I'm not in flux, *I swear*," she whispered, trying to get him to relax and trust her. She could literally feel his eyes close . . . but then, yeah, right, of course . . . he had to make it look like a real feed. All right, he was gonna be cool, was in the game. Her fingers stroked his hair as she welded her body to him, bit down and sucked for a few minutes, then pulled away, and spoke into his ear just like a vamp female would have.

"Now, listen, I'm going downstairs before McGuire gets into his room to position myself, I will dust McGuire, then you and J.L. and Dan . . ." His hands traced her back, and the deep swallow he took stifled a moan she felt through his chest. She pulled back and looked at him. There was no mistake about what she saw in his eyes, or what she felt when her body fit against his. Oh, my God . . .

He looked away but his hands were still on her, had slid to her hips. "I'm sorry, D. But you're gonna have to find another way to have this conversation." His gaze came back to her, but he still hadn't moved. "I'm only human, for real, for real." Then he let her go.

"What happened out in the hallway, at the hotel?"

"This ain't got nothin' to do with that," he murmured, his gaze intense. "I've felt like this for a long time . . . but they said you had to choose. I always hoped it would be me."

She reached out to touch his cheek, for the first time truly understanding just how deep the wound in his soul must be. But he jerked his head away from her touch, not with anger, just self-preservation.

"Don't," he said quietly. "Like Carlos told you, it only makes the burn worse."

She nodded. Wanted to hug him, but couldn't now. He didn't want a big-brother platonic hug. He knew she was pregnant by another man, and still loved her, still wanted her. Would even take her if she had fangs. And he was standing on a ship with his life hanging in the balance, an unequal match for four master vampires and Carlos—there for different reasons than all the other Guardians.

Her hand found her mouth and she turned away from him and walked a few steps in the opposite direction, just so she could get some air. When she turned around, Jose was just staring at her, weapon dangling in his hand, his will openly shattered, and his hope gone. Oh, my God . . . what had she done? What was happening to her team? It was like everything was shifting, was mad-crazy, and there was no way to fix all the breaks in the family dam.

She went back to him, kissed his cheek quickly, and stepped away. "I love you, Jose. Like a brother, but trust me, I don't want anything bad to happen to you on this ship. *That* will break my heart, you hear? Get with Dan and J.L., and watch your back. When we get home—we'll talk. Just me and you, like old times. Cool?"

He didn't say a word to her as he stepped past her, and walked slowly toward the others a few yards away, leaving her guarded but alone until she was ready to go downstairs to McGuire's room. They both knew that it would never be like old times. A private confession had permanently changed everything. This couldn't be fixed and there was nothing to say now or later. That was the worst part of all.

"Mr. Councilman," McGuire said fast, poking his head into Carlos's room as a massive security guard opened the door. "Uh . . . a word?"

Four female vampires glowered at McGuire as they slowly drew back from Carlos. Evelyn nearly hissed when Carlos scooted her off his lap and got up off the red velvet sofa. Lai cut him a nasty gaze and went back to snorting the black powder off the coffee table. Alani stretched out on the bed, and crooked her finger at Kiersten who sauntered over to her and joined her.

"I'm really busy, man. Now is not a good time."

"He *truly* is indisposed, Harold," Evelyn crooned. "Go find somewhere else to play."

But Carlos went to the door, anyway. McGuire didn't need to get a contact from the black powder. His own blood wouldn't affect him, but another male might have a bad reaction. Carlos ushered the Aussie out of the suite and slammed the door behind them.

"Wha'did you give 'em to make them respond like that?" McGuire asked, sounding impressed. "I know they're vamp females, and all, but my wife acted like—"

"Where is *my* wife?" Carlos said, drawing out each word separately and holding McGuire by the lapels. "She's supposed to be with you at all times!"

"No worries," he said fast. "I left her on deck with one of your monsters and her bodyguards. I also have three of them in place now to guard my door, my men on the periphery."

Carlos let go of McGuire's lapels and gave him the hit he was seeking. "Go get her, then take it, and keep her in your room."

Damali picked her way down the stairs, and gave Dan the all-clear as Shabazz flanked her. The three younger Guardians took up a post by the top of the main stairs, waiting for Shabazz.

"You ready, baby-girl?" Shabazz murmured under his breath as he escorted her to rendezvous with Rider and Mike in front of McGuire's suite.

She nodded. "You see Master Amin, yet?"

Shabazz shook his head. "Haven't in the last forty-five. So you look alive in there. This joint's about to blow. I can feel the hair standing up on my neck."

"You seen Carlos?"

For a moment Shabazz didn't answer. "Nah. Ain't seen him."

"He's got the wives on lock?"

"Yeah," Shabazz murmured, walking with his eyes forward and not looking at her. "Time to rock and roll."

She kissed his cheek as she joined Rider and Mike, needing to do that before he went back to his post. "Be safe, 'Bazz. I love you."

"I love you, too. But ain't nothin' safe 'bout my job." Shabazz petted her hair and put his hand back on his gun, then glanced at Rider and Big Mike. "The Aussie in there?"

"Yep," Rider murmured, "and high as a kite. He stumbled right through the door without opening it, taking off his tie and ripping his shirt while walking. He asked one of us to go 'fetch' her. You believe that? The bastard is blitzed."

Mike leaned in real close. "Listen, this motherfucker is flip-top high. Full fang, four inches dropped, 'bout ready to howl at the moon for baby-girl. I say we shoulder cannon our way in and get this party started righteous."

An agonized wail made them stop talking and stare at each other.

"Hold the line," she whispered. "Too many of us are at risk if this doesn't go right."

Before they could argue with her, Damali had slipped through the door.

Carlos brought his head up from Evelyn's throat the moment the assassination registered in her system. She covered her hand where he'd left the kiss but no bite.

"Don't stop," she said, her voice so thick she was slurring. "I'm tired of foreplay, take off your clothes. *Please*."

Carlos stood, four females surrounding him, eyes hungry. "Somebody just dusted your master, Evelyn—one of my lieutenants. I felt the current run cold through your system, didn't you?"

"What I felt was you," she said, loping toward him with the others, fondling her breasts as she walked. "Don't worry about it."

"Somebody just smoked him," Carlos said. It was going down. The dominoes were falling.

"I hope you feel them dust Amin," Alani murmured, her

hands running up his chest as she slid against him. "But right now, the only thing you need to *smoke* is *me,* baby. Just do me."

Evelyn had run her hands up his back beneath his suit jacket, nipping his shoulder through it as she pressed herself to his spine, sandwiching him between her and Alani.

"If you kill Xe, can I watch?" Lai whispered through a drug shudder. She was on him in seconds and gyrated against his leg, then climaxed as she nipped his ear and drew blood.

Kiersten had him by the hand, and began leading him away from the sofa. "Don't worry about them. We need your total focus, Mr. Councilman. *Please* come to bed."

"Yo," Carlos said, pulling out of the serpentine knot of flesh surrounding him. "If a master got dusted, on my watch, I need to find out what happened. Take another hit, and I'll be back," he said, bolting for the door. Damn.

He couldn't even open it to get away, they were on him again so fast. His only recourse was to simply walk through it and seal it with a transport block. He knew the black powder was strong, but shit . . . This was a precarious position for a married man. For a second, he glanced at the door, then at the security guard.

"Keep them in here," he told the courier, then vanished, materializing in front of the Aussie's room.

Rider and Mike drew fast, and Carlos held up his hands.

"It's me. It's *me,*" he said quickly, knowing it would take a second for their human reflexes to pull weapons back. "She smoked him," Carlos said quietly, with a nod of his head. "How long she been in there?"

"Less than two minutes," Rider said with a smile. "You smell something burning? Our girl is *good.*"

Carlos nodded, but he was very concerned. "She wasn't in there long enough to do that, no matter how good she is."

The Guardians hadn't even drawn a breath to respond and Carlos was through the door. His eyes scanned the room fast. A pile of ash lay in the center of the bed, still hot, smoldering, next to her blade. Damn . . . maybe she did? But then, where was she?

Again, he scanned the room for a tracer. Two male scents battled for his attention. The ship rocked and a loud boom cracked the ceiling above. Rider and Mike were in the doorway.

"Upstairs, all hands on deck. It's on." Then Carlos was gone.

Amin had Tetrosky by the throat and had body slammed him into the bridge deck so hard that the wood gave way. Hell-dogs took flight, flew, and dive-bombed the two combatants, snarling as Amin ducked, and caught one of them square in the jaw, dropping it from the air into the sea. Sharks tore at the hound, eating it alive as it struggled and flapped and bit at its tormentors, tail slashing, heavy claws slashing through the water. The weight of the water pulled at its leathery wings, trapping it too long under the surface as Great Whites disemboweled the yelping creature chunk by chunk.

An excited crowd had gathered. Tetrosky was back up with lightning speed, pushing Damali behind him. Carlos reached for her, but Tetrosky zapped her to the other side of the battle with a surge of dark current. Big Mike aimed his shoulder cannon at Amin, fired, and missed, as the huge Master ducked and glared at Mike, then blew him across the deck with a thought. A rail bent and immediately broke away from the side of the yacht, filled Tetrosky's hand, and whizzed past Carlos toward the center of Amin's chest as he charged. It caught Amin in the shoulder, slowing him down, nearly severing his arm.

A deep, echoing yell issued from Amin as he extricated the long section of metal with fury. Mike was back up on his feet, reloading. Rider took direct aim with Shabazz, but the ship lurched and made them all fall. An invisible energy burst sent the remaining dog sliding across the deck, its claws pulling up wood as it tried to break the momentum of the slide. A fireball headed directly toward J.L., Jose, and

Dan to stop their frenzied shooting, and Carlos deflected it, returning his attention to Damali to try to draw her to him fast. But Amin sent a counter-wave, making both masters struggle for a second to break the magnetic lock they had on each other.

Tetrosky used the distraction and charged Amin with both claws aimed at heart level, but Amin pulled out of the force-lock with Carlos and deflected Tetrosky's advance with a scissor kick. There was no way to get in between them. They had too much space to maneuver and were at maximum hype.

The Guardians couldn't get a clear shot as the masters moved like lightning in a death grip, changing positions as they wrestled for each others' throats, shifting constantly with Damali at their backs and in danger of taking a bullet. Each time Carlos charged toward her, the two battle-locked masters would momentarily stop combat, and in unified intent place an energy wall between him and his target. Together they were strong enough to hold him back.

But they were getting tired, needed to feed. The winner-takes-all struggle was consuming massive amounts of their energy. They had to not only fight each other, but Carlos and a Guardian team. It was only a matter of time before one of them wavered, he could feel it.

As soon as an opening presented itself, Carlos headed toward Damali as the ship lurched again from the weight of the mortal combat that took out the helm when the two masters collided with it. He saw it happen in slow motion.

Dan was knocked off his feet and was sliding, J.L. toppled and was skidding, Damali fell and hit the deck in a slow slide on her bottom trying to reach him and Dan, Jose righted himself and ran, then hurled himself to hit the deck on his belly right behind her—going for her and trying to save her from the shark-infested waters in a fast slide. J.L. had stopped forward momentum by catching on to a bent piece of railing, then reached for Damali, and missed.

No barrier from the others, Carlos's focus divided on blocking them and getting her. Master Xe appeared, and instantly vanished with Damali—but Jose and Dan were still going over the side. Rider, Shabazz, and Mike were right behind Carlos as Dan slid past the missing rail, taking Jose with him.

The ship lurched again, and Carlos was over the side of it, holding Jose's arm while Dan had both of Jose's legs. He'd brought his knees up and slammed his legs down to break into the deck and anchor himself. Carlos could feel Rider's arms around his waist, trying to help ground him, obviously forgetting for those few hectic seconds that he didn't need that type of help. His dog had sunk its teeth into his shoulder to hold him from going over the side. Instant pain shot through Carlos's system, but he held onto Jose.

"I got them!" Carlos yelled. "Go find her and smoke Xe."

Rider pulled away fast with the dog. Shabazz and Big Mike already had a head start on him, running with weapons raised down into the bowels of the vessel. The dog never left Carlos's side and barked wildly at the still warring masters on deck, standing between them and Carlos.

The ship lurched again, almost making Jose and Dan lose their grip on Carlos's hand. Carlos yanked hard on the young Guardian, and glared over his shoulder at the dog. "Do 'em!"

Tetrosky yelled when the remaining Hell-hound suddenly rushed him and tore his leg out of its socket. The wounded Transylvanian rolled out of the way of Amin's thunder stomp. But the splinters left from the impact of the stomp made broken wood available to Tetrosky's instant reach. When Amin came close to rip out his heart, Tetrosky staked him. The boat stopped rocking the moment the battle ceased, and Carlos slung the two Guardians up hard, catching them by their T-shirts. Tetrosky vanished.

Billowing black plumes from Amin's ashes made every vampire on top deck choke and heave. Carlos was gone. He was air.

"He chose to worry about saving two male human-helpers and didn't come for you? Foolish choice. What a pity. How can you be loyal to a man like that?"

Xe had her against the wall of a stateroom, his foul breath like a knife against her skin, and his incisors caressing her shoulder through her dress. Her Isis was in McGuire's suite, where she'd been before Tetrosky had come in behind her like vapor and pushed it into McGuire's heart from across the room.

With both hands against his chest, she flat-palmed Xe and pushed him up off her with all her might and walked away, furious. The aggressive, fearless action stunned him. That she had no fear, only rage, intrigued him. She could feel it, and she'd use it to buy seconds of precious time.

"Did my husband make a side deal with you without telling me?" Damali snapped, glaring at Xe.

"That's right," he murmured. "Get angry, just like you did in the parlor. Do that for me, baby."

"Did, I repeat, did Carlos Rivera—and I will *kick* his *ass* if he did without telling me—make a side deal?" She knew this was what he wanted, that this sick bastard was titillated by aggression. Liked it rough. All she needed was a few moments and a little working space to get to a table leg to stake him.

He circled her, breathing heavy, so unfocused on everything else but her that taking him down was not out of the question. She positioned herself near the coffee table, easy wood.

"Talk to me," she said, pointing at him. "He gave me away to McGuire for one night, so explain this bullshit *now*."

"We made a side deal," Xe said, trembling where he stood, captivated by her rage. "If McGuire couldn't make it through the night, then winner takes all."

She smiled. "Carlos know anything about this?" She'd lowered her voice to a seductive level when Xe shook his head no. "How treacherous . . . I'm really impressed."

He walked toward her slowly, stalking her, his smile glistening with razor brilliance. She could see how high he was in his eyes, and by the very obvious fact that none of them had tried to transport her off the ship. She had to keep him talking, just a quick stomp of the table to knock out a leg when he rushed. She'd take out his heart through his back while he covered her, would let him think it was rough fore-play. She studied his eyes and backed up until the table kissed her calves.

"You don't think Carlos will come in here, do you?" she murmured, glancing around.

Xe shook his head. "Don't worry. I have this room tem-porarily concealed from his senses. He's divided right now, battling two masters. And, if he does, I have a stamped agreement between the others," he said, producing it for her like a bouquet of roses. "He's a man of his word. He fool-ishly gave you away for one night. McGuire couldn't handle the privilege . . . winner takes all."

She forced a smile. "My husband can be a very irrational man, at times. Why didn't you take me somewhere . . . more private?"

Xe sighed. "We'd all considered that, but your husband is also very astute. This is his vessel, and he blocked all trans-port off of it. Council-level does give him some minor ad-vantages." He put the document away very carefully, his line of vision holding hers. "Now, Huntress, let us get to know each other on a less-formal basis. He'll observe protocol, a genuine agreement forged on his own ship . . . don't worry, baby, I'll take care of you tonight."

Big Mike's shoulder collided with the door three times be-fore it gave way. Rider and Shabazz were in first, weapons drawn, just like they'd broken down all the other doors be-fore this one. They scanned fast, saw no Damali, and were out. But this time Rider hesitated.

It took a second for all his senses to align and propel him back out the door. All three Guardians stood transfixed as they watched four naked female vamps feed off a massive security guard in a tangle of writing bodies.

"Oh, shit," Rider murmured, backing up slowly. "I think we found the wives."

One lifted her head from the guard's throat, blood drip-ping down her chin and fangs. Shabazz glanced back at the door, but there was no opening, just solid wall. Two of the females lifted their heads from a sixty-nine position, and grinned, mouths wet, full fangs glistening in the low light as they blew an air kiss toward Big Mike.

Another female riding the dead man smiled and wiped her mouth with the back of her hand. "Oh, look, how romantic. Carlos sent dinner."

Xe moved a lot faster than she expected and was on her as she crushed the table, leaping straight up, and coming down on it with all her weight. Machine-gun fire was echoing throughout the ship, then a huge boom shook the room. It rocked her where she'd landed, wood underfoot, and she fell. The wall blew out of the side of the ship, sucking everything in the suite out behind it into the now-visible ocean, except her and Xe.

"This is *my* ship, *my* house, motherfucker," Carlos yelled, slapping the center of his chest as he materialized and walked into the room with the ocean at his back. "That's *my* wife," he said, pointing at Damali and slow stalking Xe. "How long did you think it would take me to figure out that a blind spot was where you were?"

"Everything is in order, I assure you, Mr. Councilman," Xe said, backing up, but not unnerved. He produced the parchment and flung it at Carlos. "Winner takes all—we made the pact in the stateroom after you left! All the masters have stamped it, and you can't override the contract." He glanced at Damali and smiled. "You gave her to a master for one night. *Tonight*. It is of no consequence whom she ultimately ends up with—you know how this works."

"Take your complaint to Hell!" Carlos roared. "I want a legal review at council level!"

"That could take nights," Xe growled, "and my patience eludes me."

A shoulder-cannon blast rocked the ship as the two masters squared off. Damali grabbed a makeshift stake from the broken table leg, and backed up deeper into the suite. All she'd need was to get bumped into the water. Reading her slow movements, both Carlos and Xe looked up.

"Get out of here," Carlos ordered, his eyes trained on Xe. "I'ma kick this bastard's ass."

"Tell her to stay away from the edge," Xe said through his teeth. "Once I dust you, I don't want to have to waste time reconstructing her from shark bait."

The suite door blew open as Carlos lunged for Xe, sending Damali through it. She was hurled against the far wall so hard that her head hit it and made her bite her tongue. She could taste blood in her mouth. Xe and Carlos had stopped combat for a moment, looking to see if she was all right. She hawked and spit. Carlos froze.

It happened in slow motion. The saliva and blood from Damali's mouth falling, falling, about to hit the floor of a vampire vessel sanctioned by the council as a part of his territory. A perfect DNA sample telling them everything they needed to know about Damali. Everything. Xe was moving toward him, but that wasn't his biggest concern. Xe's fist collided with his jaw. His head snapped back, and he couldn't send the power to catch her spit fast enough. The splat on the floor sounded like thunder, and spread out as she stood slowly, looking dazed. As he was going down he saw it sizzle on the floor and draw in, getting smaller and smaller until it was gone.

Time truncated instantly. Xe was in midair and coming down on him. Carlos held up his hand, paralyzed Xe's motion to a dead stop, ripped out his heart, and sent a table leg through it, staking it against the wall, then let him drop and burn. Carlos rolled away from the cinders, stood up fast, rushed to Damali, and grabbed her by the arm.

"My cover's blown. I have to get you and your men to a speedboat while I still have some power left."

She grabbed the back of his shirt, trying to slow him down. "Berkfield is in the hull of the ship," she said through her teeth. *"He's the key."*

Carlos stopped, spun on her quickly and held her by both arms. "Talk to me fast. We don't have a lotta time. I know the key is in the hull, but I don't have time to save him and you."

"Our seers located him from your concert transmission.

The sacred blood," she said quickly between pants. "It's been injected into him—he's a *living* key. They'll put him on the seal and crucify him to bleed him out. As soon as his blood separates and hits the seal, the biblical gate opens."

Panic collided with terror within Carlos as he felt his energy waning. "I can't save you both. You're my top priority, D. Period. Send one of the Guardians after Berkfield, but *you* have got to get off this ship, and then your men can blow it. I can't worry about it if they don't get to him in time. If it's him or you, you know my choice." He began pulling her behind him but her resistance was slowing their forward progress.

"No! Don't you understand? He's an innocent. One with your mark. None of my men can break the hold on him within that hull—only you can, if Tetrosky performed a dark ritual. Only a vampire of higher level than him can break it to open that casket, or we have to find Tetrosky and behead him. If you let the man drown, they can still get to his body and drain him, but your soul will be lost forever with us going into the Armageddon!" Tears streamed down her face. "There will be no world, no future for humanity, including our child, if that sixth seal is opened."

Her voice fractured and split his conscience, making him grab her to him, then lift her to keep running toward safety no matter what she'd told him.

"Carlos, don't do this," she begged him as he carried her. "If you cross over, at least you can be a warrior angel, still on our—"

"You, the baby, that's all I care about, D!"

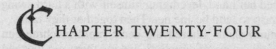

CHAPTER TWENTY-FOUR

IT WAS like history repeating itself, coming full circle. He'd become so fatigued that at one point he'd nearly dropped her. Now she was running by Carlos's side, her steps hard and sloppy from exhaustion, gasping breaths through a blinding pain in her abdomen that felt like someone was examining it, ruthlessly invading it. Carlos was wounded. Both of them were practically staggering and hitting the sides of the walls while running and as the ship continued to shift, listing, like they were, her man was too tired to transport, too tired and unfocused to heal himself, half dragging her toward her team.

As they rounded a corner within the behemoth vessel to escape through the exit left by the fallen stairs, they saw a wide smoking hole in a wall and three smoldering vamp dust piles. A dead man was on the bed with a table leg in his chest. Carlos glanced at the grisly sight and his panic shot through her system, nearly blinding her.

Without a word, he wrapped his hands around her waist and thrust her over his head so she could grab a bent rail and pull herself to deck level.

"Run!" he yelled, but she watched him struggle to pull himself to safety with his uninjured arm.

Ignoring his command, she knelt, hooked her arm securely on a brace, and extended her hand. She reached for him harder, holding her breath as new tears formed in her eyes and fell. Their eyes met, no words needed, and he grabbed her hand, leveraging himself with a hard swing and her grasp to land beside her. Then together they ran.

Ammo shells littered the deck; rapid machine-gun fire sent shells in every direction, making them run low and in a zigzag pattern to avoid getting hit. Her team was pinned down behind a twisted section of metal and wood that was once the helm. A Hell-hound was assisting, keeping nearly fifty top-deck vampires held at bay at the bow from leaping at them airborne, patrolling the expanse with razor-sharp jaws and a slashing tail.

J.L. had rolled away, fly-kicked an encroaching male vampire, and mowed him down with a hail of bullets while sliding on his back. Dan was dead aim and capped two females, then smoked another to give J.L. cover, while Jose stood, a Glock in each hand, giving Dan a chance to reload another magazine.

Shabazz, Rider, and Big Mike were hemmed in at the stern, out of ammo. The rail was at their backs, and a long she-serpent with Lai's body atop, a thick, black coil swayed from side to side. Mistress Xe's six bulked arms were reaching for the trapped Guardians with claws. Mike stepped forward and took a swing at her with the butt of his shoulder cannon, catching her in the jaw, chipping one of her fangs and splitting his weapon in two. In a swift pivot, six hands snatched Mike, squeezing him into a snake's death grasp as she freed her claws to combat the others by thrusting him into her coils. As he struggled to break her hold, she screeched and screamed her fury, making his ears bleed, crushing him with constricting serpentine strength.

Carlos was on her tail in seconds, grappling with the end of it, making her turn, drop Mike, and focus on him. The Hell-hound swooped in, slicing her back open, making her screech, sending black blood everywhere that the huge Guardian had to avoid as he rolled away from the splatter. Then the dog flew off to circle and come in again.

"Carlos . . ." Lai hissed, furious, her thick, muscular tail-body slamming him to the deck. "We ran out of product, but we'd picked your pocket and found one more pill. Shame you didn't stay."

The dog stole the female vampire's attention for a moment as she swiped at it with a free hand.

"The red pills," Damali yelled, her eyes going to Jose.

Jose nodded, and flung a Glock end-over-end to her. Damali missed, but Rider caught it as Master Xe's wife reared back, swaying, to deliver a death strike to Carlos. J.L. tossed Shabazz a full clip as the dog landed behind the female vamp, distracting her again, and stalked toward her.

With complete synchronicity, Rider and Shabazz shadowed each other's movements; they were one. Each brought their arms up, extended, at the same time.

"Yo, sis," Shabazz hollered, making the female vamp turn away from the approaching hound.

Carlos had both hands around the female's throat, but she was a full head taller than he, and more bulked. His back was to the Guardians as she pivoted him with her, and her multiple arms were crushing his rib cage.

"He's family," Rider said, releasing the hallowed-earth-packed rhino shells at the same time Shabazz released his.

Carlos felt sudden heat whiz over his shoulders. Mistress Xe released him, writhing, twisting, and screeching. The dog stopped its advance, then he heard two more simultaneous gunshots, ducked, and shielded his head as her chest exploded, leaving only ash.

He stood fast, glanced back at Rider and Shabazz, and nodded a nonverbal thanks. But his condition was real. Big Mike's gun butt had had more of an effect on the female vamp than he did. If the dog hadn't been there and assisted, if the Guardians hadn't had his back . . . He had to get Damali and her team off the ship while there was still time. Council was taking away his power.

Drawing together like a magnet, the team instinctively formed a ring around Damali. The hound howled and stood by Carlos. The ship leaned at a harder angle and groaned.

The lower-level vampires who were left backed up and sought cover.

"She's going down," Carlos said, his terror unmasked as his gaze swept the group, then the open sea. "I have to bring it to a full stop and reverse engines."

Damali touched his face, her fingers tracing Master Xe's blow, which still bled, then she looked at his ragged shoulder. "You have to feed. You don't have that much energy in you—your wounds aren't sealing."

He shook his head. "There's nothing on the boat to eat." He stared at her, refusing to look at anyone else in the group.

"Save the key, Carlos. Don't worry about me!" She extended her arm and he glanced at it and staggered away, going to the stern. He held onto the rail and closed his eyes. He could feel energy draining away, making it hard to breathe as the ship slowed to become dead in the water. He pushed off of the rail, his hands forward, concentrating everything within him to a pinpoint of fury, then fell back as the listing vessel lurched and jettisoned in the opposite direction going toward the harbor.

Gasping, he lay on the deck. It was getting too near dawn. Hell was siphoning him hard for answers, draining him. He could smell the putrid stench of Hell-hound saliva and the creature nuzzling him back to consciousness. Footsteps echoed from the deck wood into him, pain. Hands pulled at his body. Sweat blinded him, but he managed to stand. His vision was fuzzy, unfocused for a moment, but he could feel the speed by the rate of the wind passing him. A pair of tender arms held him upright. Sydney Harbor Bridge was coming into view, and he could hear the speedboats rushing to rendezvous in the distance.

"Get on the boats," he said, his speech slurring from fatigue as he weaved. "I can't stop it from hitting the harbor."

"We all do this, man," Shabazz said.

"No," Carlos said, almost unable to lift his head. "Protect the package," he croaked, pushing Damali away from him, staggering backward, and snapping his fingers for the dog.

"No acid," he yelled at the creature. "No harm. Do not bear down—carry her for me. Be my arms."

"We are not doing this again," Damali yelled. But as she took a step forward, the Hell-hound rushed her, grabbing her in its massive jaws, and flew off without biting down, and dumped her into Marlene's fast-moving skimmer. Then it circled back to the ship.

Marlene rubbed Damali's back as she jumped up and leaned far over the side of the speedboat, straining toward the larger vessel. Father Lopez made a U-turn in the water and came alongside the rocketing yacht. Father Patrick and the other clerics flanked Marlene's speedboat, all eyes looking up, trying to keep from bumping the vessel beside them, but also urging with their eyes for the rest of the team to quickly join them.

"Jose, J.L., Dan," Carlos yelled, not looking at them, but sending the order to the dog, who responded instantly. Carlos looked at Jose. "The others are too heavy now, the dog hasn't been fed, is exhausted, and might drop them. Don't fight me. Remember what I told you. Hallowed ground. Deliver the package intact."

All the Guardians glanced at each other. The dog hadn't eaten. Jose nodded, and nervously complied on trust alone, committing his body to the dog's jaws. They all watched as the animal brought the three lighter-weight Guardians and dropped them with a soft thud. But on each pass, the animal visibly slowed its return, the exhaustion clear as it strained harder with each delivery.

"We ain't leaving you," Big Mike hollered. "We'll jump, Mar can circle back."

"The sharks," Carlos said. "I can't hold them back."

"We are one," Rider said.

"Carlos, throw a line, and let Rider and—"

A swirling black cloud silenced Damali's urgent demand. It was headed in a direct path, perpendicular to the port side of the listing yacht. Carlos turned slowly, knowing exactly what it was. Council transport.

The dark tornado cut the water in two frothing sections that made the speedboats bounce and have to pull away from the yacht to avoid collision. Black lightning zigzagged through the Hell-sent mass, flashing hints of red-eyed courier bats within it before going dark again. The angry screeches sliced his eardrums and made Big Mike hurl. Carlos glanced at the cloud and then at the horror in Damali's eyes.

Gale-force winds made it hard for them all to stand. The remaining lower-level hiding vampires and helpers that cowered at the bow took their chances against the sharks, leaping off the yacht like lemmings. Angry jaws from beneath the water's surface abandoned their chase of the speedboats and headed back toward the yacht. Their instant feeding frenzy colored the water, turning it black and red and sizzling. Vampire extinctions and human cries rent the air as lieutenants and helpers fought against the impossible—nature's efficient garbage disposal system.

With his last ounce of strength, Carlos slung his arm in the three ship-trapped guardians' direction, knocking them overboard from the starboard side, jettisoning them forward, his mind connecting them with the two speedboats, separating their landings as his fists opened, his fingers craned, and the veins stood up in his neck—they could not fall wrong and die, it would break her heart.

Instantly, he saw Berkfield's terror-stricken face within his mind's eye and felt a small surge of light enter him as he grappled to get past the dark current shackling the man's arms and legs within one of the four coffins hidden in the engine room. Deck board splintered; a hole opened in the ship all the way to the hull. The boat listed at the invasion, and a frightened, weary man bubbled up with a froth of sea water, choking.

The exertion brought Carlos to his knees. The cloud was calling. Carlos looked at Berkfield, unable to even speak. He glanced at the speedboats and used the last that was in him to slam Berkfield into the getaway vessel closest to the yacht. Carlos stopped breathing. His heartbeat slowed to a crawl and then died.

His dog was now circling him, growling, stalking him. He'd lost favor. His throne had been revoked. Power drained from his hands, the cloud was calling. He looked up at the waning moon. He'd had a good run, had played it to the bone, but it was time to ante up and pay the band. Carlos closed his eyes, feeling the foul wind on his face. He was oddly at peace—the lie was out, he'd been busted . . . the night was on his face. Damali's sobbing voice begging him to jump was a stabbing pain in his temple.

"We don't leave our own!" Shabazz hollered. "You're one of us—always were. C'mon man, you're a Guardian!"

Father Patrick's loud, fervent prayers made his ears ring, but didn't slow the cloud. Marlene's, and prayers from all the others, blended in and became chants that only made the tornado pick up speed. Damali's voice was drowned out by the turbine winds. Berkfield was weeping as the clerics whisked him toward the shore. This was Hell's concern, he was theirs, he'd used their credit at the table. A deal was a deal. All the power to play by their rules. He'd reneged, now it was their turn to do said same. It was nonnegotiable.

He could hear futile gunfire whirring through the cloud. A rocket-propelled grenade lit the cloud like the Fourth of July, but it kept coming. Hell's debt-collection system had a score to settle.

Father Lopez pulled away, Father Patrick's boat on his flank. They were giving up! Damali's eyes filled.

"No!" she screamed, her voice breaking with a sob. "Don't let them take him!" Strong hands held her from the boat's edge—she'd swim if she had to but she wasn't letting him die alone, not like that.

She reached out, and opened her hand—the Isis filled it as Carlos looked back at her slowly one last time. Then the cloud collided with the yacht, and the fireball explosion sent splintering cinders everywhere, rocking their careening speedboats almost out of the water.

Marble broke his fall, shattering his kneecaps. Carlos rolled over on his side, his legs jelly, as agony shot up his thighs, into his groin, and stabbed his abdomen. Three sets of black robes swished by him—he could hear them near, hovering, repressed fury making the air around him crackle and pop. He opened his eyes slowly, his face a hot poker against the icy floor.

He peered up at the chairman, then focused on the other two councilmen. Tetrosky stood by the council table, his expression triumphant.

"Stand and face me!" the chairman bellowed, raising Carlos to his feet by sheer will and an outstretched claw. Then he flung him to a far wall and hurled two stalactites at him, spearing his arms to keep him hanging against it.

The instant agony made Carlos close his eyes and release a long yell that echoed and bounced through the chamber, his body convulsing and burning until his muscles stopped twitching.

"I don't even know where to begin," the chairman said. His voice was even, level, controlled as the vampire tribunal approached Carlos. He grasped Carlos's jaw in his gnarled hand, forcing Carlos to look at him, squeezing his face until his fangs dropped. "You don't even deserve to possess these," he whispered, seething, then let go of Carlos's face, pacing away. "I am *so* disappointed," he said with his back to Carlos, his voice escalating in volume with every word, his hands now outstretched, gathering strength, curling in, rattling thrones until the huge pentagram-shaped table shuddered.

When he turned around to face Carlos, black tears of rage shimmered in his eyes, nearly eclipsing his all-red pupils. Breathing hard, the chairman paced over to Carlos again, reared back, drew his arm far over his shoulder, and released a backhanded slap that took out one of Carlos's fangs, leaving blood in his mouth. "Ingrate! Infidel! Heretic! Treasonous bastard, I *made* you!"

The blow had shattered his jaw, and a long trail of saliva mixed with blood oozed to the floor from where his left fang used to be. He shut his eyes tight, hurt as much from the blow as he was from the humiliation. He could feel a claw dig into his wet scalp and thrust his head back, forcing him to stare into furious glowing eyes. Then his jaw repaired, minus his fang, as the eyes narrowed on him.

"Speak to me!" the chairman bellowed. He dropped Carlos's head from his grasp and walked away, pacing hotly, drawing smoke from the floor as he waited for an explanation.

Carlos glanced around the room, looking for anything to cling to, a place to begin. Tetrosky's sly smile dug into his pride. "I made the drug because—"

"Silence!" The chairman was trembling, and the other councilmen backed up, hissing. He stretched his arm out behind him and pointed to Tetrosky. "He brought a valid complaint to my chambers about my most trusted, most promising councilman!" The chairman closed his eyes and made a tent in front of his mouth. Then he lowered his voice to a murmur. "I do not care about a little masters' territory squabble."

The elderly vampire swished away and walked up to Tetrosky, grabbing him by the throat so fast that Tetrosky hadn't been able to avoid the snatch. The chairman studied the fear in Tetrosky's eyes with casual disdain. "We were debating the futile," he said, speaking over his shoulder to Carlos while holding Tetrosky. "I explained to him that I didn't give a *centuries damn* about his losses, or the fact that my own turned councilman had bested him and the others in a blood hunt. Winner takes all. Those are the rules. And I told this pathetic topside master that if power was to concentrate, then let it be with the better vampire—so be it. And if my turn was conniving and shrewd enough to use a drug, or whatever ruthless methods to deceive him, then that truly showed who was the better vampire."

The chairman dropped his hold on Tetrosky and let out a long sigh. "I was so proud of you, son." The chairman shook his head as he stared at Carlos. He drew a deep, shaky breath, and let it out slowly. "So, I told this sniveling, Old World bastard to get used to a new empire—Carlos Rivera was progressive, street savvy, had shown *even me* something new . . . and I cannot tell you how long it's been since I've seen something new!" He turned his attention back to Tetrosky. "Didn't I?"

Tetrosky nodded. "Yes, Your Excellency," he said, genu-flecting and backing away.

"And I told him to take his pathetic, pampered, betrayal-ridden carcass out of my chambers and away from my sight, and to never darken our threshold down here again—not over some bullshit about his feudal rights over a woman!" The chairman whirled around, snapped his fingers, and brought a transport cloud down to collect Tetrosky. "But now, I may have to cede Europe back to him! Perhaps the *entire* topside empire! Why? Because as the only topside master that has survived this fiasco, he told me that *you* pos-sessed the key that would open the seal—that it was your treachery! It was hidden in *your* marked human. And he let me witness with my own eyes how you sent that key away with clerics en-route to hallowed ground to protect him. And you also impregnated our vessel—stealing daylight and power from me not once, but twice!"

His gaze narrowed on Tetrosky as the smoke gathered around him. "Although I have not decided to give him all that he asked for yet." The chairman glared at Tetrosky. "So do not get comfortable even lusting over the idea. You did yourself a disservice. Instead of taking your losses like a true master and being clever enough to bide your time to win your losses back, you came to council like a child, wanting your territory handed back to you on a silver platter." The chairman shook his head. "You disgust me. Our kind, from the old days, would have seen that as a challenge, raised an army, embedded intrigue in Rivera's own courts, but we would never have whined about our misfortunes. *Youth!* What is happening in our world? You had the perfect oppor-tunity to show me something new—your worst deceptions through creativity!"

With that, he bitch-slapped Tetrosky. "*You* dishonor Dracula's line, and will *never* descend to a throne under my rule for bringing this information to me that breaks my heart about my favorite—I will *never* forgive you for that."

The chairman stepped away from the cloud. Tears of humiliation glittered in Tetrosky's eyes and burned away as he glanced at Carlos while the dense cloud consumed him.

In the quiet moments while the chairman took deep, stabilizing breaths and Tetrosky disappeared, a new awareness entered Carlos. He clung to the acquired knowledge like a life raft. The chairman had said he was his favorite. Had called him *son*. Like an heir apparent to the top seat, someone being groomed for further descent. Even in his wrath, the old vampire's spirit had hesitated to exterminate him. He'd felt it in the blow, in the crushing hold of his hand, the way he'd held himself back from ripping out his heart, had repaired his jaw to hear his side of the dispute.

Their eyes met, one pair older and seeming broken, one pair hopeful.

"Carlos," the chairman whispered, and then looked at the two seething councilmen by his side. "Leave us," he ordered, and waited until the others begrudgingly vanished. He returned his focus to Carlos. "Have you *any* idea how much pain this causes me?"

The chairman shook his head slowly, coming to Carlos without fury. "No, you don't. You never will." He walked back and forth slowly with his eyes closed and his hands behind his back.

Carlos knew it was useless to try to offer an explanation in his own defense, no matter what Tetrosky had done, or how he'd been set up. The balance of the evidence was damning. He could feel his mind being torn open from the lethal probe. Blood began to run down his nostrils, burning, stinging, and making him gag. The pain was so intense from the brutal invasion that he could barely hold his head up. But there was one thing about a mind probe, it always worked both ways.

"My Neteru . . ." the chairman said, his voice far off as he chuckled and took another deep, stabilizing breath. He looked at Carlos. "I was midsentence, tongue-lashing Tetrosky, when her blood dropped onto my council table and the light in it burned a hole straight through the marble."

He smiled and pointed. "Right on the crest." Then chuckling, he rubbed his hooked hand over his bald scalp.
"Burned right through the table and went all the way to
level seven."

Carlos blinked and sniffed back blood and mucous. "History is repeating itself, isn't it, sir?"

The chairman nodded. "I thought you could beat the cycle," he whispered. His gaze was eerily tender. "You had become so intertwined in their lives . . . so trusted, that you
could roll over prayer lines and live. I had seen a new era.
Not even hallowed ground could stop you. I nearly wept with
pride. For a moment I tasted the elusive thing called hope."

The old man walked away and gave Carlos his back, his
breaths shuddering his body as he spoke. "You were with
ripe Neteru on hallowed ground, about to start an empire."

"Sir, she was just in false flux and—"

"Do *not* mock me at *this* juncture!" The chairman spun,
his arm outstretched, pointing at Carlos so hard that his
chest started to groan, ribs snapping slowly, his heart tearing
away from the surrounding tissues. He drew back his arm in
a fast jerk, and Carlos's body slumped. "You think I do not
know the *true scent* of ripened Neteru?"

Agitated, the chairman paced back and forth quickly,
stuttering as he spoke, lather forming at the corners of his
mouth, his fangs dropping three additional inches. "I don't
know because I am an old man?" He paced some more, stopping in front of Carlos. "I bit the *first* Neteru on the planet.
Eve!" The chairman slapped the center of his chest, and spit
on the floor. "Human prayer lines? Please!"

Pure, unadulterated shock held Carlos against the wall
harder than the rock spears the chairman had hurled. "Eve?"
The question came out on an awed whisper filled with genuine respect.

"Yes!" the chairman yelled as he opened his arms and his
voice fractured. "In Paradise, I crossed barriers that you cannot fathom, gained her trust against the one who shall remain nameless, took her from a male Neteru!" He was

breathing hard as the recollection swept through him. He pointed at his chest. "It was *I* who began our race. Cain was mine. That is why *I* sit here as your chairman." He took a heaving breath and swept away from Carlos's unblinking gaze. "She was *gorgeous,* the first woman on the planet . . . flawless, innocent, a warrior, and I brought her pleasure that she couldn't even comprehend." He covered his face with his back to Carlos. "And they took her from me," he added quietly. "She went back to her people. She made a choice that even I couldn't control."

Black tears stained the chairman's face as he turned around and stared at Carlos. "Can you fathom that? She went right back into Adam's arms, and carried his human seed right next to mine. Gave up every luxury I could have offered her, all for desert, hardship, and hope." He slowly went to the abandoned table across the room and touched the burn hole in it. "It was a hollow victory when Cain slew Adam's part of her womb fruit, Abel. She probably died human—I wouldn't know. I got demoted from the left hand of my father, and was sent here to rule a lesser realm in the darkness."

The elderly vampire glanced around the cavern. "That's why our kind cannot bear the light, and we have been made death-sterile, except if we can be shrewd enough to beguile a Neteru—to right the earlier wrong." He offered Carlos a sad smile. "My father's wrath knows no bounds . . . but he did leave me a conundrum, a puzzle if you will . . . a challenge loophole, an opportunity that only presents itself every thousand years." His voice dipped to a dangerously low whisper. "You had solved the puzzle, were so close . . . and *then* . . . she bent your will. A council-level master!"

Again, two pairs of eyes met. A terror filled Carlos like he'd yet to experience. Information was power, but his mind was not ready for this black box that he'd opened within the chairman's. He now understood to whom he was speaking, understood who he'd been playing games with . . . oh . . . shit . . . and the baby . . . Damali . . . this was who he was employed by . . .

"Uhhmmm-hmmmm," the chairman said with a sly smile. "Rude awakening, isn't it?" He sighed and studied his nails. "But you were excellent, Carlos. In thousands of years, I had never seen a man with such balls. Absolute defiance." The chairman chuckled. "You delighted me so. Reminded me so much of myself. I had my night where I angered my father by doing the Paradise job while he was in heavy negotiations, and fucked up and lost." The chairman laughed harder, amused at the wicked memory. "So like me. Here we are on the brink of the Armageddon, and you are cutting side deals left and right, light and dark, all because of a woman who is making you crazy . . . making you lose perspective, forgetting all about what we can really do to you down here. You even gave her the key." He shrugged and sighed. "Not to worry. We've sent an escort to reclaim it. No matter. It's your intent that pains me so, going against me, the one who made you."

He waved his hand. "Ahhhh, youth. I did it, too. My father was stalling for time with his primary adversary when I breached Paradise; his demon legions were not built up, he hadn't harvested enough dark souls . . . he was not prepared to do battle—but my ill-timed seduction almost made the Light eclipse the Dark and withdraw from sensitive negotiations. It almost began the final battle while our side's forces were just forming."

The chairman shook his head. "Just like you have done— while our vampire forces have sustained heavy losses, our empire is in shambles with the loss of all topside masters but one—with only a weak one left . . . two open thrones at a table that requires five, only lower realms filled, and lower-level vampires topside that cannot create more masters . . . and you fall in love." His smile evaporated as he let out a frustrated breath and stared at Carlos hard. "My father was *very* displeased . . . much like I am now. Timing is everything. Son, you just screwed yourself by attempting to screw us."

He pushed away from the table and licked the finger that had touched the burnt hole. "But the difference between you and me is this. All I could create, given the times and the bargain on the table my father had made, was an evil spirit within a man—Cain." He pointed at Carlos now, his fury slowly building as he thought about what he was saying.

"But *you* could have released our kind to dwell in sunlight as well as live forever. It would have sealed the rift between level six and level seven—there would be no boundary between those realms! Even the other councilmen have no concept of how close you were to that, what power you held in your arms as you loved her—only one who has been there could ever fathom that . . . no other, but you and I, Carlos, has had a Neteru willingly give herself by choice."

The old vampire became very still, his voice dropping to a murmur of madness as though addressing himself. "The fair exchange would have been made—the Eve fiasco possibly forgiven. If I had delivered night eternal by opening the sixth seal and swayed the Armageddon, my debt to my unholy father would have been paid in full. We would have broken the backs of all Guardian teams worldwide, as well as the Covenant; hope would have finally been banished from the face of the earth . . . and my father's army would have spoiled it, unchallenged—harvested souls in numbers that are frightening. The power you walked away from . . . power that I would have never given up. That's the critical difference between you and me. You've ruined everything!"

Suddenly becoming quiet, the chairman stopped walking, shook his head, his voice a mere whisper as his weary eyes searched Carlos's. "Carlos, why? Why would you give them both the Neteru and the key . . . what did they offer you that was so great? Salvation? What is that anyway? Why?"

"I didn't know . . ." Carlos said quietly, the truth in his words no ploy, no game. "I didn't—"

"You didn't think as you released!" the chairman yelled, his mercurial emotions now thundering his voice through the chamber. He swept in to Carlos fast, grabbing his tattered lapels. He gazed at Carlos, his eyes filled with hurt. "You loved her like *a man*." He dropped his hands away. "You filled her with hope, love, faith, trust, everything that keeps the human choice whole and the spirit unbroken." Near sobbing with regret, he touched Carlos's face. "You let *her* turn *you*. And you *prayed* for her . . . and prayed that if she ever conceived by you, the baby would be like her, human. You let her give you the virus of humanity—a conscience . . . compassion. And you disgraced everything I've ever known."

The chairman walked away from Carlos. "Even now, down here, so crystalline a plea is in your heart . . . a prayer to end this, take you, but spare her. You brought a prayer into *my* chambers, staked to my wall, bleeding, broken, defeated—the absolute *gall* of it, and you come in here with *hope*?" Incredulous, the chairman's voice dropped to a whisper. "Your last wish, the only thing on your mind is not survival, but to see her one last time . . . not power?"

He placed his hand over his heart and closed his eyes. "She has polluted my protégé and has driven a *stake* through my heart." Then he chuckled and shook his head. "And, I can't kill her. She's still the only vessel we have, unless I can extract the key. But even then, I must still find the seal— which could take centuries!" His withering gaze held Carlos. "You played our entire realm into a winner-takes-all position where she's temporarily won. Unbelievable."

He began walking again with his eyes closed and his hands behind his back. "What to do, what to do with you, my wayward, wayward son? The sins of the father shall be visited upon the son—that's the law of all realms, a point not negotiated . . . and I'm sure my father had to ask himself this same question. Irony."

"It wasn't her fault," Carlos said, sheer panic in his voice as a million different horrific options entered his mind.

"Oh, yes . . . there was total, clear intent in her desire to save your damnable soul . . . to snatch it from our clutches, to *convert* you to her side—*Dark Guardian*. She wanted to bring you into the Light." The chairman tilted his head and nodded. "So be it. Grant the lady her wish, and let her see what the Light does to our kind." He walked away from Carlos. "I hope she likes her decision."

Carlos could feel his body relax. It would be painful, but it would be an end, and be over quickly. She'd survive, so would the baby. Maybe, under the right circumstances, Marlene could help guide it, anoint it, keep it from being evil.

The chairman put one finger to his lips before speaking. "Over quickly? No . . ." He made a little tsking sound as he slowly shook his head. "And, we do intend to be sure that she sees your death in the Light—just where she wanted you to be, to place a scar on her heart where she left one on mine."

Carlos closed his eyes.

"And, the baby . . . the Neteru is our vessel, and it has to be cleaned out. I'm not going to risk—"

"No!" Carlos yelled, straining against the rock stakes in his arms.

"Yeessss . . ." the chairman said. "Just like you showed her. The blood separation—yours to one side, hers to the other . . . we can't harm her, we can't infect her blood, but we can take back that which is rightfully ours—your blood and your DNA . . . and we will drain it out of her womb until the fetus detaches from—"

"Oh, God, no! *Compassion*," Carlos cried out, sobs now choking the mucous-trapped words, "*Dios, por favor, compasion*—don't let them do that to her! Take me, do whatever, don't hurt her—not like that!"

Horrified, the chairman stepped back as the black marble floor split between them, sending a hiss of thick, black sulfuric smoke up from the widening gully. Tears, smoke, blood, burned Carlos's eyes. Hysteria made him tear at his own flesh to free himself from the wall, nearly severing his arm.

"*Never* in my chambers—that name!"

Screeching, howling, spitting creatures climbed over the edge of the dark pit in the council floor. Squatting, gargoyle-faced entities appeared, their gray-green skins mangled and fused into contorted features as though keloid scars from burns. Their long, scaled hands had gleaming yellowed hooks on the ends of six appendages that mocked fingers. Their tails swished back and forth like a cat's, a razor barb at the end. They had no eyes, just bloody black sockets, and from behind jagged yellow teeth, they flicked a long, black serpent's tongue. Gray wings with razor edges and spikes spread out to help them balance in a slow scamper forward. The creatures huddled around Carlos's feet, touching his legs with one finger, poking him, tilting their heads, their short black horns catching the torch fire as they conferred with each other.

"I might have been moved to some dark level of mercy," the chairman said calmly, backing further away as the entities turned to him and screeched. "May have struck a deal," he added, which returned their focus to Carlos when the chairman gave the only acceptable answer in Hell. "But you cried out *down here*." He shook his head, his voice filled with strange compassion and yet respect. "I can't help you now that the harpies have come to investigate. You will have to tolerate an Inquisition."

She couldn't see as she stumbled up the dock, half running, half jogging with her team. The tears wouldn't stop flowing, then she heard it. A piercing wail that ran through her soul. She turned to the others and covered her face. Brutal images flashed in strobe in her mind, made her vomit, and drop to her knees. "They're torturing him!"

A sharp tug on her shoulder, arms lifting her, reinforcing her grip on Madame Isis, and making her stand. The sea was spewing a dark, whirling funnel cloud, electricity sparking inside to reveal the razor-toothed flying creatures within it. Instantly they all knew it had come for the living key, Berkfield.

The Guardians temporarily halted their retreat, holding a line at the edge of the dock to slow down the hellish cloud. Weapons drawn, the clerics began to half drag, half carry the semiconscious Berkfield to a Jeep. Then the team froze. The clerics surrounded Berkfield.

"Damali, come to me!"

She wiped her face fast and focused on the deeply pained male voice, and gasped.

"Steady aim," Rider whispered. "We got us an amped master."

"Stand down," Damali ordered, her back to her team. She spun on them when they wouldn't lower weapons. "Me and Tetrosky had a deal! Stand down if it's the last thing you do. Now!"

"He's in her head," Shabazz said, his voice steady. "Take aim—"

"No," Damali said fast, backing away from her team to stand between them and Tetrosky. She ignored their stricken confusion and blocked their aim.

"Neteru," Tetrosky said. "Your team stood with me against Amin. I saw them try to take him out to assist me. They're confused, they're human—but we need them to clear away the hallowed earth over close-by lairs. Don't harm them. It's near dawn. Send the chairman his key and we shall find favor, still, in the empire. It's not too late. All my primary forces are gone. After the battles, and the transports, I need to feed just to have you in my arms and protect you." He wheezed but stood tall, passion and yearning glittering in his eyes. "We'll rebuild the empire, you and I, one turn at a time. All the chairman wants is the living key, but it will take him eons to find the seal to open it. None of us know where it is. That leaves us as his only future. Tell them to lower the weapons that can hurt our kind."

"You hear that?" Damali said, pointing her sword toward her team, sheer force in her eyes as she held each gaze closely, trying to transmit information, then she looked at Marlene and nodded slowly. "He is the *last* master vampire topside," she said carefully. "All the second-levels, including wives, went down with the ship. Winner takes all. I made this man a deal in the castle parlor . . . I actually made him more than that—I made a *promise* that I would honor with my Isis—now *stand down*—and do not be confused. *Trust me*."

Her team cautiously followed her lead and lowered their weapons, but their muscles twitched with readiness. She watched Tetrosky visibly relax, his breathing labored as though he'd just been through Hell.

"Where's Carlos? I have to know before I honor our pact. I have to know if you've truly won the blood match."

Tetrosky took a step forward, but she lowered her blade, making him stop, and keeping him twenty feet away from her.

"He is down in council chambers, Damali," Tetrosky said, his voice becoming a plea. "He's staked to the chairman's wall and is getting his innards ripped out. I am the last master vampire standing." He opened his arms. "Don't make it a hollow victory for me."

Damali slowly brought her hand to her mouth, her Isis lowered a bit, and she fought the chill that ran through her. She refused to allow tears to build in her eyes and found an old inner rage to cling to in order to anchor herself. Without looking back at her team, she held her hand up to them, knowing they were ready to unload what was left of their ammo. Timing was everything. Not yet. He was still a master, and still dangerous. Especially now if he panicked.

"Gustav," she said, allowing her voice to become soft, and using his first name on purpose. "The victory will not be hollow."

She could see tears of relief, pent-up desire, self-doubt, tension—so many things all at once glittering in his eyes. She knew where he was, could sense it with everything Neteru and female in her. He was male. And he had led her man to the worst nightmare imaginable.

"I remember what you asked me to do just before the master's hunt," she said, slowly approaching him as her grip on her blade tightened. "You wanted me more than all the others, and you played your hand so very, very well."

"Yes," he whispered. "For you, McGuire. For you, a visit to council to survive the chaos on the boat. Now come to me. We still have time before dawn, you and I."

She nodded, walking forward. "Skill, shrewd strategy, deception . . . let the best man win."

He nodded, approaching her slowly, still cautious about her nervous team and unwilling to make a sudden move that could spook them. "Winner takes all, and you still smell so good."

"I'll come to you, just as you wanted. With Isis in hand," she murmured, allowing her gaze to rake his body until he briefly closed his eyes.

A sob stole his breath for a moment. "Do you have any idea what I went through to acquire you?"

She nodded, her steps moving forward steadily, her eyes locked with his, gaze unwavering, stalking, hunting. Then her voice dropped to a breathless whisper. "Just ask me once again like you did in the parlor, just so my memory can fuse with the new image as I give you my throat now that my husband is being extinguished. Just let me see it raw. I need that now." Tears filled her eyes as she referred to Carlos, and that devastated Tetrosky, sent insane fury through her system like a rocket.

Tetrosky opened his arms wide, trembling, dropped to his knees, leaned his head back, and another sob of sheer relief entwined with blatant longing caught in his throat. "With all that I have, take everything—and my throat. You extinguish me."

Damali swung so hard that it felt like her shoulders were coming out of their sockets. Each vertebra in her back expanded, twisted, and snapped as the blade connected with Tetrosky's throat, slicing in a ringing wind chime through skin, and muscle, and tissue, and cartilage and bone. She kept spinning in a full three-hundred-and-sixty-degree circle and almost fell from her own momentum. She heard the head thud and bounce, rolling away from the body, the eyes in it stunned open, before the body fell back and made a loud thud—then burst into flames.

"Gladly, you bastard! As promised!" she screamed, going to the ashes and kicking them, hysteria bubbling in her. "The last man standing is staked to a wall in Hell! They're torturing him because of you!" Screaming sobs made her vision blur, her ears ring, and her hands grasp at the air as her team drew her away from the site.

Her team was pulling her away from the cinders, lifting her off her feet to keep her from repeatedly stabbing the ground where Tetrosky had been. The team was yelling about the cloud of evil that was only a quarter mile away. She didn't care! She snatched away from them, going back to where Tetrosky had been, beating the ground with her sword, trying to kill this motherfucker over and over again.

"He was the better man. He is the better man. I'll kill you! I'll kill you! Oh, Marlene, I will kill this bastard. Shoot him, Shabazz. Mike, blow this fucker up! Oh, my God! Heaven help me! I will kill him!"

The team backed off for a few seconds, their gazes monitoring the darkening horizon, but they gave her those few heartbeats to let her rail at the nothingness. Immediately the remaining ash and dust from Tetrosky blew away from her foot stomps and the mere wind. Then in an eerie moment of clarity, she stopped, wiped her face with her dress sleeve, closed her eyes and breathed deeply, and really cried hard in earnest. They were torturing her man . . . oh Lord . . . make them stop.

A female hand touched her shoulder, and then female arms encircled her. Yes, they had just wiped out the entire vamp empire and had saved an innocent containing the living key—but what a bitter victory it was. Mission accomplished, but to what end? So what there were no more master vampires left topside? Who cared if all that were left were probably thirds and fourths, and minor entities that could be easily conquered? As long as there was Hell, there was a manufacturing plant to make more. What was all of this for, then? All the battles against something that just kept coming and coming and coming—evil? They were *torturing her man,* ripping her heart out . . . and there wasn't a thing she could do about it.

"Why?" she said, her question so piteous even to her own ears as she looked at her team, looked past Marlene's shoulder, then broke away from her to face the clerics.

"Damali, we've got to get out of here!" Shabazz yelled. "Marlene, Mike, Rider, Jose, tell her, it's time to go!"

"Why? You answer me! Why!" She stormed away from them when they took two seconds too long to answer her, and she approached her bewildered Guardian brothers and opened her arms. "Why?"

"Baby, we ride," Rider said, going to her to drag her away from the battle she couldn't win as she raised her blade and took a stance as though bracing for the incoming cloud.

She saw her team about to go to her, then Berkfield stumbled toward her, his eyes wild, his hands bleeding. Clerics began yelling, soaking his wounds in their robes.

"Stigmata!" Father Patrick shouted. "Bind up his wounds, do not let a precious drop of sacred blood hit the ground! She beheaded the master and broke the vessel ritual," he said, huffing and working quickly with the others to wrap Berkfield's wounds.

The turbine whine of the dark cloud made them all hold their ears. Surf crashed into the pier, lightning and thunder lit the sky, and wind made it difficult for them to stand, but the team noted that for some eerie reason, the evil contained within the dark tornado momentarily stayed back.

"He's going into shock," Father Patrick yelled over the storm. "This man's blood is separating from the Lamb's and the sacred blood must be returned to the key keepers! He is our priority. We must get him, and the sacred blood, to sanctuary!"

Berkfield convulsed, stopping their retreat, his forehead dribbling blood, his eyes running tears of blood, his palms pierced and dripping blood, his feet broken and bleeding. Then he arched, cried out, and began bleeding at his side. There was no way to keep all of the blood that fled his body from splattering the ground. The clerics were frantic as they worked against the inevitable. They couldn't get it all, sacred blood would surely hit the earth. But the second a drop hit the dirt, it was as though they were all watching the scene in slow motion.

Dark crimson drops transformed into golden-silvery-red iridescent orbs that gathered together and rose off the ground's surface a few inches. Blood splatter immediately gravitated to the hem of each cleric's robe. Stupefied by the sight, the teams watched the process of the sacred blood key going to holy vestments, staining them crimson within the folds as it crept upward away from the ground, concealing itself in the fabric of them. Once the last of it had been absorbed and hidden, a ray of light broke through the black horizon. It drew a line of white fire in the water offshore, sending a message for the cloud to stay back, halting its advance.

To the group, it seemed to be a momentary standoff, but like all things, they also knew that the dark side was willful and would exhaust all possibilities before it ever surrendered to defeat.

As the last of the stigmata began to disappear from the detective's agonized body, Berkfield convulsed again and passed out. Imam Asula caught him and carried him to a waiting Jeep. The line of light withdrew, and the black cloud began a slow advance that began to rapidly gain in speed.

Numbly, Damali watched the clerical team speed off with the limp body of an innocent man on the seat. Berkfield was their priority now. Who was there to help Carlos? New sobs accosted her, made her push Big Mike away as he tried to pull her to him and stroke her hair. It was the wrong set of arms, the wrong person to stroke away the pain. There was only one right body to fit against and weep, and he was trapped in Hell.

She spun on Shabazz and Rider, their tears making more of hers fall. "So what that we won? Who cares! We all didn't make it back—we aren't supposed to leave our own! We left him," she shrieked, her voice strained, popping, fracturing with each question. "We can't get him out, and he's still alive! But what they're doing to him isn't human . . ."

The images tore at her brain, made her walk away from the group, bend over and dry heave, then spew bile.

She stayed there, standing alone for a quick moment, one that she needed to regain her battle readiness for the team. Her eyes closed, she bent over, still breathing hard, staving off the chills, and just trying to figure out the Rubik's Cube of the universe. Why?

"We have to go to hallowed ground," Rider said quietly after a moment. "We still don't know what's coming. And it's starting to pick up speed and come fast."

Marlene went to Damali and collected her. This time she followed her mother-seer's lead. She allowed Marlene to deposit her on Jose's bike. She didn't fight or struggle, there was no resistance left in her.

"Rider, you watch my back, we're faster than the Jeeps," Jose said in a far-off tone, then stomped down on his bike and revved the motor.

"Done," Rider shouted, stomping down on his black Harley. Shabazz tossed him a sawed-off shotgun from the interior of one of the waiting Jeeps, and he caught it.

"Precious cargo, gentlemen, ride fast but ride her easy." Marlene turned away, and jumped into one of the two waiting vehicles. She threw Damali's sword belt to Jose. "So she can ride strapped."

"We got y'all's backs," Big Mike said, pointing a freshly loaded rocket-propelled grenade launcher out the window. He tossed Rider and Jose more clips. "Hallowed ground, then home."

Moving like a robot, without feeling, Damali put on the belt and sheathed the Isis. Her hands grasped Jose's waist, and she rested her cheek against his back. Soul weary, she didn't care that silent tears wet his back, or that she could barely feel the wind catch and lift her hair. The noise of the motorcycle wasn't loud enough to block the agonized male voice in her head. Just let it be quick . . . that's all she could hope for him now.

CHAPTER TWENTY-FIVE

SLIMY, VIOLATING hands held the sides of his head, raping his mind, tasting it, peeling away skin from muscle from bone, creating a bleeding fissure in his scalp so their flicking tongues could gouge into his gray matter and siphon his brain with their tongues. Pressure behind his eyes bulged them forward and almost out of the sockets, ripping his retinas, blinding him, stealing back his night vision and normal vision; blackness was now his captivity. One vampire and human sensory lost to their endless probe.

His cries went from intelligible to primal as they strip-searched every hope and dream and desire and private thought he had ever possessed. When they burrowed down to find images of her, the arch of resistance broke one of his arms away from the wall, halving it, his blood splattering everywhere.

"Don't fight it," the chairman said soothingly from across the room. "It only makes them work harder, and the process take longer."

Heckling, screeching laughter assaulted his ears, snakelike tongues entered them, taking back his once-superior hearing, leaving him deaf. Then they entered his mouth.

A hot, fecal-smelling vise clamped down over his nose

and mouth, tearing the soft tissue and forcing a long, slithering tongue down his throat, suffocating him, gagging him, making him dry heave as it wrapped around his Adam's apple and snatched it out, while claws slit his torso, threading snakes through his intestines and spleen.

The convulsion began at the base of his spine, where a serpent had entered it and threaded up his spinal cord, hemorrhaging it as it slid up his back, snapping and cracking vertebrae away from each other, one torturous disk at a time. His legs were jerking, every muscle twitching, and hundreds of tiny snakes ran under his skin, setting it on fire from the inside out.

But he had no voice to scream. No eyes to see his tormentors. No faculty to listen to anticipate the next vile act to be committed against his flesh. There was no breath in his lungs—now filled with a dense substance that he could only imagine to be his own blood—and there was no peace.

Then, just as it had started, it stopped.

Evil little hands left the sides of his head. His skull slowly closed, his sight returned. He could slowly begin to focus on the chairman, who held a grave expression. Dozens of tiny tormentors huddled by his legs. He could slowly begin to hear their disorganized murmurs. Smiles of sinister glee and triumph were no longer on their faces. Air rushed into his lungs suddenly, making him cough, heave, and vomit up a bloody mass of twisting black adders, but he'd heard his voice. Something magnetic pulled his shoulder back and his arm joined the bloody stump, reattaching the severed limb.

Weak, sweat running off him like a river, the cuts in his skin healed as thousands of threadlike snakes exited his body through his pores and dropped to the floor.

Carlos stared at his innards on the black marble floor. It was an out-of-body experience, they had tortured him to the point where he might as well have been looking at lint in a carpet—everything was so disconnected, so painfully surreal. With exhausted disinterest he watched his entrails slowly recede from the floor, up and into the ragged, gaping hole, tugging him forward as sections of organs reattached to the dripping cavity, and then sealed.

Water . . . if he could just have water. They'd even taken away his blood hunger for a moment. Then the burn for blood scorched him through. Panting, he tried to close his mouth to make saliva come, and then bit his tongue when both fangs scored it. He closed his eyes, tears running down the sides of his face; they had left him whole.

"They're impressed," the chairman said quietly. "There was much to dredge from your brain, so much dishonorable intent against our realm and so many despicable acts committed while alive . . . but with such conflicting emotions . . . such an embrace of your power, but then, not." The chairman walked near him, tiny beasts hanging back. "They could not break your seal around her or dredge any information about the seal and lost key. How absolutely incredible." He glanced back at the harpies, and laughed. "You couldn't, could you? He had a prayer around her and the information about the upper realms the entire time?"

Carlos stared at him through bloodshot eyes. There was as much deep respect there as hatred, a conflict. They understood each other.

"I know," the chairman nodded. "I have so much respect for the willpower shown, the utter defiance, the stubborn refusal to just give in. But I so despise the reason why you have this strength." He brushed a damp wisp of hair away from Carlos's forehead. "We so needed someone like you on our side. I hate that you're not. Thus, my conflict."

He strode away from Carlos with purpose. He pursed his lips, and brought a finger to them, studying him. "Torturing you would grow tiresome. That no longer amuses me. We have tortured millions, after all. And with you, Carlos, the one thing that always delighted me was that you brought me something new to study, to wrap my mind around, to envision. You are a worthy adversary—and that is *definitely* rare down here."

He glanced at the harpies who were now becoming agitated and screeching in frustration.

"Oh, yes . . . this is *very* new, because we never have one down here with all of the qualities of a saint and all the qualities of a demon so deliciously blended and in our clutches. How did you manage a fusion in your system like that?" He tapped his fingers on his lips. "What do you want?"

"To die with dignity," Carlos croaked. "Just let this be over, and let her live."

"You wasted part of your wish," the chairman said, his expression amused. "We had every intention of allowing her to live. That was never an issue. But we are going to flush her womb—you understand that we have to clean out our vessel for the future."

Carlos let his head drop. "Then make it swift, and don't bring her pain . . . *please*." He looked up, renewed defiance entering him. After what he'd just experienced he knew that the memory of physical pain could fade, but the scar on a soul could last forever. "Don't wait until she starts showing and feels the life grow within her. Do it now."

"Honorable," the chairman stated flatly. "She's a worthy adversary, in fact, turned our best master—a councilman at that. We have protocols, too, and a worthy opponent should be addressed with swift dispatch of their sentence. So be it."

Tears ran down the bridge of Carlos's nose as he watched a puddle of his blood on the marble floor bead up and separate into two halves, one black, and one red with iridescence. His shoulders shook as he leaned his head back, closed his eyes, and wept, the refrain "I'm sorry" echoing through his mind. His abdomen constricted, and a sharp pain scored his lower belly. Then the mild cramp passed and took up residence in his heart. Breathing hard through his opened mouth, he waited for the heaviness in his chest to lift, but it wouldn't. "I'll carry that for her, too," he murmured.

"You. Are. Making. Me. *Ill!*" the chairman shouted. He

turned and walked away from Carlos and spoke to the harpies at his feet. "Send him into the Light to be with her, to die with honor as a warrior—but let her see what she did to break the most promising master vampire in my empire!"

He circled them and his words seethed scorched smoke as he railed. "*My registers just ran blood tonight.* The entire topside empire is gone! Wiped out, leaving only lower-level vampires. She is responsible for exterminating five of my best masters—yes, I am even counting the rogue, Nuit, in that number, plus a very old councilman, Vlak—and countless turns in our realms! At least Nuit would have stood for our side—traitor that he was, he didn't side with humans!"

As his wrath congealed, sulfur smoke plumed out from under his robe, making the harpies back up. "Now, she has ruined *my* true vessel, Carlos . . . and I want her to witness what she created, what she did by her own hand to something she supposedly loved. I want a wound on her heart so deep, so lasting that she will never be able to raise her blade against one of my own—not like this, ever again."

The chairman's voice trembled with rage and bitter defeat as he pointed at Carlos. "We would have made him *a king,* and she could have ruled at his side, but look what she did to him!"

The chairman leaned back, his arms opened wide, his eyes closed, his dark energy swirling to a critical mass of sulfuric smoke, blowing open the ceiling above the council table, scattering the courier bats, a funnel of electrified black smoke sucking up harpies and Carlos and goblets, and wall fixtures, and torches, and rock, and anything not nailed down into the vacuum. "Take him out of my sight!"

Seventy miles an hour and climbing through near-dawn streets, zigzagging past corridors they'd never traveled, they hit the straightaway of Macquarie Street, then gunned the motors to eighty—St. James Church at the edge of Hyde Park, near Queens Square, was the goal. That's when the awful cramp hit her. Stole her breath. Pain so swift and blinding that she almost dropped off Jose's bike. She knew what was happening the moment it began. The wind whipped tears from her eyes like a slap and warmth ran down her legs, splattering blood on the ground and Jose's chrome exhausts.

Rider looked down, bringing his bike next to Jose's. Marlene stood up in the Jeep behind them, wiping at her face with fury. Then the sky darkened, blotting out the coming dawn. A thundering tornado cut a path of rage behind them, then split in two, one half of it heading toward the harbor, the other coming for them.

"Drop the colloidal silver bombs in your packs, Jose!" Rider shouted. "Damali, baby, you have to reach the side packs and break the bottles on the ground!"

If she leaned over, she was going to fall. She could barely breathe, much less move. They'd taken everything from her—what was the point? She just shook her head no and buried her face deep into Jose's back and held him tighter.

Mike was standing in the second Jeep, releasing holy-water vials, splattering the roadway behind them, but the cloud changed course. It just cut a path between the Jeeps and the motorcycles, making the Jeeps swerve to get out of the storm's wake.

"Take her to the church, man, keep going!" Shabazz hollered over the howling wind to Jose. "You're almost to St. James—or St. Mary's Cathedral, ride hard and we'll meet you."

"We can't go that way," Marlene shouted, turning the drivers around. "The Jeeps have to go back past Sydney Cove to Holy Trinity Church by the Rocks."

Each direction they turned to get close to the churches rimming the park, the cloud would separate, cutting them off, and force them to go in another direction. Rider outstretched his arm, firing behind him, dropping three gray-winged creatures that came out of the cloud, soaring toward Jose's bike. Damali drew her blade as something scrabbled at her back, Rider couldn't get a shot off without risking hitting her or Jose, but her blade severed the clawed hand, leaving it to smolder and catch fire—still attached to her dress—before dropping away.

Then the cloud separated again, cutting Rider off and leaving a line of fire down the center of the road so wide that breaching it was impossible. She looked back and saw him go into the slide, firing two-handed. His bike wipeout eminent, he had a Glock in one hand and a shotgun in the other, unloading rounds and screaming at the flying beasts, splattering gook—going down with a fight to the bitter end as his bike tilted, was stripped out from under him, and he hit the ground in a hard, bone-snapping roll.

His black Harley slammed into parked cars, twisted, flipped, and careened off a parked truck to take out a store window before it exploded. Rider didn't move.

"We have to go back! They'll eat him alive!"

"No," Jose shouted. "They don't want him! They want you!"

Jose swerved the bike to avoid the epicenter of the cloud, taking the bike up onto sidewalks, jumping curbs, landing hard and skidding into turns, leaning, using his weight, their weight, as a shifting rudder, tearing through parks not on the safety-zone grid. Disoriented and turned around in the frenzied getaway, his bike headed toward King's Cross.

"Darlinghurst Street, no!" Damali yelled. "This is taking us toward the red-light district. No hallowed ground there, Jose!"

She could feel claws pulling at her, attempting to lift her from the back of the bike, and she swung her blade wildly over Jose's head, breaking the unseen hold as he swerved, pivoted, and headed back in the opposite direction.

"I'm going past where Rider dropped his bike," he hollered over the screaming wind. "They're cutting us off from the sanctuaries at Hyde Park, but daylight's coming!"

She held him tight, her glance behind her as the cloud gained speed, mass, and density, fanned out and a large funnel set up a roadblock. Jose popped a wheelie at a hundred miles an hour, she leveled her Isis, closed her eyes, and they charged it—exploding through the mass of billowing sulfur, leaving entrails in their wake.

He kept going, riding like the wind, burning down the street where Rider had fallen. She felt him swallow hard as they raced by—no sign of Rider, just the smoking destruction left by his bike. Sirens were now blaring in the distance. Everything became a blur as tears flew from her eyes and they skidded onto Cahill Expressway, burned down it, and then went into a hairpin turn to eat up local streets on the way to Holy Trinity Church by the Rocks.

So much was gone . . . her family destroyed, two Guardians lost—Carlos, and now Rider, and someone she hadn't even named yet. And God only knew if the rest of the team had made it to sanctuary. An innocent cop was in the back of a Jeep bleeding to death, a man with a family, children, a wife . . . Pain and tears blinded her. She burrowed her face in Jose's back.

Jose rode the bike up the steps, through the church doors as he saw Mike's arm sling it open and step back and they came to a sliding thud as the bike went down, he and Damali with it, her sword clattering and rolling, skidding toward the altar—stopping five feet in front of it. For a moment, they laid there just breathing.

Fast hands gathered them up, assessed them, hugged them, hard exhales of relief entering them from warm bodies huddled near.

"Where's Rider?" Damali said fast. Jose's grip tightened on Damali's waist.

"Talk to me, Mar. Where's our boy?"

Marlene shook her head and looked away. "I saw him go down, we went back . . . they took him to the Rocks in the cove. I can see it." Marlene covered her mouth with her hand and breathed deep.

"No!" Jose shouted. "They wanted her, not him." He broke away from Damali, and went to go get his damaged bike. "I'm going to get him. Who's riding?"

Shabazz and Big Mike stepped up. Dan and J.L. shoved new clips into their guns.

"Let's do this, we're bringing everybody home," Shabazz said, picking up a weapon and pulling out the keys to the Jeep.

"He's bait," Father Patrick said carefully, his eyes sad as they locked with the other clerics. "The key is safe and the detective has been taken down to our sealed vault where he's receiving medical attention. You all need medical attention . . . Rider is bait to get you all to leave this sanctuary."

"So, fuck it," Jose said. "I'm hooked. But we're gonna go get our man."

"You don't understand," Marlene told them, her voice firm and tender at the same time. "They needed to take one of us hostage and put him close to Carlos so we could track him—to get her to—"

"Carlos!" Damali shouted. "You know where he is?"

"No. Rider is telling us no, stay back, not to let you see it, no matter what they do to them. Baby, this time—"

"We ride," Big Mike said, overruling Marlene.

Marlene and the clerics formed a human shield barring the door.

"Tell her," Marlene said to Father Patrick.

"It's ten minutes till dawn. They want you to see him die. Rider will live; he was only put there to draw us. It's a trap to break your spirit. We won't lead you to him . . . and only Marlene and I can see where he is. No. You don't need to see it." Father Patrick folded his arms and looked down at the floor and swallowed hard.

"Break my spirit," Damali laughed, the tone of it hollow and bitter. She held the sides of her ragged, wet dress, and lifted it to her knees. "Look at my legs," she said. Her voice broke, new tears streaming down her face as she showed Marlene the wind-dried blood staining them. She dropped her dress, her arm flinging outward to point at Jose's bike. Hysteria bubbled within her chest and came out in a near scream as she implored them. "Look at his bike! My spirit is broken and splattered in the streets of Sydney!" A sob caught in her throat as Marlene went to her.

"We ride," Shabazz repeated. "We don't leave our own."

She kept her gaze fastened on the Heavens. Time, time, all she needed was time. *Daylight be still. Heaven, hold down your curtain and delay dawn just this once. Please God, have mercy.* Damali closed her eyes and covered her face with her hands, rocking.

When the vehicle slowed, she didn't even wait for it to stop before she propelled herself from it, feet bare, shoes lost a long time ago on the boat. Footsteps sounded behind her but lost distance as she raced ahead of the others, clutching her abdomen.

Stone pavement, then gravel, then jagged edges cutting into her flesh, running, becoming wind itself, her heart beating out of her chest, her blade not long enough or big enough to conquer what she saw. Standing so close but so far from where she needed to be, blade chiming the air, hitting nothing. Rage. Hurt. Pain. Not like this! They couldn't kill him like this!

Each time she ran forward, huge swooping predators that had a dark invisible force around them that stunned like a sonic boom, knocked her back.

She was an ineffective witness to laughing, circling hawk-like creatures, gray-green tormentors, ripping at Carlos's chest, flying with massive spans of leathery wings, talons outstretched, diving and opening his abdomen, pulling flesh from his bones, sending his cries to rent the air, designed to call her, draw her, torture her—be her worst nightmare.

Rider was struggling in tethers, but unmolested. His voice a long holler for the team to get back, screaming curses at the demons; hysteria in him flashing fight-hormone through every Guardian. Weapons firing, trying to clear a path to get to their own, plugging the things that just multiplied and dug into Carlos's stomach harder, coming away with dripping organs and meat before stopping, hovering, looking directly at Damali—triumphant, their job done, they then flew away into the waiting tornado.

Big Mike and Shabazz had run to Rider to recover their fallen brother. Jose was in a flat-out chase behind Damali with Father Lopez and Marlene behind her.

Damali suspended breath as she ran. He was so far away—at the edge of a dangerous crag, pinned to solid rock over the waves. She went down flat on her belly, hands reaching, her eyes connecting with deep brown ones that had been defeated, done unmerciful. She could feel more Guardians at her side, reaching. Her head snapped up as daylight refused to wait. "Noooooo!"

Carlos's gaze slowly left hers and went to the sun. He arched hard, and the sound of a slow sizzle blending with his agonized wail almost sent her body over the edge of the crag to reach him. Brute strength lifted her from the ground, and tried to carry her away, but she twisted out of the hold, to resume her futile reach. "Cover him!" she shrieked. "Get a blanket! Something! A jacket! *Just cover him.*"

Her request was irrational to her own ears but her voice carried nonetheless. No one moved. They, like her, were transfixed. Carlos was facing her, hand outstretched, transforming. Fangs lowered, eyes red, skin charring and crackling, her name a long echoing cry as the full sun broke the horizon. But she couldn't turn away, her voice had transformed too, becoming a constant long scream echoing back the word *no,* turning it into bitter hiccupping sobs as every wound he'd ever sustained as a vampire, every horror they had visited upon him mutated, manifested, and twisted his once whole body into a writhing mass of torn carnage and decay.

She felt her body lift again, strong arms attempting to carry her away from the gruesome scene, making her fight against family. "No, I won't leave him until it's over!" She wept and she was released. "We don't leave our own to die alone, no matter how horrible."

Jose was down a cliff side, Father Lopez sliding, skidding along the perilous rocks beside him, trying to get to what was quickly becoming ash with a suit jacket against the sun. Futile. Human. The last of Carlos's distant line responding to instinct beyond their own comprehension. Her tears dropping off her nose, hitting cinder with a sizzling pop as Carlos torched, his head still turned toward her, his hand reaching as it crumbled away.

Father Patrick's last rites were a far-off drone in her ear. A woman's hand on her back, rubbing, trying to heal the impossible, was of no use. Brothers beside her on their knees, calling Jose and Lopez back to safety, shouting that it was too late, begging them to come back, were just background noise. It was full daylight.

Two futile hands clutching ash before it all blew away, sobbing, not caring that they were men, worked and glanced up at her. Jose and Lopez were stuck on a crag as Sydney began to come to life in the morning, holding hope in their fists, wanting to put some of what they held on hallowed ground . . . allowing brothers to pull them to safety but refusing to let go of the ashes. It all seemed so remote, like watching the very end of a movie without a frame of reference . . . who were these people?

There was a woman screaming. She sounded very far away, too. She kept saying, "Please, God, no!" Damali thought she knew the woman's voice, recognized it from some distant place in her mind, wasn't sure who she was, though, as Big Mike picked her up and began walking to a Jeep. She looked up and saw Jose and reached for him, making heads turn, making Big Mike put her down easy, making Rider and Shabazz wipe their eyes. Made clerics stop walking to stand still and pray. Made Marlene close her eyes and turn her chin up to the sky, as Damali ran to the only person who would understand what this was like.

Arms opened for her, a fist of dust pressed against her back, her plea went into a shoulder that she knew had shared the same pain.

"Don't let him die," she said, shaking her head, her whisper a fervent, irrational, impossible request.

Another pair of hands touched her shoulders, and kind

brown eyes stood with her and Jose, opening her hands. Jose's face stained wet. Father Lopez's stained, like hers. Eyes red. Three together, all knowing the same hurt. Male hands pouring a funnel of dust into her cupped ones. A ring forming around them, Guardians.

"He wasn't supposed to die, not like this," she murmured. "He was a good man . . . he was a Guardian—like one of us."

"We'll bury him righteous, D," Jose whispered. "I promise."

"On hallowed ground, we'll scatter these ashes," Father Lopez said.

But their words fell on deaf ears and she dropped to her knees as she let the ashes fall into the dew-drawn grass. Everything she'd ever believed in was a lie. The good died young. The dark side had won, and they'd tortured the man so terribly . . . and those she worked for, those she held faith in, those she'd fought for—her side, the Light, hadn't interceded. She could feel the circle widen to allow her space to grieve. She opened her arms and let her head fall back. "Where were the angels? Where was the Light? Why didn't you help him?" Another sob stole her breath. "I prayed and you didn't come! Where were you when I needed you most—he needed you most?"

She stood and walked away, leaving Father Lopez and Jose to stoop and touch the fallen ashes, saying good-bye through their fingers, their last connection to his matter. The teams didn't move. She was done. She'd never pick up the Isis again in battle for the Light. *Never again.* She ran to the Jeep and retrieved it, and stormed back to where they had all gathered, ignoring the pained, stricken expressions around her, brushing past Marlene with fury. She looked down at the ring Carlos had given her, and wept. It never went back, didn't dematerialize.

How cruel of them to leave her his heart—blue ice, and not one with a true pulse. She snatched the solitaire off, and flung it into the pile of ash, raised her sword, and plunged it into the ground through the ashes, sending the ring into the soft earth. "I give it back! I wanted his *real heart*!" The Isis could be his headstone, his marker, something worthy left for a true Neteru, her equal. It belonged now to him.

As she turned away, she saw a flash of static from the corner of her eye. Jose and Lopez stood slowly and stepped back. Marlene and Father Patrick moved forward to retrieve the sword, but the others didn't move near it. They, like her, watched as a current arced between the sword, Father Lopez, and Jose. The wind gathered and the dust swirled around the blade of the sword near the ground. Particles of dust connected, tiny granules of matter flashed static, magnetized, drew together, and began to take shape and form. Marlene rushed toward it and pulled the Isis from the earth, and walked backward slowly as the tip of it dripped red blood.

"His heart," she whispered, holding the blade up to the light.

Father Patrick crossed himself and began murmuring a silent prayer as the dust continued to gather. The clerics fanned out, each taking a directional position of the earth. "*Her* heart," he said, his gaze locking with Marlene's.

"His line," Marlene said, her eyes going toward Jose's and Father Lopez's, and then going to Damali. "His hope."

"His prayer," the elder cleric said quietly, gazing at Damali. "His faith."

"His love," Marlene and Father Patrick said in unison, holding Damali in their sight, slowly bringing it back to the mass on the ground that was now large, spreading, connecting, shifting, darkening to coal-colored matter.

Damali ran to it and went down on her hands and knees, hope careening through her, watching a body form from the skeleton out. Muscles and tendons slowly covering bones, even olive-brown skin covering muscles—her hand went to her mouth, and she dared not move, breathe, hope too much, tears making what she was witnessing blur before her eyes, no fear, just awe, reverence, her soul recanting the anger, quietly begging forgiveness for her arrogance, her momentary loss of faith, her lack of understanding, her forgetting about miracles.

"We don't know what's coming back, Mar—get her outta there and away from it, until we know." Shabazz lunged forward, but Big Mike stopped him.

"Faith, brother. Faith." Big Mike closed his eyes, total reverence in his huge countenance. "Believe in things unseen."

"Hope," Rider said quietly, going near but not all the way. He touched Dan's shoulder. "A collective prayer in trinity."

"Love," Jose said, stepping back to stand by Shabazz, then he turned away. "He'll never leave her, and will *never* hurt her."

Shabazz's hand went to Jose's shoulder. "Destiny, brother. This was written before we were born."

Damali looked down into a serene face that she dared not touch, and started when it drew a sudden gasp of breath, short fangs catching sunlight, then retracting up and into his gums. She could feel every Guardian behind her tense, but she couldn't move. Her hand reached out, trembling fingers touching the side of a face she remembered, had given up on, needing to be sure she wasn't hallucinating and that he was real. Carlos.

A pair of intense, deep brown eyes opened and looked at her, then the irises burned out silver, glowing. His gaze slid from hers to the horizon as he sat up slowly, bracing himself on a shaky arm. His breaths steady, expanding his naked back, his voice low, awed, and far away.

"Can't you see them, D?"

Necks craned, eyes shot to the horizon, then back to the quiet man sitting still, and naked, and damp on the ground.

"See who?" she whispered, her voice almost nonexistent.

"There's so many of them, and they're beautiful," he said, tears running down his face as he slowly clasped her hand. "Warriors . . . angels . . . they never left me, never left you, never left their Neterus, us . . . the future."

Damali strained to see what held Carlos rapt, but her eyes were only human. All she could make out was brilliant, golden light. Her gaze went to him instead, redemption . . . her hand stroked his hair, and her body came next to his to stare out at the sun with him as he leaned against her and quietly wept with her.

"Damali . . . I'm finally free."

TURN THE PAGE FOR
A SNEAK PEEK AT THE NEXT
VAMPIRE HUNTRESS LEGEND NOVEL

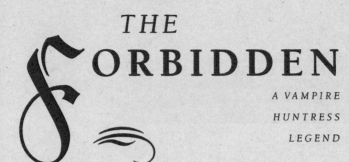

THE FORBIDDEN

A VAMPIRE
HUNTRESS
LEGEND

NOW AVAILABLE FROM
ST. MARTIN'S PAPERBACKS

DAMALI FELT like she was flying, the images whirled by so fast. Her skin crackled with electricity, and she gasped as she landed on her feet with a thud. She crouched down, instantly on guard, and glanced around herself. She quickly patted her side. Damn. Her blade was back on the plane.

The question was, where was she and how did she get here?

It was clearly an industrial area. A river lay to the south of her and to the north was a wide street, but there was no traffic. The moon shone like a perfect silver disk in the sky, not a cloud in sight. This was the hunting hour, not a good time to be without a blade. Damali glanced down at herself. Black leather pants, black halter top, and steel-toed boots. Perfect for kicking vamp or demon ass.

She walked forward slowly and cautiously. The large, dark buildings loomed silent and empty. A bridge towered in the distance, looking blue and skeletal in this half light. She saw a street sign and narrowed her gaze. Delaware Avenue. She was in Philly.

She rounded a corner and saw a purple neon club marquee that read "Club Egypt." Damali stopped walking and folded her arms over her chest. She stared at the sign, then noticed the hieroglyphics that had been spray-painted on the sand-colored exterior of the building.

"All right, then," she muttered. She crossed the wide boulevard and walked toward the club with purpose. Standing on a corner wringing her hands wasn't going to get her any answers.

When she got to the door, a huge bouncer stopped her. "ID?"

Damali looked him up and down. He was a big, burly brother who looked like he was straight out of the motherland. His blue-black complexion gleamed, blending almost seamlessly into his black muscle shirt and jeans. Brother wasn't moving. She could do this the hard way, and simply kick his huge ass, or do it the easy way. She smiled. Finessing her way into a club had never been a problem for her.

Still smiling, Damali caressed his broad chest and said, "Now you know you need to stop playing. You know a sister just wants to get her groove on."

"No ID, no getting into this club."

Damali licked her lips and moved in closer to him. She looked at him from beneath her eyelashes. "Oh, come on. How about it I say pretty please?" Then she pressed herself against him oh so slightly, leaned in, and breathed in his ear, "Please?"

He stared down at her, his face blank, his eyes icy. Damali gave a little wiggle and smiled at him again. The ice cracked. Almost reluctantly, he moved his mountainous girth out of the doorway. Damali blew him a kiss as she hurried past.

Once inside, she squinted through the purple lights and hazy clouds of smoke. The interior seemed fairly normal. The place was jumping, the music was thumping, and people were freestyling on the wide, polished wood dance floor. The DJ was all right. The bars were loaded. People were seated at round tables or lounging stylishly on purple or black mini-sofas. She couldn't sense anything preternatural or demonic. Very weird.

Damali carefully made her way to the bar and slid onto a tall brass and leather stool as she continued to scan the club. When the female bartender came toward her, she remembered—she was broke like a mug.

No problem. There were plenty of brothers sipping at the rail to make that a nonissue. But if they were offering drinks with a shot of color, she wouldn't be drinking anyway.

Damali studied the tall, older woman as she walked over to her. Girlfriend looked good. She had on a metallic gold bustier that served up her double-Ds like trophies. A gold filigree waist chain that moved ever so slightly above her tight, gold lamé pants as she walked accentuated her flat belly. Her complexion was of burnt cinnamon, but her eyes were a smoldering dark brown, matching the color of her shoulder-length braids. A gold serpent bracelet circled her sleekly muscular upper arm. She looked like she was in her late thirties. Her walk was so smooth, she almost looked like she was moving in slow motion. Damali had to shake her head to break the hypnotic rhythm. Had to be vamp.

"What are you having tonight?" the bartender asked with a smile.

Damali studied her. "What are you serving that's top shelf?"

The bartender's smile widened. "Sis, I don't roll like that. I've got a man."

Damali sat back. "Well, shit, so do I."

"Don't we all?" said a deep, sexy, female voice close to her ear. Damali quickly pivoted on the stool, ready to do battle. "But if you're angling for a free drink, just name your poison."

"First, you need to back up off me," Damali said slowly, watching a very tall Native American–looking woman slide onto the barstool next to her. She tossed her long French braid over her shoulder and sighed. Damali didn't like the odds and they were getting worse. She could feel the females moving in on her quickly and quietly as the men backed away, making room for them.

One by one the chairs filled around her. She glanced at the bartender, then the tall, older woman who was a fly-ass fifty, serving royal blue peacock and black stilettos.

"Pour this child a Jack Daniel's," the woman beside her said. "My tab."

"This ain't no bargain," Damali said, accepting the drink with her eyes but not touching it. Another older sister had slid into a chair on her right. Her dark face seemed vaguely familiar, and her intense black eyes had that same knowing quality the others possessed.

She flipped her hand to dismiss Damali's open assessment. Sister was rockin' so much ice that the diamonds were practically blinding. Pure confidence radiated from her, almost like a heat wave. She was serving red stilettos that bordered on being "fuck me" pumps. The red pants suit, killer. Her aura demanded respect.

Damali raised her glass to them. Her gaze surveyed what she quickly counted as eight women, all older, of varying hues, and dressed to the nines, so confident and cocky that they hadn't even worn good battle shoes . . . All of them, obviously, professional assassins who could be patient and wait to do their hits. "Well, I have to hand it to you, ladies. You sure know how to take a sister out in style."

The one in red chuckled and sipped her martini. "So dramatic." She looked down the bar at the others. "See what man trouble will do to you? Make you simple."

Damali gave a small smile and bumped her glass, spilling the contents into the woman's lap. "Yeah. It'll do that. So, let's get this party started."

She'd expected the woman to attack and braced herself for it. Instead she just looked at the stain and the liquor running down her shapely leg, dabbed it with a finger, tasted it, made a face, and shook her head.

"Now that was just tacky," she said in an even tone. "Why don't we step into the ladies' room?"

Damali stood. "After you."

The bartender cleared the bar in one lithe leap to stand before Damali with a sly smile. "Shall we?"

"It's your house," Damali said through her teeth. "You lead the way."

Martini glasses, champagne flutes, and rocks glasses were calmly set down in unison as the women flanking the leader stood.

"Baby girl, do you have any idea who you're up against?"

Damali stepped back, one hand on her hip. "No, do you?"

It was the first time she saw a flicker of rage cross their faces.

The women simply turned on their heels and walked away, their heads high and their shoulders back.

Damali stared after them. Was she hallucinating, or had these female vamps just marched off toward the bathroom like a bunch of offended church ladies? Something did not fit, big-time. Curiosity got the best of her and Damali cautiously followed their regal promenade.

The sister in red swung open the heavy door, almost yanking it from its hinges and making it slam against the wall. Bright fluorescent light greeted them. Damali entered the now tightly packed space last. She made a quick assessment. No windows. All white metal stalls and tile with pink accent borders. Who knew vamps liked pink? Then she stopped as they stood before a huge mirror, every one of them casting a reflection.

Okaaay. They weren't vamps. So then, who the hell . . . ? Damali opened her mouth, then slowly closed it.

"That's right, damn it!" the woman in red said. "You'd better recognize who you're talking to. I ran empires before you were even thought of, sister!"

"*Chica,* this is bad," another said, shaking her head. "We're gonna have to kick your behind for real now."

"Aw, ladies," a third tall beauty said. "You know that's not why we brought her here."

The bartender stepped forward. "We've got bigger problems."

"All right, Eve," the sister in red said, giving Damali a hard glare. "This is your territory. School her fast before I snatch a bone out of her narrow behind."

Damali's attention jumped from one woman to the next. Did one of them just call the sister serving drinks *Eve*?

"Yeah, yeah, yeah. Long story, baby. But hey, you know how this goes. You find Mr. Right, fall in love, get your head twisted around by some other fine bastard, then you have issues. Feel me?"

Damali couldn't stop herself from gaping.

"Take a walk with us," the one named Eve said, moving toward the mirror. "You game for some insight?"

Damali nodded numbly. Eve turned and touched the mirror, melting into it as if it were water. "We had to strip your blade from you, hon, until you could learn to use it correctly. Because you can't fight what's coming for you like you just did out there. A common street fighter."

The others nodded.

"You will get your ass beat down if you go after her like you just did, hear?" the woman in red said, obviously still salty about her dress. "Lilith will fuck you up good if you don't watch your back, and no man is worth all that."

Damali's eyes were so wide that she couldn't blink. Then someone behind pushed her forward and she was suddenly alone in a vast stone enclosure, standing on the landing of a massive staircase. Towering oblong windows let in the breaking dawn.

Once she reached the top of the stairs there was a wide hallway. A glasslike wash of violet light spilled across the marble.

She focused all her senses, straining to feel vibrations, to hear, all to no avail. Where had they gone?

She began to walk forward, feeling amazingly light as each footfall lifted her slightly off the floor. Soon the glasslike purple rays covered her as she entered their full beam. Suddenly she rushed forward to an open atrium filled with swirling golden-white light and women's voices.

Damali squinted as a large, opalescent table came into view. Seated before her were the eight women. Four were sitting to either side of an empty, high Kemetian throne carved in alabaster, with a falcon-winged sun disk bearing the ankh symbol of fertility. She recognized Nzinga instantly this time. The red siren's getup had completely thrown her off. Then she saw the Amazon sitting to her right and immediately dropped to one knee. Oh, dear God!

She'd been summoned to the Council of Neterus!

READING GROUP GUIDE

1. Now that Damali is twenty-one and can hook up with Carlos, do you think she should have?

2. Early in the series, what did you think about Damali's need to remain celibate until her twenty-first birthday? Would that fly in the "real world"? How do you feel about the whole issue surrounding the "choices" women must make regarding childbearing?

3. Which character in the book is your favorite hero/heroine and why?

4. What character do you love to hate and why?

5. What did you think about the depiction of the levels of Hell? Have you visited the Web site www.vampirehuntress.com to see how each level is organized by a governing structure? If so, what parallels does that possibly have to some of the "real world's" social, political, and economic infrastructure?

6. Do you believe a person can be redeemed after they've lived a wild life?

7. Are there types of characters (or creatures) you would like to see in the upcoming novels within the series? If yes, who or what?

8. Discuss the role of the Chairman versus Father Patrick as father figures to Carlos Rivera.

9. Remember that bad boy, Fallon Nuit? What did you think about his near sexual encounter with Damali on the astral plane (from the special edition scene in the mass market edition of *Minion*)?

10. Discuss the metaphor of "vampirism" as a seductive force to draw humans into a lifestyle of violence, crime, fast money—but ultimately incarceration into "a system."

For more reading group suggestions visit
www.stmartins.com/smp/rgg.html

St. Martin's Griffin